Also by Thomas Trump

Crime Fiction

Inspector Chris Hardie, Murder with a Scottish Connection
Inspector Noal, Sarah Angel or Devil
Inspector Noal, Nightmare

I dedicate this book
to all my friends in my local pub,
"THE RISING SUN"
in Winchester.

I also dedicate this book
to my wife SEVIL TRUMP,
the love of my life.

*D*uring the early 1900s, Detective Inspector Chris Hardie and his trusted Detective Sergeant George House of Winchester Criminal Investigation Department (CID), investigated the murders, which seem to have no motives or reasons. The cases were complicated, but after many twists and turns, they were able to solve the cases.

Winchester, Ancient Capital of England is a city and the county town of Hampshire, lies in the valley of the River Itchen, surrounded by magnificent green countryside.

The early 1900s, Winchester was a small compact city of about twenty thousand people, dominated by the Cathedral with many communal packed streets, all within easy reach of the main high street. The high street was long, and upwards, but most of the shops with their bow fronted windows or open fronted was situated at the bottom end, around the Guildhall, the street lights ran on gas and were lit by teams of lamplighters. Roads leading both ways from the high street, was also full of shops, pubs, barbers, rag and bone merchants, butchers and even a stable for horses all made up the bustle of the Winchester High Street.

It was a friendly town, in which most everybody knew each other. Murders and violent crimes were relatively rare, however murders, rapes, violent crimes occurred, most of the crimes were young lads scrumping apples, children on their way to school trying to pinch a sweet from the many sweet shops in the town, very few crimes were committed that warranted the birch, or imprisonment.

Detective Inspector Chris Hardie and his team Detective Sergeant Fred Willett and Detective Sergeant George House, investigated the murders, investigations were not always straightforward, range from the very simple straightforward to the very complex and complicated, the detectives were taking a meticulous approach to gathering the information needed.

BOOK ONE

INSPECTOR
CHRIS HARDIE

MURDER WITH A
SPY CONNECTION

"It's a lovely view of Winchester from here Chris, I often take a walk over here and sit," Elizabeth said, clutching Chris's arm as they sat together.

"It certainly is, it's the first time I've been up here, the Statue of King Alfred, couldn't have been put in a better place, he seems on guard," Chris replied.

"Yes, I was about five years old when they put it up, I can just vaguely remember it, I know it was around 1901," replied Elizabeth.

Chris patted her arm that was clutching his. "You must have been a beautiful child," Chris said a smile playing around his eyes.

"No I wasn't, I was long and thin, and had braces on my teeth," Elizabeth smiled at him.

"Well you have certainly changed from that, you are beautiful now," Chris flattered with a smile.

"That's very nice of you to say so Chris, do you really think so?" Elizabeth asked, her face blushing a little.

"I would not say it if I didn't," Chris replied. "As far as my eyes are concerned, you are the most beautiful woman that I have ever seen."

With her arms still grasping Chris's arm, Elizabeth laid her head against his arms.

"I could sit here forever with you," she said. "You say the sweetest things, no one have ever said those things to me before."

Chris was about to answer, when Elizabeth continued.

"Why don't you smoke your pipe, I like the smell of a pipe, and with your moustache you look very handsome," Elizabeth said straightening herself up. "Tell me Chris why have you never married, you must have had a lot of chances?"

Chris laughed. "You think so do you, well I haven't, in fact I have been out with very few girls, never had time, but I have to admit I feel nervous around a woman."

"You feel nervous with me?" Elizabeth smiled looking at Chris with love in her eyes.

"No not you, in fact I am surprised at myself, I feel relax with you."

"Have you ever thought of marriage?" Elizabeth asked blushing.

"A wife of a policeman, especially one in my position can find it very hard. I could never make any arrangements with a sureness of keeping that arrangement, for instance, I would say to you I'll be home for dinner at six, then something comes up which needs my attention, so I let you down, and the dinner is ruined. We could make a date, say to go to a show, or go to friends for dinner, or even invite friends to our house, but something comes up, then I have let you down," Chris paused, as he took out his pipe, and lit it, puffing out clouds of smoke.

"Are you trying to put me off marrying a policeman?" Elizabeth scolded him smiling.

Chris took a deep puff of his pipe, it was now or never, he took the pipe from his mouth, and put it behind him on the bench, he looked at Elizabeth, his face serious.

"No I'm not trying to put you off," Chris spoke. "I'm just letting you know what you can expect, if you accept my proposal of marriage?"

Elizabeth's eyes sparkled with the tears that build up into them.

"It's taken you a long time to ask," Elizabeth sighed, the tears shone in her eyes. "It's been agony waiting, now kiss me," she said brazenly offering her lips.

There in the warm evening, they clung to each other, they were oblivious to the world around them.

"Mum and dad will be pleased I'm sure," Elizabeth said as they relaxed.

"I'm sure they will," Chris laughed. "I have already asked them."

Elizabeth punched Chris on the arm playfully. "You sneak," she said, offering her lips again.

Chris sat at his desk, it was hard to concentrate, with Elizabeth on his mind from the evening before. His Sergeant, Fred was already at his desk, busy scribbling.

"How is the wife settling?" Chris asked, trying to focus his mind.

Fred turned his head and faced Chris. "Trouble I'm afraid, she hates Winchester, she likes the big cities you know, I think, I'll have to think about retiring," Fred shrugged his shoulders.

"I hope not Fred, just as we are getting used to each other," Chris replied.

"My feelings exactly," Fred remarked. "But," he hesitated trying to find the right words. "As I told you before, we spend our lives making the little women happy, always at our expense."

Chris smiled, his thoughts were on Elizabeth, a knock came on the door, Sergeant Williams poked his head in.

"I have a gentleman outside, a Mr Marchant, he says he wants to see someone with authority," he said looking at Chris.

"About what?" Chris asked.

"His housekeeper has gone missing," the sergeant replied.

"Can't you see to it, it's routine isn't it?" replied Chris.

"Yes, but he is insisting," Sergeant Williams replied.

Chris looked at Fred, who was looking at him and saw no suggestion in his face. "Very well sergeant, show him in."

Mr Marchant proved to be man of substance, smartly dressed in a three piece suit, carrying a briefcase and umbrella, he wore no hat, and was clean shaven. Chris thought him good looking.

Chris stood up, offering his hand, which Mr Marchant took, and shook warmly.

"I am Detective Inspector Hardie of Winchester CID, and my colleague is Detective Sergeant Fred Willett," Chris introduced themselves.

He smiled as he indicated the interview chair for him to sit. "Now how can we help?"

"I am pleased to meet you both," replied Mr Marchant. "I hope I am not wasting your time, but the truth is, I came home last night, and my housekeeper Miss Thompson had disappeared, she had taken all of her clothing, and not a word of explanation."

"Where do you live?" Chris asked leaning on his desk.

"I have rather a large house in Christchurch Road, just the first one in from St James Lane," Mr Marchant explained.

"Are there anyone else in the house?" Chris asked as a matter of routine.

"No, just myself," replied Mr Marchant.

"What about her friends, family etc have you tried them?" Fred butted in.

"That's the trouble Sergeant," Mr Marchant answered. "She has no friends or family, what I mean is, I don't think she has friends that she is that close to."

"You know of course that we have a tried and tested routine with regards to missing people Mr Marchant, she has only been missing for a few hours, perhaps she will turn up again, but you can rely on us Mr Marchant, we will do all that's necessary to find her," Chris replied picking up his pencil to make a note on his pad. "You can rely on us," he repeated himself.

"I know I can Inspector," Mr Marchant replied. "The reason I wanted to see someone with authority, is because this is the second time it has happened in the last year."

Chris leaned back in his chair, fingering the pencil he held between both hands.

"Did you report the last one?" Fred asked.

"No I didn't Sergeant, with my last housekeeper Miss Osman, I was very surprised that she had gone, but I guessed that she had her own reason for going, so I let it pass, and lucky enough got myself another."

"So you have lost two housekeepers in the last year, both leaving with all their clothing, both without leaving a letter or a note to explain," Chris summed up.

"That's about it Inspector," Mr Marchant replied.

"I think that's strange as well, but I'm sure there is an explanation, we must try to find it," Chris remarked looking at Fred getting no response.

"What work do you do Mr Marchant?" Chris asked.

"Dennis, Dennis Marchant Inspector, I own several textile shops and a factory."

"So you are a busy man, Mr Marchant," Fred spoke up. "Do you get home at nights?"

"Most nights, unless I'm travelling," replied Dennis. "But I must tell you the truth," Mr Marchant shifted in his seat. "I have a special relationship with my housekeepers, yes they look after my house, and when I am there, they wait upon me. I treat them however like a wife, they have no set hours, and can go wherever they like, with plenty of money to spend, in return they act like a wife in all ways," Dennis found himself in the embarrassing position of explaining.

"Now I know people look down on this sort of thing, but it's my life, which I might add is full of work, I am much too busy to go out looking for woman, so I settle on this way, and I am quite happy with it, like everyone else, I do have my needs."

"I'm not worried about your morals Mr Marchant," Chris replied. "But it do put a different slant on the case, are you sure these housekeepers didn't leave you, because they did not want to stay with you any longer?"

"Perhaps they found someone they loved?" Fred butted in. "It do happen."

Chris leaned back on his desk, a smile playing around his eyes. "My sergeant is right Mr Marchant, one could guess a number of things that could have made the housekeepers go, but both going without an explanation is puzzling."

"It's not only that Inspector, I am a very rich man, I have more than I can spend in a lifetime, I am not mean to my housekeepers, in fact both of them would have loved to marry me, however I do offer them a substantial wage for every month while they are with me, these housekeepers left without collecting their wages becoming due."

"Can you tell us how much we are talking about?" Chris asked.

"Thirty pound a month, remember they also get a good housekeeping money of several pounds a week, out of which they buy the food etc, plus their full board. I buy some of their clothes, so I am not mean to them."

"Sounds as though you are very fair with them at least Mr Marchant," Chris replied. "I can't think why they should leave within a few weeks of getting their wages, which is quite a lot of money, tell me," Chris continued playing with his pencil on the desk. "Have you only had two housekeepers?"

"No I have had several, but the others have always had a good reason for leaving me, and none have left me before their wages became due," Mr Marchant gave a weak laugh.

"What about the first one Miss Osman to go this way, did she have any friends or family?" Fred asked.

"I'm not all that sure Sergeant," Dennis answered.

"She was an assistant in my Andover shop, actually we were having an affair, before she took the housekeepers job. I don't have an address for her, but I do believe she had a mother, or a father living, I did make enquiries at the shop after she left, but she had not been seen," Dennis shifted again in his chair. "Look Inspector, if these women left their job for any reason, fair enough, but for two to leave without any explanation seem strange to me, and that's why I brought this to you."

"I'm glad you did Mr Marchant, have you photo's of the women?" Chris asked.

"I'm afraid not, I never had photographs taken with them, whatever they had, it went with them," Dennis said apologetically.

"Perhaps then you can give us their names, and possible addresses," Chris requested. "Plus the names of two or three of your past housekeepers that left in a reasonable manner."

"Allow me a few hours to go home, and I'll have all you want delivered to the station later today, at the moment, I do have an important meeting to attend, which I do not want to miss," Dennis said with a hint of urgency in his voice.

"Leave everything with us Mr Marchant," Chris said standing up and offering his hand. "I am grateful to you for coming in, let's hope there is a reasonable explanation."

"Thank you Inspector," Dennis shook the offered hand. "I'll see that you get everything that might be helpful," he looked at Fred and nodded as he left the room.

Chris looked at Fred, who was looking at him his face blank.

"I know it's a routine job, but we are quiet at the moment, it won't hurt to dig it a bit will it?" Chris said a smile on his face.

"It will pass the time I suppose," Fred answered without enthusiasm in his voice.

Chris waited for Elizabeth at the Butter Cross being situated in the High Street in the centre of Winchester, he watched her as she approached, dressed in a brown two piece, her long slim skirt, covered by a knee length matching coat. Her hat balancing correctly on top of her well combed hair. She walked gracefully towards him, a smile already on her face, Chris scoffed, as he saw a couple soldiers who was walking the other way, eyeing her up and down, then smiled to himself.

"It was only natural for men looked at beautiful women," the thought had crossed his mind.

Elizabeth grabbed his arms, after giving him a very quick peck on the cheek.

"Have you been waiting long?" she asked, as they started to walk down town.

"Waiting for you will never become a chore for me," Chris replied. "No, I have just got here, you have been in my mind all day."

"Same as me, I must have made several mistakes with my arithmetic today," Elizabeth admitted.

Chris stopped outside a jewellery shop. "Let's have a look in here, you might find a ring you like?" he said.

Elizabeth did not answer, as she followed Chris into the shop, but squeezed his arm tighter.

Almost an hour later, Chris and a smiling Elizabeth emerged. "It's not very romantic," Chris said looking at Elizabeth, who was happily looking at the gleaming ring that was now on her finger. "But it seems that you took to that one."

"It's beautiful," Elizabeth said happily, still looking at the ring on her outstretched finger. "I love it so much, but it was expensive."

"I wanted to give you a small party, before I gave you the ring, but I had to have you with me when I bought it because of your finger size," Chris replied ignoring her remark.

"I find this romantic," Elizabeth smiled squeezing his arm tighter. "It was such a surprise you taking me in that shop, I truly did not expect it, won't my mum be jealous when I show it to her," she said happily, her eyes sparkling.

"Perhaps we can all go for a drink after tea," she suggested, looking at the ring on her finger.

Chapter Two

*D*etective Inspector Chris Hardie, sat at his desk, a broad grin on his face as he told Detective Sergeant Fred Willett, about his engagement party, the evening before.

"It just happened, I wanted a proper party," Chris explained. "But once she saw the ring she wanted, she wouldn't take it off, her mother went crazy with excitement, and when two women make up their mind, we men might as well accept."

"I've told you that," smiled Fred.

"Anyway," continued Chris. "After a meal, we all went to the Rising Sun, that's our local, or what we call our local, and had a great time," Chris was full of happiness as he spoke. "So I am an engaged man."

"Well I wish you all the very best Chris, a man needs a woman to go home to," Fred said offering his congratulations.

"How is your wife anyway Fred, any signs of settling yet?" Chris asked.

Fred shook his head.

Chris decided to make no comment as he opened a letter on his desk, that had been delivered late the night before by Mr Marchant, and read it.

"A letter here from Mr Marchant who came in yesterday regarding his housekeepers, he has given the names and detailed descriptions of the two missing housekeepers, a Miss Doris Thompson, and a Miss Doris Osman, both Doris," Chris explained. "Coincidence I suspect."

Fred looked up from his writing. "Any addresses?" he asked.

"Only a couple addresses of past housekeepers," Chris murmured.

"He should have been a horse," Fred commented with a laugh. "He certainly liked his oats, if you can believe what he told us."

"Didn't you believe him Fred?" Chris looked up from the letter and asked.

"I'm not sure," Fred replied. "It was a boast in a way, women are not all that easy, at least not the well brought up ones, but he seemed to be able to get a string of them, I was thinking last night," Fred continued. "Would the soldiers have anything to do with their disappearance, after all the town is full of them?"

Chris thought on the matter before he answered. "Anything is possible Fred, but all these soldiers are just passing through on their way to France, they are only here a few days, and I wonder where would they take the women even if they had time to meet them."

"Deserters," Fred gave his opinion.

"I suppose, but they are all volunteers, no one is forced to join the Army, so why join then desert?" Chris hesitated.

Fred made no comment, his arms laying across his desk, twiddled a pencil around his fingers.

Chris passed the letter from Mr Marchant over to Fred.

"How would you like a train trip to Andover tomorrow Fred?" he asked.

Fred took the letter, and studied it. "You want me to go to his shop in Andover?" he asked.

"Well yes, but I thought you could take Mrs Willett with you, give her a change so to speak, she may appreciate it."

Fred smiled. "Thank you Chris, she can do some window shopping, she will like that while I pop into shop it will take all day, the wife is bound to make a day of it."

Chris smiled. "Have a meal while you're there, it will be a good day to go, we are eventually having a telephone installed tomorrow, and workmen no doubt will be all over the office."

"It's about time," Fred remarked. "What will you be doing?"

"I shall get on my bike, and go to those other addresses on the list, but now I'm due in court, that sheep rustling case," Chris shook his head as he tidied his desk. "How someone can steal a sheep, then try to sell it to a butcher he don't know, beats me," he smiled as he left his desk.

"I'm not sure how long I shall be, but if I don't make it back today, I see you the day after tomorrow, make sure Mrs Willett enjoys her day out," Chris ordered, taking his trilby from the stand. "If anything important turns up, you know where I am," he smiled leaving the office.

Chris stopped at the desk sergeant's desk on his way out. "Sergeant, who have you bobby on the beat in the Christchurch Road area?"

"Constable Higgins," replied the sergeant looking down his list.

"What's he like, I mean is he sensible?" Chris asked.

"All our policemen are sensible Inspector," the sergeant scolded. "What do you want of him?"

"Can you ask him to get as much information as he can about a Mr Marchant, who lives in a large house, the first one in Christchurch Road from St James Lane, I'll have to sharpen my wits a bit, I did not ask him the number," Chris smiled a little embarrassed. "Anyway, I want it done discretely, I don't want it known that questions are being asked."

"You can rely on uniforms Inspector, I'll see to it," replied the sergeant without a smile.

Chris thanked him. "As soon as possible, if that's possible," he added with a smile as he left the station.

The following day, Chris parked his bike at the curb, checking his list, to assure himself that he was at the right address, he took off his cycling clips, and shaking his legs, walked up the short garden path and knocked on the door, hoping that someone would be in. The door opened, and Chris found himself confronted by a slim attractive young woman.

"I am Detective Inspector Hardie, from Winchester CID," Chris introduced himself. "I am looking for a Miss Brenda West."

"I am Miss West," came the reply. "What would a Detective Inspector want from me?"

"If I may come in, I would like to speak to you about your time with Mr Marchant, of Christchurch Road, I understand that you once worked for him," Chris replied.

Chris thought that Miss West was a bit unsure of herself as she opened the door wider for him to enter.

"I don't understand what you would want from me, I left his employment many months ago," she replied, acting a little worried.

"I understand that Miss West, nothing to worry about, I need couple of questions to be answered," Chris replied as he entered a small, but tidy looking front room.

15

"Well," remarked Miss West, still unsure of herself. "Please take a seat, would you like tea?"

"No, thank you," Chris replied taking a hard chair to sit on. "Can you tell me why you left Mr Marchant's employment?"

Brenda West seated herself opposite the Inspector, a small dining table between them.

"I'm not sure that I understand your question inspector, I wanted to leave, and gave my notice."

"But why Miss West, you must have had a reason?" Chris pushed gently, watching colour appearing on Miss West's face. "If it will help you Miss West, I do have an understanding of the terms of employment with Mr Marchant," Chris continued politely.

Brenda West fiddled with the edge of a white table covering that was spread over the table.

"I don't know what to say," she answered. "I was there less than a year as his housekeeper, he was away lot of the time, he was kind enough for a man, not dominating, I had the run of the place," Brenda let go of the table clothe, and shrugged her shoulders. "I left Inspector, because he wanted too much from me, me being a woman, if you understand."

Chris nodded his head. "But you stayed just long enough to get the monthly wages?" he asked.

"You mean my yearly salary don't you, but he did pay monthly," Brenda remarked.

Chris leaned forward. "He didn't give you a weekly wage as well then?"

"Only food money, he was generous with that, you see he would not have any tradesman apart from the coalman calling, all his food even bread and milk had to be bought fresh, I spent most of my time shopping. Milk had to be fresh every day, used or not and the bread no more than three days old, used or not. Because he was away a lot, and only came home late at night when he did, much was thrown away, it was a shame when you think there are many who are starving."

"I see," Chris said, his mind racing. "Did he happen to buy you clothes?"

Brenda laughed. "Oh yes, he would buy me a gown when he needed me as a host, when putting on a party for his business friends, but he would pick them himself, they are not clothes that I could wear out, even now I have left, the odd gown that he bought for me I have no opportunity to wear them, they were for the society class."

"But thirty pounds a month is a lot of money Miss West," Chris said.

"I suppose it is, I could never earn that amount now, but I think I was sensible with the money, it's only two down and two up, but I managed to buy this house with it," Brenda said with a smile. "I never had the need to spend my wages, because I was getting so good housekeeping money."

"I think you were very sensible Miss West," Chris agreed. "Tell me are you in work now?"

"Only part time, I do cleaning jobs for several houses, brings me in enough to pay the bills, and buy the food, I also take in the odd lodgers, on the short term basis so I feel comfortable," Brenda smiled weakly.

"You are not married then?" Chris asked.

"No Inspector I'm not, I am what people call a soiled woman," Brenda said her face colouring. "But I don't regret what I done, I have my home which no one can kick me out of."

Chris pondered choosing his words.

"So I take it Miss West, you left because you did not want to act as his wife any longer, apart from that, the house was a respectable house?" he asked.

Chris saw Brenda nod her head yes.

"Would you have known his housekeepers since you left, a Miss Doris Osman, and a Miss Doris Thompson?" Chris asked.

"No I wouldn't," Brenda answered, she seemed a bit nervous. "I have no idea who he might have had since I left, I haven't seen or heard of him since I left."

"That's fine Miss West," Chris said rising. "Thank you for being so frank with me, I wish you luck for the future."

Chris left the house unsure what he was feeling, he was sure that Miss West had not told him the whole truth, Chris checked his list, decided to pay a visit to Miss Hilda Johnson as well. Chris cycled to the other end of the town, to the remaining address on the list, and once again, the woman who answered, Miss Hilda Johnson was also a slim, attractive woman, she also owned her house, and had stayed single. With the story she told, more or less matched that of Miss West. By the time the interview was over, it was well pass midday, and Chris decided to go back to his office, where he found his telephone had been installed.

"Call me if you don't know how to use it," Sergeant Williams said who had entered the office with Chris. "I'll make you out a list of important numbers just in case," he offered.

"Thank you Sergeant," Chris smiled. "Now did this bobby on the beat find out anything, or is it a bit too early?"

Sergeant Williams looked at Chris unsmiling. "Never too early for uniforms, Constable Higgins will be calling in about four this afternoon," he said.

"That will be appreciated," Chris said, watching the Sergeant leave.

Chris wondered how Fred was getting on, as he scribble down details of his interviews with Miss West and Miss Johnson that morning, he was almost finished when Sergeant Williams poked his head around the door. "Constable Higgins is here Inspector," he said politely.

Chris took out his pocket watch. "Dead on time," he thought replacing the watch. "Let's have him in."

Constable Higgins, was a middle-aged man in his late 30's, he was heavy build like Fred his Sergeant, and noticed that the black leather belt around his waist seemed a bit tight. Constable Higgins took of his helmet as he entered and stood to attention in from of Chris's desk.

"Relax constable," Chris said. "Take that chair, and tell me what you found out?"

The constable sat, and placed his helmet on his knees, looking a bit unsure of himself. He reached into the top pocket of his tunic, and took out a hard cover black notebook and opened it, he cleared his throat.

"During the morning, I proceeded," he began.

"Cut that out constable, just tell me what you have learnt, in your own words, you are not in court," Chris smiled.

Constable Higgins coloured up, looking at Chris, then a smile appeared on his face.

"Yes Sir," he said respectfully. "Well I asked a few people that during my beat, I stopped and have a chat, sometimes over a cuppa, and during these conversations, I brought up about Mr Marchant," constable Higgins coughed. "He is known to be a millionaire, but very few people in the area know him, he seems to be a very private man. No one speaks bad of him. Now the house that Mr Marchant lives in, seems to be two houses knocked into one, that is why it's larger than any other in the road. However it keeps its two entrances, both entrances as you know are four steps up from the ground."

"No I didn't know, but please go on," Chris smiled.

Constable Higgins continued. "Well it seems that the housekeeper, and any caller during the day, uses only the first entrance nearest to St James Lane, while at night the other entrance is used, according to one of my informers who walks his dog late at night, he has a sleeping complaint, suffers with insomnia or something like that, anyway, because he can't sleep, he walks his dog very late at night, and he sees people use second entrance to enter the house, he thinks it's a bit odd," constable Higgins explained.

"Men or women constable?" Chris asked.

"He didn't say Sir, and I did not want to push him, I was told to be discrete," replied the constable.

"Anything else constable?" Chris asked.

"That's the lot Sir, but I'll keep my ears open for you," he replied respectfully.

Chris thanked the constable. "You have been very helpful, remember, I don't want it known that questions are being asked, but anything you find out, let me know, you can even phone me constable," Chris smiled looking at newly installed phone.

"I'll do that Sir," replied the constable standing, holding his helmet under his arms.

"Off you go then constable, and thank you," Chris said as he watched the constable walk awkwardly out of the office.

The following day, Chris was early in the office, he had met Elizabeth on her way to work. Fred was already at his desk, he looked up as Chris entered and hung his trilby.

"How did it go yesterday?" Chris asked crossing to his desk.

"Great," replied Fred. "It cheered the wife up no end, with the weather being good, it was a trip worth taking. I see we got our phone installed as well, while I was away."

"I'm glad about that," Chris replied. "Did you learn anything?"

Fred told Chris all he had found out. "I went to the address in Andover and found that Miss Osman has a father still living, he is perhaps in his mid-forties. He told me his daughter had disappeared, since she went as Mr Marchant's housekeeper. He agreed that she once worked in Mr Marchant's shop as an assistant, but he refused her daughter having an affair with him, he believes that it would go against her moral upbringing. He has no idea where she is now, he has been to the local police, but with no result. He showed me letters he had from his daughter while she was working in Winchester, she always sent him a pound note in them, then they stopped coming."

"Did the letters tell you anything?" Chris asked.

"They said she did not like working there, the only thing keeping her there was her wages, and she would leave as soon as she got it."

"We now know that she did not wait to collect her wages," Chris voiced.

"I called in Mr Marchant's shop, while the wife was window shopping, and spoke to a couple of the girls who work there, they didn't seem to open up, rather secretive I thought, and wondered why," Fred paused. "One of them did tell me that Miss Osman was a very likeable girl, got on with everyone, but she was inclined to think she was flirty, the shop girl said that she did not do anything wrong, in fact the girl said she would not believe that Miss Osman had an affair with Mr Marchant."

Chris then told Fred of his two house calls and what Constable Higgins had reported.

"It's very confusing," Chris said. "On the face of it what I was told, Mr Marchant seems to be above suspicion, but he has lied to us, making us believe about the wages, which we now know was the yearly salary, it was only partly true about him buying their clothes, but the rest seems to be true. Why I wonder do I sense I was not told the whole truth by the women I saw," Chris paused thinking of Constable Higgins.

"Constable Higgins intrigued me about the house, why would he use two entrances, one in the day time, and one in the night time, for what reason?"

"Perhaps he uses the house for a different reason during the night," Fred voiced.

"Then why didn't Miss West or Miss Johnson mention it, they must have known, after all they were the housekeepers who would have to clean the place. Also if there were people going in and out during the night, they must have drink or eat, Miss West was particular when she pointed out to me that she threw a lot of food away."

Chris fell silent for a while, then gave a shrug of his shoulders. "Let's concentrate on Miss Osman for the moment, how do we find her?"

Fred looked up. "Put it like this, it's just a chance, but we know that Miss Osman left her employment several months ago, since then Mr Marchant has had another housekeeper, has any woman been found dead, or has any woman made any complaints in the last months that has been brushed aside, I think it might be worth checking," Fred suggested.

Chris's face lit up. "Good for you Sergeant, why didn't I think of that, I knew yesterday that I will have to sharpen my wits, get on with it Fred, get that sergeant off his backside."

Fred left the office with a grin on his face. "I won't tell him what you said."

Chris met Elizabeth at the Butter Cross, and got the expected quick kiss on the cheek. "Have you had a busy day?" she asked gripping his arm.

"So, so, I have a complicated case on at the moment, in fact, I'm not sure whether or not it is a case," Chris replied.

"I'm sure you will work it out Chris," Elizabeth said smiling up to him.

"It might stop me seeing you for a day or two," Chris hesitated. "Apart from meeting you going or coming from work like tonight, but I won't be able to stop at your house, I need to have a pint."

"A pint is more important than me Chris?" Elizabeth pretended to sulk.

"I would give it up for you," Chris laughed, squeezing her arm attached to his. "But I find I do my thinking better when I am alone, with a pint in front of me," he smiled. "Do you think it's silly?"

"No I don't think it's silly," replied Elizabeth. "Anyway you told me once what I could expect being a detective's wife, and I accepted, I won't go back on my word. I'll miss you, but I am not going to be jealous of a pint of beer," she laughed.

"Ron might be in there," Chris replied.

"You sure you haven't arranged this with dad?" Elizabeth asked.

Chris patted her arm again. "Would I do that?" he laughed.

Chris left Elizabeth at the bottom of the path leading to her house. "I'll try and see you in the morning," he promised kissing her fully on the lips. "I love you, give my thanks to your mother," he said about to leave her.

"Thanks what for Chris?" Elizabeth asked with a puzzled expression.

"For giving birth to you, silly," he smiled. "Now off you go."

Chris entered the Rising Sun, and did not see Ron, Elizabeth's father, but Alfie with his always smiling face greeted him, with a pint glass already under a pump.

"Boiler or straight?" Alfie asked.

"Make it straight Alfie, I'm already mixed up in my mind without my drink being mix."

Chris watched as Alfie pumped furiously on the pump, forward and backwards, until the liquid started to fill the glass.

"Any new cases?" Alfie asked, as he took the money.

"I thought you would be able to tell me that," Chris smiled at him, taking his glass to the small table by the window, where he always sat.

"Give me time, just give me time," Alfie repeated himself. "I'll soon know."

Chris smiled at him, as he took a drink, it had been a warm day, and the bitter tasted good, Alfie always kept a good pint.

Chapter Three

Chris met Elizabeth the next morning on his way to work. "I'm sorry about last night Elizabeth," he said, but I really needed to do some thinking.

"Don't be sorry Chris, I understand, it being female you know, we are jealous of everything that takes our man away from us, when it comes to our men we can be real animals protecting them, from anything that might be a competitor."

"You have no fears in that way, I can assure you," Chris smiled at her. "I would like to be with you twenty four hours a day, but I have to earn, in order to give my wife, the life she deserves."

"You say the sweetest things Chris," Elizabeth said smiling as she gave him a quick kiss on the cheek. "I have to rush now, see you tonight."

Chris watched her hurry towards her bank, then putting his hands in his trouser pockets, whistled a tune, as he made his way to the Police Station.

Fred already at his desk, was still going through a thick wad of papers.

"Any luck yet regarding the missing housekeepers?" Chris asked as he hung his trilby.

"I think so," Fred replied. "At least I do have a murdered woman, some six or seven months ago, wonder you didn't remember," Fred said, handing Chris a paper report.

Chris read the report, about a young woman, was found in a storm ditch, out in the country, she had been strangled. Chris placed the report on his desk.

"I have a vague idea about this Fred," Chris admitted. "Inspector Noal and myself did everything possible to identify the woman, but we couldn't, so it was left unsolved in the files. At least now we can find out if she is Doris Osman, we have a name, and someone who can recognise her if she is, we must have a photo of her?"

"Yes I have it here," Fred replied passing a photo to Chris. "Will this mean another trip to Andover?" he asked.

"I'm afraid it will," Chris said as he studied the brown and white photograph in front of him. "She looks young and attractive don't she."

"When do I go?" Fred asked looking at Chris.

"Now if you can get a train, if this is Doris Osman, and we can only guess at the moment, then we have a case," Chris replied.

Fred got up. "I'll phone the railway station to check the train times."

"Use our new installed phone Fred, it's got to be christened," Chris smiled.

Fred dialled and spoke to the railway station, putting the phone down within minutes.

"There's one at eleven," Fred said. "That will give me time to get home and tell the wife I might be late, so I better get off, and I'll see you tomorrow," Fred smiled wondering what his wife will say.

"Let's keep our fingers crossed Fred, a lot depends on it, should you need any help from the local police, give them my name, or tell them to phone me," Chris advised.

"Will do, well I'm off then," Fred stood up and put on his jacket to leave.

"Good luck," Chris smiled as Fred left the office.

With Fred gone, Chris suddenly felt alone, with nothing important to do, he thought about phoning Elizabeth at her work, then decided against it. He took his pipe from his pocket, and filling the bowl with tobacco, lit it, sitting back in his chair, puffing out clouds of smoke, all the time thinking of Elizabeth.

The desk sergeant poke his head round the door, he seemed agitated.

"A body of a young woman been found Inspector, you better get on your bike."

Chris took the pipe from his mouth. "Where?" he asked.

"Just pass the turning in Easton Lane to the Gasworks," the sergeant explained.

"Get in touch with the police surgeon Mr Bob Harvey, tell him the story, I'm on my way," he said putting his lit pipe in the ashtray.

Chris took his trousers clips from his desk drawer and clipped the bottom of his trousers, then hurried out the back way to the bicycle shed, where he chose a bike, he started pedalling as soon as he was out in the Broadway. Easton Lane was not far, he knew it very well on another case. All the time his mind wondered, could this be the other housekeeper.

Chris looked down on the fully clothed body of a young attractive woman, seeing a red mark around her neck, Chris assumed that she had been strangled, but kept an open mind. He looked around, and saw a constable standing a little way off.

"Constable," Chris raised his voice in order to be heard. "Who found the body?" he asked as the constable approached him.

"A horse rider who stopped to have a pee," replied the constable. "He is standing over there," the constable pointed a man who was in riding clothes. "Do you want to see him?"

"In a moment, is this your patrolling area constable?" Chris replied.

"Yes, I cover the Winnall area," replied the constable.

Chris knelt down looking at the woman, then scanned the surrounding area, apart from flattened undergrowth he saw nothing that would help. "Did you see a handbag around constable?" Chris asked the constable who was standing behind him.

"No, I have kept the others away from the scene, nothing has been touched," replied the constable.

Chris stood up, looking towards the road. "This is a long way in for someone wanting a pee," Chris said to himself.

"He's a rider Sir," replied the constable hearing what he said. "Their riding breeches has no fly buttons, he has to drop his pants down before he can have one."

Chris forced a smile. "Thank you constable," Chris said. "I do know that."

The sound of a motorbike, attracted Chris's attention, knowing who it was, he walked towards the sound, not being able to see the road.

"Hello Bob," Chris greeted the Police Surgeon. "Sorry about this, at least it's not a weekend."

Bob Harvey returned his greeting, as Chris turned to walk back the way he had come.

"I haven't had time to congratulate you on solving that treble murder case, I think Inspector Noal would be proud of you," Bob remarked.

"Just luck," Chris said modestly with a shrug of his shoulders.

"I don't think so, going all that way to Scotland, I don't think that Noal would have done that," Bob replied. "What's Scottish Police force like?" he asked.

"I didn't see it a lot, Inspector McNally was my chaperone, I had no authority whatever in Scotland, it's completely separate from the English force. However, I made a lot of good friends in Scotland," he answered.

"Good for you Chris," Bob replied stopping, and looking down at the body. "What a waste," he muttered to himself, as he knelt turning the head of the woman.

Chris did not interrupt as he watched Bob examine the body, who eventually stood up.

"Well, it looks like she was strangled," Bob remarked still looking at the body. "She has been dead, I should say about four or five days, I don't think she has been abused in a sexual way, her clothing is too tidy and neat for that, she was not killed here, she was carried here," he paused twisting his lips.

"I agree," Chris remarked. "The undergrowth points to that, no struggle."

"No, do we know who she is Chris?" Bob asked.

"No handbag has been found," Chris replied.

"Well I might find out more when I do an autopsy in hospital," Bob remarked. "I'll let you know the result as soon as I can, can we take her now?"

"There is nothing I can do here," Chris said.

"I might have someone who might recognise her, how long will you keep her there?" Chris asked.

"For the next two days at least," Bob replied. "Then she will go to Magdalene Hill Mortuary, I have the wagon coming, perhaps your constable will keep the scene secure until then, can I give you a lift back to town?" Bob offered.

"Thanks, but I have my bike," Chris replied with a smile watching Bob take his leave.

Chris cursed, he had put his nib pen too deep into the bottle of ink in front of him, and as soon as the nib had touched his paper, it had blotted. Chris screwed up the report he was writing of the body found the day before, and threw it into the waste basket. Just about to start again, he looked up as Fred entered.

"Morning Fred," he greeted him, putting his nib pen down, waiting patiently.

"Morning," replied Fred going to his desk. He sat, then turned to Chris. "Mr Osman recognised his daughter straight away," Fred said.

"I have had to take bad news many people during my time in the force, but Mr Osman," Fred shook his head. "I expect women to burst out in tears, but somehow, when a man do it, it seems more tragic. It took me some time to get him calm, he idolised his daughter, and the few questions I managed to get him to answer tells us no more than we already know. She was brought up in a happy surroundings, and when her mother died, she took over. I had to get the lady next door to look after him for a while, I had to leave to catch the last train," Fred explained. "This one upset me."

"I'm sorry Fred," Chris said, not knowing what to say. "It must be upsetting, even for us, who deals with this kind of thing all the time."

Fred nodded his head. "Anyway," he said forcing a smile. "How did your day go, we now know that at least one of Mr Marchant's housekeepers was murdered and has been found."

"Perhaps the other one as well," Chris said watching Fred's face look of surprise. "We found another body of a young woman yesterday."

"Murdered?" asked Fred.

"Strangled we believe," replied Chris.

"Identified?" asked Fred.

"No not yet, nothing was found," Chris said.

Then Chris told Fred all the details. "I shall be wanting Mr Marchant to look at the body, I have already sent a message for him to be at the hospital at three this afternoon, he don't live far from the hospital."

"That's if he gets the message, he's not often there is he?" Fred replied.

"Keep our fingers crossed, the message was sent last evening, so let's hope it was one night that he came home," Chris remarked. "Still he may not recognise her," Chris said thoughtfully.

Chris and Fred watched Mr Marchant approach them as they stood outside the main hospital entrance.

"Inspector, Sergeant," Mr Marchant spoke coming up to them. "I did have a meeting this afternoon, but managed to cancel, now what's all this about?"

"A body of a young woman was found yesterday Mr Marchant," Chris said. "She had no identification with her, and we just wondered if it could be one of your missing housekeepers, after all without any photo, you are the only one who can identify her."

"I see Inspector," replied Mr Marchant. "Well of course I want to do all I can to solve the mystery."

"Have you ever seen a dead body before Sir?" Fred asked politely. "It's not a pleasant task."

"I'm sure it's not Sergeant," Mr Marchant replied. "No I've never seen a dead body, but I will survive."

Chris lead the way into the hospital, they went down stairs, and walked into the passage way until they came to swing doors, and were greeted by Mr Bob Harvey.

"This is Mr Marchant he will see if he can identify the body we found yesterday." Turning to Mr Marchant. "This is Mr Harvey Police Surgeon who has carried out an autopsy on the body," Chris introduced.

Mr Marchant offered his hand, which Bob accepted.

"It's not a pretty sight, she has been dead about four and half days, and with this warm July, her body is a little decomposed," Bob spoke.

Mr Marchant nodded his head, as he was led into the hospital mortuary. Chris, Fred and Bob, all watched as Mr Marchant looked at the body, Chris sensed straight away by the look on his face, that he knew her.

"That's my last housekeeper," Mr Marchant said in a cracked voice. "Miss Doris Thompson, how did she died?" he asked looking away from the body.

Fred took Mr Marchant's arm, and led him out of the room, where there was a chair that he could sit and calm himself.

"Would you like a cup of tea?" Chris asked coming to his side.

"Thank you, no," Mr Marchant replied. "How did that poor girl died?" he repeated.

"We want you to come to the Police Station now Mr Marchant, I need more questions to be answered," Chris informed.

Mr Marchant nodded his head. "Anything," he said.

Back to the Police Station Chris and Fred sat behind their desk, while Mr Marchant was drinking a cup of tea, sitting in the interview chair. He forced a smile, as he put his cup on Chris's desk in front of him. "Thank you for the tea," he said.

"Now Mr Marchant," Chris began. "We have found both of your missing housekeepers, Miss Doris Osman, and Miss Doris Thompson, they had both been murdered, both strangled."

"Now," Chris continued looking straight at Mr Marchant. "Miss Doris Osman, had been an unsolved murder case on our books for several months, she was never been identified, and was eventually given a paupers funeral."

"How dreadful," remarked Mr Marchant.

"It could have been prevented had you reported her missing when you found she had disappeared, as it was we could not connect her to anything or anyone," Chris spoke in all seriousness.

"I'm sorry, I had no idea," Mr Marchant said softly.

Chris continued. "I have spoken to the two past house-keepers, that you put on your list, and it seems that you have mislead us."

"In what way Inspector, I hope you are not trying to involve me in any of this?" asked Mr Marchant, who suddenly sat up straight.

"You mislead us regarding their wages," Chris continued ignoring his question. "I understand that their wages were in fact your housekeeper's salaries for the year, which although you did pay monthly, you were not doing something wrong paying monthly, but could hold your housekeepers for a year without paying."

Mr Marchant shrugged. "I suppose you could call it that, however it was a lot of money, even for a years work, I took it that they helped themselves to the generous housekeeping money that I gave them every week."

"It's either one or the other Mr Marchant," Fred interrupted. "You can't call wages a salary, at least we can't, we need honest facts, and you misled us."

"I'm sorry," replied Mr Marchant. "What else can I say."

"The truth from now on please, whatever you called what you paid them, means very little, but shows us that you can mislead us," Chris said who then waited but got no reply.

"Do you have any idea, or reason, why both your last two housekeepers were murdered, it seems very strange to us, and must seem the same to you, as you brought it to our notice, two previous housekeepers of yours are now living in a house that they own, while your two last housekeepers were murdered."

Mr Marchant sat up looking straight at Chris. "I have no idea Inspector, as I told you before, they were free to do with their time as they wished, if they did make any friends it's doubtful, that I would have been told," he said.

Chris leaned back in his chair, a slight smile playing around his eyes. "Tell me Mr Marchant, you have visitors to your home on occasions, always I believe during darkness."

"My, my Inspector," Mr Marchant remarked with a smile. "I am impressed, I cannot imagine how this will help your investigations, but it's simply that every week, we have a late night cards game."

"I see," Chris replied. "But I understand that you have two entrances to your house, one is never used during the day, only at night when you have this cards games."

"That is correct Inspector," replied Mr Marchant.

Chris waited for a deeper explanation, but did not get one, he realised that Mr Marchant was not going to volunteer information.

"Would you mind telling me why?" Chris asked.

"Not at all Inspector," replied Mr Marchant. "I have two large houses built into one, one part is used daily by my housekeeper, and myself when I am home. The other side is shall we say closed, I use it only when we play cards, and as we play late, we use the second door, so that the housekeeper is not disturbed. I also use this part of the house when I am hosting a dinner table," he said lifting his arms wondering where this questioning was going.

"I see," remarked Chris. "Can you tell us who you play cards game with?"

Mr Marchant thought for a while. "I play with a group of Winchester dignitaries Inspector," he finally said. "All highly respected people, magistrate, solicitor, council official, even a high ranking Army man, but before I give you their names, I wish to get legal advice."

Chris chewed over in his mind what he had been told, and decided to leave it for a while. "Very well Mr Marchant, whatever you wish, thank you for coming in voluntarily, you must understand, a missing person is one thing, but murder is very much different, and we have to follow our routine,"" he said standing up and offering his hand.

Mr Marchant took the Inspector's hand, and nodded to the Sergeant. "I understand Inspector, should you wish to contact me again, would you please phone my solicitor," he said, taking a card from his waistcoat pocket and handing it to Chris. "A little notice would be appreciated, as I am often away outside of Winchester."

Chris smiled his agreement as he watched Mr Marchant leave.

Chris looked at the card in his hand, then put it in the small drawer of his desk. "He started to clam up with the mention of his night visitors," Chris remarked. "I'm wondering if I can dig anything in to it."

"We won't get those names, if they are not relevant to our case," Fred argued. "Especially if they are who he says they are, anyway, we don't want to get on the wrong side of a Magistrate do we," Fred smiled.

Chris gave a force smile as he took out an envelope from his inside pocket.

"When you took Mr Marchant out of the mortuary, Bob, gave me this envelope of the post-mortem," Chris said opening the envelope, and unfolded the sheet of paper inside.

A small piece of paper, fell from it onto his desk. Chris let it stay on his desk for a while, as he read the report.

"She was strangled, she was about twenty to twenty-five years old, with no identification marks on her, she was not a virgin, but in his opinion, she was not raped. In his opinion, she had been dead for about seven days," Chris looked at Fred and continued.

"Let's see, she was reported missing last Monday, today is Friday, so that makes it five days, but we deduct a day, because the autopsy was carried out Thursday, so it must be seven days including Thursday, which makes it that she died Thursday or Friday, about a week today," Chris explained to Fred who was watching him.

"Well if that's so," Fred said. "Mr Marchant reported it almost at once, given it was the weekend in between, but then again, didn't he miss her over the weekend?"

Chris nodded his head in agreement, and picked up the small piece of paper that had fell from the report. "It looks as though you and me will have a liquid lunch today Fred," he said handing the paper to Fred, who read it.

"That will make a change," replied Fred. "Where did this come from I wonder?" he asked.

"It seems that Miss Thompson was wearing bloomers which had a small pocket in them, and Bob found that bit of paper in the pocket, it was a footnote on his report."

"Mr Stanley Millard, The White Horse Canon Street," Fred read out. "Do you know it?"

"I know where it is, but I've never been inside," Chris answered. "But there is always a first time," he smiled.

The White Horse was not a large pub, which was separated from the road, by a narrow pavement. Chris and Fred entered, it was just midday, and the pub had only two customers.

"Gentlemen," smiled the youngish man serving behind the bar. "What's your pleasure?" he asked.

Chris looked at Fred. "What's yours Fred?" he asked.

"I'll have a bitter," Fred replied, looking around.

"Then two pints of bitter landlord," Chris said.

"I'm not the landlord Sir, I'm a barman," the youngish man corrected.

"He's upstairs, I only work here," the barman said as he placed two pints before Chris who offered him the money.

Chris sipped his pint. "Do you think I can have a word with the landlord, his name is Stanley Millard?"

"That's him Sir," replied the barman. "I'll just shout for him," he said going through a door at the rear of the bar, soon to return. "He'll be down in a sec," smiled the barman.

Chris looked around the bar, and saw a small table to the right away from the two other customers. "We will sit at that table barman," Chris said to him pointing in the direction. "Please ask Mr Millard to join us."

"Will do Sir," smiled the barman, as he started to clean glasses.

Mr Millard was a man about forty, very good looking, his hair greying at the temples, he wore a well trimmed moustache, was slim, with average height. Chris stood as he reached their table.

"I am Detective Inspector Hardie, and this is Detective Sergeant Willett," Chris introduced themselves. "You are Mr Millard, landlord of this pub?"

Mr Millard nodded his head. "Yes I am, what can I do for you?" he said in a pleasant polite voice. "It can't be for a licence offence, normally policeman come for that, so I take it this is serious, with someone of your rank, how can I help?" he asked, sitting at an empty chair at the table.

"Tell us what you know about Miss Doris Thompson if you will," Chris asked.

"It's been a week since I've seen her, is she in trouble?" replied Mr Millard, his face showing concerned.

"When did you last see her?" Fred asked.

Mr Millard screwed his lips as he thought. "I'm not sure, it was either last Thursday or Friday," he answered.

"Can't you be sure?" Fred asked.

Mr Millard turned his head towards the bar. "Jim, when did Doris come in last, can you remember?"

"It had to be Friday, I was not here Thursday," the barman called back.

"It was Friday then," Mr Millard replied to Fred. "It would have been dinner time, she never came in night times."

"That's helpful Mr Millard," Chris remarked putting his glass on the table. "You keep a nice pint of bitter Mr Millard," Chris praised him smacking his lips.

"Thank you, we do our best," Mr Millard replied smiling.

"How well did you know Miss Thompson Mr Millard?" Chris asked.

"You are talking in past tense Inspector, has anything happened to her?" Mr Millard replied, his face serious.

Chris cursed himself for that slip, most people he would ask questions to, would not have noticed, he had to consider Mr Millard educated above average.

"I'm afraid she has been found dead," Chris said. "According to the post-mortem she could have died some-time last Friday, can you remember what time she left?"

Mr Millard, wiped his hands in the half white apron he had around his waist, he was shaking his head. "I just don't believe it, I just don't," he murmured.

"Doris would come in most days after opening time, during the dinner hours, after I closed at two thirty she would come upstairs with me, and stop about an hour, so it would be about three thirty that she left here last Friday."

"You were very close to her then?" Fred butted in.

"Nothing romantic, if you understand, just two people enjoying each other's company," Mr Millard said. "She would shop during the morning, and on her way back to where she worked, she would spend much time in here with me, she always seem reluctant to go back up there, I don't think she liked the man who she worked for," he added.

"I take it that you are not married Mr Millard?" Chris said as he finished his pint.

"No my wife passed away two years ago," he said in a sad voice. "Inspector, Sergeant, let me fill your glasses up," he offered.

"That quite alright Mr Millard," Chris said, not wanting to accept his offer.

"I insist, you obviously have other questions to ask, so you might as well have a drink, Jim," he called the barman.

"Refill please," he said as the barman looked at him. "Bring me a whisky as well," he ordered.

Having sipped their fresh drinks, Chris looked at Mr Millard, and thought he looked honest enough, but one can never be sure.

"She worked for Mr Marchant in Christchurch Road," Chris said. "As you were both close enough to have a this unromantic relationship, did she ever talk about Mr Marchant to you?"

Mr Millard gulped his glass of whisky down fast. "Tell me inspector, how did Doris died?"

Chris hesitated. "I'm afraid she was murdered," he replied.

Mr Millard called to his barman for another Whisky.

"On the way here I see you have a stable at the side Mr Millard," Fred butted in again. "I would have thought that this pub was in the wrong position to have one," Fred remarked.

"I have a horse and trap," Mr Millard admitted. "It's useful should I run out of bottle beer, I have my own transport."

"When did you last run out?" Fred pushed.

"I think it was Friday, I don't know, Inspector how exactly was she murdered?" Mr Millard asked again.

"She was strangled Mr Millard," replied Chris.

"Oh my God," replied Mr Millard. "I hope you get the bastard," he swore.

Chris studied the face of Mr Millard for a while then asked. "Did you by any chance know of a Miss Osman, she worked at the same place as Miss Thompson?"

Mr Millard shook his head. "Not that I recall," he said. "But then so many people come in here that I don't know the name of, why do you ask?"

"She suffered the same fate as Miss Thompson," Fred replied sharply.

Mr Millard stared at both of the detectives with disbelief on his face. "Well that's a turn up, two young women, working for the same person turns up murdered," he said looking at his whisky glass, which he was twisting in the palms of his hands. "When did this other murder happen?" he asked lifting his eyes.

"About six months ago," Chris replied. "It must have been reported in the papers."

Mr Millard continued to roll his whisky glass in the palms of his hand, as though deep in thought. "Yes, yes, I think I do remember something about a woman's body being found in a ditch, that must have been about six months ago come to think of it."

"That's probably the one," Fred remarked.

"No Inspector, I'm sure I did not know her, and had she been in this pub, I am sure that someone would have said so at the time, no Inspector I'm sorry."

"You have been very helpful anyway Mr Millard, and thank you for your drink, perhaps one day when off duty, you will allow me to return the kindness," Chris stood up and offered his hand.

Chapter Four

*I*t was Saturday, and Fred's day off, Chris ambled his way to the Butter Cross, and sat on the steps, hoping to meet Elizabeth, who would be going in to work, just for the morning. His mind pondered over the case he was on, it was now almost a week since it was brought to him as two missing persons. He had found the two women, by just the connection that they had worked for Mr Marchant, but instead of a missing persons case, it was now a murder investigation. He pondered over the bits and pieces of information that he had, but none of it told him who could have murdered the women, no one would strangle themselves.

"Day dreaming again Chris?"

Chris dismissed his thoughts, and looked up to find the smiling face of Elizabeth.

"I was waiting for you," he returned her smile.

Chris stood up, and Elizabeth gave him a quick kiss on the cheek, and grabbed his arm, as she always did. "Are you free today?" she asked as they started to walk towards her bank.

"No, my Sergeant is off today, so I'm on duty," Chris replied. "I have a lot of thinking to do."

"Are you bothered by this case?" Elizabeth asked, concern evident in her voice. "I'm sure you will solve it in the end, like your last one."

"Let's hope so," Chris replied patting her arm. "I am off tomorrow."

"Lovely," replied Elizabeth. "Mum will be pleased, you will be coming to dinner?" she asked looking up in his face. "Why don't you call in the Rising Sun about twelve, and have a drink with dad before you come, I'm sure he will enjoy that."

"That's a date," Chris replied.

They stopped outside the bank, Elizabeth let go of Chris's arm, and stood facing him. "You're a handsome man she said giving him another quick kiss on the cheek." "Sometimes good will come out of something bad," she smiled.

Chris understanding her meaning smiled at her. "We will have a good future together," he assured as he let her go into the bank.

Chris sat at his desk, writing carefully with his ink pen, when the desk sergeant poked his head around the door. "I have a Mr Osman outside Inspector, he wants to see Sergeant Willett."

Chris put his pen down. "Show him in Sergeant, and will it be possible to have two cups of tea?"

"I'll see what I can do Sir," replied the desk sergeant, as his head disappeared.

Mr Osman was just how Sergeant Willett had described him, Chris stood up as he entered, and offered his hand.

"Please sit down Mr Osman, I am Detective Inspector Hardie, Sergeant Willett have told me everything, and let me say from the outset, how very sorry I am about your daughter."

"At least you found her Inspector, not knowing where she was all these months, was very stressful, she was a very good girl," Mr Osman said.

"I'm sure she was Mr Osman," Chris said, as the desk sergeant brought in two cups of tea.

"Ah Sergeant thank you, put them here on my desk," Chris indicated. "I am sure Mr Osman will accept a cup of tea."

Mr Osman smiled his thanks, as the desk sergeant left. "That's kind of you Inspector, I have come straight here from the railway station."

"Then you will need a cup, please feel free," Chris watched as Mr Osman picked up his cup and drank from it.

"That was lovely," Mr Osman said replacing the cup on its saucer.

"Have you come here for the day Mr Osman?" Chris asked.

"I'm stopping with a relation of mine, just until Monday, I want to find out where Doris's grave is," he said a sadness creeping into his voice.

"I'm afraid it will be an unmarked grave Mr Osman," Chris said politely. "When your daughter was buried, no one knew who she was, our routine enquiries came up empty handed, so to speak, I am very sorry Mr Osman."

Chris saw tears come to Mr Osman's eyes. "Still, if you will call again during Monday morning, Sergeant Willett will only be too happy to go to the Council with you, with him along things might move quicker."

"That's decent of you Inspector," Mr Osman said with a sniff.

"I will do that, I did have another reason for calling, I wanted the Sergeant to have these letters," he handed Chris a small bundle of letters. "I did allow your Sergeant to read one of them, but after he went, I read the lot again, I am a silly old man Inspector, I don't know much, but I am sure there are bits in everyone of these letters that may help you find who killed my little girl."

Chris took the letters. "Thank you Mr Osman I'll read them myself."

"You will see that the last letter is dated January of this year," Mr Osman said.

"Thank you Mr Osman, you say you are stopping with a relative, I am wondering, how did your daughter get on with them?"

Mr Osman smiled. "I'm sorry Inspector, Harry, that is the man I shall be stopping with, is really no relation, but during the Boer War, we were like brothers, I'm sorry for that misunderstanding, Doris would have heard of him, but I doubt if she would have met him."

"I see," Chris said. "So you were in the Boer War Mr Osman?"

Mr Osman smiled as he nodded his head. "Yes, it was scary."

Getting no further reaction, Chris did not push for any. "Well Mr Osman, shall we say about ten o'clock on Monday morning," Chris stood up. "Sergeant Willett will be ready for you," as he offered his hand.

Chris spent the next two hours reading and re-reading the one page letters, and he felt that Mr Osman was not the fool he made himself out to be, the letters between them gave Chris a good idea of her life, while she was housekeeper. Chris bundled the letters together into a neat pile then looked at his pocket watch, it was midday.

He got up and went to the desk sergeant's desk. "I going out for a while, but I should be back by about two or thereafter."

"Right you are Inspector, no way of getting in touch?" the desk sergeant asked.

"I shall be on my bike, I have a couple of calls to make," Chris replied, seeing the sergeant nod his head understanding.

Chris clipped his trouser bottoms, and went out to the cycle shed, picking a bicycle, and was soon cycling towards the White Horse Public House. Reaching it, Chris dismounted, and removing his clips, stood his bicycle against the wall leading to the stable, and entered the bar.

"Ah Inspector, glad to see you again," the barman said.

"Thank you barman, a pint of bitter please," Chris replied.

After being served Chris stayed at the bar. "Mr Millard around?" he asked.

"Upstairs, do you want him?" asked the barman grinning all over his face, and Chris wondered if the grin was stuck on.

"No, I'm just in for a pint, it was a good one yesterday, go long way to get one just as good," replied Chris pleasantly.

"That what makes a good manager," the barman explained boastfully.

"Really," Chris replied. "So you're the manager not just the barman," Chris smiled as he took a sip of his drink.

"You can call me Jim, Inspector," the barman offered.

"So Jim, have you been the manager long?" Chris asked. "It must be a big responsibility?"

"This is my first week," Jim said still grinning. "But I'm learning."

"I'm sure you are," Chris replied. "Do you remember when you were asked yesterday, when was the last time you saw Doris and you replied Friday, could you have been mistaken?"

"I don't think so," Jim replied. "She was in here every day, and weekends, as I was off on Thursday, it had to be Friday."

"Thank you Jim," Chris answered. "What do a man like you do on your day's off?"

Jim laughed out loud. "Go for a drink," he said thinking it was funny. "I don't drink while I'm behind this bar, strict rules," he said pointing a finger to the upstairs. "He don't like it," Jim whispered.

"You don't come in here then?" Chris asked sipping his drink. "I suppose you get fed up with the place working here all the week as the manager, you are bound to get fed up with the place, where do you drink?"

"No, no, I come in here we have a game of push halfpenny, I enjoy being that side of the bar," Jim replied.

Chris finished his drink. "Well thank you Jim, I'll see you again, now back to work," he said, as he left the bar with a satisfactory smile on his face.

Chris, clipped his trouser bottoms, and mounted his bike, he wanted to see Miss West again, but when he got there, there was no one in, disappointed, he made his way back to the Police Station, where he found constable Higgins waiting for him with a little old lady, who was wearing a tummy for a hat. Chris thought that only children wore them, he shook his head, as he opened his office door inviting them both in. Chris held the interview chair for the woman to sit in, and brought a chair from the rear of the room for the constable to sit, then seated himself behind his desk.

"Well constable," Chris smiled.

"This is Miss Burton Sir," the constable said. "I bumped into her in town, she remembered that I asked her if there was any noise in the road during the dark hours, she could not remember then. When I bumped into her in town, she said she remembered something, that she would only tell a high ranking policeman, if they promise she would not be involved. So I brought her in to see you Sir," the constable ended, his face having gone a red colour.

Chris looked at the old lady, she reminded him of the woman who was always behind the net curtains, but she looked intelligent.

"Thank you constable, you did well," Chris replied. "Now Miss Burton, thank you for coming in, I am Detective Inspector Hardie, you can tell me what you want to, I promise you will not become involved."

Miss Burton's face beamed with a grin, she looked at the constable then looked seriously at Chris.

"Inspector," she said in all seriousness. "I am by nature a private person, I don't interfere with people, as long as they leave me alone, I am not the one for peeping behind blinds wanting to see what is going on, even if I was," she scoffed. "Little happens in Christchurch Road that might entertain peeping toms," she smiled.

"Anyway, it was early in the year as I remember, around January I would think, I remember I had gone to bed, you see I always go to bed at nine, you know," she tried to explain. "Early to bed, early to rise, that saying, anyway I went to bed at my usual time, then I awoke with a start when heard a sound," she said throwing her arms about. "It was pitch dark, but I can walk around my house blind folded, you see I was born in that house, and have lived in it all my life, I never married you know," she said looking at the Inspector.

"I'm sorry to hear that Miss Burton," Chris replied, not knowing what to say. "You were saying you awoke with a start."

"Oh, yes," continued Miss Burton. "I had forgotten to put out the saucer of milk for the hedgehog, you see," she went on to explain. "I have a hedgehog, that comes to my front every night for its milk."

Chris looked at the constable, who was fiddling with his helmet that rested on his lap, Chris looked back at Miss Burton and sighed.

"So," Chris ventured to say.

"Well I had to open my front door, to put out the milk, and I was greeted with a rumpus, that would wake the dead, I am sure that it was heard by other householder in the street, as I said," Miss Burton continued caught up in her own story.

"It was very dark, but the gas lamp opposite Christchurch road, seem to glow more brightly, yes I remember, because I was able to see two covered carriages in their small driveway, one carriage was half way in the road, the noise was deafening," she said flinging her arms in the air again. "I heard screaming and shouting, but I remember thinking at the time, they don't sound like joys screams, they sound more like agony screams."

Chris saw that Miss Burton had ended her story, as she laid back, and smiled at the Inspector.

"Where do you live in Christchurch Road?" Chris asked.

"I am the forth house in from St James Lane," she replied.

"You're able to see the first house in from your own?" Chris asked.

"Not the entrance door Inspector, but I can see all of the front garden," Miss Burton answered with the feeling of being important. "Have I been of help to you Inspector?"

"You certainly have Miss Burton, and I must thank you very much for telling me what you know," Chris said, a smile around his eyes.

"I told the constable here, what I have to tell is for the ears of high ranking policeman only, I was right wasn't I Inspector?" she asked excitement of the moment showing in her face.

"You were certainly right Miss Burton," Chris said getting up. "Will you be alright getting home?"

"Don't you worry Inspector, I shall be alright, I have a little shopping to do first, I am glad that I have been able to help you," Miss Burton said, as she shook Chris's outstretched hand.

Chapter Five

*I*t was quarter past the hour when Chris entered the Rising Sun, he looked to his left, and saw that Ron was already sitting. Ron rose as Chris entered and offered his hand, which Chris took and shook warmly.

"You have missed a quarter of an hour drinking time," Ron said to Chris with a smile. "I've ordered a bitter for you is that alright?"

"Perfect," Chris replied.

"All ready for you Chris," Alfie smiled. "Don't like to keep my customers waiting, I hear that you have found a woman's body," Alfie continued with his usual smile.

Chris took his pint from the counter. "I'll have to employ you Alfie," he smiled as he took his pint to the table.

"I heard that as well," Ron said. "Another case?"

Chris kept his voice low. "Yes I'm afraid, it's actually the second body we have found, both murdered."

"Oh dear," Ron said putting his pint glass to his lips. "Still I'm sure that you will solve it."

Chris drank from his pint before answering. "I hope so, it's a bit complicated."

"Have you any opinion, or shouldn't I ask?" Ron said.

"No that's alright," Chris replied. "I don't believe in opinions, you see, you and I could have a different opinion on the same subject, but opinions are only what we think, so both of our opinions are, shall we say equal, and I don't think that anyone should argue over an opinion."

"But you do have a couple of facts to go on?" Ron queried.

"Well yes," replied Chris, but then it become an assumption, opinions are made without facts, assumptions are made with a few facts."

"I never thought of it that way," Ron admitted.

"Well let's take a doctor," continued Chris. "When a patient goes to him, he makes a diagnose, on the facts that he is told, but it's still only an assumption, because many patients leave out vital information. If a doctor gets his diagnose wrong, it could mean a life, if I get mine wrong, it could mean an innocent man spends time in prison."

"I see," Ron said as he raised his glass again. "So if you don't have opinions, and you are wary of assumptions, what makes your mind up."

Chris smiled. "Deduction and detection I suppose, mixed with common sense."

"But what's the difference between deduction and assumption?" Ron asked as he finished his pint.

Chris drained his pint and turning to Alfie ordered two more. "The way I see it, deduction is what I can reasonably deduct from the facts I know as a waste of time, even though I will follow them."

Chris got up and picked up the two pints that Alfie had put on the counter. "Have one yourself Alfie," Chris offered paying over the money.

"Your mind must be in use twenty four hours a day," Ron said lifting his pint. "Bit too heavy for me."

"It's training," Replied Chris. "I had a good boss, all the fact had to fit, before he would committed himself."

"I'm afraid we will have to go after this one," Ron said. "I did say we would be home around one, if that's OK with you."

For Chris, the rest of the day went too quick, after being welcomed like the prodigal son, by Olive and Elizabeth, Chris enjoyed the roast beef dinner, served to him by Elizabeth, followed by apple pie and custard, after which he was made comfortable in a armchair, and encouraged to have his pipe.

"I could get use to this," he said smiling at Elizabeth as he settled.

"You will be after we are married," Elizabeth replied to the smiles of her parents who had heard her.

"We'll go for a stroll over the hill when you're ready," she suggested.

"I'll enjoy that," Chris replied. "I ate too much, a walk might help my digestion."

Chapter Six

C hris was seated at his desk when Sergeant Willett came in. "You seem happy," he said to Chris. "Had a good weekend?"

"I had a great Sunday," Chris admitted. "A couple pints at the Rising Sun, and great roast dinner, and a stroll with the lady I will marry."

"No wonder you're happy," Fred replied without a smile. "I wish I could say the same, my misses moaned continuously."

"About Winchester?" Chris asked.

"Yes, I am afraid, she will never accept living here," answered Fred as he made his way to his desk. "Still what can I do, anyway, what's on today?" he asked trying to cheer up.

Chris felt sorry for Fred, he was a much older man than Chris, with loads of experience, and Chris was getting used to him, he brushed his thoughts to one side.

"A friend of yours called Saturday," Chris said. "A Mr Osman from Andover, he wants to find out where his daughter is buried, I told him that you would take him to the council and help him find her, I know this is not a part of your duty, but he asked especially for you, and as you know, she was given a paupers burial, I hope you don't mind."

"No, not at all," Fred replied. "He's a nice old man, what time?"

"Around ten this morning."

"That's OK then, gives me a half hour."

"When you have finish, can you make the rounds of estate agents, find out if you can, who sold the homes of Miss West and Miss Johnson, and who bought them?"

"Will do," Fred replied. "What will you be doing?"

"I have the Superintendent Fox calling on me during the morning, no idea what he wants," Chris replied.

"What's he like?" Fred asked.

"I've met him a few times, when Inspector Noal was here, but not since I took over."

"That's strange," Fred remarked. "You would think that he would have welcomed you, perhaps he wants to congratulate you on your last case," Fred said.

"Perhaps you're right Fred," Chris replied his mind wondering.

Fred had gone with Mr Osman, some half hour later Superintendent Fox entered the office. He was a tall slender man, full of authority, he stood six foot, looking very smart in his white collar shirt, and blue uniform. He took of his peak cap, as he entered and offered his hand to Chris, who was already standing.

"It's about time I darn well called," he said as Chris shook his hand. "I haven't welcomed you, or congratulated you on your promotion, and for that I apologise," he continued seating himself in the interview chair.

"Now Hardie," he said resting his hat on his knees and holding his short cane. "You are not conforming to darn rules."

Chris taken back a little, did not understand his meaning. "I'm sorry Sir," Chris replied politely. "If I am not, then it is ignorance."

"Darn it Hardie, you went to Scotland, without authority, I had this darn Superintendent from Fort William phoning me asking if your visit to them was authorised, and darn it Chris, I had no idea that you had gone, and at the time had no darn idea what he was talking about, however," Superintendent Fox said with a vain smile on his face.

"With quick thinking, I cut the line, and quickly phoned your desk sergeant here, who told me you had gone to Scotland, to get information on a darn case, I then phoned back this Superintendent apologising about the line being cut, and lied for you."

"I apologise Sir," Chris replied. "When I took over, I had the understanding that I had a free range."

"God damn it Hardie," interrupted the Superintendent. "You went to another country, you were absent without leave, and on top of that you put in a claim form for expenses. It's not my darn way of working, to be watching my chaps all the time, going to Andover or Basingstoke, I would overlook. But to go to Scotland, without authorisation," the Superintendent stared at Chris.

"You were really pushing your darn luck, and mine, you must remember it was on Inspector Noal's insistence that I forwarded your name to the Chief Constable to take over, and the first thing I had to do was to cover your darn ass."

Chris found himself going red, realising that he had really made a bloomer. "What can I say Sir," Chris murmured with a movement of his shoulders. "I can now see that I was wrong, I should have run it through with you first."

"Yes you darn well should have done, and make sure that you darn well do in the future," the Superintendent rolled his short cane across the top of his hat, and a smile came to his face. "The Chief Constable wants me to congratulate you on solving the case, I might add that Inspector Noal would have been proud of you, as we all are in the force."

Chris felt a surge of relief go through his body, he had just been reprimanded, and had expected the worse but instead had been congratulated. "Thank you Sir," was all he was able to say.

"Now Hardie this new case that you are on, my darn telephone has been going all the time, run me through it?" he asked.

Chris told the story as he knew it. "It started as a missing housekeeper, and ended up as two murders, both had been housekeepers for Mr Marchant, who seems to be a very wealthy person, with highly respected friends."

"It's these darn highly respected friends that is my darn worry," the Superintendent said. "We don't want to upset powerful people if it's not necessary, the Chief Constable has to live with them, and you will be surprised of the darn aggravation that they can give him."

"I understand Sir," Chris replied. "What is it you would like me to do?"

"God damn it Hardie you run your case as you see fit, all I'm darn well saying is that unless these names coming out are irrelevant to you getting a conviction, there are other ways that they could be known, if you get my meaning, a prosecutor will often bring out hidden factors," the Superintendent stood up. "I have a meeting in the Guildhall at eleven, so I must dash."

Chris looked at his pocket watch. "Quarter to," Chris said with a smile around his eyes, I am really sorry for the bloomer I made Sir."

"We are all entitled to one darn mistake Hardie, you saved your ass by solving the case, I have granted your expenses by the way," the Superintendent smiled as he left the room.

It was midday when Fred re-entered the office.

"Not much luck I'm afraid Chris," Fred said sitting at his desk. "I've been to all the estate agents in Winchester, no one sold these women a house. One estate agent did remember selling these houses to a man, who paid cash for them, they said they had sold him several, all around three hundred pounds each, just normal two up and two down."

"But no name?" Chris interrupted.

"They said that they would find out if possible, should he come in again," Fred replied.

"How about Mr Osman?" Chris asked interested.

"It seems paupers graves are marked by numbers, we found Mr Osman's daughter easy, it was the only body buried without a name."

"So he's happy," Chris remarked.

"I suppose," Fred replied. "But it was the Parish that buried her, so if he can afford it he will have to repay the cost, if he do, then he can make a proper grave of it.

"How did you get on with the Superintendent?" Fred asked curiously.

Chris looked up with a little smile on his face. "Well it was a strange meeting, first I got a reprimand."

"What for?" Fred interrupted.

"For not telling him I was going to Scotland, he also told me that I was absent without leave, and that I went to Scotland without authorisation," Chris replied, as he saw Fred shaking his head.

"Christ Chris, I thought you had arranged it all with the Superintendent, you mean you went without him knowing?" Fred said with alarm.

"I'm afraid I did," Chris admitted.

"What happen then?" Fred asked still shaking his head.

"Then he congratulated me on behalf of the Chief Constable, and himself," Chris said a broad smile on his face. "He has granted my expenses."

"Good job you solved the case Chris," Fred remarked. "You could have got suspended."

"That's more or less what he said," Chris confirmed. "But at least that's all cleared up, it leaves us free to concentrate on the latest case, I shall think in future before I act."

Fred handed Chris a paper. "You remember Mr Osman saying that he had gone to the Andover Police about his missing daughter, well I have looked through the records, and I found that in February this year, a request was made by the Andover police, for one of our chaps to go and see Mr Marchant, regarding Mr Osman's daughter. A constable finally called at the house, and it was answered by a Miss Brenda West, who told the constable that Miss Osman had left the house without giving notice, nor her future where about, nothing else was done, and this report was passed back to Andover."

"That's strange Fred," Chris remarked. "My understanding is that Miss West was a housekeeper there before Miss Osman, Miss West also told me that she had not seen Mr Marchant since, and did not know Miss Osman."

"We are being lied to," Fred remarked.

"It certainly seems that way, I shall be calling on Miss West this afternoon, she better be in," Chris remarked, his face serious.

In the afternoon Chris arrived Miss West's house, he took off his cycle clips, after knocking the door.

"Come in Inspector," offered Miss West who had opened the door. "I've just made a pot of tea."

Chris entered taking off his trilby. "Thank you Miss West, I called two days ago, but you were out."

"Sorry about that Inspector, sit yourself down, while I pour."

Sitting opposite each other at the small dining table, Brenda West poured out two cups of tea. "Help yourself to sugar Inspector," she said passing Chris a cup.

Chris spooned two teaspoons from the sugar basin, stirred, then sipped the tea before replacing the cup in the saucer.

"Well how can I help you Inspector?" Brenda asked, as she lit a cigarette, took a deep drag, blowing out a cloud of smoke. "Do you smoke Inspector, I like a smoke with my cup of tea."

"I smoke a pipe," Chris replied.

"Feel free Inspector, I like to see a man with a pipe," Brenda smiled.

"Thank you, but I'm fine," Chris replied. "The reason I have called again Miss West, is that some of your story you told me last time do not add up."

"Oh," replied Brenda who was replacing her cup to the saucer. "In what way?"

"You told me that you had not seen Mr Marchant after you left his employment, but it's now my understanding that you were working there after Miss Osman disappeared."

Brenda West smiled as she took another drag of her cigarette, and blew out the contents. "When I told you that I had not seen Mr Marchant since leaving, I was meaning after I took over for a while after Miss Osman's disappearance, I told you the truth Inspector, I have not seen Mr Marchant since," Brenda put her butt end in the ashtray, and took the last sip of her tea before continuing.

"When Mr Marchant found that Miss Osman had left, I was asked if I could just go and see to the refreshments for the cards games until he was able to get a new housekeeper. I did not go back to live, only stopping the nights when there was a cards game. I take it you are referring to that time that the police called regarding Miss Osman, I was there preparing for the cards game, and I told the constable the truth, that Miss Osman had gone, and no one knew where."

"I see," replied Chris a smile playing around his eyes. "Tell me did you serve the members of this cards games?"

"No, no, Inspector," Brenda replied. "My job was to spread the green beige table cloth, and put out two or three new packs of cards out. I would make several trays of sandwiches, and place them on the sideboard covered over."

"No drink?" Chris asked.

"None was never delivered to the house, but there was plenty in the cards room, my guess is that every time they came, each one brought a bottle, when I clean up in the morning, there was always many half bottles left."

"So you never saw any member of the cards players?" Chris asked.

"Right Inspector, remember the cards game were played next door so to speak, these people did not enter my part of the house," Brenda replied.

"How many bedrooms would there be in the two houses?" Chris asked.

"Six, three in each house," Brenda replied.

"Apart from the three in the house part that you lived, were the beds in the adjoining house ever used?" Chris asked emptying his cup.

"Not that I know, I always had to inspect and keep the house clean, and the beds in the second house were always made, I cannot remember have to make any beds after a cards game."

Just two more questions Miss West, and I leave you alone. "Why do you think Mr Marchant changed his housekeepers so often?"

Chris saw Brenda's eyes drop to the ashtray, she fingered the cigarette end that was in it.

"I have no idea Inspector," she answered without further comment.

"The cards players, were they always the same men, every week?" Chris asked.

"As far as I know Inspector," Miss West replied. "You must remember that it was always late when the cards game was held, but it was my understanding that they were regulars."

"Well thank you Miss West," Chris said getting up.

"You have been very helpful, and thank you for clearing up that little misunderstanding."

Chapter Seven

*D*ennis Marchant, looked around his smoke filled cards room, he was very depressed, as he watched the smiling faces of the men in the room, drinking and eating while chatting to each other. He wondered what they would say, when he told them his news. He sipped the whisky in front of him, wondering where it all had gone wrong.

"Right gentlemen, let's get started shall we," he said. "Bring your drinks to the table."

Dennis watched as the chatter stopped, and the four men found their places at the table, where they waited for him to speak.

"The news I have for you tonight is very depressing," Dennis said. "We have lost several agents last month."

Dennis waited for the murmur that started to ease before he continued.

"As you all know that Agents Roggen, Melon, Lody have all been shot in the Tower of London this year, they gave their life for their belief, they will be honoured and remembered by Germany when we win this war."

Again a murmur went around the room, agreeing with what Dennis was saying.

Agents Muller and Hahn, are both waiting for their trial, which I believe will be a Court Marshall, rather than a proper Court Case. Dennis waited again for the murmur to subside before continuing.

"One would have thought that we have had enough of bad luck, but I am afraid that from the thirtieth of May until the ninth of June, four more of our agents have been arrested."

A loud murmur, with talking followed, and Dennis waited for it to ease.

"Who were they?" came a voice.

Dennis looked down at the paper in front of him. "I can tell you," he continued.

"That agent Jassen was arrested in Southampton on the thirtieth of May and charged with offences against the Realm, agent Roos was arrested in Edinburgh, Scotland on the second of June last month, and with those agents goes most of our Navel intelligent."

"Who else?" came a quiet voice from around the table.

"Well," Dennis continued. "Agent Bushman was arrested in South Kensington on the forth of June, and Agent Breeckow was also arrested in London on the forth of June."

"Good Lord," came an alarmed gasp from around the table. "We must have a spy in our midst," another said. "Any more?" asked another voice.

"We lost our only female, Wertheim on the ninth of June," Dennis replied.

Dennis watched as the four men, sipped their drinks, deep in thought and not conversing.

"What are we doing wrong?" a voice asked.

"My opinion," Dennis replied. "Agent Jassen and Roos were working together on British Navel ships, I believe that Special Branch or CID Scotland Yard suspected one, and when he was arrested they found the name and address of the other one, this is also same about Breeckow, when he was arrested they found the name of Wertheim in his flat. This broke the strict rules, never meet your partner at his or her address, nor keep names and addresses in your home, for someone to find, one thing is sure," Dennis continued.

"Fluid for invisible ink, is a give away if found in your home, also if you are writing on rice paper, hiding it in your shaving brush or toothpaste, or walking stick etc, is no longer safe, Special Branch know all these tricks. But to cap it all, I believe we have lost our agents because of the letters they send abroad, which were intercepted."

"So what are we going to do?" asked a voice.

Dennis thought for a while, then spread his hands open on the table. "With the lost of so many agents since we set up a year ago in August 1914, we have to re organise at the moment," Dennis paused and looked at each agent in turn. "You are the only four agents left, and I don't want to lose any of you."

"Can't we get more across?" a voice asked.

"That will be up to Number One, who ever he is."

"Don't you know?" a voice asked.

"No I don't," Dennis replied. "I carry out his instructions, I'm the paymaster, but I have no idea who Number One is."

"So what is his instructions?" a voice asked.

Dennis looked at the speaker, and gave a sigh. "This is a safe city, that is why we are able to meet here every month, since I have settled here I have held cards games nights every week with well known dignitaries, so that these weeks every month is covered. I also have two safe houses, each one run by a past housekeepers, I have other houses, but with no housekeeper at the moment. We are going to stop all activity for the next two months, to give us time to re-organise, and hopefully to get more agents."

"So what do we do in these two months?" a voice asked with urgency in his voice. "Just sit around doing nothing."

"No," Dennis replied. "You will go home now, destroy whatever you have that may give you away, let it be known around that you are travelling for a couple of months, because you will be going back. Then you will all come to this city, and take up lodgings, the addresses will be in your pay envelope. It is no need to tell you that you must memorise these addresses and destroy the written addresses. Two of you will stop in each address, then after a month you will swap over, just a little extra security," Dennis looked at the glum faces around the table. "No need to tell you that when you come back to Winchester, you will take the same precautions as you always do, I don't want any suspicions forming here."

"What about these housekeepers, can they be trusted?" asked a voice.

"Yes," Dennis replied "But remember they are not agents, they don't know you are agents, so act normally, and do not speak about Germany in any way. You will have to pay them bed and breakfast however," Dennis said with a smirk on his face.

"Yes what about money?" came a voice.

"Don't worry, I don't want to see you now for two months, just do what anyone would do while on holiday, travel if you want, but do nothing that may involve you. You will get two months pay this time, that's one hundred pounds each for the two months."

Silence followed for a time, while those around the table filled their glasses. Dennis got up and refilled his whisky, then re-seated himself.

Dennis laid in bed, he could not sleep, he wondered how it will all end. He had followed Number One's instructions, while wondering who he could be, but in his mind he was worried about the murdered housekeepers. He had not told the agents about the murdered housekeepers, for fear that may have panicked. He had told his cards games members about the disappearance of the housekeepers, he had no reason not to do so. With the disappearance of the second housekeeper, the solicitor had advised him to report it to the police, this was endorsed by the magistrate, and the councillor who both advised that if these housekeepers had been hurt, or abducted, the police might think it strange that you did not report them missing. He had spoke on the phone to Number One the next time he had made contact about it, and he had agreed with what he had been advised to do, so he had. But it worried Dennis, he hoped that the murders would be cleared up, he knew that the police had called on his two past housekeepers, and he was worried in case the police suspected his other activity. Dennis fell into an uneasy sleep.

Chapter Eight

*C*hris signed the last document in the folder with care, using his nib pen. Then closing the file, placed it with several others to his left, replacing his pen beside the inkwell, he looked at Fred who was reading the paper.

"Well that's all the odds and ends done," he informed.

Fred placed his paper down on his desk. "Pity we can't say that about the Marchant case, it's now at the end of August, no headway for over four weeks."

Chris leaned back in his chair, and sucked on his unlit pipe. "Noal always said that sooner or later, someone, somewhere will say something that will give you a clue, if that's the case, I wish that someone would do it soon, we don't even have a suspect."

"You win some, and lose some," Fred was saying as the phone rang.

Chris lifted the receiver from its stem, and eased himself forward, enabling him to speak into the mouthpiece. "Inspector Hardie," he spoke onto the receiver.

"Superintendent Fox here," came the reply. "Darn it Chris what are you up to?"

"You have me at a disadvantage Sir," Chris replied a puzzled look on his face.

"I've just had a darn Special Branch Officer here, I had no idea you were dealing with a spy case darn it."

"News to me Sir," Chris replied.

"You mean you're not aware?" asked the voice over the phone.

"I'm not aware of it Sir," Chris replied, then waited a few seconds before getting a reply.

"Well he's on his way down to darn well see you, his name is Inspector Harris."

"What is he like Sir?" Chris asked with a smile playing on his face.

"What is he like," exploded the voice on the other end of the phone. "What do you darn well mean what is he like?"

"I mean in appearance Sir," Chris replied, the smile still on his face.

"He's about forty, about five foot, ten inches tall, seems in good shape, he is average looking with dark hair. He wears a suit and tie, covered with a overcoat, and wears a trilby, oh and he wears black shoes with his brown suit. Why do you want to darn well know that, you will be seeing him soon."

"Just to be on the safe side Sir, if we are dealing with spies," Chris replied.

"Well keep me darn well informed," Superintendent Fox grunted replacing his receiver.

"You winding the Superintendent up?" Fred asked as Chris replaced his receiver.

"We are having a visitor from Special Branch," Chris explained. "It's about spies."

"What was all that stuff about his appearance?" Fred asked.

"Just a tease," Chris laughed. "The Superintendent has a good memory and a good eye, this chap wears black shoes with a brown suit," Chris smiled. "Anyway let the desk sergeant know Fred who to expect, and tell him to check his ID.

An hour had passed when the desk sergeant knocked and entered the office.

"Inspector Harris to see you Sir," he said.

Thank you Sergeant," Chris replied as a man with black shoes, and bearing the same description he had already been told entered the office, with his overcoat undone, and his trilby in his left hand. Chris stood, as the man approached him.

"Harris of Special Branch, you are Inspector Hardie?" he said holding out his hand.

"Yes," replied Chris taking the hand, then introducing Sergeant Willett. "Please have a seat Inspector," Chris offered indicating the interview chair.

Harris took the chair, then looked at Chris, and then the Sergeant Willett.

"What can I do for you?" Chris said breaking the silence.

"I'm here Inspector on a matter of security of the Realm, and what I have to say must not be repeated," he said once again looking towards Fred.

"What I know Inspector Harris, so do my Sergeant, we are the only two CID at this station, and work as a team," Chris said.

Inspector Harris smiled, knowing that Chris had suspected that he wanted the Sergeant out of the room. "I'm sorry Inspector Hardie, old habits die hard, Sergeant Willett is welcomed to hear what I have to say," Inspector Harris twisted in his chair before continuing. "I have seen your Superintendent Fox, and I have his permission to work with you, in your area."

"I'm still in the dark Inspector," Chris said.

"Well to put it bluntly Inspector," Harris said. "I am a spy catcher, and we believe you have spies in Winchester."

Chris looked at Fred, who had a bewildered look upon his face. "I am not aware of them," Chris replied, his confusion was plain on his face.

"That's understandable, spies do not advertise themselves," answered Harris. "But you do have them here, let me explain. We have been very lucky this year, already we have caught nine, three have already been trialled and shot, the others are awaiting a Court Marshall. During the interrogation of these spies awaiting trial, the name of Marchant has popped up, I believe you are investigating a murder case, that involves a Mr Marchant."

"That's true," Chris replied leaning back in his seat full of interest. "But there must be many Marchant across the country, unless you have a specific address."

"No I don't have that Inspector," Harris replied his face unsmiling. "What I do know about this man is that he is rich, and because of his businesses, travels the country and his headquarters is somewhere around Southampton. We have checked every Marchant known, and your Mr Marchant seem to fit. He is what we call the paymaster, as he provides the pay of the spies, and other funds, it goes without saying that there is a meeting place somewhere," Harris paused for a moment. "If his headquarters is in Winchester, then you would have spy trouble here, they need a small town."

"But this is an Army Town," Fred spoke up. "Surely this is one place spies would not operate."

Harris smiled at Fred. "No, not really, Winchester is known in Germany as a Army Garrison, they are not worried how many soldiers are stationed here, but they are worried how many leaves our shores. Spies are found around sea ports, Southampton, Portsmouth, and even at Edinburgh in Scotland, all taking notes of our troop-ships, and warships leaving, so you see that Winchester could well be a safe town for them, as there will never be a hint of any spying, so no investigation."

Chris still leaning back in his chair, interested in what was being said, sucked on his unlit pipe. "If this Mr Marchant of ours is the paymaster, you must believe that he meets here with spies, in order for him to pay them, do you have anything to back this up?"

Inspector Harris stood up, and took off his overcoat. Fred left his desk, and took the coat, and his trilby from him and hung them on the stand.

"Getting warm in here," Inspector Harris smiled as he re-seated himself.

"I'm sorry Inspector," Chris said leaning forward. "Can I get you tea?"

"No, no thank you I'm fine," replied Harris continuing. "Spies are normally travellers selling one sort of goods or another, usually for a firm abroad, so they travel a lot, and stay at hotels, so we never really have an address for them but we do know that there are at least four spies operating in this area, we actually know them."

"Why not arrest them like you have the others this year?" Chris asked, leaning back in his chair again.

"We need to find out who the paymaster for this area is, also we hope to find out who is Number One, no one, even the spies we have caught, have any idea who he is?" "So we tracked them," Inspector Harris commented.

"Back to Winchester?" Chris asked.

Inspector Harris gave a laugh. "If it was only that simple, yes we do track them, but we lose them. It seems that at least once a month, they all leave for a station in London, don't matter where they are, one could be in Southampton, but he would first go to London, then we would lose him in the crowd, he could from London catch transport to anywhere, we do not have the man power for this type of tracking. If we know where the paymaster is, then we will find safe houses, for spies to hole up for a while. If of course we can find Number One, who recruits all the agents, then we could say, this country will be free from spies."

Chris took the pipe from his mouth, and leaned forward, as the telephone rang, lifting the receiver from its stem, Chris leaned forward to speak. "Inspector Hardie," he said into the mouthpiece.

After a minute, Chris replaced the receiver with a thank you, and looked at Fred.

"A man been found badly beaten, can you see to it Fred, the sergeant has all the details."

Fred got up feeling disappointed, but he knew that Chris was not getting him out of the office on purpose. He nodded to Chris and Inspector Harris as he left the office.

"Good man is he?" Inspector Harris asked referring to the Sergeant.

"Yes, and he has years of experience," replied Chris. "Anyway Inspector, what is it you want from me, what you have told us, makes me think that you could be right about our Mr Marchant."

"Just tell me what you know if you will," replied Inspector Harris.

Chris leaned on his desk, his hands clasped. "Mr Marchant himself came to us, over the disappearance of two of his housekeepers, they had both disappeared without trace, leaving nothing in their rooms at the house. Our Investigation, found that they had both been murdered, one six months earlier than the latest. On the investigations of their murderer or murderers, we have come to a full stop. Mr Marchant has two houses in Christchurch Road here, that has been knocked into one house. One side, or one house is where he lives, and sleeps, with the housekeeper, the other house or half of the two houses, is used for his cards games that he holds every week. I must say that I don't think the men he plays cards with every week are spies," Chris picked up his pipe and fingered it.

"I have interviewed two of his past housekeepers, they both have a house, both single. I have had Mr Marchant's home and the houses of the two housekeepers watched over the last four weeks, and reports are that the two housekeepers have two male lodgers each, and the cards game held every week, did not occur last week, now while," Chris spread his hands over his desk. "I feel you may be on the right track as to your spies, I do not think Mr Marchant will turn out to be my murderer."

Inspector Harris looked at Chris with a smile on his face. "You know what Inspector, I think you are right. The housekeepers are not agents, but their cause is with Germany, they provide safe houses, Bed and Breakfast, without asking questions, and their houses are normally bought for them by the paymaster. Mr Marchant's cards games every week, hides the real purpose of his agents meetings with him, which takes place on the forth week. Are you sure that you will not find the answer to your murder investigations with these people?" Harris asked hesitating slightly. "Because if you are sure, I would like your permission to put my own men on watch."

"This station will give you full cooperation Inspector," Chris said. "If I need to interview any of the people we have spoken about, I let you know, as long as you keep me in the picture should you have to do anything other than watch."

"Agreed," replied Harris.

"Where are you staying?" Chris asked. "I take it you will be staying in Winchester for an unknown time?"

"I shall stay at a hotel tonight," Inspector Harris replied. "I shall call about four of my men down here tomorrow, don't know of any pub out of the way that do Bed and Breakfast, we don't like to stick out in our job."

Chris thought for a while. "I do have a local which might do for you, I'll asked the landlord if he can do it, I'll let you know tomorrow if you call in."

"I'll be on my own tonight," Inspector Harris said. "Can't we have a drink together?"

"I don't see why not," replied Chris. "Meet me outside about six thirty, and I'll take you to my local. But now if there is nothing else, I need to find out what has happened to Sergeant Willett," Chris opened his desk drawer, and took out a thick file. "This is my only copy of my investigations to date about Mr Marchant, if you have time, and want to, you can stay here and read it, take notes of all the addresses and so forth."

"That is very generous of you Inspector, yes I would like to," Inspector Harris answered.

"Call me Chris," Chris offered the Inspector.

"I'm George," replied Harris with a smile on his face.

"Take my chair, and make yourself at home George" Chris smiled. "I'll get the desk sergeant to bring you in a cuppa, his name is George as well."

Chris spoke to the desk sergeant, informing him that his office would be occupied, also enquiring about the beaten man.

75

"A man badly beaten was found in a house at Wharf Hill, where the man was a lodger, he could not speak as he was unconscious. He had been taken to the hospital, and that is where I sent Sergeant Willett," the desk sergeant explained.

"Well when the Sergeant Willett returns, tell him who is in the office, I shall be back within a hour," Chris informed.

"You can rely on uniforms," remarked the desk sergeant without a smile.

"Take the Inspector a cup of tea will you sergeant, and remember he is Special Branch."

"So is a thorn branch," remarked the sergeant, as Chris left the station.

Chris dug his hands into his trouser pockets, as he made his way up the high street towards the bank where Elizabeth works. A few weeks ago she had invited him into her office, where she did accountancy. "Don't be shy Chris," she had said to him. "You can visit me anytime you like, I am usually here on my own."

Chris had never taken the offer up before, but today he had to contact her, and did not wish to phone. Chris entered the gas lit bank, and moved to his left, where he knew Elizabeth's office to be. He tapped the door lightly, opened it and pocked his head in. Elizabeth was sitting at her desk, studying papers in front of her. She looked up, and a smile filled her face seeing who it was.

"Chris darling, what a lovely surprise, come and sit," she said getting up inviting Chris inside.

Chris walked across the small office to her desk, where there was a chair available.

Elizabeth leaning forward planted his expected kiss on his cheek, before re-seating herself. Elizabeth, looked at

76

Chris, and the love she felt for him surged through her body, she knew he was having difficulty in telling her that he had to cancel their meeting that night, and knew because it was hurting him, he would take hours to explain.

"I'm glad you called in darling," she said her eyes full of twinkles, which Chris called smiling eyes. "I have found myself overloaded with work, I have all these accounts to get out by tonight," she said indicating the sheets of paper on her desk. "I was wondering, would you be too disappointed if I asked you not to see me tonight?"

Chris sighed a silent relief, he forced a smile, thinking that every moment away from her was a moment that he could never make up. "Well I do have work to do," he said looking at her, and finding her face a distraction to what he wanted to say. "I have these Special Branch people down from London, I do have to find them a place to stay, and I was thinking that I could get them billeted in the Rising Sun, which means I shall have to go there after opening time, so it would help me as well," he said with a feeling of regret.

"That sound serious," remarked Elizabeth. "Special Branch, are they really special?"

"They are trained for special jobs, and although I am not supposed to say, they are here in connection with spies, but you must not mention that to anyone."

Elizabeth smiled. "Whatever you say to me about your work darling remains confidential, could these men not go to a hotel?"

Chris hesitated. "Well I have to find some place, where they won't stick out, but they have their own reason."

After a few moments of chit chat, Chris took out his pocket watch. "I'm sorry Elizabeth, but I will have to go,

I have a man in hospital who was found very badly beaten, I must look into it."

"My poor Chris," Elizabeth smiled getting up. "Will I see you tomorrow?"

"Also every day after that," Chris smiled as he walked with Elizabeth to her office door.

Chris stood looking at Elizabeth before opening the office door. "I love you very much," he said as his hand crept around her waist.

"I love you too darling," Elizabeth replied offering her lips.

Elizabeth stood there until her office door closed behind him, then went back to her desk, picking up a paper from her desk. "Well I will have to wash my hair tonight," she thought.

Half hour later Chris entered his office, and found that Inspector Harris and Sergeant Willett there, both men greeted him. Inspector Harris, closed the Mr Marchant's report that he had been studying, and got up allowing Chris to take his seat. Inspector Harris went to the hat stand, and put on his overcoat, and took his trilby, then sat in the interview chair facing Chris.

"Your report is very informative Chris," Inspector Harris said. "Do you know the names of these five people who play cards with him?"

Chris spread his hands. "Interference from the top I'm afraid, not to go near them unless I can prove their involvement."

"You mention in your report that five people play cards weekly at his home. A high ranking army officer, a solicitor, a magistrate and a councillor, that's four, do you know the occupation of the fifth?"

Chris shook his head. "No idea, all I know that they are all local people."

Inspector Harris thought for a while. "If that's the case, then they are not who I am after, we know where the men we are after live, even when they change their lodgings, we know, as I told you at least once a month we follow them, only to lose them in London."

Chris looked confused. "What you're saying if your assumption is right that they all descend on Winchester, at least once a month, three weeks an above board cards games do take place, which is done to cover up the forth week, which is not a cards game but a meeting for the spies."

"You have it," Inspector Harris smiled. "However, regarding your murder inquiry, there is not much in the report to help you, the only connection you have with Mr Marchant is that both your murdered women were once housekeepers for him. What I would want to know is the names of these cards players, even if you keep them quiet I mean, where sex is concerned for men good honest and respected men can lose their reasoning, could not these housekeepers got on a good relationship with one of the cards players?"

"As far as I have been told, the housekeepers never met the cards players," Chris replied.

"So you are told Chris," Inspector Harris said rising. "Anyway, I'm off to get a bite to eat, is our date still on for around six?" he asked.

"I'll see you outside," Chris assured him as he left the office.

Chris pushed the folder in front of him to one side, looking at Fred with a smile. "What do you make of it Fred?" he asked.

"It seems to me that our murder investigation, will be hampered with his investigation. We do not have any suspect, as regard to the murders we are investigation, but we do have a link, Mr Marchant, who Harris believe is the paymaster of the spies."

"Do you think otherwise?" Chris asked.

Fred shrugged his shoulders. "He is able to travel without suspicion, it seems to me he could be the right type of man for the job, but did he kill his housekeepers, and if so, why did he bring the missing housekeepers to our attention, he's no fool, and must have realise, that had he done the murders our investigations would eventually connect him, my opinion is that he could well be the paymaster."

"I suppose we will know in time," Chris replied. "Anyway what about your hospital case?"

Fred smiled. "You will never guess who it was beaten up, he's in a coma at the moment, and the hospital will notify us when he is out of it and able to talk, they expect him to recover, although almost beaten to death, perhaps he was left to die."

"Well who was it?" Chris asked.

"Jim, the barman of the White Horse," Fred blurted out.

"You mean our White Horse?" Chris asked sitting up.

"That's the one," Fred replied.

Chris thought for a while. "Another link do you think?"

"When he comes around we will soon find out," Fred answered.

"Well while we are waiting I'm going to phone the Superintendent Fox," Chris said as he took an address book from his desk drawer, and scanned through the pages. "It's something that Inspector Harris said."

Fred did not answer as he watched Chris phone the number.

"Afternoon Sir," Chris spoke into the mouthpiece. "Inspector Hardie here."

"Yes," came the reply.

"Just keeping you up to date Sir," Chris remarked. "It seems that Inspector Harris case is tied up with our own murder case."

"Well darn it, you can both work together can't you?" snorted the reply.

"We are Sir," replied Chris respectfully, a smile playing around his eyes. "When I said tied up, I should have said that there was a strong link between the two cases, but I am hampered, by not knowing who the fifth person is that plays cards with Mr Marchant?"

"Darn it Hardie, I thought you understood," the Superintendent Fox replied.

"Oh I do Sir," Chris cut in. "But I have a couple of questions that needs answering."

"I am not interfering with your case, darn it Hardie, if you need to know their names, that's up to you, but I am disappointed, what are these questions, perhaps I can help?"

"Well Sir," Chris replied, a smile now over his face. "I really need to know, how many times they play cards together, were the games continuously every week, or was there a break every so often?"

"What the other questions?" the voice at the other end cut in.

"I know the profession of four of the card players Sir," Chris answered. "I have no idea of the fifth player."

A few moment of silence followed, Chris looked at Fred and smiled.

"These darn questions are important to your case I suppose," Superintendent Fox murmured.

"They are to me Sir," Chris replied.

"Very well, leave it with me and I will get back to you darn it," Superintendent Fox promised.

Chris replaced the receiver, as the line went dead.

"What was all that about?" Fred asked.

"I don't think Inspector Harris is concerned about the cards players," Chris explained. "He knows the men he is after, but thinks however that they play cards as a cover up to the true reason, however if they do play every week, then his assumption is wrong, also," Chris continued. "I know we have a Army man, a Solicitor, a Magistrate, and a Councillor playing in these games, but what do the fifth man do?"

"How will knowing his profession help us?" Fred asked.

"No idea," replied Chris. "But if a name comes up during our investigation, connected with one of these professions, it could give us a lead."

"Why not just demand the names from the Superintendent, or Mr Marchant come to that, they have to be a part of our investigation don't they?"

"It may come to that Fred," Chris answered, but at the moment I want to keep the Superintendent Fox sweet, I am sure that he knows the magistrate of this game."

"The afternoon wore on, Chris looked at his pocket watch, well it's gone five, and no word from the hospital yet," Chris said. "I have to get lodging for Inspector Harris's men, so I shall be late, but you might as well go."

Fred stretched his arms. "Might as well," he said as the telephone rang. "Might be the hospital?" he said as he watched Chris take the receiver in his hand.

"Inspector Hardie," Chris spoke into the phone.

"Superintendent Fox here," came the reply. "I have the answers to your darn questions. As far as the playing of cards are concerned, the games continuous sometimes for three times every month weekly basis, then a week off, sometimes they go on four weeks without a break. As to your other darn question, the professions are as follows, Magistrate, Solicitor, Councillor, Army Officer, and a Publican."

"Very good Sir," Chris replied.

"Satisfied," said the voice on the other end.

"For the moment, yes Sir," Chris replied before hearing the phone go silent.

Chris laughed as he explained what had been said to Fred. "Inspector Harris could well be right in his assumption that the cards games are only a cover up for the real purpose but what do you think about the fifth profession, a pub Landlord."

"The White Horse," replied Fred.

"Exactly," smiled Chris.

"When do we go there?" Fred asked with excitement.

Chris took out his pipe, he felt excited, he filled the pipe and lit it before answering.

"We are not certain that the fifth cards player being a landlord is the landlord of the White Horse, but it is a coincidence, especially with the manager of the White Horse in hospital being beaten up, I wonder, what is the connection, if there is one, but before going there I want to see Jim at the hospital," Chris sat back, and blew out clouds of smoke.

*I*t was early evening when Chris followed by Inspector Harris entered the Rising Sun, and was greeted by a smiling Alfie, who already had a glass under the pump.

"Evening Chris, still alive then, what's it to be straight or mixed?"

"Straight tonight Alfie," Chris smiled. "This is a friend of mine, George," Chris introduced Inspector Harris.

"Any friend of Chris's is a friend of mine," replied Alfie with a smile, as he worked the pump forward and backward until the glass was full, which he placed on the counter before Chris.

"What would you like George?" he asked.

"I'll have the same," George replied with a smile, watching Alfie again starting on his pump action.

Chris looked around, the bar was empty, he paid for the two pints. "We'll sit over here George," Chris said pointing to his usual seat, then turned to Alfie.

"Alfie, the pub is quiet, do you think I could have a private word with you, and your better half if you wish, because I'm going to ask you a favour, which will involve your wife as well."

Wondering what it could be about Alfie agreed. "I'll call her I doubt if we will get any customers for the next ten minutes, you sit with your friend, while I get her."

Although Chris had become a regular at the Rising Sun, he had never met Alfie's wife, and was very surprised, when Alfie brought her to the table and introduced her.

"This is my wife Liz," Alfie introduced her, as both Chris and George stood up.

"This is Chris, this is George," Alfie said to his wife as Chris and George offered their hand.

George watched as Liz slid her tall slim well shaped body into the seat facing him, he thought her a very attractive woman, with her hair mixed of both light and dark brown, flopping attractively over her forehead.

"You have me at a disadvantage, and full of curiosity," Liz smiled.

Chris smiled at her. I wanted to talk to you both, I need a favour, you do know my type of work I take it?" Chris asked Liz who nodded. "First can you tell me how many bedrooms you have?"

Liz did not know what to think, strange questions, which made her more curious.

"We have five bedrooms here, but only use one," she saw a smile appear on Chris's face.

"I will tell what I am able," Chris started to explain. "But whatever I tell you must be in complete confidence, you must not tell a soul."

"Agreed," Liz replied. Chris looked at Alfie. "Agreed," he said.

"Good," replied Chris. "Now George here is responsible for the security of the Realm."

"You mean catching the enemies?" Alfie said with a surprised tone.

"Yes but in this case spies I would say," remarked Liz. "Please carry on Chris."

"You are very quick Liz," George butted in. "Yes you are right, I'm here to catch spies, but I have four men coming tomorrow, and I need rooms for them, this place of yours would be ideal, for unlike a hotel that has many guests staying, and not knowing who they are, my men would be your only guests. I take it you don't rent out your rooms?" George added.

"On occasions," Liz answered.

"Would you be able to give my men and myself rooms, my four men apart from breakfast they can buy their own meals out."

Liz looked at Alfie, who nodded his head. "What about other customers asking about them?" Alfie asked.

"Just tell them they are travellers, or something like that," George replied.

"Would they need anything else?" Liz asked.

"Do you have a back way in?" George asked.

"Yes, but you have to go into station approach, our back door is just below the station entrance on the right or left, according to which way you are going," Alfie replied.

"Is it possible for my men to have a key each, they could be out all night, but whatever, they will be keeping odd hours, you don't have to worry about them, they are all high officers in the police."

Liz smiled. "I think we can grant your favour, Alfie here will have to get some back door keys cut first thing in the morning, I take it you will be here sometime during the afternoon?"

"That's right Liz, put the cost of the keys on the bill, should you be in doubt or have a worry, phone Chris at the police station if you unable to get me."

"I will," replied Liz.

"Good, that's all settle then," Chris said smiling. "Now Liz, this is the first time I have met you, will you allow me to buy you a drink, we haven't touched our own yet."

"Thank you, I'll have a brandy and baby sham if you don't mind," Liz smiled.

"Not at all," replied Chris. "Alfie get one for yourself."

Alfie stood up with a grin over his face. "Are you alright for tonight George?" he asked.

"Yes, not knowing where I was going, I booked into a hotel for tonight thank you."

With the drinks in front of them, and Alfie staying behind the bar, the next half hour passed with small talk. George eventually finished his pint. "Let's have another," he said taking Chris's glass that was empty." "Liz, the same?" he asked.

"No, no," Liz replied putting her hand over the top of her glass. "I am not a drinker, perhaps one a night, but I do enjoy my particular drink."

"You are very welcome," George said trying to change her mind.

"I know," Liz replied. "But I have work to do now, starting on the bedrooms, by the way, how long do you expect to stay?"

Chris looked at George, who seemed hesitant. "A week, perhaps two," George replied with a shrug of his shoulders, will it prove a problem?"

"No, stay as long as you like," Liz replied.

Both George and Chris, watched as Liz walked away from the table, George wondering just how far her waist was from the ground, it was obvious to him that she had long legs.

Chapter Ten

"You certainly have been given a brutal beaten," Chris said looking down at the badly swollen face of Jim, and not expecting an answer. Chris gently touched his shoulder, as he saw two slits through the swollen eyes, that was surrounded like his face with the colours of black, blue and yellow.

"We will leave you for a while, come back another day," Chris murmured.

Jim's head did not move, and he did not make a sound. Chris left the bedside, followed by Fred.

"He took a beaten there," Fred said, as they made their way out of the ward. "Wonder why, do you think who ever it was tried to kill him?"

Chris saw a doctor talking to nurse, and made straight for him. "It certainly looks that way," he answered Fred as they reached the doctor, stopping short until the doctor had finish talking to the nurse.

The doctor turned towards them as the nurse left. "Can I help you?" he asked.

"Are you taking care of badly beaten man in this ward?" Chris asked indicating the ward behind him.

The doctor looked at his clip board. "You mean Mr Jim Saunders, yes he was brought in yesterday, badly beaten, are you a relative?"

Chris showed the doctor his badge. "I am Inspector Hardie, and this is Sergeant Willett, we are investigating the beating, can you tell me his injuries?"

"Pretty extensive I'm afraid, in fact he is lucky to be alive, but what his future holds, I can't say," the doctor answered.

"How do you mean?" Fred asked.

"Well," replied the doctor looking again at his clip board. "His kidneys are damaged, he had a good kicking, he will have trouble with them in the future. He has two ribs broken, they will heal eventually, he has lost two teeth, and his nose is broken, apart from that, his body is covered with bruises, have you seen him?"

The doctor saw both Chris and Fred nod their heads. "Then you can tell he's in a bad way."

"We have not disturbed him on this visit doctor," Chris remarked. "How soon do you think he will be able to talk without pain?"

"It will take several days for the bruises to go, as the swelling goes then he will be able to speak, we will take care of his broken ribs, and nose, but it will be a few weeks before he will leave hospital."

"Thank you doctor, I will phone in a couple of days, to see if he is able to talk, if in the meantime anything else happens, please let me know by phoning Winchester Police Station."

The doctor nodded as he wrote the number down on the clip board that Chris was given him.

Both detectives left the hospital in silence, turning left towards the covered cycle shed, where they left their bicycles, and started their journey back down Romsey Road to the Police Station.

Seated at his desk, Chris took out his pipe and lit it blowing out a cloud of smoke.

"What now?" Fred asked.

Chris took another puff on his pipe, and blew out the smoke before answering. "I want you to get all the background you are able on Mr Millard, the landlord of the White Horse, see how long he's been at the White Horse, if possible find out where he originated from, that sort of thing, I'm going to Jim's lodgings, and have a look at his room."

Chris took out his pocket watch. "It's now just eleven, I'll see you at the White Horse about one, we will have another liquid lunch," he said taking his trilby from the hat rack.

Chris parked his bicycle at the kerb, and took off his cycle clips, before knocking the door of number nineteen Warf Hill. The door was answered by a stoutish lady of about fifty, she had a jolly looking full face, that was smiling below the dust cap she was wearing on her head.

"Good morning," Chris said raising his trilby an inch. "I am Inspector Hardie, from Winchester Police Station, would you tell me your name please?"

"Mrs Sparks," the woman informed Chris. "Are you here about poor Jim?" she asked her smile leaving her face. "However anyone can do that to another human being is beyond me."

"I am investigating it," Chris said politely. "If possible I would like to look at his room?"

"Of course Inspector," Mrs Sparks replied stepping aside and allowing Chris to enter as he removed his trilby.

"I'll take you to his room, he is a very clean man," Mrs Sparks was saying as she led Chris down a narrow hall, to the stairs.

90

Chris following her, noticed that to the right of the hallway was three closed doors, which he took as entrances to the living quarters.

"You have a large house here Mrs Sparks," Chris remarked.

"Yes too large for me and mine, now that the children have grown and flown from the nest," she replied. "I have three bedrooms, and I let out one of the rooms, it helps with the money you know, but I get out of breath, and with my rheumatism I have to take things slowly, but as I said Jim is a very clean man, that helps me no end."

Mrs Sparks stopped at the bottom of the stairs, the walk along the hall had made her breathless. "You tell me which door Mrs Sparks, no need for you to climb the stairs," Chris suggested. "I only need to look around his room, I won't disturb anything."

"Thank you Inspector, it would help, you will find his room, first door to the left at the top."

Chris entered the room, he found it as Mrs Sparks had said, neat and tidy. The large double iron frame bed was against one wall to the side of the window, underneath of which stood a marble top wash stand with a plain white jug and basin on top, along side the wall at the other side of the bed, was a large single wardrobe, and a chest of drawers, between the wardrobe and the bed was a cast iron frame fire place. The floor was wood, covered mostly with a single carpet, where the carpet did not reach the walls, the wooden floor had been painted black. From the picture rail some eighteen inches from the ceiling hung a large gold colour picture frame, showing the brown and white photo of a soldier.

Chris opened the door of the wardrobe, it contained a brown pinstripe suit, plus a odd pair of grey trousers, and three ties were hung over the rail, looking down Chris saw one pair of polished brown shoes. He closed the door, and went to the chest of drawers, he opened the two small drawers, apart from a couple pair of socks, and a couple vest, there was nothing else. He felt the newspaper lining of the drawers, and was satisfied that nothing was below the newspaper. Closing them, Chris then open the top of the two larger drawers, in the first he found just three shirts, and in the bottom drawer found a couple of jumpers. Going around the bed to the wash stand under the window, Chris open the two small drawers, the drawers were empty. Chris looked gently under the pillows, and eased up the corners of the palliasse. He looked under the bed, and saw a suitcase and a chamber pot. He pulled the case out, it was empty. He looked around the room, then shaking his head, left, making sure that the door was shut behind him.

Chris saw Mrs Sparks at the bottom of the stairs. "I've made a pot of tea Inspector, come and have one," she said, her jolly face now showing a smile.

"Thank you Mrs Sparks," Chris replied following Mrs Sparks into the kitchen.

"Sit yourself down Inspector, anywhere," Mrs Sparks offered, as she busied herself pouring out the tea. "Sugar and milk, help yourself," she said.

Chris sat at a well scrubbed kitchen table, and drew his cup towards him taking a sip before speaking. "Mrs Sparks, how long has Jim been with you?"

"Almost two years now," replied Mrs Sparks. "As I said, he is no trouble to me."

"Just before the war started then," Chris replied.

"Oh, several months before Inspector, he seems a fit young man, and when the war started I wondered why he did not join up," Mrs Sparks replied. "Would you like a piece of cake Inspector, I make my own?"

"Thank you no, Mrs Sparks, I'm going to dinner when I leave here, perhaps he do not agree with the war," Chris added.

"He never talks about the war Inspector, at least I have never heard him."

"I find his room very strange Mrs Sparks," Chris said after taking a drink of his tea.

"He has no personal effects at all, no letters, not even a photo of himself, apart from his cloths, you would not think that anyone was living in the room almost two years, I mean one would expect to find something."

"I can't account for that Inspector," Mrs Sparks replied. "He has his own key, he comes and goes whenever he likes, my husband and I go to bed quite early, nothing to keep us up, so I would not know when he is in or out."

"What about cleaning his room then?" Chris asked.

"As I said he is a very clean and tidy young man, he makes his own bed, he tells me not to climb the stairs, you see he knows my condition, he's very thoughtful."

"So you never go into his room then?" Chris asked sipping the rest of his tea. "You never really know whether he is in his room or out?"

"You could say that, you see I don't see a lot of him, apart from when he pays his rent, and he is always punctual with that," Mrs Sparks agreed meekly.

"So what do you know about the night, when he was beaten?"

"Well it took place outside the blacksmith shop at the top of the road you know, it seems that he was passing when a group of men came out of the pub next door, and set about him, I don't know why. Anyway, although it was late, my husband heard the noise and woke me, the next thing we knew was a banging on our door, my husband went down to see who it was, and when he opened the door, he found Jim, who somehow must have crawled down from the pub. We took him to the front room, and put him on the sofa, he was in a very bad way, bleeding all over. I bathed his face, but he was really in pain, my husband went to see the landlord of the pub, who had a phone, and he called the doctor, and the doctor got him to hospital, that's about all I know."

Chris nodded. "I see," he said. "Tell me Mrs Sparks there is no hairbrush or comb in his room, not even a toothbrush?"

Mrs Sparks smiled. "Inspector, he don't have to wash in his room," she replied getting up from the table, and going to a small wall cupboard to the side of the sink.

"This is his cupboard, he washes here," she said opening the cupboard door.

Chris cross the scullery to where Mrs Sparks was standing, and peered into the cupboard. Hair brush, comb, toothpaste and brush, plus bottles of scented stuff, together with packet of aspirin were all in the cupboard. Chris could accept this, after all in his own lodgings, he washes and shaves in the scullery.

"Thank you Mrs Sparks," he said patting his pocket. "I seem to have left my pipe upstairs, do you mind if I go and get it."

Mrs Sparks seemed alarmed. "Of course Inspector," she said.

"Don't worry Mrs Sparks, it was not alight," Chris said as he made his way from the room.

Chris made straight for the wardrobe, inside was the suit that he had not searched. He felt the side pockets of the coat, finding nothing, he felt the inside pocket, and he smiled, at last he thought. Chris took out three envelopes, he opened the first and read it. A smile crossed his face, it was a love letter. Chris returned the letter to its envelope, then putting all the letters in his own pocket, closed the wardrobe door. Chris left the room, as he took his pipe out of his coat pocket, and it was in view as he met Mrs Sparks at the bottom of the stairs.

"I'll be off now Mrs Sparks, thank you for your cooperation," Chris said as he made his way along the passage and opened the front door.

"Inspector," Mrs Sparks pulled him to a halt. "Have you seen Jim?"

"Yes I have Mrs Sparks, I was at the hospital early this morning," Chris said turning to her. "I was unable to speak to him, his face was too swollen. I can tell you that the doctors are pleased with him, but it will be a few weeks before he comes out."

"Well at least it's a little good news," Mrs Sparks replied, the smile absent from her face. "I will go up and see him."

"He will be pleased to see you I'm sure," Chris tried to comfort her. "But leave it a couple days, swellings take time to go."

"Thank you again Mrs Sparks," Chris said taking his cycle clips from his pocket, and putting them on. He cocked his leg over the bar, and sat up straight on the saddle, taking out his pocket watch. "Just about right," he thought to himself, putting the pocket watch back. He looked at Mrs Sparks again, who had stood there watching, he touched the brim of his trilby, then pushed himself away from the kerb.

Chris cycled at a steady pace through Wharf Hill, then the road straightened for a while at Blackbridge. To his right was just barren ground, but to his left, he was cycling along the meadows, which was separated from the road by a narrow river. He saw college boys in their straw hats, walking around the college enclosed swimming pool, that was built on the other side of the river, then he turned right, turning left again into College Walk, as he came opposite to the entrance of Wolvesey Castle. He passed High College houses on his right, and on his left the first impressive stone buildings of Winchester College. He turned left into College Street, and immediately turned a sharp right into Canon Street, the White Horse was about half way along Canon Street. As the pub came in view, Chris saw Fred waiting for him.

Chris parked his bike next to Fred's by the entrance to the rear of the pub, then taking off his trouser clips, walked around to the front where Fred was waiting. "Been here long?" he asked.

"Just arrived, thought I would wait for you," Fred replied following Chris into the pub.

"Mr Millard was behind the counter, he smiled as they entered. Inspector Hardie, and Sergeant Willitt, how nice to see you again, business or pleasure?"

"Just a little business," Chris replied putting his hand in his trouser pockets. "Not all that important, so let's have a couple pints of your best bitter please."

Chris paid for the pints that was put in front of them, both taking a sip, as Mr Millard gave Chris the change.

"Where's Jim?" Chris asked as he put his pint down.

Mr Millard shrugged. "He hasn't turned up for the last two days," he replied. "But he is one for mood swings, so I don't worry much."

Chris studied Mr Millard's face, and wondered if he really did not know. "Then you don't know that he is in hospital?" Chris said.

Mr Millard's face became serious, his smile disappeared, and Chris was sure that he did not know.

"In hospital, how do you mean Inspector?" Mr Millard looked at Chris in total surprise.

"He was given a severe beaten two nights ago at Wharf Hill," Fred informed him.

Mr Millard stared disbelieving. "But why, by whom, for what reason?" he asked.

"We have been to the hospital this morning to see him," Chris said ignoring his questions. "He is badly swollen, and was unable to speak to us."

Mr Millard poured himself out a measure of whisky and drank it straight down. "Is he badly hurt?" he asked.

"A broken nose, a couple teeth missing, a couple broken ribs, and a severe kicking in the kidneys, yes I would say he is very badly hurt, but the doctors seem to be pleased with him, he will be in hospital for some weeks," Chris explained.

"Lord, do you know who is responsible?" muttered Mr Millard.

"We have just started our investigation, naturally you are the first person we come to," Fred answered.

"I don't see how I can help you Sergeant, this is the first I have heard of it."

"That is reasonable," replied Chris. "I doubt if you get many customers here from Wharf Hill would you, so how would you have heard?"

"That's true, but in Winchester these things soon gets known, but I had not heard anything," Mr Millard agreed.

"It happened late last Tuesday night, was he in here during the evening?" Fred asked, as Chris took a drink.

"He only works regular for me dinner times," Mr Millard replied. "He do come in at nights, and should I be busy he will give me a hand, yes, I am sure he came in Tuesday night."

"Does he drink a lot, when he is not behind the counter?" Fred asked. "I mean, if he had a lot to drink, would he get nasty, anything like that?"

"No he is not a big drinker, he spends most of his time in here playing shove halfpenny, and as for getting nasty, he hasn't a nasty bone in his body."

"You rather like him don't you Mr Millard?" Chris asked.

"He grows on you," Mr Millard replied with a forced smile. "He's cheerful, and honest, if he has a flaw in his nature, it's being a little unreliable."

"Well he is in no state to inform you about this Mr Millard," Chris remarked. "But rest assured, we will do our best to catch whoever is responsible."

"Now if you don't mind, I need to bring up about Miss Doris Thompson again, have you thought of anything that might help us regarding her murder?"

Mr Millard shook his head. "I only wish I could, she was a pleasant woman."

"You told us, that she used to go upstairs with you to talk, after the pub closed at dinner time," Chris continued. "If as you told us it was not romantic, can you tell us what you talked about?"

Mr Millard smoothed down his white waist apron. "Just this and that, nothing important, just talk between two lonely people."

"Are you lonely then?" Fred asked finishing his pint. "I would have thought you had plenty of friends."

Mr Millard smiled. "During opening hours, you have plenty, but once the pub is shut, then loneliness comes a factor."

"Don't you ever feel like marrying again?" Fred asked pushing his glass towards Mr Millard for a re-fill. "I mean you must have plenty of admirers?"

Mr Millard filled the glass, then took Chris's glass and did the same.

"Two years since your wife died, it's a long time for a man running a pub to be on his own, is this your first pub?" Fred asked.

"I was landlord of the White Hart in Alresford before coming here," Mr Millard responded. "But tell me, am I involved in your investigations about Miss Thompson?"

"As far as we are able to tell, you were the last person that we know of, who saw her alive that Friday," Chris remarked.

"But she left here before opening time that evening, what about her employer?" Mr Millard murmured.

"Have or did you ever meet him?" Chris asked.

"No," Mr Millard shook his head. "Never had that privilege."

"Well it was her employer that first brought her disappearance to our notice, he has been ruled out."

"Well what can I say," Mr Millard spread his hands in despair. "I have told you all I know."

"Do you play cards?" Fred asked. "I mean do you belong to any cards games that plays regularly, say, once a week?"

Mr Millard smiled. "I have played, but not regularly, what time do I get off to play regularly?"

"You work seven days a week then?" Chris asked.

"Yes, but only night times behind the bar, Jim normally serves the dinner opening times," Mr Millard replied. "This week so far I have done most of the dinner times as well, and if you are right about Jim being in hospital for some week, then I won't have a time to myself."

Chris and Fred both finished their second pint. "Well thank you Mr Millard, I am sorry to be the bearer of bad news regarding Jim, I hope he will get better soon, please," Chris said, putting a coin on the counter. "Have a drink on us."

Chris leaned back in his chair, he filled his pipe, and lit it, puffing out clouds of smoke. "You know Fred," he said taking the pipe from his mouth. "We are still no further with this case than we were several weeks ago, I have several bits of information, like bits of a jigsaw, but no two pieces fit together."

Fred twisted in his chair. "Do you think, if our Inspector Harris is right, that our murder case in somehow mixed with spies?"

"I have been thinking around those lines myself," Chris replied looking at his pipe held in front of him. "I am supposed to work with him but doing what, I ask myself, besides himself he now has four men from Special Branch down here, so we must assume that he is after spies, then again," Chris continued. "These men are only for watching and following the men, these men are supposed to be spies, I fail to see how they fit in with my murder investigation."

"They could arrest them on sight, if they have the proof, but they are after the man called Number One aren't they?" Fred replied.

"Yes, and that's another thing that bothers me, we are told that no one, not even the spies know who Number One is, then we are told he does all the recruiting, so how can he do that, without being known?" Chris leaned forward in his chair looking straight at Fred.

Fred shook his head. "You would at least think, that if Mr Marchant is the paymaster, he would at least know who Number One is?"

"Perhaps we are not being told everything," Chris remarked taking a puff of his pipe. "Don't forget they have questioned several spies who have been caught, but, how the hell did Special Branch know that I was investigating a murder, that was linked with Mr Marchant, I mean it's not general information is it?"

Fred shook his head. "Puzzling," he murmured.

Chris took out his pocket watch. "It's now almost three, I have a date tonight with Elizabeth, can't let her down tonight, I did that last night."

"So what's our next step?" Fred asked.

"I'm starting from the beginning again, I shall study our report into Miss Osman's death, and the letters she sent to her father, you never know we may have missed something, and something might connect with the little bits of information we have got, what else can I do, by the way, anything on Mr Millard?"

"Actually he has not told us the full truth, the pub he had at Alresford was not his first pub, before that about ten years ago, he married the landlord's daughter of a pub at Ropley, on the Alton Road. When his father-in-law died, he took over the pub, stayed there about eighteen months, then moved to Alresford, so the White Horse here is his third pub."

"Anything else?" Chris asked.

"Not really, he was born in Alton, his family was not rich, but seemed respectable. He has kept his nose clean, but he has travelled a lot on the Continent, where he got the money from I don't know, he is not in any of our files as yet, but then I have only dealt with local files. His wife did die about two years ago natural death, apart from that, nothing."

"When did he take over the White Horse?" Chris asked.

"Just over a year and half ago," Fred answered.

"That must have been just before the war started," Chris murmured to himself.

"By the way I went to Jim's lodgings," Chris remarked as he was thinking about what Fred had just told him.

"Oh yes," Fred answered. "Did you find anything?"

Chris explained his feelings that the room was not used much, taking the letters out of his pocket, he passed the one he had read to Fred.

"Well, well, well," remarked Fred, a grin on his face. "So our Jim is the romantic type, will it help us?"

Chris spread his hands. "It's still a little more information, not known to us before."

"Anything for me to do?" Fred asked.

"Yes," replied Chris. "Go to the pub at Warf Hill next door to the blacksmith shop, see what the landlord knows about Jim's beating, you might as well knock off after that, unless you have anything to clear. Tomorrow I want you to dive into Mr Marchant's business, where he has his offices etc, I might be a little late in the morning, I want to pop into the local newspaper."

"Fair enough," Fred said getting up to leave. "Have a good date," he said with a smile leaving the room.

Chapter Eleven

*P*uffing away on his pipe, Chris spent the next two hours studying the police report of the Miss Osman's death, which was his own report, written when he had been a Sergeant under Inspector Noal. He read and re-read the letters Miss Osman had sent to her father, and made notes on a plain piece of paper. He leaned back in his chair, and stretched his arms above his head, then with a sudden thought, his hands went straight for his pocket watch.

"God," he said to himself, seeing that it was five pm. "I shall miss Elizabeth, if I don't hurry."

He put the letters back into his desk drawer, closed the file of the police report, which followed the letters. Then springing to the hat stand, took his trilby and hurried from the office.

Chris saw Elizabeth crossing Middle Brook Street, he saw her smile as she caught sight of him. "Sorry I'm late, I was reading reports, and forgot the time," Chris said standing close to her.

"Silly," smiled Elizabeth giving him a quick kiss on the cheek. "I knew it would have to be serious for you to stand me up twice in two days."

"Two days away from you too long," Chris said to her as he took her hand, and started to walk towards Morn Hill.

"How's your case going darling?" Elizabeth asked letting go of his hand and grabbing his arm, snuggling up close to him.

"I know a bit more now than I did this morning," Chris replied. "But it's slow, my main hope now rest upon the man who is in hospital."

"I'm sure you will solve it darling," Elizabeth smiled. "What are we doing tonight?" she changed the subject.

"Whatever you want?" Chris replied.

"Well it's a lovely August evening, I have already told mum to cook enough food, so I thought we could have a meal at home, then go for a walk over the hill, you can kiss me without people watching," Elizabeth giggled brazenly.

"What am I going to do with you," Chris teased. "But I'll settle for that."

The evening went well, and as they walked over the top of St Giles Hill, Chris felt his mind clear of all the bits and pieces about his case, that was jumbled in his head. He stopped at the spot, where he could see Winchester High Street way below him. He took hold of Elizabeth's waist, and pulled her towards him, pressing his lips upon hers. He felt his emotions stirred, he could not describe the feeling he felt, just holding her in his arms, it was indescribable. He knew that Elizabeth was brought up respectfully, and although he wanted to, he did not think she would accept any hanky panky but he certainly wanted her, to the point where it hurt.

Elizabeth was a outspoken girl, she said what she thought even if people took her the wrong way. "You know darling," she said still clinging to Chris after their kiss. "I can feel your love for me," she smiled as she saw Chris blush.

"Don't blush darling," she said her face serious. "I might be a well brought up woman, but I do understand human nature, and if I could not feel your love when you kiss me, I might feel disappointed."

"I'm sorry," Chris said still blushing. "I do try to control my feelings."

"You shouldn't have to darling," Elizabeth said, stroking his face. "But can you hold on until we are married, you see I look forward to my marriage and my honeymoon, with you full of excitement and expectation, I go to sleep at night thinking of us on our honeymoon, if we were to do things before we are married, then all that excitement and thought of our honeymoon would be gone. You know you are the only man I shall ever give myself to."

Chris cuddled her as he saw a tear come into her eyes, he would rather accept torture than see her cry."

"Now Elizabeth," Chris said trying to sound firm. "I love you with all my heart, I'll do anything for you, being a man, I'm afraid I might let my emotions run away now and again, I do want you, but I will wait. I have always been told," he continued taking Elizabeth's face in his hands and looking at her with a smile on his face. "That if you want a thing badly enough then it's worth waiting for."

Elizabeth sniffed, she wiped her eyes with her fingers, and forcing a smile, offered her lips.

Chris was late into the office, he had called into the local paper, and read what the paper had said about Miss Osman's death. The death did not reach the national papers, and just a few lines were written about the death in the local paper. He found only Inspector Harris in the office.

"Hello George," Chris said as he hung his trilby. "Are you settled in the pub alright?"

"Yes thank you," George replied as he twisted in the interview chair watching Chris go to his desk. "My men are here, and already on the job. Liz gave us all a good full English breakfast."

Chris smiled. "Well I'm glad all is well, now George, let's put our cards on the table."

George looked at Chris, then a smile spread upon his face. "I was wondering if you were going to ask me to," he said. "What do you want to know?"

"Everything, I believe your spies are connected to the murders I am investigating."

George nodded his head. "That's my opinion as well."

"Well tell me how Winchester became a target for you, there must have been a purpose?" Chris asked resting his arms on his desk.

George hesitated for a while before answering, he leaned back in his chair.

"Winchester has always been a target with Special Branch, but not an active one, you see we have always known about Mr Marchant being the paymaster of the spy cell in this area, we keep around the clock tail on him, he spends more time travelling the country, than he comes to Winchester, which we wrongly believed until I met you was just his resting place."

"I see," Chris replied. "But if you thought that Winchester was just a place for him to resting, what made you want to work with me?"

"That was just a stroke of luck, and we all need a stroke now and again," George smiled. "We caught a spy in Edinburgh, we had tailed him there from Southampton. It was while we were at Southampton tracing his movements, that I happen to read a small paragraph in the local newspaper about a Miss Doris Thompson, being found murdered in Winchester.

"Now," continued George making himself comfortable in his chair.

"I thought I recognised the name, but it was a couple days later that it came to me Miss Thompson was the only daughter of her parents, both now dead. She lived in their bungalow in a place called Seven Oaks, just outside London, toward Kent. Our office received a letter telling us that Miss Thompson was a spy. We checked of course, although we had not heard of her before, we found that her remarks were sympathetic to the German cause, but that was all it was. Later we found out that her grandparents were German. We did not consider her a threat, but we kept an eye on her. When I read that a woman of the same name was murdered in Winchester, I got onto London for a report on her. It was found that she had vanished from her home, which was now rented by other people, so I put two and two together, and here I am."

"I see," Chris replied. "But just exactly what am I supposed to do?"

"Catch her murderer, just that," George replied.

"Easier said than done," Chris replied. "Just how many spies are in this area?"

George thought for a while. "Well we have captured about eight this year, we only know of four others, and we believe those four are now in Winchester. Did you know that Miss Brenda West and Miss Hilda Johnson has two of them each lodging in their houses?"

"I knew that both had taken in two male lodgers but I had no idea they were spies," Chris said in a serious voice.

"Why would you," George remarked.

"You say you have captured eight this year?" Chris said.

"That's right," replied George. "Four of them have already been shot, one has been given seven years and the other three are awaiting trial."

"I can't remember seeing anything about the trials in the papers," Chris remarked.

"You won't," George informed him. "They are not trialled in a Court of Law, they are trialled by Court Marshall."

George leaned forward in his chair. "We play the game as we see it, many times the game is changed because situation changes. We now have all the known spies gone to earth here in Winchester, and we can get Mr Marchant, whenever it pleases us. All we are waiting for is you to solve the murder of Miss Thompson. It might lead us to Number One, who we want badly."

"Let's say that I solve the case," Chris said. "The murderer turns out to be a spy, do your power precede mine, I mean do I charge the person with murder, or do you charge the person with spying?"

"In war time Chris, our powers regarding spies, precedes all other power."

Chris looked down at his desk, this is what he had been afraid of.

"But in this case Chris, it will be different," George said with smile.

"It can't be easy for you to solve this case, without any clues. But if you do I will allow you to charge the person with murder, then your work on the case will be in your personal record. Then if he is a spy, I will take him from you with the spy charge, but I must be here when you charge him."

"Agreed," Chris replied with a smile. "But I have two murdered victims, and for the life of me I cannot imagine Miss Osman being a spy, she was far too young."

"I understand Chris, she was not known to us, you are sure that the two deaths are linked to the same person?" George asked looking a little concern.

"Both were strangled," replied Chris. "And both are linked to Mr Marchant as his housekeeper. Tell me if what you assume is right, and Miss Thompson was being groomed to be a safe house, like our Miss West and Miss Johnson, why would they murder one of their own kind?"

"That's my thinking," George smiled. "This is another reason why I am waiting for you to solve the case, I have no idea."

"Are you calling in the Rising Sun for a drink tonight Chris, I can introduce you to at least two of my men who will be off duty."

"I think I might," Chris replied. "I have told my intended that I will be busy for a few days."

"So you are courting are you?" George teased. "Bring her with you."

"She's not a drinker, but her father might be there."

Fred entered the office, and smiled a greeting at George, looking at Chris with a wink.

"Well I'll be off," George said getting up. "I'll keep you informed, but I don't expect much action for a time, we will just watch and follow for a while," he smiled lifting his hand at Fred, as he left the office.

Chris informed Fred what had taken place that morning. "Now I want to interview Jim, but I think I'll leave it another day, let him heal properly."

Fred nodded his head. "I have been checking Mr Marchant, but first, I saw the landlord of the pub at Wharf Hill last night, he was very cooperative. He told me that four men had started an argument over the war, he being sure that there would be trouble, told them to go. They stopped outside on the pavement still arguing, and it was at this time, he thinks, that our Jim pushed his way through them to get home. The men angry with their argument took it out on Jim, for no reason apart from him trying to go through them blocking the pavement. The landlord know them, and gave me their names, he only knew the area they lived in. I have given their names to the desk sergeant, and told him to see to them."

"So it was a one off, nothing to do with our case," Chris said. "What about Mr Marchant?" he asked.

"I have put out a few fingers," Fred replied. "Just a matter of waiting now."

Chris nodded, he leaned back in his chair, took out his pipe and lit it, filling the office with smoke.

"I have a few things I want to talk over with the sergeant," Fred said getting up, and left the office.

Chris met Elizabeth as usual on her way home from work, he received his kiss on the cheek, and as they started to walk home, Elizabeth grabbed his arm as usual snuggling up to him.

"I fell fast asleep last night dreaming of you darling," Elizabeth giggled.

"But I did feel guilty" she continued gripping his arm tighter. "You know, about what we agreed last night."

Chris looked at her a smile playing around his eyes, he loved this woman on his arm, and could not help his feelings in other ways. "Don't let it bother you Elizabeth, I have forgotten it," he lied. "From now on I will control my feelings."

"I hope not," Elizabeth replied with another giggle. "I did not say that I did not want you, I do, it's just that I want my honeymoon to be special."

"Elizabeth," Chris sighed.

Chris heard a slight giggle from her, she squeezed his arm tighter. "What are we doing tonight, can you be with me?"

"Not for long," Chris replied with disappointment in his voice. "I have to meet Special Branch for a talk."

Elizabeth felt annoyed, but did not allow it to show. "Will you leave me alone a lot when we are married?" she asked.

"Not if I can help it," Chris replied. "I did warn you about marrying a policeman."

"I know, but although I accept it, I don't like it," Elizabeth replied. "Why do you have to work during the evenings?"

Chris patted her arm. "Usually cases can be investigated and solved during normal hours, but every so often a case comes along where you have to continue during the evenings, but try not to be upset, after all Saturday is the day after tomorrow, and I'm off, we can make a day of it."

"You mean a afternoon of it, remember I work Saturday mornings," Elizabeth replied as they reached her house in Alresford Road.

"Why do you have to work, when I am off," he smiled as he allowed her to walk in front of him up the path towards her front door.

It was seven thirty, when Chris entered the Rising Sun, and found George sitting, where they had last sat.

"Ah Chris, I have told Alfie to give you what poison you want," George greeted getting up.

"Chris smiled as he went to the bar, where Alfie was already pumping his pint." "That's right Alfie, I'll have a straight bitter tonight."

"How long do you think his men will be staying here?" Alfie asked pumping the pump.

"I don't know," Chris replied "Why is it a problem?"

"No," Alfie replied having filled the glass and putting it before Chris. "These men are good drinkers when they are off duty, I just wondered."

"It will be at least another week," Chris replied taking the pint and tasting it. "But Alfie it's hush hush, no talk, do you understand."

"You can trust me Chris, I never make comments, I only listen, that's why I know what's going on," Alfie said with a smile.

Chris smiled as he took his pint to the table, where he sat opposite George. "How do you find Alfie?" Chris asked after saying cheers. "He has been quite helpful to me sometimes, it surprising what information he gets."

"It's a pub," George replied. "People talk, especially after a couple of drinks, he seems nice enough."

Chris looked around the bar, there were a few other customers, but no one near enough to hear them talk, but Chris lowered his voice as he spoke. "Tell me George, this Number One you are on about, just what is his job?"

George rested his glass on the table. "As far as we are able to tell, Number One is called such, because he is not known to anybody. He controls all the activity that spies carry out. He deals straight from Germany, we don't know how yet, who he is?" George spread his hands. "He could be anyone, even one of the people we know."

"Well how does he communicate with his spy cell?" Chris asked.

"He has more than one cell Chris," George went on to explain. "He controls the whole of the cells in Britain, we believe he has deputies, whether they know him or not, we are just guessing. As far as we know, the network was set up several months before the war. It was always on the cards that war would one day break out between Germany and Britain, but knowing that once war started all German nationals would be rounded up, none of the spies could have any connection with Germany."

"So they have to be recruited from here?" Chris cut in.

"Yes," George replied. "They would pry on people who did have past relatives in Germany, but to correct myself, there must be a few well hidden agents from Germany itself. But they have not been too successful, they only had a dozen or so recruited when the war started, we believe that the only spies left in England, are all in Winchester at the moment, we have been very lucky this year."

"I still don't get how he communicates with the cells?" Chris said.

"They use safe letter boxes, these letter boxes known only by the paymasters, who pass on his instructions on pay day, but there is always a special one in case of emergencies," George replied.

"Where are these safe letter boxes, do you know?" Chris asked.

"Lord no," George replied. "If we did we would be watching them day and night. But they could be a hole in a tree, or behind a loose brick, in an old wall, but you can be sure that they are safe. With regards to getting instructions to his deputies, we do believe he has them, because his instruction reaches the four corners of Great Britain. He must either send them letters, which of course would be posted from a town, far from where he is living, or telephone.

In turn the deputies write his instruction down, which they post in a safe letter boxes in their area."

"Clever wouldn't you say," Chris replied.

"Of Course," George replied. The problem for us is that Number One, none of his deputies are involved with any spying activity, they are usually well respected people."

George lifted his glass and swallowed. "By the way Chris, none of my men are here tonight," he said resting his glass. "It looks as if the lodgers of Miss West and Miss Johnson are swapping their lodgings, I have all my men out there watching."

"Why would they do that?" Chris asked. "Unless they know you are on to them."

"You said it yourself Chris, the Germans are a clever race, not to be underestimated, it's not because we are here, or your murder investigation, it is security."

Chris took a drink, his mind racing with interest.

"Would spies normally hole up together in one town?" Chris asked after a while.

"That is strange," George replied. "Spies normally work on their own, it's very easy for one spy, not to give another away if one of them is suspected. No, I think they are holed up for a while, breathing space so to speak, we have captured quite a lot this year."

Chris drank the last of his pint. "Well let's have another, then I must move, I have thinking to do."

The following days, remain quiet. On Friday Chris told Fred all that had been said between George and himself, keeping Fred up to date with investigation. Fred waiting patiently for results from his enquiry about Mr Marchant, which did not come.

On Saturday, Chris met Elizabeth, and took her home. Her mother fussed over Chris as though he was a new born baby, while her father sat reading the paper, now and then looking over the top of his glasses and smiling to himself while Elizabeth washed and changed. Chris took her shopping, and then to a meal, had a great lunch at the new Italian restaurant. They had such a wonderful time, Chris felt so happy, he had forgotten about his investigation, and did not want Saturday to end. On Sunday Chris sat at his desk most of the day studying, but the hectic week, and the weekend was catching up on him, his mind was tired. Leaving early, went straight to his lodgings, and straight to bed, without eating.

"You look chirpy Chris," Fred said to Chris as he entered the office on Monday morning. "Did you have a good weekend?"

"Great, and today I feel like a new man," Chris replied. "But after work yesterday, I went straight home to bed, I was so tired."

"Thinking and answering questions in your head can do that to a man," Fred commented.

"I can believe that," Chris replied. "Now have you anything on Marchant yet?"

Fred gave a smile. "Came through this morning in the post," he said handing Chris a sheet of paper. "All his offices are there."

Chris scanned the list of addresses on the paper, and his eyes did not miss Seven Oaks address. "Seven Oaks is one of his addresses, that is where our Miss Thompson lived, I bet you ten shillings to a penny, it was Mr Marchant that brought her to Winchester," Chris said to Fred.

"For what?" Fred asked.

"To groom her as a safe house proprietor of course," Chris replied.

115

"Do it help us?" Fred asked.

Chris thought for a while. "It's another piece of the jigsaw," he replied. "It might fit in, Mr Marchant seem to have offices in many counties, I know he has a textile business, but I fail to see why he needs all these offices, after all they each take money to keep, with staff."

"He can afford it, if it's true what is said about his wealth," Fred voiced his opinion.

"True," replied Chris. "I am just wondering just where he gets all his money, if he is a paymaster, he certainly cannot draw from a German Bank account over here, so he must be using his own money, perhaps with the promise that it will be repaid after the war is won."

"In that case then, he will never get repaid," Fred smiled.

"Now Fred," Chris said clearing the papers on his desk. "I want you to spend sometime in the library, see if you can find a book about the German High Command, I would particularly interested in a book, that deals with their spying organisation."

"Do you think they will have such a book?" Fred asked wondering why he should need such a book.

"You never know, it might be a book published well before the war, still we can try," Chris suggested.

Fred smiled. "OK," he said. "It will pass a few hours away, what are you doing?"

"I'm going to see our friend Jim in hospital," Chris replied as he took out an envelope from his desk drawer, and put it in his pocket.

Chris entered the hospital ward, and found Jim sitting up in bed, the few days that Jim had been left alone seem to have done good, his face was no longer swollen, and although half of his body was wrapt in bandages, he smiled as Chris stood beside his bed.

"How are you doing Jim?" Chris asked.

Jim smiled as he looked up at Chris. "On the mend Inspector," he replied.

"That's good Jim," Chris smiled. "You took a nasty beating, you could have been killed, I can tell you we know the men that did it to you, you will have to sign a complaint however."

"It's my teeth and my broken nose," Jim explained. "I wish they had not done that."

"Well you are in the best place, by the time you come out you will be a new man," Chris tried to cheer him up.

"So they have told me," Jim replied. "But my nose will not look that same."

"You are a handsome young man Jim, with a nice attitude to life, your nose will not effect that, and soon, you will accept it."

"It's nice of you to call Inspector," Jim answered. "Have you a reason to call?"

"I'm sorry Jim but I do, I have been to your lodgings, and seen Mrs Sparks, she seems a very nice person."

Jim nodded his head.

"She also let me look at your room, voluntarily I might add. At the time I did not know any reason why someone would beat you up, so I had to investigate, and sometimes looking around a room, one can get clues. But as I later found out you were beaten by a group of angry men for no reason, but I did find some letters in your suit pocket."

Chris saw Jim's face go white, there was fear in his eyes. "So you know as well," Jim said softly. "What are you going to do?"

117

"Well if you help me Jim, then I will help you," Chris answered.

For a while Jim did not answer, Chris knew that although he was a nice reasonable man, Jim was not all that bright. Chris did not know which way to take his silence before he asked his next question.

"What did you mean, by saying that I know as well?"

Jim looked at Chris, there was still fear in his eyes.

"I meant Mr Millard found out about me as well," he murmured.

"Look Jim," Chris said trying to encourage him to speak. " I know you are frightened being what you are, could land you a few years in prison with disgrace, but tell me the answers to my questions, and I promise I will help you, you see whatever you have done, I believe you were blackmailed into it."

"You're right, Inspector, when Mr Millard found out, I had to do all what he wanted, including hiding the two bodies, I did not want to go to prison. But he did let me run the pub dinner times, I was in charge, and then after your first visit to the pub, he made me his manager," Jim said.

Chris took the envelope from his pocket, and pull out a photograph, and pass it before Jim's eyes. "Now this is the picture of Miss Doris Thompson, who you told me was in your pub every weekday dinner time, how did you get her to where she was found?"

Jim looked at the photo, an expression of uncertainty appeared over Jim's face.

"That's not Doris," Jim said. "I don't know her, never seen her."

"Are you sure Jim, now take a good look, this is Miss Doris Thompson that was found dead at Winnall, who you told me as well as Mr Millard she came into your pub every dinner time, now be absolutely sure Jim?" Chris almost begged.

"I tell you Inspector, I have never seen that woman, you must be wrong," Jim insisted.

Chris felt bewildered. "Describe the Doris you know," Chris demanded.

"I don't know Inspector, she was slim, had a nice figure, she had a lovely laugh, and she was prettier," Jim tried to describe.

Chris's mind raced as he replaced the photo back into the envelope, his mind not understanding. "But you did take a body to Winnall and hide it in the small hole?"

"I had to Inspector, Mr Millard threatened me to inform the police about me. I did not see the body, like the first one, I don't like seeing dead bodies" Jim replied, his eyes watering. "Inspector what's going to happen to me?" he sobbed.

"Calm down Jim," Chris said. "You don't need to worry, when did you take the body to Winnall?" Chris asked as Jim calmed himself.

"I slept at the pub that night Inspector," Jim went on. "I did not want to drive the horse and buggy, I was frightened, but Mr Millard insisted, it was first light on the Saturday morning, no one was about, we went straight there and back, hardly met a soul."

"What about the first one Miss Doris Osman?" Chris asked.

"I can't remember the day Inspector but it was six or seven months ago, the same time, first light in the morning, I never did see what the first one looked like," Jim answered.

"So you and Mr Millard, tried to hide two bodies, during the last six or seven months," Chris said gently trying not to upset Jim any more. "Tell me Jim, did Mr Millard tell you how did they died?"

"Mr Millard said that the first one had fallen down the cellar, while the flaps were open, and she was walking on the pavement, he told me he would lose the pub if the police found out, and wanted me to help move her body away from the pub. I told him it was wrong and that he ought to report it to the police. But, he insisted, and when he understood I was not going to get involved, he told me that he knew about me, and wondered if I wanted the police to know as well, he said we were both in the same boat."

"The second one, Miss Thompson, how did she died?" Chris asked.

"He didn't tell me, he just said that another accident had happened, and that it was Miss Thompson, who also had to be taken far from the pub," Jim replied nervously.

"You are sure that the person in the photo is not the Miss Thompson that you know?" Chris asked again.

"I'm sure of it Inspector," Jim replied.

Chris could not concentrate on the questions he wanted to ask, his mind was too full of Miss Thompson. The dead woman was Miss Thompson, verified by Mr Marchant who had employed her, so who was the woman that Jim knew, and, Chris thought Mr Millard.

"Now Jim, you take it easy, and rest without worry, you can trust me, Mr Millard will not know of our talk, but once I get things straight in my mind, I might have to see you again," Chris spoke very gently.

"Thank you Inspector," Jim replied trying to force a smile. "Thank you."

Fred was at his desk, when Chris stormed angrily into the office, and threw his trilby onto his desk, Fred looked at him amused. "What up?" he asked.

Without answering, Chris sat at his desk, and took out his pipe, lit it and drew hard, blowing out clouds of smoke.

"Sorry Fred," Chris said leaning back into his chair. "It's this damn case, it gets crazier and crazier."

Then re-counted his meeting with Jim.

Fred shook his head as Chris finished. "But it was Doris Thompson that died, Mr Marchant did view the body, and confirmed it, and don't forget she must have been connected to the White Horse, she had the address in the pocket of her bloomers packet," Fred said.

Chris leaned forward, he put his pipe in the ashtray, and leaned on his desk, his hands clenched into a fist.

"We were told by Mr Marchant that it was Miss Thompson, we had to accept that, but then Mr Millard knew who he had murdered, if indeed he did murder the woman, so I am going along with Mr Marchant's confirmation that the woman was Miss Thompson," Chris paused and looked at Fred before continuing. "But then again, if Jim did not know the woman, who was it that was calling herself Miss Thompson and why?"

"Baffling," Fred offered.

Chris unclenched his fist. "How did you get on at the Library?" he asked.

"Not good," Fred replied.

"Never mind, it was a try," Chris replied just a little disappointed.

"Any bearing on our case?" Fred asked.

"I'm not sure, it's jumbled in my mind at the moment, and this new evidence don't help," Chris replied.

"Go and have a drink tonight and forget about the case," Fred advised. "It might give you a fresh start in the morning."

"I don't know about that, but I do find that left alone I think better with a pint in my hand," Chris smiled.

Chris's mind still occupied with the case as he met Elizabeth, walking home from work. As he took her hand, she reached up and gave him a kiss on the cheek.

"What's wrong darling?" she asked letting go of his hand, and clutching his arm. "You look very depressed."

"Just a problem, I've not yet sorted," Chris replied.

"Is it to do with the case you're working on?" she asked.

Chris nodded his head. "Yes it's a hard one."

"Tell me about darling, if you can," she offered.

Chris looked at her and smiled. "Since when have you been interested in detective work?"

"Never," Elizabeth replied. "But if I am going to marry one perhaps I can help, two minds are better than one they say," Elizabeth ended with a giggle.

As they walked towards her home, Chris related the story. More out of something to say, rather than wanting to, he did not feel very romantic, but he was glad, she was clutching his arm. "So give the answer," Chris smiled at her.

Walking in silence for a while, Elizabeth spoke, hoping that she was talking sense. "Well it seems to me, that who ever was impersonating this poor girl, wanted people to think that this poor woman was shall we say a boozer, they perhaps wanted to discredit her, even though, they knew they were going to eventually murder her. But who ever impersonated the woman must have been very close to the murderer, they might have murdered her together. One thing is clear however, who ever it was must have been trying to get people to have a bad opinion of her."

It was a warm night, Chris pushed his blankets away, and covered himself with just the sheet, as he laid in bed wrestling with his thoughts. He smiled to himself, his mind recalling what Elizabeth had said about the case. Without knowing anything about the case, her thinking had not been too far off the mark, but she had added one word, that he had not thought of, and that word was Close. His mind twisted and turned, who could be this close to Mr Millard, there was only two live women linked to the case, and that was Brenda West and Hilda Johnson. Jim had told him that the woman he knew was slender and dark hair, which did not help a lot, as both the women linked were slender and dark, if his investigation was tied up in espionage, then he would choose Brenda West as the woman, but then Hilda was more of a German name. But then again, there was no evidence that Mr Millard was seeing a woman. With his mind twisting and turning, Chris fell into a uneasy slumber.

Chapter Twelve

*C*hris was busy at his desk, when Fred entered. Chris had risen early from his uneasy sleep, and felt as though he had not been to bed. He had gone to the scullery, washed and shaved, and had eaten a bacon and egg breakfast, that his landlady had cooked for him, after which he had lit his pipe, his mind still occupied with the case. It was another fine summer day, as he strolled hands in pockets towards the bank where he would see Elizabeth for a few moments.

"Did you sleep well darling?" she said as she kissed him on the cheek.

"Not very," Chris replied. "It's this damn case, it seems to be crazy, but, I will solve it," he said a smile coming to his face.

"I know you will darling, you must not let it upset you," Elizabeth said with sympathy in her voice. "Will I be seeing you tonight?"

Chris hesitated before answering. "I'm not sure, can I phone you?"

"Of course you can darling," Elizabeth said, planting another kiss on his cheek. "I don't want you making yourself ill."

Chris had entered the Police Station, and found the desk sergeant talking to a person, so Chris entered his office, without saying good morning.

"You're early," Fred remarked.

"Couldn't sleep, I had this case on my mind all night," Chris replied.

"That will keep you awake alright," Fred smiled. "You have to learn to forget work when you are at home, but it's hard to do."

Chris smiled, knowing that he would never be able to master that, his mind was always active, only Elizabeth had been able to make him forget work.

"I was thinking about Doris Thompson myself," Fred was saying. "I cannot help asking myself, why, Inspector Harris would come to Winchester, then bring his entire team because of a woman, who he said was of no threat to the Realm, I mean many people are now talking against the war because of the casualties we are getting, and don't forget Jim, the men who beat him up were arguing over the war, but points of view don't make you an enemy of your country."

"I have thought of that as well," Chris replied. "But I can only go on what the Inspector Harris told me."

"With Special Branch, it's on a need to know basis," Fred continued. "One has to learn not to take everything at face value, one must always have a little suspicion, at least in this game."

Chris fell silent, his mind jumped into top gear, he looked down at his desk, and played with a pencil.

"Do you think that this Doris Thompson, could be a undercover agent?" Chris asked. "I mean we are led to believe that Miss Thompson was being groomed to run a safe house, I have always wondered that if this is true, why they would kill one of their own, you know Fred, you might have something, at least it would give us a motive for her killing, but how do we proceed on this opinion?"

"You could always ask Inspector Harris straight out," Fred offered advice.

"Oh no, no, " Chris replied a smile around his eyes. "If I find I have been lied to by Inspector Harris, then if I do solve this case, he will be in for a big surprise, I hate lies, especially lies that hold me up."

"I have been under many Inspectors during my time," Fred said turning towards Chris in his chair. "The best of them, have always used a little bluff, in order to get to the truth."

Chris thought of Inspector Noal, he would detect, deduct, twist all his information around in his mind, often coming up with different answers. He would pick the answer, he liked the best, and without any proof would go ahead and bluff, often getting the proof he wanted. Chris wondered if he were capable or experience enough to do that.

"I'm glad I have you as my Sergeant, Fred, you are teaching me lessons, that I shall not forget."

"I'll send in my bill," Fred replied a blush covering his face.

"If Doris Thompson was undercover," Chris spoke saying his thoughts. "Her killing must be that she was discovered some how. She did have the note in her bloomers, with the name of the White Horse on it. Is it possible that she had never been in the White Horse, but found out that this pub had some connection with the spy cell."

"Could be," agreed Fred.

"Fred," Chris said sitting up straight in his chair, having made up his mind.

"Wrong or right we will carry on with that line, it would fit better with the information I have, in fact I can see my case being solved. I have only one thing to find out before arrests start."

"What's that?" Fred asked a smile on his face, seeing the excitement on Chris's face.

"Why they need to impersonate her in the pub?" Chris in a serious voice.

"Also who?" replied Fred.

"Maybe, but I think I already have an answer to that," Chris smiled.

Chris felt elated, in his mind he had solved the case. He phoned Elizabeth, it always hurt him to cancel a date, but in this instant he knew he would have to, he decided he would not see Inspector Harris until he made charges, so he would not go to his local the Rising Sun. While Fred had a little local trouble to sort out, Chris busied himself with all the information he had. He could not remember saying goodnight to Fred, as he made notes on pages and pages of paper, many he screwed up and threw away in the dust basket. Chris burnt the midnight oil, and it was two o'clock in the morning before he went to bed, falling into a exhausted sleep.

Fred entered the office on the Wednesday morning a little early, he was not surprised that Chris was not there. He looked at the waist paper basket by Chris's desk, it was almost full of twisted papers. Fred smiled as he made for his desk, and picked up a note that Chris had left for him in pencil.

"Fred," the note said. "I think I can close this case. Go to Mr Millard, Miss West, Miss Johnson, and get in touch with Inspector Harris, tell them I want them in the office at ten o'clock tomorrow morning. I will also want Mr Marchant here regardless of wherever he is, so it will be best to get on to his solicitor early, in case he is away. I may be late in today, if you get any trouble, as to why they have to be here, *you can tell each one not to worry, because they will not be arrested by me." Chris*

Fred pouted his lips, and wondered, as he made his way to the desk where the telephone stood, and finding the number, made a call to Mr Marchant's solicitor.

"Good morning Sergeant," the voice said after Fred had introduced himself. "What can I do for you?"

"Mr Marchant told us, that should we ever want to see him again, to get in touch with you. We need him at the police station at ten o'clock tomorrow morning," Fred he spoke onto the receiver.

"I see," spoke the voice. "Can you tell me what about?"

"It's to do with our investigation Sir," Fred replied.

"I see," the voice said again. "Is Mr Marchant involved in this investigation?"

"Naturally there is a link Sir," Fred replied. "No reason why you can't come with him, but I can tell you," Fred giggled a little over the phone. "He will not be arrested by Inspector Hardie."

Fred heard the reply in a lighter tone of voice. "Well thank you Sergeant, I am sure Mr Marchant will be able to make it. I take it that your Inspector has solved the case, and is just clearing up the lose ends."

"I'm sure you are right Sir," Fred agreed politely hearing the line go dead.

Fred cycled to the White Horse, and taking off his cycle clips, stood his bike against the wall of the pub. It was a long way off opening time, so Fred banged the door.

"Sergeant Willett," Mr Millard said opening the door. "I wondered who it could be at this time of morning, we are not open, but please come in," he said leaving Fred to close the door. "Would you like a drink, on the house of course?"

"I'm on duty I'm afraid Mr Millard, but thank you anyway," Fred said.

"Sit yourself down Sergeant," Mr Millard said offering Fred a chair, at a small bar table. "What can I do for you?"

"We are asking all those linked in someway to our investigation to be at the police station by ten o'clock tomorrow morning," Fred explained.

"Am I included?" Mr Millard asked, all smiles having left his face.

"Well Miss Thompson did visit this pub, and as you told us you were very friendly with her."

"That is quite true," Mr Millard replied. "So I suppose I am involved in your investigations, is everyone who knew Miss Thompson involved as well Sergeant?" Mr Millard asked.

"To be frank Mr Millard," Fred replied, a little caught off balance by the question. "Apart from her employer, you are the only one that we know, who knew her."

"What about Jim my barman, he knew her, so did many of my customers," Mr Millard argued without a smile on his face.

"I know Mr Millard, but your barman I believe is in hospital, and like the rest of your customers who knew her, they did not spend quiet afternoons with her as you did," Fred replied with a light tone of voice.

"Don't worry Mr Millard, my Inspector want to tidy things up, that's all, he is not going to arrest you," Fred said forcing a laugh.

Fred sensed that Mr Millard was not happy at the thought of attending the police station, but Fred's last words seemed to have calmed him.

"Very well Sergeant I shall be there," he said as he rose from his chair.

"Voluntarily?" Fred asked and watched as Mr Millard nodded.

Fred's next visit was to Miss West, he knew he had to be careful what he said, knowing that the two lodgers she had were spies, her door opened to his knock.

"Yes?" she asked.

Fred produced his badge. "I am Sergeant Willett, I am here to see Miss West, Miss Brenda West," Fred repeated himself.

"I am Miss West," she admitted.

"I wonder Miss West can I come in and speak to you for a few moments?" Fred asked.

Brenda seem unsure, she turned her head looking into her front room. "It's a bit difficult Sergeant, you see I have gentlemen guests staying here, can't you just tell me what you want?" Brenda asked.

"Of course Miss West," Fred replied. "You are needed to attend the Winchester police station tomorrow morning at ten o'clock," Fred told her with a straight face.

"Please do not be late," he said as he started to turn to leave.

"Just a moment Sergeant," Brenda said hurriedly. "Perhaps I have been a bit hasty, perhaps you could come in for a few moments," Brenda stood to one side of the door, and allowed Fred to enter. "Please sit anywhere."

Fred took a hard chair, not expecting to stay very long.

"Now Sergeant if you please, what is all this about?" she asked.

"Inspector Hardie, who I believe you know, wants all the loose ends tidied up, with those who are linked or even slightly linked with the case we are investigating," Fred obliged.

"Do this mean he has solved this murder case?" Brenda asked.

"I'm only his Sergeant," Fred said with a slight smile. "I have no idea what he has in mind."

"But I didn't even know the girls," Brenda said her voice sounding annoyed.

"Perhaps so Miss West," Fred said politely. "But you were at Mr Marchant's house when the police called regarding the disappearance of Miss Osman."

"But I told your Inspector how I came to be there," Brenda replied. "Are there going to be anyone else at this meeting?"

Fred spread his hands over his lap. "I only do as I am told Miss West, but don't look so worried, Inspector Hardie is not going to arrest anyone."

"That's nice to know," murmured Brenda. "Well it's a bit late informing me, I have house guests you know, but I'll be there, ten o'clock you say?"

Fred nodded his head as he rose from his chair to leave.

The next port of call for Fred was Miss Hilda Johnson. Fred pulled up outside her house, taking off his cycle clips, he parked the bike by leaning it on a small hedge outside. Miss Johnson opened the door, and when Fred showed his card, she became very nervous. She did not offer him in, after he had told her to be at the police station the next morning, just nodded her head, saying that she would be there.

Fred decided then that he would have to see Inspector Harris, his last call. He flicked his wrist so that he could see the time on his wristwatch, it was gone twelve. "At least the pub will be open," he thought as he parked his bike just inside the coach house of the Rising Sun.

Fred entered the empty bar of the Rising Sun, a few paraffin lamps were burning, Alfie was behind the counter polishing glasses.

"Afternoon," Alfie greeted him with his broad grin. "I know you, don't I?" "You've been in here with Chris, Inspector Hardie," he said lowering his voice in the empty pub.

"I came in once with him yes," Fred replied with a smile.

"Chris don't like me calling him Inspector, he says that if I did, I would lose a half of my customers," Alfie smiled.

"In that case," Fred returned his smile. "You had better call me Fred."

"OK Fred," Alfie replied. "Now what can I get you?"

"Well, I am on my break, so I am allowed, I'll have a Black and Tan beer," Fred answered. "Do you do food?"

"No, I haven't got time, I'm here on my own, never gets a break, but seeing we are empty at the moment, I'll make you a nice cheese sandwich if you like," Alfie answered.

"That will be great Alfie," Fred replied watching Alfie pumping the pump. "I don't suppose Inspector Harris will be in?"

"Yes he is," Alfie replied as he took a bottle of stout, and poured it into the half fill glass of beer. "Do you want me to call him?"

"I would be grateful," Fred replied. "How much is that?"

"Twopence for the drink, and a penny for the sandwich, that's threepence please."

Fred paid for the drink, and took the glass to the table he had sat at when he had been with Chris, while Alfie left the bar.

"What a nice surprise Sergeant," Fred looked up from his drink, and saw Inspector Harris standing before him.

"You wanted to see me?" he asked as he took a seat opposite Fred.

"Instructions from the boss," Fred smiled. "Can I get you a drink?" Fred offered.

"Not that I wouldn't like one," Inspector Harris replied. "But unlike you I don't have breaks, so I'm on duty."

Fred gave a smile as he took another sip of his drink, as Alfie came and gave him his sandwich.

"There you are Fred," Alfie said. "That will fill a hole."

Fred smiled his thanks at Alfie, and waited for him to go, before he spoke. "My boss has call all who are linked with the murders we are investigating, to his office tomorrow at ten o'clock."

"Has he?" Inspector Harris replied a little surprised. "Has he solved the case?"

"He hasn't told me," Fred replied. "I haven't seen him today, I believe he was working last night well into the late hours on the case, he's very thorough man, this could be the end of the case."

"I'm impressed Sergeant, am I invited?" Inspector Harris asked.

"That's my reason for being here, to tell you to come," Fred replied.

"Can you tell me any more Sergeant, I find myself very curious," Inspector Harris asked.

"Not a lot I'm afraid, I am carrying out his instructions, I have been told to tell everyone coming that they will not be arrested," Fred said, wondering just how much he should tell the Inspector.

"Of course this might stop them bring solicitors with them, Inspector Hardie always get annoyed with them when he is summing up the case, with their interfering questions," Fred continued. "Perhaps it will be best if you see Inspector Hardie before the meeting, which is at ten tomorrow morning."

"Thank you Sergeant," Inspector Harris replied with a murmur as though his mind was elsewhere. "Would it be possible to see Inspector Hardie today?"

"You know his door is always open to you anytime, but I don't know if he will be in today, my instructions for today was left by letter, but you could always phone."

Inspector Harris stood up. "Thank you Sergeant, I will do that, can I get you another drink?" he offered.

Fred looked up at him with a smile. "No thank you Sir, this one will do me nicely."

Fred picked up his sandwich, as he watched the Inspector disappear from the bar, and bit into it, having to open his mouth wide, owing to the thickness of the bread.

Chapter Thirteen

*E*very one had turned up for the ten o'clock meeting. Fred and Inspector Harris sat at Fred's desk, also sitting around the same desk was a young woman who would be taking minutes of the meeting in shorthand writing. On the last case, Chris had a typist, but she had been noisy, so this time he had gone for a person able to write in shorthand, who could then type up her minutes later. Mr Millard sat in the interview chair next to Mr Marchant, and his solicitor who was introduced to Chris as Mr Wonston sat a little behind, Miss West sat to the right of Chris, and next to her Miss Johnson. Chris sat at his desk, facing them all.

"Thank you all for coming, do you know each other, Mr Marchant?" he asked.

"You know that I know the two young ladies," Mr Marchant replied.

Chris waited a few moments getting no further comments from him. "You do not know Mr Millard then, Mr Millard is the landlord of the White Horse, Canon Street, not far from your address."

"I'm not aware that I know him," Mr Marchant replied.

"Really," Chris replied turning to the two women. "I know you both know Mr Marchant, do either of you know Mr Millard?" Chris watched getting no reply apart from the shake of the head from both women.

"Then Mr Millard," Chris said. "It looks like you are the odd man out, but never mind," Chris said watching Mr Millard shrug his shoulders.

"Mr Marchant brought to our notice the disappearance of two of his housekeepers. My Sergeant and I do not investigate missing persons, we have a special routine for this that is normally carried out by uniform police. However we decided to look into it, and we discovered both missing housekeepers, both had been murdered, at least six months apart, it then became our case," Chris looked around the room, all eyes were on him as he continued.

"However, with no clues, the case put us in limbo, and the question of money paid to these woman by Mr Marchant, and the food intake of the house explained to us by Miss West and Miss Johnson, muddled our minds. We now know that we were given this information in order to do exactly what it did do, confused us."

"Are you saying I lied to you Inspector?" Mr Marchant spoke up.

"No Mr Marchant, I know what you paid these women and others now, but if you will allow me to continue, I am sure all will become clear. As I was saying, we was not getting anywhere with these murders, but then two things happened, which would not have been expected by anyone in this room. The Special Branch became interested, having read in the local papers about the murder of Miss Thompson, and Jim Saunders, the barman at the White Horse, was beaten up."

Chris looked over to Fred and Inspector Harris, who winked at him, the silence was broken with a murmur, from the rest of the people in the room.

"What would interest Special Branch in these murders Inspector?" Mr Marchant's solicitor asked.

"Espionage," Chris replied.

"In that case Inspector, I do not feel the need for my client to stay around any longer, he is a busy man, and he came here to help you clear up the murders, now you are talking about espionage a very different matter, which is no concern to my client."

Chris looked sternly at the solicitor. "As I understand it Mr Wonston, your client came here voluntarily, to help us with our investigations, and as it turns out, espionage is a part of that investigation."

"He was also told by your Sergeant that you would not be making any arrest," Mr Wonston added.

"That is correct Mr Wonston," Chris replied. "So please, I want your client to stay, but feel free in your advice to him regarding any questions I shall ask him."

Mr Wonston turned his head to Mr Marchant and whispered to him.

"What I don't understand," Mr Millard burst out. "Is how my barman getting beaten up can help your investigation?"

"Please give me time to explain," Chris asked leaning on his desk. "Now Mr Marchant," Chris continued ignoring Mr Millard's black looks. "I understand that you play cards once a week with five well respected people of Winchester."

"That is correct," replied Mr Marchant.

"These cards games started I believe just before the war, or sometime around June, last year 1914."

"That is again correct Inspector," Mr Marchant said glancing at his solicitor.

"These people you play cards with," Chris said picking up a pencil and twirling it between his fingers. "One is a army officer of high rank, a solicitor, a magistrate, a councillor and a landlord, all from Winchester, and highly respected."

"Again you are correct," replied Mr Marchant.

"I also take it, that you came to us about the disappearance of your housekeepers, on the advice from these people, as at least two, the magistrate and the solicitor would have advised you to see the police, both being connected with the law."

"I did tell them about the disappearance, I saw no reason why I shouldn't, we were all friends, yes I was advised by them, particularly it being the second one."

"It was good advice Mr Marchant, did they all agree to this advice can you remember?" Chris asked.

Mr Marchant spoke to his solicitor before answering. "I really can't remember, I think they were all in agreement," Mr Marchant answered.

"Tell me Mr Marchant," Chris continued. "You played cards once a week three times every month, then missed a week. Tell me who did you play with on the weeks you missed?"

Chris could see that Mr Marchant was clearly taken back by the question, he spoke hurriedly to his solicitor. "I have no idea what you're saying Inspector, on the weeks that I did not play cards I must have been away on business," he said after a while.

"Really Mr Marchant," Chris said amused at his defence. "Are you quite sure, only I do have evidence that on the weeks that you did not play cards a meeting took place in your address."

"That is incorrect," Mr Marchant replied.

"Mr Marchant," Chris said. "When Special Branch intervened in my case, because you brought the matter to my attention, you had to be watched. Would it surprise you to know that, men known to Special Branch as spies, were followed to your address."

"Inspector this is ridicules, you are accusing my client of being an enemy agent," Mr Wonston stormed. "I would like to see what proof you have?"

Chris looked around the room, every eye was on Chris as he continued.

"Certainly Mr Wonston, as soon as this meeting is over."

"Let me tell you a story, many months before the war, Germany and Britain knew that war would eventually break out between the two countries. Although you are educated Mr Marchant, you do not come from a rich or middle class background. You did visit Germany when you were young, visiting relations which are no longer alive. You met and married a Major's daughter while in Germany, which has been kept out of the British records. It was your Major, now your father-in-law that converted you to their way of thinking. However, you were educated, and you were married to a Major's daughter in the German Army, so you were not to be, how shall we say," Chris pondered for the right word.

"A common spy, you were set up in business in England, and became very successful, and very rich, rich enough to become the paymaster of a spy cell, who every month paid the wage bill. You covered up meetings with the spy agents by running a regular cards games once a week three times every month, as a cover up to the true reason, then missed a week which takes place on the forth week it would be a spies meeting rather than a cards games."

Chris saw Mr Marchant and his solicitor both with open mouths unable to answer, and switch quickly to Miss West. "What I can't understand about you Miss West is why you joined this spy cell. I know you are not a spy, but you are groomed to run a safe house, for the protection of any spies who have to seek shelter. Why Miss West would you do that, these men are ruthless, their information they get from the spies do destroy your own countrymen. They are filth, scum of the water pond," Chris went on, his voice sounding hate. "These men are not fit to live, they should be all shot."

Chris fell silent as Miss Johnson stood up.

"Swine," she burst out with venom in her voice. "What would you know about men, real men," her voice trailed off, and she almost fell down upon her chair, as she realised, she had lost her temper, and given herself away.

Chris leaned back in his chair, this is the reaction he had wanted with his outburst to Miss West, the room was silent, and as Chris looked around, he saw all eyes were on Miss Johnson, who so far was the only one who had given herself away.

"Thank you Miss Johnson," Chris spoke, a smile around his eyes. "Or should I call you Miss Hoffman, Miss Hilda Hoffman," Chris repeated looking straight at her. "I shall call you that anyway, even though by law you are Mrs Marchant."

"Swine," she replied as she began to sob.

"When I first called upon you Miss Hoffman," Chris continued taking no notice of her sobbing. "I saw a photo in your front room. Major Von Hoffman and Tochter Hilda. I was then investigating a murder, I did not take particular interest in it at the time, even though my second visit to you I noticed the photo had gone. It was only with the intervention of the Special Branch, that I remembered, thinking that it may be important," Chris decided to ignore Miss Hoffman, who was sobbing into her handkerchief.

"Now let me tell you another story," he said watching all eyes upon him, as he gave an amusing smile. "We will deal with the murder of Miss Doris Osman first."

"About time, I do have a pub to open," interrupted Mr Millard.

Ignoring the remark Chris continued. "This investigation was six months old, there were no trails, I know because I investigated the murder at the time. However when Mr Marchant brought this case to me, my Sergeant and I investigated it. We looked back all the unsolved murders of young women, and Miss Osman's name came up. I had my first lead, my Sergeant visited Mr Marchant's shop in Andover, and we found that Miss Osman had a father, still living in Andover. He was shown Miss Osman's photo, and he confirmed that it was his daughter."

"This also brought in Miss West and Miss Hoffman, who had been past housekeepers for Mr Marchant. Investigating this murder, I was told many plausible lies by both Miss West and Miss Hoffman, they did fuddle my way of thinking, so to speak. Both told me that they did not know the members of the cards games, not being allowed in the rooms where it was played. Then my Sergeant was given some letters by Miss Osman's father, Miss Osman wrote letters to her father every week, she mentioned that there were men coming to the house that she did not like, and would be leaving as soon as she received her month's wages. This told me that housekeepers were not kept away from the visitors, as I was led to believe."

"When I asked you all if you knew each other none of you knew Mr Millard. All of you must have knew him, because he was the landlord that played regularly in the legitimate game."

Chris looked around the room again as he paused, with the sound of chairs being scuffled against the floor. He looked at Fred and Inspector Harris, who seem to be very amazed.

"Where did you get all this rubbish from?" Mr Millard fumed. "Of course I know all of them, it's no secret. However when Mr Marchant came to you, he was asked to keep the names of the cards players out of it, as we men had no involvement in his housekeepers, and was no concern of ours, it's as simple as that."

"Apart from one thing Mr Millard, none of them knew that you were a part of the spy cell, not even the paymaster himself, as your pay was paid into a bank in Germany."

"Rubbish," Mr Millard cried out as he stood up.

"Please sit Mr Millard I haven't finished," Chris said politely. "Now let's come to the murder. I told you that the beaten that your barman took, although it was a one off and brutal, and had no connection with the case or even Jim himself, he was in the wrong place at the wrong time, was in itself a stroke of luck. Jim confessed everything when I saw him in hospital."

"The boy is backward," shouted Mr Millard. "I treated him like a son."

"Only to keep him sweet Mr Millard, you were blackmailing him because of his sexuality."

"Rubbish," Mr Millard stormed.

"I have his confession, it says that you made him go with you driving your horse and buggy, and dump the body of Miss Osman, you told him that she had fallen down your cellar while the flaps were open, and you did not want the police to know, because you may lose your licence."

"There you are then," interrupted Mr Millard.

"But Miss Osman did not fall down your cellar, there were no indication at all that this had happened, she was in fact strangled. If you did not kill her, why did you dump her body, she must have been killed on your premises."

142

"You can't prove that I killed her, and who will take the word of a backward boy?"

"I think you killed Miss Osman, Mr Millard, and I know you got rid of her body, when I asked you if you knew Miss Osman, you told me you didn't, but you knew she had been found in a ditch, you told me."

"So," replied Mr Millard. "I could have heard that from one of my customers, or from the newspapers?"

"No Mr Millard, it was never mentioned in the newspapers, it's only on police reports that the rain ditch is mentioned, I wrote it myself."

"You still can't prove that I killed her," Mr Millard said more quietly. "More to the point, why would I, for what reason?"

"With all the lies I have been fed, that puzzled me, I can only assume that you knew Mr Marchant was having an affair with this young girl, who you thought would be a danger to the organisation. Somehow you got Miss Hoffman to get on good terms with Miss Osman and bring her to the pub, where she would be killed. Miss Hoffman did not know about her husband's affair with Miss Osman until you told her, not knowing yourself that Miss Hoffman was the wife of Mr Marchant. Miss Hoffman became a very willing partner in crime. Through one of your safe letter boxes you instructed Miss West to clear her room of all evidence that Miss Osman had ever been there. Miss West obeys orders without question, and did as she was told during the absence of Mr Marchant. She did have a key to the house."

Getting no response from Mr Millard, Chris continued. "Let us now move on to Miss Doris Thompson."

"Oh dear I killed her as well did I," Mr Millard stormed again.

"Of course you did Mr Millard, I would say in the same way. Jim your barman was again blackmailed into helping you, and you could have got away with it but for one thing," Chris looked at Inspector Harris who was listening intensely.

"Somehow you learnt that Miss Thompson was a undercover agent for the British, you had to get rid of her, having got rid of Miss Osman with no comeback, you decided to repeat it with Miss Thompson. You did not search Miss Thompson before you dumped her, because in her bloomer pocket, we found a small note with your name and address on it."

"Proving what?" asked Mr Millard.

"Nothing in itself," Chris granted him. "But it brought you and your pub into the investigation. You however were never sure, just what Miss Thompson knew, or what she had passed on to her superiors, so you had to discredit her name. She had to be known as a drinker, this you did by getting Miss West, again through your safe post boxes to impersonate her in your pub, after you had killed Miss Thompson. Miss West still not knowing that you were a part of the spy cell, because as I have said she only followed orders. By doing this, you and your customers could verify the what type of woman she was, which would hamper any investigation as to your own activities."

"Agents, spies, murder, this is all a bit far-fetched isn't it," Mr Millard said, his voice telling Chris that he was beginning to get alarmed.

"It would seem that way," Chris smiled. "Nevertheless it's true."

"Well you will never prove that I murdered these girls, why don't you ask the solicitor present?"

"No need to Mr Millard, I am not arresting you on these charges. As Mr Wonston knows, in time of war the Special Branch has priority over murder, when it involves spies."

"I think you are right Inspector," replied the solicitor. "Are you saying that my client is a spy?"

"In a way, he is certainly an enemy agent, the same as Miss West and Miss Hoffman, but he is important because he is the paymaster for the spy cell."

"You are able to prove this with facts Inspector?" Mr Wonston asked.

"Five minutes after Miss West and Miss Hoffman left their house in the morning for this meeting, the two lodgers they both had, were arrested and charged as spies, do that answer your question?"

Mr Wonston nodded and looked at his client, who defiantly shrugged his shoulders, with the rest of the people being questioned seem to be tongue-tied.

"Well as you are not arresting anyone, and you have cleared up all the agents, perhaps we can go and get on with our own business," Mr Millard said.

"One moment please Mr Millard," Chris answered. "You seem to have overlooked the fact, that I told you, that you had got in touch with Miss Hoffman to get Miss West to impersonate Miss Thompson in the White Horse, in your Pub."

"You said it was done through these safe post boxes whatever they are," Mr Millard replied.

"But Miss Hoffman knew that you were the landlord of the White Horse, she knew you while you played cards during her time as housekeeper, wouldn't it be suspicious to her getting this message, after all, no one knew that you were a member of the team, so why would a ordinary cards player with no connection want a murder committed on his premises."

"But we only have your word that the murders were carried out in my pub," Mr Millard replied. "I don't know, I can't keep up with what you are telling us."

"Let me clear it up then Mr Millard," Chris offered. "When you were young, before you were married, you travelled Germany. You met Miss Hoffman, and had a brief affair. Through her, you met her father Major Von Hoffman, who at the very moment is sitting in his Berlin office, wondering how most of his spies had been caught in England. He is in charge of the Secret Service is he not?"

"How do you know that, I don't know any Major Von Hoffman," Mr Millard replied meekly.

"It was Major Von Hoffman that converted you into working for them, the promise of big money, but you had to start a business, a business where you could meet people. You chose a pub, you married a daughter of a landlord at Ropley, after a time you moved to Alresford, then here to Winchester. You were accepted as a respectable person. You knew that Miss Hoffman would eventually run a safe house. Now Mr Millard to put an end to this meeting, it is my opinion that only the very highest authority would have the power to order these two murders that could and did become a danger to the spy ring, no ordinary member would have the power. In England it would be the man they call Number One," Chris paused allowing the murmurs, he looked at Inspector Harris who had his mouth open.

"You are Number One Mr Millard, and Miss Hoffman can confirm it," Chris nodded to Fred, who rose, and left the office, re-entering followed by the four officers of Inspector Harris. "I bid you all good morning," Chris said.

"Now I hand you over to Inspector Harris, who is from Special Branch."

Chris heard a few bits of slander, as he stood up, and walked over to Fred, rubbing his hands, as Inspector Harris and his men, charged all those in the room with being an enemy agent, a danger to the Realm, with the exception of the solicitor.

Chapter Fourteen

alf hour later, Chris sat at his desk, with Fred and Inspector Harris sitting at Fred's desk.

"Chris," Inspector Harris remarked. "That was perhaps the best summing up I have ever heard, when one considered, there was very little facts to verify your stories."

"I know," Chris replied with a smile, but you once told me that we all need a little luck now and again, and Fred here told me that the best Inspectors he ever worked under, always used a little bluff. But although my story had little foundation, and a good solicitor could break easily what I had. He will be unable now, with all involved arrested."

"How the hell did you know that Miss Thompson was a undercover agent for us?" Inspector Harris asked. "I never told you."

"I know you didn't," Chris replied. "It was a suggestion from Fred here, he could not understand why you would bring a team of four officers here, just because of a girl's death."

"I'm impressed Fred," Inspector Harris said turning to Fred.

"How did you know that Mr Marchant and Miss Hoffman was married?" Fred asked curiously.

"It was the book you brought me back from the library. It was officers uniforms, also German Coats of Arms. Now I believe that Von means similar to our title Lord, and knowing that his name was Hoffman because of the photo I saw, I found his Coat of Arms."

"How did that help?" interrupted Fred.

"Mr Marchant and Miss Hoffman both wore the same ring with the Coat of Arms on it," Chris answered. "For both to wear the same ring, they had to be family, I chose the right relationship."

"You certainly got a good memory or eyesight," Fred laughed.

"It comes in handy," Chris replied.

"OK," Inspector Harris said. "How did you know that Mr Millard and Miss Hoffman had an affair?"

"Now that was pure bluff," Chris admitted. "I considered that if Major Von Hoffman had converted our Mr Millard, how did he meet this powerful man, after all we know he came from a poor family from Alton, he had no money, so that he could eat and drink at the places that Major Von Hoffman would, how would he have been invited to their parties, balls etc, I could only come up with his daughter. As for him being Number One of the spy ring, I reasoned with myself, the normal spy would not murder deliberately, they might if they were caught in a tight spot, but otherwise, only one man could authorise a murder, that was Number One, Mr Millard."

"But what about Mr Marchant, he could have been Number One?" Fred said.

"I did think of him," Chris admitted. "But I don't think he has it in him to kill in cold blood. I watched him when I accused his wife of having an affair with Mr Millard, he was clearly shocked."

"Well, Fred was right in this case, about a bit of bluff, do you both realise what we have achieved here today, we have cleared England of all known spies," Inspector Harris said. "Credit will go to both of you," he expressed his admiration.

Chris and Fred smiled, but did not comment.

"Your cells will be full for the next few days at least to Monday," Inspector Harris remarked before leaving. "I'll get them transferred to London on Monday."

"My uniform will be pleased, we have just enough cell," Chris smiled.

"They have had to double up, so don't have anyone arrested for a few days, and saying that, I am going to be very busy over the weekend, but perhaps you and Fred can join me and my team for a drink before we leave Monday. I'll see that the government pays for it," Inspector Harris offered.

Chris looked at Fred. "We shall be honoured," he said.

Chris met Elizabeth from work, she kissed his cheek and grabbed his arm, as though it was going to disappear. "You look like the cat who have got the cream," she said with a giggle. "Have you had a good day?"

"Well it worked out OK in the end," Chris said smiling at her.

"You've solved the case," she said looking up at him with pride.

"I don't know about solved, but it's ended, case closed," Chris said.

"I knew you would do it Chris," Elizabeth said. "Mother said you would, mother is never wrong."

Chris patted her arm, as they reached her house. "You are coming in tonight aren't you?" Elizabeth said.

"Of course, and Saturday is my day off, so will go shopping, and have a meal out, I must do that paper work about this case while it's fresh in my mind, so I shall be busy tomorrow," Chris replied, playfully chasing Elizabeth up the path to her front door.

Elizabeth's mother quickly set a place for Chris, and fussed over him, while her husband Ron, looked on with amusement.

"You will get used to it Chris," Ron said seeing Chris a little uncomfortable. "Women need to make a fuss, it's a part of their nature."

"I've lived on my own so long, I am not used to it," Chris smiled. "My landlady is incline to be a bit fussy with me."

"How is your case?" Ron asked putting aside his newspaper, and taking off his glasses. "Getting any luck with it?"

"It's a close case now," Chris replied all smiles.

"Good for you Chris," Ron replied. "It seems that my daughter's confidence in you have turned out to be true, but I suppose you do have cases that they are not solved?"

"We do, the one just closed, went back six months, and was on our books as unsolved, but of course now it has," Chris admitted.

"Have you any ambition to get on in the Force Chris?" Ron asked. "Or is that a silly question?"

"I would like to get to Chief Superintendent if I could, I may be the youngest Inspector in the force, but that is due to the war, but it gives me a good leg up, all I need now is to be successful in solving cases."

"Good for you Chris, I'm sure you'll succeed," Ron replied. "I have no idea how the war is going," he added. "We are losing a lot of casualties, I doubt very much if the war will be over by Christmas, it will be a few more years yet I'm afraid."

"I haven't had a lot of time keeping up with the news," Chris explained as Elizabeth and her mother came into the room. "Perhaps I should be pleased that my flat feet kept me out, although I would have liked to have gone."

"Being a Detective Inspector, with your own office, is far better than being out in France in a muddy old trench," Elizabeth said on hearing what was being said as she entered.

"I agree," voiced her mother. "Now Ron, leave Chris alone and sit at the table."

"I was not getting on to him," Ron muttered as he did as he was told.

Chris and Elizabeth, after the dinner things had been washed up spent the evening playing snakes and ladders.

"I suppose I better let you win," Chris said with a smile.

"Yes," replied Elizabeth. "That's what gentlemen do."

On the Friday morning, after Chris had seen Elizabeth into her bank, he made straight for his office, knowing that he would be all day filling in forms etc. Although he himself had made no arrests, his reports of his investigation would have to be ship shape, in case they would be needed at the trials. He wondered how the police were coping with their police cells full, he got his answer as he entered, with the frosty good morning from the desk sergeant, who seem to have overlooked his morning offer of a cup of tea.

Chris put his trilby on the rack, and smiled, as Fred who was already at his desk greeted him.

"The desk sergeant is not too happy," Chris said making for his own desk. "No tea for us this morning."

"They have plenty of tea to make for our eight prisoners, perhaps they have run out of tea, meals are brought in I suppose," Fred voiced his opinion.

"I assume so," Chris replied. "I can't ever remember more than one or two in the cells before, most of those over night. We are bound to have a load of solicitors today, Special

Branch must have a lot of pull, to be able to keep them locked up until Inspector Harris takes them to London."

"Well there is a war on Chris," Fred said. "As you told the prisoners, Special Branch have priority over them, being spies."

"What are we doing about Jim Saunders, the barman?"

Chris leaned back in his chair, took out his pipe, filled it and lit, blowing out smoke gently. "I can charge Jim with homosexuality, if I did he would be the only one in this case, that I am able to arrest," Chris said enjoying his pipe.

"He would get a few years in jail if proven, but you know Fred, I feel sorry for the chap, because of his sexuality he was blackmailed, and made to do crime, that he did not want to do," Chris added taking his pipe from his mouth and looking at it.

"I have never known whether homosexuals are born or they chose to be like they are, but it do warn us of one thing, and this is mainly because it is illegal, agents, spies, whatever are always open to be blackmailed if they are that way," Fred said.

"I agree," Chris admitted. "In this case however Fred, I am incline to forget that Jim is a homosexual, he helped us no end with our investigation, and he was certainly very badly beaten for no reason of his own. Would you be with me if I ignore him?"

"Of course I would Chris, I am glad you feel that way," Fred agreed with a smile.

"But there is one other thing, If Mr Marchant is the son-in-law of this Von Hoffman, and Von Hoffman is in charge of Espionage, why didn't he make Mr Marchant Number One?"

Chris thought for a while. "It's my guess that Mr Marchant is not brutal enough, but ideal for the job he has, which is the paymaster. Number One's job, is mainly to protect the spy cell in any way necessary, which in our case included murder. Mr Marchant is not capable of doing that, at least not cold blooded."

"But it seems his wife is," Fred remarked.

Miss Hoffman, or Mrs Marchant, whichever, must have wanted to be here with her husband. Her father gave her a job as a safe house landlady, and although she was a enemy agent, if caught would not mean a hanging offence, however as you said, she must have been in agreement with Mr Millard about the murders, she must have some of her father in her, I am told he has no pity."

Chris worked all day on reports, often referring back to Fred regarding certain events. He tidied the papers on his desk, and patted them.

"Well Fred I am off tomorrow, I will finish what is left on Sunday, I expect it to be quiet."

"I will follow you soon I am meeting the wife, we are going for a meal," Fred replied.

"Good for you Fred," Chris replied as he reached for his trilby. "How is Mrs Willett?"

"No change there," Fred admitted with a sad smile. "But it's more peaceful."

Chris smiled his reply. "See you Monday then Fred," he said leaving the office.

Chris entered his empty office on the Monday morning, feeling weary. On Saturday he had spent most of the day at Southampton, window shopping with Elizabeth, and while they were there, they had a meal, arriving back in Winchester by train, half way through the evening.

"Don't let us go back to my house Chris," Elizabeth had said. "Let's take a walk over the hill, it's a pleasant evening, and still quite light."

Chris had agreed, although he would have rather gone straight back to Elizabeth's house. Walking over the hill, with Elizabeth clutching his arm, her closeness, Chris knew that he would feel his emotion of wanting her come on. However sitting on their favourite seat overlooking the high street Elizabeth told him to light his pipe and relax.

"I like the smell of your pipe darling," she said. "It looks so manly."

Chris was pleased, it helped him take his mind off of wanting her, at the moment he had to control himself, knowing that sex between them would only happen after they were married, due to the respect Elizabeth and for her parents.

"Did you enjoy today darling?" she asked clinging to his arm, as he drew on his pipe. "I felt wonderful," she smiled.

"It was different," Chris admitted. "It's purely a woman's thing, window shopping isn't it?"

"We women are strange creatures," Elizabeth said with a giggle.

"Can't argue with that," Chris replied taking his pipe from his mouth. "But then woman likes to shop."

"For clothes and such like," responded Elizabeth. "But most of their shopping is for food, to fill their spoilt husband's belly," she giggled again. "But it will make me happy when I am able to do it for you darling," she continued trying to snuggle closer to him.

"You know darling, I am so full of excitement and expectations, that I want to give you anything that you want," she sat up straight and looked at Chris.

"When do you think we should get married?" she asked. "I already have my bottom drawer filled up."

Chris looked at her, he thought her the most beautiful woman he had ever met, and he knew the answer to her question, he wanted her so badly, so sooner the better.

"You are telling me," he teased. "That you and your mother have not discussed it, or picked out a date?"

"Of course we have silly," she replied with a smile. "My mum is as excited as I am, well almost," she said after a moment thought.

"Well I tell you what," Chris went on as he sucked at his pipe. "You and your mum pick out a couple of dates, and let me have them, then I can find out which is most suitable for me, I just can't slam the office door, and leave for a fortnight."

"A fortnight?" Elizabeth asked in a shocked voice.

"Well I was thinking of the honeymoon," Chris said with a smile on his face. "I need time to enjoy our marriage, tell me what do you keep in this bottom drawer?" Chris asked, teasing her.

"Bed clothes, and many things that I can only wear to bed, which I hope will help you to enjoy our honeymoon," Elizabeth replied looking sternly at Chris wondering if he was teasing her or not.

"That's OK then," Chris replied sucking contentedly on his pipe. "What sort of things are we talking about?"

"That's for me to know, and you to see," Elizabeth answered, smuggling up to his arm again. "I think we better go now darling," she said. "I don't know just how long I will be able to keep the trust my parents have in me," she let go of his arm, and pushed her face towards him, as she offered her lips.

Sunday, Chris was on duty, he had hoped for a quiet day, but just as he was about to leave, he had to go out on a motorbike accident, that took a couple hours. During the day he had visited the police cells, their voices, told him that he was not welcomed, but he had to ask a few question in order to finish his report, but they were uncooperative.

Chris found that Mr Marchant and Miss Hoffman had been put into the same cell, after all they were married, and space was limited. Miss West had a cell to herself, as did Mr Millard, with the four spies sharing two to a cell.

"You know Inspector, that was a stroke of deduction, finding that I was Number One, and me making that slip about the trench, I must go back to training," Mr Millard said.

"I didn't pick it straight away Mr Millard, it wasn't until I went to the local paper, to read about the Miss Osman's case, what they had printed you know, that I realise that there was no mention of a trench. From then on I had you in my sights," Chris replied walking away, and allowing Mr Millard to curse his mistake.

Fred came into the office a bit late. "Went out last night for a drink with the wife," he said as a greeting to Chris. "Must have overdone it, I woke up with a hangover, don't feel like work at the moment."

"Did you have a quiet Saturday?" Chris asked.

"Well apart from a couple solicitors, I put them in touch with Inspector Harris, it's not our case anymore is it?"

"No," Chris replied, then told him of his day out on the Saturday.

Chris lifted the receiver as the telephone rang.

"Inspector Hardie," Chris spoke onto the receiver.

"Morning Hardie," came the voice of the Superintendent Fox.

"I've had some darn good news about you, how you do it I don't know, darn it Hardie, you are to be congratulated, spies and murderers, as well as clearing up cases for the Special Branch."

"I had help from Sergeant Willett as well Sir," Chris replied respectfully.

"That's another darn thing I want to tell you, you are going to lose him, he's going back to the Big City, this time as a Inspector."

Chris looked at Fred and winked. "Does he know about this Sir?" Chris asked.

"No darn it, but conformation will be on his desk in the morning. You will be getting a new Sergeant, discharged from the army after a few months he was in hospital, wounded in France. He will be with you a week today his name is George House. Now I must go, you're doing the Force well darn it keep up the good work," the line went dead.

"Who was that, the Superintendent Fox?" Fred asked.

"Yes it was Fred, we have been congratulated, but he also gave me bad news, at least bad for me, you are going back to London Fred. Conformation will be here tomorrow, and you leave Friday."

"That's my wife I bet a pound to a penny," Fred answered with anger in his voice. "Well I just won't go, I am happy here."

"You're going back as a Inspector Fred," Chris said with a smile on his face. "I'm pleased for you Fred, although I will miss you," Chris left his chair and walked over to Fred with his hand held out. "Congratulation on your promotion."

"I have only about three years left to do," Fred replied unable to believe the news. "I wonder why they have picked me?"

"Don't think about it Fred, just accept, anyway with your experience, you deserve it."

Fred calmed a bit after the news had sunk into his brain.

"I'm sorry Chris I was happy here under you, but this will give me a better pension, and certainly make the wife happy," Fred said with a broad smile. "I can hardly believe it, still I shall miss here."

"So tonight when we have a drink with Inspector Harris, we also have your promotion to celebrate," Chris said, seeing a grin spread over Fred's face.

THE END

BOOK TWO

INSPECTOR
CHRIS HARDIE

NO PEACE FOR
MRS BROWN

Chapter One

*A*part from all the paper work he had to complete, regarding his previous case that had been solved, Detective Inspector Chris Hardie felt a little sadness. Sergeant Willett, who he had become close to, was moving to a station, not in London as first thought but at Poole just outside Bournemouth, where he would be promoted to Inspector. His replacement was Sergeant George House.

Chris read Sergeant's House documents with interest. He had enlisted in the army at the outbreak of war in 1914, having been a serving Detective Constable in the MET. He was single and twenty seven years old, two years younger than Chris. He had passed his Sergeant's exams, but had enlisted before his promotion was through. He had been sent almost immediately to France with just a few weeks training, and put straight into the trenches. Chris lifted his eyes from the records, his mind thinking of his last Inspector and friend, Inspector Noal who had enlisted just ten weeks ago, and Chris not having heard from him, wondered about him.

Chris continued reading, Sergeant House wounded in the thigh, and he was brought home to Netley, a hospital just outside Southampton, where he was operated on and eventually recuperated. On leaving the hospital, George House had applied for reinstatement in the police force, and was eventually given the rank of sergeant, his station being Winchester, under Inspector Hardie.

"I see that you have been in the war George," Chris said with a smile around his eyes looking at George who was sitting in the interview chair. "Your wound completely healed?"

"Yes Sir," George replied. "Weather plays it up a bit, otherwise it's OK."

"Well George," Chris remarked. "Apart from on the job, where one has to be professional, we use first names here, please call me Chris and I'll call you George, now, you take Sergeant Willett's desk there, you may have to clear it out," Chris said standing and offering his hand. "Welcome to Winchester."

"Thank you Chris," George replied taking the hand. "Where is Sergeant Willett now?"

"He is transferred to Poole, near Bournemouth, and promoted to Inspector," Chris replied with a smile.

"He deserved it, he is nearing retirement, gives him a better pension. I see you were serving in the MET before you enlisted, didn't you want to go back to London?" Chris asked as he watched George check the drawers of his desk.

"I spent quite a time at Netley," George replied without interrupting his search of the desk. "Eventually I was allowed out in Southampton, and I like the area. I have no need to go back to London, apart from friends, I have no parents, or wife," he said with a smile.

"Are you married Chris?" George asked politely.

"No, but heavily engaged," Chris replied with a smile.

With questions going backward and forward between them, the morning went quick, and both soon realise that their working relationship would be agreeable.

"Have you got a place to stay?" Chris asked.

"I have, I got here Saturday, and had a look around, I got lodgings in Middle Brook Street, they seem suitable," George replied. "It's a nice little city, although I haven't seen a lot of it."

"Reminds you of being in the army I expect," Chris answered. "With all the soldiers around."

"There do seem to be a lot of them," George agreed.

Sergeant Williams knocked and entered the room.

"Body been found Inspector," he said without a smile. "You are wanted, the body has a knife in it."

Chris looked at him. "Have you met Sergeant House?" he asked indicating George who was also looking at Sergeant Williams.

"When he first came in I did," remarked the sergeant. "Do you need anything from me?"

"The number, and the street would be handy," Chris smiled looking at George.

"Number 16 at Lower Brook Street," Sergeant Williams replied apparently without interest. "It's just a few minutes from here," he added.

"Who's at the scene then?" Chris asked, as he started to rise from his desk.

"Sergeant Bloom, and Constable Bowman," answered the sergeant. "Do you want me to inform the Police Surgeon for you?"

"Where there is a body, you know the drill Sergeant," Chris replied a little unpleasantly.

Sergeant Williams retreated from the office without another word. Chris looked at George and smiled. "He's as good as gold really, you just have to get used to his ways."

"Well this will be your first case with me, whatever it turns out to be, not far from your lodgings, in the next street up," he rose from his desk and crossed to the hat stand taking his trilby.

Lower Brook Street, was about two hundred yards long, before Tanner Street took over. One side was a row of bay window houses, with a small walled garden in front of each. Opposite was a row of terrace houses, where the front door, and the single front window to one side of the front door opened onto the pavement. Number sixteen was one of these.

Carrying his murder bag, and followed by George, Chris stopped and knocked on number sixteen, constable Bowman opened the door.

"Inspector," he greeted him respectfully.

"Constable this is Detective Sergeant House, he is one of us," Chris introduced George.

"Now where is Sergeant Bloom?" he asked, watching the constable and George nod at each other with a smile.

"He's in the scullery with the father," constable Bowman replied. "Shall I get him for you?"

"If you will," Chris replied.

Sergeant Bloom came out of the door, and walked down the narrow passage toward the detectives.

"Inspector," the sergeant greeted.

"Sergeant," Chris replied to his greeting. "This is Detective Sergeant House, he has just been transferred to us."

Sergeant Bloom held out his hand to George, who shook it. "Glad to have you aboard," sergeant Bloom said gracefully. ·

"Now sergeant bring me up to date," Chris asked.

"The dead body belongs to Gloria Newman, she's unmarried and lived here with her father, she is twenty five years old," the sergeant replied.

"Where is the body?" Chris asked.

"Up the stairs first door on the left," the sergeant replied.

"Well, I will take a look," Chris said with a foot already on the stair. "When the police surgeon gets here show him up, keep the father in the scullery, we will want to speak to him."

Chris and George entered the bedroom, the body lay face down across the iron frame bed, dress only in a nightdress, that had been pulled up around her waist, about nine inches down from her shoulders, and knife stuck out.

"Not a pretty sight George," Chris said as he looked at the body.

"No," replied George. "It's murder, she could not have stabbed herself, the nightdress could provide a reason."

"You mean rape," replied Chris. "We know who she is, so let's try to find a bit of background," Chris continued. "Take a look into those chest of drawers, will you George," Chris asked pointing to the dresser.

It was a front room bedroom with one window, over looking the street, against the far wall, stood a heavy looking dressing table and wardrobe to match. Chris made his way to them. "I hope Bob gets here soon," he muttered as he made his way across the room. "At least we can cover her up."

"Who's Bob?" George asked, opening a drawer of the chest, and moving items of clothing around with his hand.

"The police surgeon," Chris replied looking at the dressing table. "He's a decent bloke."

Chris studied the dressing table top from left to right, a ashtray, which it contained two cigarette stubs, and some peanut shells. His eyes moved to the centre of the dressing table, where a glass tray was placed under the small swing mirror. Chris studied the contents of the tray, a few pieces of jewellery, a ring, earrings, and a bracelet lay in the tray, plus a lipstick, to the side of the tray laid a hair brush, with a comb stuck into the bristles. Leaving the tray, his eyes fell upon a pair of pink lace gloves, there was nothing else on the table top.

He opened the small drawers of the dressing table, and just moved the contents with his hand, feeling the bottoms, that was papered with old newspapers. Satisfied that the drawers held no information, he opened the wardrobe doors, and screwed his eyes as the smell of mothballs hit him. The hanging clothes he saw was several dresses most with a floral design. There were three two piece suits, blue, dark red, and a brown. He looked at the shelf above the hanger, and saw three hats, one for each colour of the suits. Looking at the floor of the wardrobe, he saw several pairs of shoes in different colours.

He closed the wardrobe doors, he strolled around the room, and keeping his eyes from the body, checked the area around her side of the bed, a coin laying on the floor caught his eyes, and he bent to pick it up, it was a coin of some kind he thought, but not one of the real, absently he pocketed the coin as the police surgeon entered the room.

"Hello Chris," Bob smiled as he entered the room, and his eyes fell upon the victim. "Gee that's nasty."

Chris returned his greeting. "This is my new sergeant Bob," Chris said introducing George. "Not a nice start for his first day is it?"

Bob looked at George and smiled offering his hand, which George took. "I'm supposed to know your name am I?" he smiled.

"Sorry Bob," Chris apologised. "Meet Detective Sergeant George House."

"Well George," Bob said with a smile on his face. "We are a small team here, so call me Bob, everyone else do."

Bob turned to Chris. "Well, let's have a look at the young woman."

Bob took his bag to the bed, and carried out his routine check of the body. The knife had not been plunged in fully, and an inch of the blade was visible below the hilt. Bob put on a pair of gloves that he took from his bag, and holding the blade that was showing, pulled the knife out.

"That's a kitchen knife," Bob remarked lifting the knife up to show them, but still holding it by the blade. "I should say about six inches."

"I agree Bob," Chris replied as he bent and took out a brown bag from his murder bag, and opening it, allowing Bob to carefully place the knife in it. "At least I have the murder weapon, don't I?"

"I would say so," Bob replied. "We can turn her over now."

"She's a pretty girl," George said. "Would it take a lot of strength to plunge that knife?"

Bob puffed his lips. "It did not connect with bone, it came out easy, I would think any adult could have done it, male and female."

Bob looked at Chris. "What do you know about her?" he asked.

"I haven't talked to her father," Chris replied. "At the moment I know her name is Gloria Newman, twenty five years old and single."

"I can't do a lot here Chris, I need her in hospital for post mortem," Bob said as he pulled a sheet over the body. "Can I take her, I have the wagon coming."

"Well the photographer has already been so I'm told, be my guest Bob," Chris replied. "Any idea how long she's been dead?"

"I'll let you have a full report tomorrow, but a rough guess, I would say about twelve hours."

"As long as that," Chris muttered.

"Anyway Chris," Bob said removing his gloves, and putting them in his bag. "I have work elsewhere, people like me cutting them," he smiled. "I'll see you again George, I hope you settle in well."

"I'm sure I will," George smiled back.

Bob looked at Chris, as he opened the bedroom door. "Murder seem to follow you Chris, many more like this and your name will be too big in the force."

"I have to solve them first," Chris replied with a farewell.

"You'll solve it OK," Bob smiled as he left the room.

Chris walked to the window, and stared out onto the street.

"What are you thinking Chris?" George asked as he closed a drawer.

"Just possibilities, if it was an intruder, how did he get in here, come over here take a look," Chris spoke.

George crossed to the window

"Bob said that Gloria could have been dead for at least twelve hours," Chris said taking out his pocket watch. "That would make the time she died around midnight, it's almost midday now," Chris scratched the back of his neck before continuing. "To enter this room from outside, one would have to have a ladder, this window is at least twenty feet from the pavement."

"Risky," George replied. "It would be dark, but there is a gas lamp just across the road, that would throw some light, bit risky if you ask me to put a ladder up in a residential street like this."

"You're right," Chris agreed. "I think we can dismissed this way of entry. Now the window below us is the front room, and at street level, the way would be easy enough, then again he could have come in from the front door, he would need a key however, there was no key hanging behind the letter box."

"What about the back way?" George asked.

"Backdoors are normally locked and bolted during sleeping hours," Chris replied. "When we question the father, I will ask Sergeant Bloom to check around the outside."

Chris turned from the window. "Did you find anything of interest?" he asked George.

"Mainly personal stuff," George replied. "I did find a album, which I took out, but no diary, which you were hoping I might find."

Chris smiled at George, who had guessed his thoughts. "Well let's check under the pillows and palliasse, then we'll see the father."

Chris followed by George entered the scullery, Sergeant Bloom who had been sitting, he rose as they entered. A man who was sitting opposite him, holding his head in his hands, looked up, his eyes were red and his cheeks tearstained.

"This is Mr Newman," the sergeant making the introduction.

Chris sat at the table in the chair that Sergeant Bloom had vacated.

"Mr Newman," Chris spoke in a soft sympathetic voice. "I am sorry about your daughter, it must be very hard to bear, and I understand, if you do not feel up to answering questions at the moment."

"It's all right," replied Mr Newman, his voice trembled with his grief. "It's best to get it over with."

"Thank you Mr Newman," Chris replied. "Please understand that I would not asked these questions, if they were not important."

Chris watched Mr Newman nod his head in reply.

"Where were you last night about midnight Mr Newman?"

"I was at work," he replied. "I work as a night watchman, from seven to seven."

"You were home then just after seven this morning?" Chris asked.

"About quarter past," Mr Newman replied, now with his arms folded on the table, looking at Chris.

"I work for the gas board, we are laying pipes at Bar End, about a hundred yards of trenching left open, I make sure that the trench is lighted by paraffin lamps, I stay there all night, making sure that the paraffin lamps do not go out, by the time the labourers get there in the morning, I have collected all the lamps from along the trench, and stored them."

"That must be a cold job," Chris remarked.

"No, not at all, I'm quite warm, I have my little sentry box that I sit in, and my coke burning brazier in front," Mr Newman replied.

"Tell me your daily routine please Mr Newman," Chris requested.

Mr Newman thought for a while, then spread his hands open across the table.

"I leave the house in order to get to the trenches by seven at night, at seven the next morning I leave and arrive home, mostly before seven thirty, then I go straight to bed. I get up about twelve, and pop down to the Wagon Inn and have a pint, then about two, I come back, have my dinner that Gloria has ready for me, then I go to bed again until about six, when I have another bite to eat, and get ready to set off, that's about it," Mr Newman said with another spread of his hands.

"Do you see your daughter when you arrive home in the mornings?" Chris asked.

Mr Newman forced a weak smile. "No Gloria is not a early riser."

"She don't work then," Chris remarked.

"Don't go out to work, not in the way you are asking, she looks after me and the house, and takes in sewing and washing, she has enough to do," Mr Newman said, his voice dropping to a whisper.

"I'm sorry that I have to ask these questions Mr Newman," Chris said softly. "But I do have to get a background picture."

Chris looked at George, who was leaning against the sideboard taking notes. "So you first see your daughter, shall we say, when you get up a midday to go to the pub for a pint," Chris continued. "So what happened this morning?"

"I got up as usual, Gloria who is usually busy doing something was not around, I called for her, but got no answer, then I began to get worried, Gloria is always here with a cuppa when I get up, I thought she may be ill, so I went up to her bedroom, and found her like that," Mr Newman sobbed, and tears ran down his cheek. "It was a terrible sight, who could have done it, who would leave her like that?"

"Mr Newman," Chris spoke in a quiet voice. "Would you have noticed whether this back door was unlocked when you arrived home?" he said indicating the door with his hand.

"No, I go straight to my bedroom," Mr Newman replied.

"What about when you got up around twelve you said, did you notice then?" Chris asked.

Mr Newman shook his head.

Chris had other questions to ask, but he was feeling a little of the man's grief, so decided they would have to wait.

"Mr Newman, I have other questions I need answering, but they will wait for another time but before I finish, I have to tell you that your daughter's body will be taken to the hospital shortly, do you want to see her before it happens?"

Chris saw a tear run down Mr Newman's cheek as he answered with a shake of his head. "No, I'll have her home when the hospital is finished with her," he sobbed.

"I need to take a couple of things back to the station, from her room," Chris said getting up. "Would you have any objections?" Chris saw Mr Newman shake his head, as he pushed his chair under the table.

"Thank you, I'll send in my constable to make you a cup of tea, he will stay with you a while," Chris spoke gently.

Chris left the scullery, nodding to George and the Sergeant to follow, he made straight for the front room which he entered, making straight for the window which he tested.

"Well it's a locked window," Chris said. "Of course anyone could have got in had it been opened, then locked the window after, and made his way out by the front door."

He turned to George and the sergeant standing behind him. "This is a straight street, someone may have seen or heard something, George, take Sergeant Bloom, and knock doors, ask questions, and try to find out if she had any real friends in the street, I want to have another look at the room, before the wagon comes, and Sergeant, get constable Bowman to sit with Mr Newman for a while, have him make a cup of tea will you, but first Sergeant, what about the back entrance?"

"The garden is run down, it's quite long, but narrow, to get into it, one would have to climb a wall of six foot, however, I would not like to navigate the garden in the dark. I spoke to Mr Newman about it, he told me that after he leaves for work, the back door is always locked and bolted. The bedrooms all have chamber pots in them, so his daughter would have no need to go out the back to the toilet. All the back gardens are separated by a three strands of wire fence, pull tight through concrete bearers, however, there is a pathway right the way through the back of the houses from each end, perhaps because of the dustman, but one can walk by any of the back doors."

"When you went out into the back garden, was the back door unlocked, or did you have to do it?" Chris asked.

Sergeant Bloom thought for a while. "I'm sure it was unlocked," he said.

Chris re entered the bedroom, and tried to avert his eyes at the sheet that covered the body, he wondered where the wagon was. He took out two paper bags from his murder bag, and crossing to the dressing table, he emptied the ashtray into one of them. He picked up the pink gloves, and put them in the other bag. Crossing to the chest of drawers, he picked up the album that George had found, and after a quick look at the pages, put it into his murder bag. He wondered about dusting for fingerprints, then dismissed the idea. Gloria's murder he was sure, was carried out by someone with intermit knowledge of the house, if he had not worn gloves then the prints would be on the knife handle.

His thoughts were interrupted with the arrival of two men, each wearing a peak cap, and a blue uniform.

"Come for the body, told is alright to take it," remarked one who tipped his hat with his hand.

"Correct," replied Chris firmly. "I expected you some time ago."

"It's the horses playing up," replied the man who had previously spoken. "They smell death you know."

Chris decided to ignore the remark as he watched the man who had not spoken, open a red blanket, without removing the sheet that Bob had covered the body with proceeded to cover the body in the red blanket.

"Well be on our way then," remarked the man. "We'll have her in hospital within a jiffy."

Chris held the bedroom door open, and the men carried the body down the stairs, he overtook them in the passage leading to the front door, so that he could open the front door for them.

"Thanks," said the speaker. "Our wagon doors are already open, we'll say goodbye."

Chris closed the front door behind them.

hris left the house, and made his was back to the station, where his thoughts were on Elizabeth, he would have to cancel their meeting that night. He took the receiver off the telephone stem and dialled her office number.

"Chris here," he said hearing her voice.

"Chris," said a happy sounding voice. "Lovely to hear you, you are not seeing me tonight are you?"

"I'm going to have to be careful with you," Chris replied a smile playing on his face. "You seem to be able to read my mind."

"Why else would you phone me at work darling," she replied. "I only saw you this morning."

"I could be phoning to tell you how much I miss you and love you," Chris teased. "But seriously, I'm sorry Elizabeth, I have a new sergeant, and a new case, I have to get my thinking cap on, without any distraction."

"Am I a distraction to you darling?" Elizabeth replied with a little giggle.

"You know very well you are, when I'm with you the only thoughts I have is holding you, apart from that I lose all my concentration," Chris scolded.

"You say the sweetest things darling, but never mind mum and I will find something to do, I will miss you," Elizabeth replied.

"Me too," responded Chris. "Sure you don't mind?"

"Will I see you in the morning?" Elizabeth asked.

"I'll do my best," Chris assured her.

"Don't tire yourself out darling, get a early night if you can, I love you," Chris heard as the line went dead.

Chris smiled as he put the receiver back, then took out his pocket watch, it was two, and although he did not feel hungry, he realised that he had not eaten any dinner. He snatched the receiver again and dialled O.

"Sergeant," he said as the desk sergeant answered. "Any chance of a cup of tea, I've had no chance for a breakfast."

"I'll get you one in," came the reply. "Constable Bowman is here, do you want to see him?"

"Yes, send him in," Chris replied replacing the receiver.

Chris put his pencil down as the constable came in, and placed a cup of tea before him.

"Take a seat constable," Chris said as he lifted the cup to his lips. "I have been dying for this," he said as he drank a half of the cup.

"Now Constable," Chris said putting the cup back into its saucer. "How did you leave Mr Newman?"

"Sergeant House brought a Mrs Simpson in after you left, she lives opposite, and when I left she was fussing over him like women do, you know," constable Bowman replied.

Chris smiled to himself. "How was he?"

"In a state of shock I would say, I told him to go to bed and keep warm but he would have none of it. He said if he went to bed, he would be awake thinking of his daughter, so he said might as well go to work, as it might help him take his mind off of it."

"I see," Chris remarked feeling sorrow for Mr Newman. "It was not a very good start for any of us on a Monday morning, are you alright?"

"I've never seen a murder before," constable Bowman answered. "I still feel a little shaky."

"I'm sure you do constable, but thank you for your assistance, and tell the desk sergeant, I said you must have a cup of tea before you go back on duty."

"Thank you Sir," the constable replied. "I will do that."

It was two hours later, when George entered the office, followed by Sergeant Bloom. George went straight to his desk, while the sergeant took the interview chair.

"Have you two have a cup of tea, or anything?" Chris asked.

"I've had a couple," George replied.

"The same with me," sergeant Bloom replied. "I had to refuse a few."

"Good," Chris said with a smile. "Have we learnt anything with door knocking?"

"I met a Mrs Simpson who lives at number thirty, she is a widow, and a very nice lady, all she wanted to do was to go over and take care of Mr Newman," George smiled. "Apart from that not a lot of use, everyone was shocked of course, Mr Newman is considered a quiet, private sort of chap, and no one really had a bad word to say about Gloria his daughter."

"Mine was pretty much the same," sergeant Bloom spoke. "However number twenty, I was told was good friend with Gloria but they were out, a Mrs Sharpe lives there. Number eight told me that her daughter was close friend with Gloria, but she was in service. I'm told she sleeps at home, that was Mrs Hanks, no one I met heard anything out of the ordinary."

"Nor mine," George confirmed.

Chris leaned on his desk, thinking over what had been told him. "Well thank you sergeant Bloom, you have been very helpful, what are you on this week, I might have need for you again."

"I'm relief sergeant all this week," he replied.

"Good sergeant, if you will let me have your report on your door knocking I would be grateful," Chris smiled. "By the way, I told constable Bowman to have a cup of tea, he seem to be a bit shaky, you might look in on him."

"I'll do both of that," replied sergeant Bloom standing up to leave. "I'll be around if you need me."

"Thank you sergeant," Chris said as the sergeant left.

Chris looked at George, who was looking through his pocket book. "Any opinion?" he asked.

"Full stop," replied George with a slight smile. "Not a glue in sight."

"I agree," Chris replied thoughtfully. "You can check the knife handle for prints if you will, although I don't hold any hope, even if you find some."

Chris picked up the bag from his desk top, that held the knife, and handed it to George. "Last time I done that, I left my own print on the gun," Chris added, a smile playing on his face.

George looked but made no comment as he took the bag.

"There is no sign of a force entry," Chris continued as he watched George with the dusting powder. "So I am thinking that who ever the murderer was, was known to Gloria, and was let in by her, there is no other explanation."

George nodded in agreement. "I see you brought the album, will it be of help?"

"My first case after I took over, was more or less solved by a photograph, at least it put me on the right road, one never knows," Chris replied.

"Fingers crossed then," George replied, blowing on the powder he had smothered on the knife handle. "This knife handle seems clean," he continued as he stroked the handle with a soft brush.

Chris looked at George and shrugged his shoulders. "What I expected," he said. "So who ever it was wore gloves, I wonder if the murder was intentional or done on the spur of the moment, I'll be interested in getting the Police Surgeon's report."

"Do you have anything to do tonight George?" Chris asked. "If not we could call to those two houses that Sergeant Bloom found no one at home. Then if you like a pint, I'll take you to my local for one, you'll like Alfie the landlord of the Rising Sun."

It was five thirty, when Chris and George knocked on the door of number 8, at Lower Brook Street. The door was opened by a slender woman, wearing a blue dress, buttoned up to the neck, which was covered with a apron. She was average height, and slender, and Chris thought she was at least forty years old. Her attractive looks however, was not enhanced by her dark hair, that was cut just below the ear, and held back with hair clips.

"I am Detective Inspector Hardie, and this is Detective Sergeant House," Chris introduced themselves.

"Are you Mrs Hanks?" he asked.

"Oh yes, I was told that I would be called upon, you want to speak to my daughter," Mrs Hanks replied. "Please come in my daughter and my husband are both in," she said making way for them to enter.

Chris and George entered the house, and found themselves in the living room, Mr Hanks a well built tall man, stood aside of the mantel piece, he was wearing an open neck strip shirt, his trousers was kept up by a wide leather belt, and he had bracers dangling to the side's of them. His size dwarfed that of his wife, but Chris thought that they were about the same age.

Chris introduced himself and his sergeant again to Mr Hanks as they stood in the front room facing the table, at which was seated a young girl, she was dressed in a button to the neck dress, covered with a apron. Her hair similar to that of her mothers, she looked quite young, in fact Chris would have said she was still in her teens.

"As you may well know by now Mr Hanks, Gloria Newman at number sixteen was found murdered this morning, we are interviewing everyone in the street. "Your wife informed one of our officers that your daughter was friendly with her, so with your permission we would like to ask her a few questions."

"Be my guest Inspector," Mr Hanks replied taking a clay pipe from the mantel and looking at it. "My daughter Linda is twenty four, but not quick on the up take, if you get my meaning, but please sit and ask what you want," he offered in a deep voice.

Chris sat facing the girl, and Mrs Hanks who had seated herself beside her daughter while George stood with his notebook out.

"Did you know Gloria Newman, Mr Hanks?" Chris asked as he smiled at the girl at the table.

"I've seen her," Mr Hanks replied filling his pipe, then sucking on it. "Can't remember having spoken to her much though, I leave early for work at six and get home about six thirty at nights, if I do see her, it's on a Sunday."

"What work do you do then?" George asked.

"I work on Abbots Barton farm, on the Worthy Road," he replied, lighting his pipe.

"Linda, is a pretty name," Chris spoke to the girl. "I hear you are in day service."

"I suppose," Linda replied, sitting with her hands held loosely in her lap.

"Did you like Gloria?" Chris asked realising that the girl was backward.

"I suppose," replied Linda unsmiling, and looking straight ahead, Chris could not make out whether she was staring at him, or over his head.

"Now you know you liked Gloria, Linda," Mrs Hanks said to her daughter. "You must tell the Inspector what he wants to know."

"Yes I loved her," Linda replied. "I suppose."

"Did you ever go out together?" Chris asked gently.

"I suppose," Linda replied looking at her mother who had cleared her throat, and seeing that her mother was not pleased, continued. "Gloria would take me to the park, on a Sunday, we would listen to the band, and watched the boats."

"You liked that then?" Chris asked.

"The boats I like to watch, I suppose," Linda replied.

"Did you ever go in the boats?" Chris asked.

"No, I suppose," Linda answered, a faint smile appearing on her face. "I was too nervous, but Gloria did once."

"On her own?" Chris asked.

"No," Linda replied that faint smile re appearing. "A boy had to row her, I walked around the path following them, I suppose."

"Did the boy stay with you after Gloria got out of the boat?" Chris asked gently.

"No," Linda replied.

"Did Gloria ever meet a special boy, around the park, while you were out with her," Chris asked, with a feeling that he was getting no where.

"No but boys used to whistle at her, I suppose," she replied.

Chris relaxed and smiled at Linda. "Thank you Linda, you have been very helpful," he looked at both Mrs Hanks and Mr Hanks. "Thank you both, you realise we have to question everyone who knew Miss Newman."

Outside the house, Chris smiled at George as he spoke. "I don't think Linda will be of much help to us, let's go to number twenty, it's just gone six, plenty of time."

"I suppose," replied George with a smile.

Chris knocked on number twenty, the woman who answered the door when Chris introduced himself and that of his sergeant were invited into the front room, which was wallpapered with many pictures hanging from the picture rail, it was furnished for comfort, and the table was to one side by the window.

Chris thought that Mr and Mrs Sharpe both about twenty five or six, were a handsome couple. Mr Sharpe about six foot tall, dressed in a blue pin single breasted suit, with a mop of dark hair. Mrs Sharpe had on a dress of multi colours, waist tight, but with the top wide open, a thin net covering her chest, her hair which was mousy was long, hanging around her shoulders.

"What a terrible thing to happen to Gloria," she said in a broken voice. "Who could have done such a thing," she dabbed her eyes.

"Please Inspector, Sergeant," Mr Sharpe offered them both a chair. "If we can help we will."

Chris noticed that George had his notebook out as they chose a chair.

"Can I have both your full names please?" Chris asked.

"I am John Sharpe, people call me Jack, and my wife is Ellen Sharpe," Mr Sharpe informed him.

"How long have you lived here?" Chris asked.

"Since we were married, about five years I would say," Mr Sharpe replied looking at his wife, who was nodding her head.

"Thank you," Chris replied. "It might be simpler if you told us what you know about Miss Newman?" Chris said. "I can ask a couple of question later."

While Mr Sharpe remained standing by the hearth, Mrs Sharpe seated herself on the sofa.

"We were good friends," Mrs Sharpe started. "We would go to the dance on a Saturday night, and occasionally she would spend a evening around here, her father is a night watchman you know, it passed the time for her coming around here rather than being stuck in her house all alone, we often went shopping together."

The door of the front room suddenly opened and a slender young man of about thirty stood there. "Oh, I'm sorry Mrs Sharpe," he said looking straight at her. "I did not know you had company, I'm off out, I'll be in about the usual time," he smiled quickly closing the door and disappearing.

Chris looked at Mr Sharpe who answered his look. "That was Terry, Terry Sarshall he lives here, as a lodger of course."

"He's a lovely boy," Mrs Sharpe started to explain. "He's been with us just over six months, no trouble is he?" Mrs Sharpe said turning to her husband, who shook his head.

"He is as quiet as a lamb," Mrs Sharpe continued looking away from her husband, looking at Chris. "When he comes in and we are in bed, we don't hear a sound, do we?" she asked looking at her husband who again shook his head.

"He is fine," Mr Sharpe agreed. "He works at the Brewery in Eastgate Street."

"You have no children Mrs Sharpe?" George asked.

"No, I'm afraid not, we are waiting until we are in a better financial position," she replied.

"Where do you work Mr Sharpe?" Chris asked.

"I'm just a dogsbody in a builder's office," he smiled. "Steady job, but poorly paid, actually I'm the only one in the office, I take orders, I do the books, I make the tea, as I said I am a dogsbody, but it gives me security, for a while anyway," he added.

"Getting back to Miss Newman," Chris continued. "Would you know if she had a boyfriend, I mean a sort of steady boyfriend?"

Mrs Sharpe hesitated. "I really don't think so," she replied.

"Most men would consider her a eyeful, she would often get wolf calls, but I never knew of a steady boyfriend even when we go to a dance, she never picked up with anyone special, we would sit around the edge of the dance floor, and if a boy or man came over asking for a dance, she would oblige, but that's as far as it went, she always came home with me, didn't she?" she asked turning to her husband, who just nodded.

Chris rose to take his leave, George followed. "Thank you both for your time, you have been very helpful, I may need to talk to you again, as you may know a murder investigation can often go in a circle."

As George said his goodbyes, Chris walked to the sideboard that was to the side of the front room door, and took his trilby that he had placed there.

Chris moved to the front door. "By the way, because of fingerprints, have either of you been into Miss Newman's bedroom?"

"No I haven't," Mrs Sharpe replied as she opened the front door. "I am sure my husband have not," she said looking back at her husband with a grin on her face.

Outside, Chris turned to George as they walked towards Union Street. "Not much help there, still as far as everyone is concerned she had no special boyfriend," he said.

"Anyway, it's almost seven, just right for a pint," Chris continued as they walked into Union Street.

George followed Chris into the Rising Sun, who walked straight to the bar, where a smiling Alfie was always waiting to welcome his customers.

"What's it to be tonight Chris?" Alfie asked holding a pint glass in his hand.

Chris did not answer as he turned back looking at George.

"Alfie meet Sergeant George House, he is taking over from Fred Willett, no need to use sergeant when you speak to him."

Alfie stretched his free hand across the counter, which George accepted. "Any friend of Chris is a friend of mine," he said smiling. "Now what's your poison?"

"Thank you Alfie," George replied. "I'll have a beer I think."

"I'll have a bitter," Chris ordered.

With Alfie working away at his pumps, Chris's eyes strayed around the bar, and came to rest on a young man sitting at a table near the open fire place.

"There we are then," Alfie said putting the pints on the counter. "These are on me as a welcome to George here, I hope he stays longer than Fred."

"I'm sure he will," Chris remarked as both detectives took their glass.

"Alfie," Chris said before moving to his usual seat. "That young man by the fire place, is he a regular?"

"Most of the time," Alfie replied. "Why, are you on the Lower Brook Street murder?" he asked.

"I expected you to know Alfie," Chris smiled. "You don't know who did it do you?"

"Can't betray my customers," Alfie smiled humorously.

"Can you tell me if that young man was in here Sunday night?"

Alfie thought for a while before answering. "Yes he was, he left at closing time."

"Is he any trouble?" George asked before taking a sip from his pint.

"Who Terry, no, he is as good as gold, only drinks lemonade," Alfie replied, "All my customers was like him, I wouldn't become rich, with him drinking only lemonade," he joked.

"Thanks Alfie," Chris said with a smile. "We'll take a seat now."

Once seated in their seat, that overlooked Magdalene Hill, Chris turned to George. "I need to have a word with that young man," he said as he lifted his pint glass to his lips.

"Let me talk to him," George offered. "Got to keep my hand in."

"That will suit me," Chris said with a smile. "I will just sit back and enjoy a pipe while you do."

George rose and crossed to where Terry was sitting. "Terry isn't it?" George said reaching his table.

Terry looked at George, wondering, then nodded.

"I am Sergeant House of Winchester CID. My Inspector and myself were talking to Mr and Mrs Sharpe tonight when you went out, you may remember."

"Oh yes, I remember," Terry replied.

"Would you mind if I ask you a couple of questions?" George asked sitting at an empty chair at the table. "It would save calling on you while you were at home."

"Why would you want to call on me?" Terry asked. "I take it you are on about the murder of Miss Newman?"

George nodded. "Did you know Miss Newman, Terry?" George asked.

Terry nodded his head. "She was often in with Mr and Mrs Sharpe," he replied.

"You wouldn't know if she had a regular boyfriend would you?" George asked.

"I don't know about regular," Terry replied. "But she had many men calling on her during the week after dark that is."

"I don't understand Terry," George replied. "Are you saying that men called upon her during the night?"

Terry took a drink of lemonade before answering, then nodded. "A path runs right through the back of our house, and my bedroom window looks out onto this path, sometimes before turning in, I stand at the window and have a fag, I have often seen men walk by and go into her backdoor."

George leaned back in his chair, he was taken by surprise at what was being told to him. "Would you know any of these men?"

189

"No replied Terry, I can see them, but always too dark for me to recognise them, they move like a shadow, I mean," Terry joked with a smile. "One could even have been you?"

"I don't think so," George replied ignoring the joke. "I've only been in Winchester a few days, tell me, she was a looker, did you ever fancy her, after all you are a young man?"

"No I never fancied her, she was a prostitute, actually it would have been very easy for me to get into her house, remember she's alone just two house away."

"Have you ever entered her house?" George asked, surprised at what Terry was saying. "Have you ever been in her bedroom?"

"Why would I?" Terry responded. "I had no interest in her."

"How long have you been in Winchester Terry?" George changed his line of questioning. "Are your parents still alive?"

"About six months," Terry replied. "I was lucky to get the lodgings I have, both my parents died when I was eight, and I was brought up by an aunt."

"Where was this then Terry?" George asked.

"Portsmouth," Terry replied, his face serious, as his childhood came flooding back into his mind.

"Well thank you Terry," George said getting up. "Seeing you here has saved me another call."

Terry looked at George and gave a weak smile. "No problem," he said as he put his glass to his lips.

George returned to his seat with Chris, and took a long drink of his pint, then watching Chris puffing on his pipe, related all he had been told by Terry.

"Interesting," Chris replied puffing away on his pipe.

"If Sergeant Bloom is correct and the back door was unlocked, for we know that Mr Newman locks and bolts the back door before he goes off to work, then Gloria must have opened it for some reason, had the door been locked, then it would have looked like a inside job."

Chapter Three

Chris, met Elizabeth on her way to work the next morning. She gave him his usual kiss on the cheek, and grabbed his arm, as they made their way to her bank.

"I miss you last night darling," Elizabeth said.

"I missed you as well," Chris replied. "I have this new sergeant, George House, and this new case, I'm sorry."

"Don't be silly darling," Elizabeth replied with a giggle. "Mother and I had the time of ourselves trying to fix a date for our marriage."

"Did you," Chris replied. "So what is the outcome?"

"Well," Elizabeth smiled holding tighter on his arm. "We decided," she giggled again as though she was embarrassed to say it. "That an April wedding would be lovely."

Chris did not reply straight away, as his mind was counting the months. "That's four months away," Chris remarked unsmiling.

Elizabeth looked at him, she felt worried. "We can always change it darling," she said.

"I don't know if I can wait four months," Chris replied, with disappointment showing in the tone of his voice and expression on his face. "I'm suffering every time I'm with you."

Elizabeth stopped and looked at Chris with alarm. "Do you really?" she asked feeling a sense of shock.

Chris realized that he had said something that had upset her, he looked at her lovely face, which looked unhappy, he smiled. "I said that wrong Elizabeth, I should have said that four months is too long for me to wait for such a desirable young lady."

Elizabeth smiled as she realized what Chris had meant. "You frightened me for a moment," she said as they started to walk again. "Is it really too long for you darling?" she asked with a serious look on her face. "You know I can alter it if you want me to?" she offered.

Chris patted her arm, as they approached her bank. "I was teasing, it came out wrong, I am sorry if I upset you, it wasn't meant, I think April will be just great, it will give you time to organise."

"You don't know mother," Elizabeth said brightening up. "I doubt if I am left much organising, mother is bound to take over."

Chris smiled as they stopped outside Elizabeth's bank.

"I love you, and yes I want you, but I am prepared to wait, because I respect you and your parents, don't be upset if I joke about it a bit," he said.

"I'm sorry Chris, I feel guilty about it sometimes, I need you as much as you need me," Elizabeth gave Chris a quick kiss on the cheek, and went inside of the bank.

Chris walked back towards the police station, and cursed himself. Still annoyed with himself, Chris entered the police station, he nodded to the desk sergeant who just smiled at him, he entered his office, and put away his trilby, then cross to his desk, where he sat for a moment without speaking to George who sat at his desk watching him.

"Sorry George," Chris eventually said. "I'm such an idiot, I said something intending to tease to Elizabeth, and it came out the wrong way."

"When do you intend to marry?" George asked.

"I'm marrying her in April next year," Chris replied. "I'm sorry I haven't had chance to tell you about her yet."

"You will have to introduce me," George replied.

"I will when I get a chance, ever since I got engaged, I haven't had much time with her, as soon as one case is finished, another one comes up."

"Never marry a policeman," George replied.

Chris smiled. "Elizabeth understands all that, I warned her before we got engaged what it will be like to marry me, but she understands," he smiled.

Chris fell silent as he looked through a few papers that was in his in-tray.

"I was thinking last night about this Terry," Chris spoke. "If she do have men visitors during the night, we know that it's done during the night time, her father is night watchman, my guess is that he has no idea what his daughter was doing. While any of these men could be the murderer, Terry was right when he told you he could have done it, I have to consider him a suspect."

"I should have asked him if he saw anyone enter late Sunday night, I'm sorry, I didn't think of the question."

"We are not supermen George," Chris replied. "We all forget at least one question we should have asked, at least I often do."

"Where do we go from here?" George asked.

"A very good question," Chris replied. "I have no idea, but I do have a job for you, I want you to dig out the background on Terry, where he lived in Portsmouth, what he

194

has done since his parents died, what his parents died of, we have to start somewhere?"

"I'll see Mrs Sharpe again then," George replied getting up from his desk. "She must know a little about him, if not I'll have to ask him straight out."

Chris nodded in agreement as George left the office, he still felt unhappy with himself having upset Elizabeth with a silly tease. The telephone rang loudly.

"Inspector Hardie," he spoke into the receiver.

"Chris darling," came the reply. "Are you alright?"

Chris smiled to himself, the sound of her voice was all that he needed to get him out of his depression. "Elizabeth," he almost shouted. "I'm so glad you phoned, I have been worried."

"Me too," came the reply. "I am so sorry I took your meaning wrong, I been thinking, perhaps I'm being a bit old fashioned, after all we are engaged."

"You must not think like that Elizabeth," Chris replied. "Although I want you in that way, it's you I love and want, not what you can give me, that comes way down the list, so don't think like that, I want you to stay old fashioned, that's the way I want my children brought up."

"Chris darling, you say the nicest things, you make me happy, see you tonight if possible, love you."

"I love you too," replied Chris as the phone went dead.

Chris was in a different mood when George arrived back at the office, during late morning.

"What's happened?" George asked seeing the change in Chris.

Chris smiled as he replied. "Had a call from Elizabeth, she is OK."

"Well I have a little news as well," George said with a smile on his face. "I managed to see Mrs Sharpe, she was a book of information, it seems that Terry was born in Gosport, just outside Portsmouth, Terry told her that his parents had drowned on a boat trip, and he was brought up by an aunt. His aunt is still alive, but as he grew older he wanted to travel around the country, and that's why he is in Winchester, which she believes is just a stop over for a few months, he is thirty two years old. Mrs Sharpe thinks he is foreign."

"Did you ask her not to tell Terry of your conversation?" Chris asked.

George nodded his head.

"What we really want is the address of the aunt, if his parents are dead, she will be the one with any information we want," Chris added.

"How do we get that, without asking him?" George replied.

"Simply by doing that," Chris replied. "After all we do have to check every detail we get."

The desk sergeant opened the office door without knocking. "You're wanted at Twyford Sir," he said his face unsmiling. "Seems a body has been discovered behind the village hall."

"Any other details sergeant?" Chris asked as he started to rise from his desk.

"Children found the body, and it was reported to the village constable, constable Shaw, he has secured the site, and awaits you."

"Twyford is it far?" Chris asked.

"About four miles out of Winchester," the sergeant informed. "The hall is at the bottom of the hill as you enter Twyford from Winchester."

Chris took his trilby from the hat stand. "Looks like we have a lot of cycling to do George," he said.

George smiled. "Why don't I take you on my motorbike?"

"Had no idea that you had one George," Chris replied replacing his trilby. "Where is it?"

"In the Brooks outside my lodgings, it will take a couple of minutes to get it," George replied.

"I'll be outside waiting for you George," Chris agreed. "While you are gone, I'll contact the police surgeon," he said as George went.

Chris took the receiver from the phone, and dialled.

"Bob," Chris spoke into the receiver hearing Bob Harvey's voice. "I have a body at Twyford."

"Naturally," came the reply. "It's lunch time, when else would you have one."

"Sorry Bob," Chris replied with a smile.

"I'll get there as soon as I can," Bob confirmed. "Where about?"

"Behind the village hall, I'm told," Chris informed him.

"I know the place, I'll be there as soon as I can Chris."

George arrived on his motorbike, almost as soon as Chris left the station.

"Hold on to my waist Chris," George said as with a roar and a bang the motorbike moved foreword. "I know which way to go, the desk sergeant gave me directions," George shouted over his shoulder.

"Chris with his arms around the waist of George did not reply, the chugging and the occasional bang from the exhaust as they made their way through the horse drawn traffic, did nothing to calm the fear that Chris felt, he had only been on a motorbike once before, and that had been with the police surgeon, but that time he had sat in a sidecar, this time he was sitting behind the driver, not feeling to safe.

Twyford village hall, was a one story building, standing some fifteen yards from the road, between the road and the hall, gravel was laid, and when George finally pulled in and stopped with a bang and a cloud of smoke from the exhaust, Chris was not slow in getting off.

"Save all that cycling," George smiled at Chris seeing his nervousness. "Safe as a house as well," he said.

Chris did not answer, he thought otherwise as he made his way to the side of the building, a small crowd had gathered, and as Chris followed by George approached, the crowd made way for them, not knowing but wondering who they were. Chris found himself at the back of the hall, in a small field, which seem to be a playground, he noticed swings and a sand pit. He looked around the area, and noticed that the field ran onto the back of a few large houses, that was dotted around.

"Inspector Hardie," he heard a voice, which made him turn, finding a constable looking at him.

"You are constable Shaw, I take it?" Chris replied. "Where is the body?"

"It's over here Sir," the constable replied. "She was partly undressed, so I covered her up with a sheet, I did not disturb anything, it must have been a terrible sight for the children."

"So it's a woman," Chris replied following the constable to the other end of the building, to where the body covered over by a sheet lay. "The children found her?"

"Yes Sir," replied the constable. "According to the teacher who runs a small infant school in the hall, she thought she would allow them out to play, as it's quite a warm day for the time of the year, they ran ahead of her and found this," the constable said pointing at the sheet.

"Is she a Twyfod woman?" Chris asked the constable.

"Yes, I know her and her mother, her father is out in France, her name is Stacey Brown lives along Park Lane, just behind the pub."

"So you are able to verify who the dead woman is?" Chris asked.

"Yes Sir," replied the constable.

Chris did not reply to the information. "Get rid of the gathering constable, you must know them, I have the Police Surgeon coming, so he will want privacy, don't let anyone back here."

"I understand Sir," the constable replied, then walked back to the side of the building, which was the only entrance.

Chris looked at George. "Two murders in two days," he remarked. "Well we better have a look."

Chris kneeled, and gently pulled the sheet away from the body, showing the face and neck. "I would assume she was strangled," Chris said looking at the dead face.

"That's a nasty red mark around the throat, but still better wait for the police surgeon," Chris added covering the face.

The constable returned. "I have put a rope across, to stop the people," he said. "They are mainly the parents of the children."

"Thank you constable," Chris replied looking at George. "The mother needs to be informed, will you take Sergeant House to the house?" he said. "I want to talk to her as well, but after the police surgeon has been."

"That's alright," replied George not really wanting the job of telling a woman her daughter has been found dead.

"It might be a good idea if she has a neighbour that can go in with you," Chris added.

"There is a Mrs Carter across from her that I believe is a good friend of hers," the constable explained.

"I'll send the constable back," George said as he followed the constable.

"Thanks George," Chris answered as he started to look around the scene.

Left alone, Chris looked around the scene, he knew he should be examining the body but the constable had said that the body was half undressed, so he decided to wait for the police surgeon. Although dry, the night had been very windy, he saw nothing that looked out of place. He slowly walked around the small playing field, his eyes on the ground. Coming to the far side, he looked and studied the houses whose gardens adjoined the field separated by a small hedgerow. Returning to the body, he was satisfied in his mind, that the back windows of the houses could not have seen the body lying there owing to the conifers growing in their gardens. The sound of a engine spluttering took his eyes from the body towards the entrance to the field, a moment later Bob Harvey the police surgeon made his appearance.

"Bob," Chris greeted as he watched Bob get off his motorbike.

"Hello Chris," Bob greeted as making sure his bike would stand up straight. "Let's see the body."

Chris led the way until they reached the body at the back of the hall.

"Well, what do we have here," Bob remarked as he took the sheet covering from the body, and revealed a young woman, with her clothes up to her waist. Her bloomers down below her knees. Bob knelt beside the body, and carried out his examination without a word.

"I don't know what the world is coming to," Bob said as he rose. "She was a pretty girl about twenty four or five I would say, do we know who she is?" Bob asked turning to Chris.

"The local constable identified her, he said he knew her and her family, her name is Stacey Brown, and lives here in Twyford."

"Have you seen the parents Chris?" Bob asked, his eyes still on the body.

"No, I waited for you, Sergeant House is at the house however."

"So you want my guess work, I take it?" Bob asked.

"Give me something to tell her mother when I speak to her," Chris replied.

"My guess is that she was strangled, it looks like she had sex, whether forced or not I don't know yet. The weather is cold, but I would put her death between ten and midnight last evening, I'm afraid that's the best I can do at the moment, have you finished with the body?" Bob asked looking at Chris.

"No I have not examined her, I was told she was uncovered and after yesterday, I thought I would await you," Chris replied.

Bob smiled. "You will have to get used to such sights Chris." "You will probably see more than this, before you retire," Bob continued pointing at the body.

Chris knelt, he examined her hands, he checked her dress, since becoming Inspector, he had seen several dead bodied, but in the last two days, he had seen two dead women half undressed, he felt sorry for the victims, their humiliation of being left in such a fashion. "Nothing there Bob," he said getting up, and brushing the knees of his trousers. "So she is all yours."

I commandeered the motorised ambulance, I knew there would be a body to bring back, with you on the case," he smiled at Chris with a grin. "It can do five mile an hour."

"Really?" Chris replied.

"It should be waiting outside for us now," Bob replied. "It followed me."

Bob, tidied the dress on the woman, and made her presentable, he then covered her with the sheet, before going and calling the driver and the ambulance attendant, who lifted the body gently on the stretcher, and carried it out of the field. Chris found that the crowd outside the front had increased, but they made way for the stretcher bearers, who took the body to the rear of the ambulance.

Chris studied the ambulance, they were not a common sight. The body was like a oblong box, the sides were panelled, and two small windows showed high up in the sides, mounted on four sound wheels with solid rubber covering. The drivers cab was completely open, no sides or front, but the painted white roof of the ambulance extended over the drivers cab like a canopy.

With the body loaded, Bob walked back to Chris. "I shall leave you now Chris, the driver will follow me back," he said. "The attendant will stay with the body in the back, it's not as cold as sitting with the driver with an open cab, I'll let you have my report in the morning, I'll tidy her up, her parents can come anytime tomorrow afternoon if they want to see her?"

"Thanks Bob," Chris replied. "Sorry to have called you out."

Bob laughed. "We'll have to get another police surgeon with you as an inspector, you wait until I see Noal again, I tell him," he grinned.

As the ambulance drew away, the constable returned. "I managed to get Mrs Carter to come with us," he informed Chris. "It's not a happy house, Sergeant House is still there."

"Thank you constable," Chris replied. "I'm just going to check the back again, and you can take me there."

Chris studied the place where the body was found, apart from the flattening of the grass, Chris could find nothing else and eventually gave up. He turned to the constable who had followed him.

"There is nothing here constable, so the playground can be opened again, you didn't see a handbag around did you?"

"Never touched a thing Sir, never saw a handbag," replied the constable.

"Well thank you constable," Chris replied. "On second thoughts, tell me what number Park Lane Mrs Brown lives in, and I can walk there myself. I would like you to ask questions to the people outside, you never know, someone may seen or heard something between ten and midnight last night, can you do that constable?" Chris asked.

"I can Sir," replied the constable. "Number nineteen, Park Lane is the second turning on the left, behind the pub."

"Thank you constable," Chris replied as he left the scene, and made his way pass between murmuring people.

Chapter Four

Chris knocked on number nineteen, the door was opened by Sergeant House. "I have not told Mrs Brown anything, except that her daughter had been found dead, she wanted to go to her, but I convinced her that it would be better for her to see her later at the hospital. I have a Mrs Carter consoling her, she has taken it badly," George informed Chris as he let him into the hall.

"Thanks George," Chris replied. "It's not a nice duty is it?"

George made no reply as Chris followed him into a room to the left of the hall. The warmth of the room hit him, outside was dry and cold, and Chris who had taken off his trilby, was only wearing his suit, the same as George. Chris noticed that the room was clean and tidy, and furnished for comfort. He saw Mrs Brown, her face buried in her hands sitting by an open fireplace that was burning brightly, standing behind her with her arm around Mrs Brown's shoulders was another woman, who Chris took as Mrs Carter. Chris thought that both women were middle ages, and neatly groomed. Chris approached the table, Mrs Brown was seated on the opposite side to the left.

"I am Inspector Hardie of Winchester CID Mrs Brown," Chris said as kindly as he could. "I am so sorry about your loss, I know your grief."

"Do you?" Mrs Brown replied with anger in her voice, lifting her tear stained face from her hands and looking straight at the Inspector.

"In my job, I see a lot of grief Mrs Brown," Chris replied kindly, dismissing her outburst of anger. "I have come to feel it myself."

"Mrs Brown dabbed her nose and sniffed. "I'm sorry," she said. "You are very kind, please forgive me."

"Can we do anything for you, what about a nice cup of tea?" he asked looking at Mrs Carter.

"I have asked her, she don't want one," Mrs Carter replied.

Chris pulled up a chair, and sat at the table, almost facing Mrs Brown.

"Have you any other children Mrs Brown?" Chris asked.

Mrs Brown, her eyes red was looking at the Inspector, the palms of her hands were placed into each other resting in her lap.

"I have no children Inspector," Mrs Brown sobbed. "Stacey was not even my child, we, my husband and I adopted her when she was a baby, I have never been blessed in that way."

"Where is your husband now Mrs Brown?" Chris asked kindly, remembering what the constable had told him.

Mrs Brown put her hand in the pocket of the apron she was wearing, and took out a yellow envelope, that Chris recognised to be a telegram, she passed it over to Chris, who took it and read it.

Chris almost choked, and felt a deep sadness, as he passed the telegram to George.

The telegram was from the war office, informing Mrs Brown that her husband had lost his life in the defence of his country. Chris shook his head, not knowing how to proceed. Chris stopped himself from reaching across the table to take Mrs Brown's hand.

"I have no words that can give you comfort Mrs Brown," he said softly looking at Mrs Brown's swollen eyes. "When did you get that telegram?"

"Yesterday," Mrs Brown sobbed. "I showed it to Stacey when she got home from work, she works in Winchester you know, I put her tea out, and allowed her to eat it, then I told her. Stacey ran to her bedroom crying, it was about an hour later when I heard her go out, she didn't say anything to me, she just went out, I haven't seen her since, and now, never will," Mrs Brown burst into tears.

Chris turned to George. "Go back to the village hall George, you will find the constable there, villages normally have a doctor, get him to show you where he lives and bring him, Mrs Brown need a sedative."

George nodded, pleased that he could get out of the house, he felt so sad and depressed.

Chris bowed his head looking at the table, he had no idea what to say, and stayed that way for several minutes before looking at Mrs Carter.

"You know where the makings are Mrs Carter, please would you make tea, it will help Mrs Brown," Chris said in the kindness voice.

Mrs Carter nodded her head, and left the room, tear filled her eyes.

"You want to ask me some questions Inspector?" Mrs Brown sniffed looking at him.

"Only if you are up to it Mrs Brown, I can call back another time."

"No, no, I want to know about my daughter, your sergeant told me only that she was dead, how did she die?"

Chris looked at Mrs Brown, he could see that she was fighting with herself to keep control, yet the only news he had for her was bad.

"Come along Inspector, I have lost my family now, what can you tell me that's worse?" she spoke with her voice trembling.

Chris spread his hands over the table. "The cause of your daughter's death is being classed as suspicious Mr Brown," Chris replied in a whisper full of sadness.

"You mean she did not die of a natural causes," Mrs Brown sobbed in reply.

"I'm afraid not Mrs Brown, what can I say?" he replied feeling hopeless.

"You can tell me Inspector," Mrs Brown said throwing back her head, and trying to force a smile. "I am not a weak woman, and nothing can hurt me no more than I am, if as you believe my daughter was murdered, you must have questions that you want answered, so let's get it all over with, once and for all."

Chris saw Mrs Brown's determination to get things over, he understood that in a short while she could have a complete breakdown, that's why he had sent for the doctor, he pushed his emotions to one side, he had to act like a policeman, but it was difficult.

"Boyfriends Mrs Brown, did Stacey have anyone special?"

"If she did, I don't know of it," Mrs brown replied. "She worked in Winchester, and she was beautiful, so she must have had admirers."

"I agree, but no one special?" Chris said softly.

"Not that I am aware of," replied Mrs Brown. "How was she murdered?" she asked tears filling her eyes again. "I mean was anything done to her?"

"I can't say at this point Mrs Brown," Chris half lied. "She is at Winchester hospital at the moment with the police surgeon, it will be tomorrow before we know what really happened."

Mrs Brown sniffed and seem to be thinking. "When can I see her?" she asked.

"Anytime after tomorrow dinner time I'm told, but you don't have to go, she is peaceful now, and she will be brought back to you here, the village constable Shaw, identified her."

"Yes I know him," she said in a absent voice. "I will have to go to Winchester to make arrangements," she sniffed. "My husband's arrangements have already been taken care of," Mrs Brown burst into crying as Mrs Carter entered the room with the tea to the relief of Chris.

It took Mrs Carter several minutes to console Mrs Brown, Chris took it upon himself to pour out the tea, one cup for each. Mrs Carter eventually got Mrs Brown to drink, when a knock on the front door was heard. "I'll see to it," Chris said getting up. "Probably my sergeant?" he murmured.

Chris opened the front door, let in the doctor and George. "This is Doctor Chapman," George introduced to Chris, I have left the constable still asking questions.

Chris offered his hand to the doctor. "I am Inspector Hardie of Winchester CID doctor, Mrs Brown's daughter has been found murdered behind the village hall."

"Yes I have heard," replied the doctor. "I was about to make myself available then I saw the ambulance arrive."

"Mrs Brown also had a telegram from the war office yesterday, her husband has been killed in action in France," Chris informed.

"Good Lord," exclaimed the doctor. "I am glad you called me."

"I am going to leave now doctor, I cannot bring myself to ask her any more questions, I'll see her another day, take care of her please she has much grief."

"Leave her in my hands Inspector," the doctor said, as Chris followed by George left by the front door. "Make my excuses please doctor," Chris asked, and gave a weak smile as the doctor nodded.

Chris felt the coldness, he pressed his trilby firmer, and turned up the collar of his jacket, digging his hands in his trouser pockets, George followed him as they turned left, heading back towards the village hall.

"Should have worn our top coats George," Chris remarked.

George nodded. "I didn't bring mine with me this morning, it seem to have got colder."

"Mrs Brown's house was very warm, that's why we are feeling the cold. I wanted to ask her several more questions, just didn't have the heart," Chris explained. "We see a lot of grief in this job don't we, perhaps I'm not cut out to be a policeman, it gets to me."

"Perhaps that's what make you such a good detective," George remarked. "You have feeling, and with that emotion comes fairness, I'm sure that you will never put the wrong person away."

Chris smiled as they came to the village hall. "I hope you are right there," Chris replied taking his hands from his pockets. "I would hate the thought."

Constable Shaw stood on the path outside the village hall looking at his notebook, the gathering of people has dissolved, and he was alone, he looked up as they approached.

"Constable," Chris greeted him. "Any luck?"

"Bits and pieces Sir," replied the constable. "Just trying to get it all in order."

"Well constable," Chris said. "Go home and write it all down as you remember it, be at my office at nine tomorrow morning, and we can go over it, I don't think I shall solve this crime tonight," Chris said in all seriousness.

"Right you are Sir," the constable replied. "Anything else?"

"You can keep asking questions, this is only a small village, don't bother Mrs Brown, but if you can find out where Stacey worked in Winchester, it will be helpful."

The constable smiled as he watched Chris get on the back seat of George's motorbike. "You will both feel the cold on that bike," he said fingering his chin.

"We are detectives constable," George replied as he was about to drive off. "We know that."

Chapter Five

Chris stood outside the police station, it was cold, and darkness was descending. Chris pulled the collar of his top coat up, he was pleased that George on the way back from Twyford had taken him to his lodgings to fetch his topcoat. He has frozen on the back of the motorbike, and wondered how George had stood it being the driver. With neither of them having had dinner, Chris told George to call it a day, as he was meeting Elizabeth, and would pass the time by looking through the album taken from Gloria Newman's bedroom.

Chris watched as a lamp lighter carrying his long shoulder pole passed, horse drawn carts passed with their paraffin lamps glowing on each side of the carts. Cyclist swerving in and out of the traffic ringing their bells passed, it seemed that everyone was in a hurry to get home. Chris crossed the Broadway, and stood outside the small tobacconist shop opposite, the dim light coming from it just penetrating the pavement, he did not want to miss Elizabeth in the darkness.

"I'm glad to see you are wearing a top coat darling," Elizabeth smiled looking up at him. "It's a cold night," she grabbed his arm, than planted a cold kiss on his cheek.

"You must be frozen," Chris said with concern in his voice.

"I'm quite warm darling," Elizabeth replied. "This top coat I'm wearing is like a green house."

They walked with their arms locked for several moments towards Elizabeth's home.

"I missed you last night," Elizabeth giggled. "It was cold in bed last night, and I was wishing that we were already married."

"Will you stop teasing," Chris scolded her with a smile. "I have that same wish every night, cold or hot."

They crossed St John Street, and passed the Rising Sun on their right.

"We will be in the warm soon darling," Elizabeth said. "A good hot meal will put warmth into you."

Chris touched her arm with his free hand.

"I'm already feeling hot being this close to you," Chris replied.

Elizabeth giggled. "I love it when you speak naughty," she giggled.

Mrs Oborne opened the front door, as they walked up the path towards it. "Come along quickly you two, you must be frozen."

Chris and Elizabeth looked at each other and smiled, then hurried inside.

"Give me your coat and trilby Chris," Mrs Oborne said. "Elizabeth will take you through to the kitchen, with the fire there it will be a warmer room to have your meal."

Pulled by Elizabeth, Chris entered the kitchen, and found Mr Oborne there reading, he looked up from his paper seeing Chris and stood up, his hand already out in a welcome, which Chris took. "Is it cold enough for snow, or is it too cold?" he said smiling at Chris as Elizabeth gave her father a kiss on the cheek.

The kitchen was like most other kitchens, a hearth with a cooking range, the heat from the range filling the room with warmth. The table was already laid, with four chairs around it.

"Now sit yourself down Chris," Mrs Oborne fussed, going to the range, and taking a lid off of a saucepan.

Chris was thankful for the meal, it had been at least ten hours since he had last eaten. The vegetable soup was hot and warming, followed by corn beef and cabbage with mash potatoes, followed by steaming hot apple pie and custard.

"There is more if you want it Chris?" Mrs Oborne offered ignoring her husband and daughter.

"Thank you Olive," Chris replied. "But honestly I couldn't eat another bite."

Mrs Oborne smiled, as she cleared the table, with the help of Elizabeth. When that was done, both the women seated themselves around the table.

"The war seems to be going badly," Mr Oborne spoke to Chris. "We seem to be getting a lot of casualties?"

Chris shrugged, Inspector Noal flashing through his mind. "I never get the chance to read a paper these days," he replied. "My new sergeant was wounded, and he tells me it's no picnic over there."

"Now Ron," Mrs Oborne interrupted. "Chris has his own worries, he don't want to talk about the war all the time," she scolded him.

"I've hardly said a word," Ron complained, looking over his glasses at Chris and smiling.

Olive ignored her husband. "You seem very quite tonight Chris, are you wrapping up warm, it's very cold these days, you must make sure you have regular meals, and keep warm."

213

Chris saw Ron smiling at him knowingly, he looked at Elizabeth, who was resting her hand on his. "Why not smoke your pipe Chris?" she said.

Chris smiled at her, and took out his pipe and tobacco, he filled the pipe and lit it, sucking in a deep draw. "I'm alright Olive," he replied blowing out a cloud of smoke towards the ceiling. "I've had two bad cases in two days, I've seen a lot of grief, and I suppose it got to me."

"Can't you tell us, and perhaps it will help you?" Elizabeth said concern in her voice.

Chris took the pipe from his mouth, he looked at it, and twisted the stem.

"Yesterday," he began. "A body of a young woman about twenty five was found murdered in her bedroom," Chris paused and took another puff on his pipe, as he heard a gasp escape both Mrs Oborne and Elizabeth.

"Poor soul," Mrs Oborne murmured.

"Yes," agreed Elizabeth squeezing Chris's hand.

"Anyway," continued Chris. "I won't go into it all, but she was the only child of a widower, who works as a night watchman. She must have been murdered while her father was at work, around midnight Sunday."

"I suppose it was her father that found her," Ron voiced.

Chris nodded his head. "It was a terrible shock for him."

"It must have been, poor man," expressed Olive.

"Have you any clues darling?" Elizabeth asked softly, with a sadness in her voice. "I wonder if I know her, we are about the same age."

"Well it will be common knowledge in a couple days, her name was Gloria Newman," Chris informed them.

Elizabeth searched her mind. "No, I don't think I know her," she replied.

"Poor man," repeated Olive.

"This morning I was called to another body at Twyford," Chris continued. "This was another young girl about the same age as Gloria, she was found murdered behind Twyford village hall."

"Oh my God," came from Olive.

"She was a Twyford girl, so it was easy to find her mother, I had to ask her where her husband was, even though I already knew that he was over in France, I had to ask," Chris said almost apologetically. "I have to confirm, she then showed me a war telegram she had received the day before, telling her that her husband had been killed."

"Oh that poor woman, oh dear, oh dear," Olive almost sobbed and she choked on her words. "No wonder you are depressed."

Ron got up from his seat, he did not like his wife getting upset. "I have some bottles under the bath Chris, what about one?"

Chris nodded, he knew he had upset everyone. "Yes, and that's all I'm telling you," he said forcing a smile and dragging on his pipe, as Ron left the room.

"Your job can be very unpleasant at times Chris," Elizabeth said. "I have often wondered why you never talk about your cases, now I understand," she admitted.

Ron brought in two glasses of beer, and placed one before Chris. "This will help you Chris," he said. "I fear that the women are a bit upset, they do not realise that what you have just told us, is a part of life in society, it happens somewhere every day, but for us it's just reading about it, for you, it's a reality."

With his free hand, Chris lifted his glass, and smiled his thanks at Ron, then took a long drink.

"I really don't know what you are talking about Ron?" Olive butted in. "Of course what Chris told us was very sad, anyone with any feelings would feel the same, I, and I know Elizabeth do, same for Chris also, who as you say deals with the reality."

"Alright Olive," countered Ron with a smile. "Let's get down to this wedding that you and Elizabeth have wrapped yourselves in," Ron saw a smile come to the faces of both his wife and daughter, then looking at Chris, winked.

"Elizabeth feel that April will be a nice month for our wedding Olive," Chris remarked, glad to lift the sad atmosphere that he himself had created. "I myself agree with her."

"I was hoping that you would Chris," replied Olive smiling at her daughter. "Naturally it was her choice, but I think it would be a lovely month."

"What we would like to know Chris," Elizabeth said smiling at him. "Is the number of people you want to invite?"

"I haven't given it any thought," Chris replied, looking at Ron who was looking at him, a smile in his eyes. "I suppose I would like Mr and Mrs Dobson who I lodge with to be invited."

"You can invite who ever you want to Chris," Elizabeth said. "As many as you wish."

"I don't know many," Chris replied. "Being an orphan, I have no relations."

"You poor boy," Olive replied. "I had no idea you were an orphan, I am so sorry."

"No need to be Olive," Chris replied. "Don't feel any sadness, if you have never known your parents, then you can never miss them."

"Have you no drinking mates, or anyone like that Chris?" Ron asked feeling pity for him.

"Well," Chris hesitated. "I was hoping that Inspector Noal and his wife could come, but he is in France, and may not be able to get home for the wedding, and then," Chris continued after a moment of thought. "I would like to invite Inspector McNally and his wife from Scotland, and of course my Sergeant, Sergeant House," he added.

"But that's only seven Chris," Elizabeth said. "Do you not have any other friends?"

Chris smiled at her. "Never had the time to make many friends," he replied. "The people I meet are criminals or their victims, and I meet plenty of them, too many in fact, if I go for a drink it's usually on my own to think, or I go with a colleague."

"What about your colleagues, wouldn't you like some of them to come?" Ron asked trying to help Chris out.

"I suppose I could," smiled Chris. "I could invite Alfie from the pub, I like him and he has helped me from time to time, he gets a lot of information behind the bar."

"That might not be possible Chris," Ron replied. "You see we were hoping that he would do the bar for the wedding breakfast."

Chris shrugged, and spread his hand, that Elizabeth was not holding. "I know very little about weddings, never been to one, never thought much about them until I met Elizabeth, so as far as arranging one is concerned I am ignorant, tell me how many people should be at a wedding?"

"There is no fix number Chris," Elizabeth replied. "But invitation cards has to be printed, and sent out, some guest might not be able to come, having made other arrangements, so it's best to get them sent out early, we thought about sending them out during January, it's not long now with Christmas almost upon us."

Elizabeth looked at her mother. "How many are we inviting?" she asked.

"Almost forty at the moment," her mother replied smiling happily. "But I am sure we will add to that list."

Elizabeth looked at Chris, her face showing concern. "I shall be inviting many more than you, it should be about equal."

Chris smiled at her. "It don't matter how many I invite or how many you invite, I have been told it's the bride's big day of her life, I sincerely hope it will be."

"Won't it be your big day as well?" Elizabeth asked softly looking keenly at him.

"Of course it will," Chris replied feeling himself blush a little. "But for me, it will mean marrying the girl I love, having a wife, a friend and a companion for life, as well as being a part of a family."

"Before you go to any expense, please let me know, I will let you have it," Chris spoke to Ron and Olive.

Ron burst out laughing, and Chris saw a smile on Olive's face.

"We will pay for our daughter's reception Chris, it's traditional, anyway, how else can we thank you for taking our stubborn daughter off our hands."

"Dad," Elizabeth scolded her father. "Chris will think you want rid of me."

Ron's face became serious. "I'm sure Chris knows that we idolise you, the same as he do, I was only joking, let's fill that glass of yours again Chris, when you are married, you will learn one thing."

"What's that then Ron?" Chris asked.

"You will never understand a woman's mind," Ron replied getting up.

"Go away with you," Olive scolded. "You haven't got a mind, go and get Chris that drink."

Chapter Six

Both Chris and George were at their desks when Constable Shaw knocked and entered the office.

"Take a chair constable," Chris indicated the interview chair after greeting. "How did you get on?"

The constable handed Chris four neatly written sheets. "I have written all the statements and the gossip that I have learnt Sir," replied the constable pointing to the papers he had handed to Chris. "It's not on the notes, but Stacey worked at London Bazaar Store, it's opposite the Bell Inn, that faces the high Street, at the passage that leads to the Bakers Arms."

Chris looked at him with a smile. "I know of it constable, I pass it twice a day coming and going from this station."

Chris scanned the notes in front of him. "You seem to have a lot here constable, thank you, it will take me time to study, because I shall read them several times. I don't suppose you know how Mrs Brown is?"

"Well Sir, I did speak to the doctor last night, he gave her a sedative to make her sleep, and arranged for her friend to stay in the house overnight."

"Thank you constable," Chris replied. "I might have need you again, it's a long way to cycle," he said looking at George with a grin on his face. "Especially with this cold weather, with you on site, you may be useful to us."

"I'm on the phone Sir," replied the constable getting up assuming that his presence were no longer needed. "If that is all Sir," he asked politely.

"Looking at these notes constable, you have done very well, thank you, no need to detain you longer," Chris replied pleasantly. "By the way constable, any idea of the population of Twyford?"

"At a guess Sir, I would say no more than hundred and fifty."

"Thank you again constable," Chris repeated as the constable left the office.

"Good man that constable Shaw," Chris said to George laying the down the constable's notes in front of him. "I'll study them, but first George any luck with your errand?"

"I saw Mrs Sharpe again last night, but she was unable to help," George replied. "So I went to the Rising Sun, and Terry Sarshall was in there, so I sat with him, and during our talk, I found out that his aunt lives in Nelson Road, Gosport, he didn't volunteer the number."

Chris smiled to himself. "The number is not important, it can soon be known, the road name was however, I'll get on to the Gosport police later, what about Monday night?"

"Terry told me he was in the pub until closing time, I verified this with Alfie, if Stacey was killed at Twyford between ten and twelve Monday night, it's hard to see how Terry could be involved," George continued. "He would have had to get to Twyford after he left the pub, let's say that it was eleven before he arrived, he would still have to get Stacy behind the village hall, which means if it was him, he had prior arrangements with her?"

"Don't forget George," Chris remarked. "Mrs Brown told us that she had told Stacey about the telegram she had received from the war office, and that after Stacey went to her bedroom, and later went out of the house, which was the last time Mrs Brown saw her daughter. My way of thinking is that Stacey stormed out of the house, in anger and grief, so there was no prior arrangement with her or who ever murdered her. I am incline to agree with you about Terry not being involved, but if he should be, we would have to find out why he was in Twyford at that time of night."

"I agree," George replied. "Mrs Sharpe did not know the time Terry returned home. Monday night as her and her husband was in bed, but as she told us before he is always so quiet they never hear him."

"Well I have these notes to go over, and I must phone Gosport, why don't you pop up the high street to London Bazaar Store, find out what you can learn about Stacey," Chris suggested.

"Suits me," replied George getting up. "I'll see you back here then," he said leaving the office.

A few moments later, Chris left his desk, and went out of the office, where he spoke to the desk sergeant.

"Do you have a number for the police station at Gosport?" Chris asked him.

"I should have somewhere," came the reply. "Do you want it straight away, only the kettle is boiling."

"As quickly as possible," Chris replied. "When you find it bring it in with a cup of the tea you're making," Chris said with a grin as he once again entered his office.

Chris picked up the papers that constable Shaw had given him, and started to read. He read what the doctor had said that Stacey was a patient of him, although he did not see a lot of her, she was young and healthy woman, and smile creased his face as he read on, many opinions from mainly women, some said she was a nice pleasant girl, others said she was full of herself, and seem to have plenty money, most said that they had not seen her out with a boyfriend, one even thought that she was now old and if she didn't marry soon she would be left on the shelf.

Chris read right the way through the notes, they told him nothing that would help solve Stacey's murder, but he knew about her, she was single and healthy, she did not have a boyfriend in Twyford, and had she one in Winchester she never brought him home. Chris thought a bit on the remarks that she seem to have plenty money, as far as he knew, she was the only earner in the house, and her job as a shop assistance would not bring in a great deal. Mrs Carter's remarks about Stacey staying in Winchester overnight two or three nights a week was perhaps the most important remark, although cycling from Twyford to Winchester, then back again every day must have been a chore to Stacey.

The sergeant entered with a hot cup of tea, and the telephone number Chris had wanted, he placed the tea on the desk and put the written telephone number on the blotter in front of Chris. "I do have other work to do, you know," he said leaving with a smile on his face.

Chris dialled the number, and was answered. "Gosport Police Station," came the reply.

"Good morning," Chris spoke into the mouthpiece. "I am Detective Inspector Hardie from Winchester Police Station, can I talk to a senior officer in your CID department please?"

"Just a moment please," came the polite answer as the phone seem to go dead.

Chris waited, humming a tune in his mind, and it was a minute later when a voice came, stopped his humming.

"Good morning Inspector, I am Inspector Dodd of Gosport CID, it's nice to hear from you, how can I help?"

Chris explained what he was after. "I do not know the number, but I am told he was brought up by an aunt in Nelson Road, do you know it?"

"Yes I know it," replied Inspector Dodd. "So you want all the information you can get on this Terry Sarshall, going back to the death of his parents, I think I can do that for you Inspector, if my information is short, I'll phone you, if it's much, I post a report to you, is it urgent?"

"Well I have two separate murders on my hands at the moment, getting nowhere?" Chris replied.

"Lucky you," replied Inspector Dodd. "But I understand, I'll get straight on to it, you should hear from me by the end of the week."

"Thank you Inspector," Chris replied feeling satisfied. "I owe you one."

It was an hour or so later when George came into the office carrying a sack, which he put down by the hat stand.

"Felt like a rag and bone man carrying that sack through town," he remarked as he sat at his desk, and combed his hair back with his fingers.

Chris smiled, but he did not speak.

"I saw the manager of London Bazaar," George remarked. "He was very helpful, but wondered why Stacey had not reported for work in the last two days, he had heard nothing, so I told him," George paused waiting for any comments, which did not come.

"He seemed very distressed when I told him what had happened, and invited me into his office," George continued.

"He told me that Stacey cycled into Winchester, but sometimes she stayed overnight at girl friends, who he did not know. Anyway, he told me that Stacey was always well presentable, and got on with the customers, and for that reason, he had allowed her to use the stock room which was upstairs to change her clothes, after all he said, she was wet through sometimes when she got there."

"I went to this stock room, and told the manager that I would have to take her things with me, he got me that sack," George smiled. "Back in his office, he gave me details of her employment, I wrote them in my book," George went on producing the book from his pocket.

George shuffled a few pages before starting to read.

"Single girl, twenty five years old, born 4/4/1890, living at Park Lane Twyford with parents, she had been employed by them since she was twenty one, that's four years," George concluded.

"Ties in with the report constable Shaw gave us," Chris remarked. "No information on any boyfriend, or who she stayed with when she stopped over then?"

"The manager did allow me to speak to the other three girls working in the shop, but it seems that although she was well liked, her life seems to be a secret, they only knew her through working in the shop," George informed.

"Let's have a look what you have in the sack," Chris said to George, who got up and got the sack.

"Just dresses and a pair of shoes, some underwear, and odds and ends," George remarked, as he took out the contents of the sack with his hands and placed them before Chris. "Nothing much."

Chris looked through the pile, he examined the shoes, black ankle lace up, he put his hand inside of each, they came out empty, he put them to one side, he took a pair of knee length stockings, and put them to one side, as he did with several bits of underwear apart from a dress, there was nothing else, and Chris did not even examine the dress.

"I can understand her wanting to change a dress and perhaps shoes should she getting wet on the cycle from home, but why all that underwear, have you ever got wet through which went through to your underwear?" Chris looked at George with wonder.

George shrugged his shoulders. "Not that I can remember," he said.

Chris looked at his pocket watch. "Well it's almost twelve, about the time Mr Newman gets up and goes for a pint, and I want to talk to him, best to put this stuff back into the sack, and somehow get it to Mrs Brown."

The Guildhall clock had already struck the hour of twelve when Chris knocked on the door in Lower Brook Street, and it was opened by Mrs Simpson. Chris took off his trilby, seeing that she smiled at George.

"This is Detective Inspector Hardie," George introduced him with a smile. "We are here to see Mr Newman, is he up?"

"Yes he is," smiled Mrs Simpson looking at Chris. "He is in the scullery, straight through."

"Thank you," Chris said as he passed Mrs Simpson who had stood aside for him and George to pass. "I need to speak to Mr Newman alone," he said in the kindness voice.

"That's all right inspector," Mrs Simpson replied. "I do have a couple of things to finish across the road, just close the door behind me," she said leaving the house.

Chris watched as George closed the front door. "He has got the key on a string behind the door now," Chris remarked looking at the letter box. "It wasn't there on Monday."

"Perhaps he has just done it," George remarked thinking of nothing else to say.

Chris did not comment as he made his way up the passage, and into the scullery, where he found Mr Newman tying his shoes, Mr Newman looked up as the two men entered.

"Oh it's you Inspector," he said. "Mrs Simpson let you in?"

"That's right Sir," Chris replied politely. "She has gone to her own house, she had things to do, according to her."

"She's been a God send to me, wouldn't know what I would have done, had it not been for her," Mr Newman remarked. "Still Inspector, Sergeant, what can I do for you?"

"Just a few more questions Mr Newman, and I have brought back you album," Chris put the album on the table.

"Please sit Inspector," Mr Newman offered.

Chris sat at the table opposite the range, the heat from it making the room comfortable sit in.

"Mr Newman," Chris spoke softly. "Have you remembered whether the back door here was bolted when you arrived home Monday morning or not?" Chris turned his head towards the back door for a moment.

"Mr Newman shook his head. "No, can't remember either way, is it that important?"

"Quite frankly, very important," Chris answered. "Still we will pass on from that, did Mr or Mrs Sharpe ever visit here?" Chris asked seeing a confuse look on Mr Newman's face.

"Not that I know of Inspector, but you have to remember that I was at work or in bed most of the time."

"I understand that Sir," replied Chris respectfully. "But to your knowledge, neither Mr or Mrs Sharpe entered this house, or enter your daughter's bedroom?"

"I know that Gloria and Mrs Sharpe was friends, they are about the same age, and got on together, but in this house, I never saw them and in Gloria's bedroom, well,

I would doubt that very much, but as I told you I am not here most of the time."

"Don't worry about my questions Mr Newman," Chris told him. "I have to clear up all the little details in order to solve the case, have you heard from the hospital yet?"

"Yes," replied Mr Newman, tear welling up in his eyes. "They are bring Gloria home tomorrow."

"Are you prepared," George asked.

"Yes, with Mrs Simpson, she simply takes over, all the neighbours have been sympathetic, yes I'm quite ready," he sniffed.

"I have brought this album back Mr Newman," Chris said reaching out and touching it. "It has a lot of happy photos in it, I know you will treasure them, but I do have one question, all the photos show Gloria being happy, yet I could not find one when she was a baby, all the photos show that she must have been seven or eight or over when taken?"

Mr Newman did not reply, he looked at the floor.

"I'm sorry to ask Mr Newman, but I have to know everything about Gloria?"

"She was adopted," Mr Newman replied a little anger in his voice. "My wife and I adopted her when she was seven, her first adopted parents had died."

"I see," Chris remarked, somewhat taken back with the news, he looked at George, who was busy writing in his notebook.

"But she was still our daughter," Mr Newman burst out. "She knew she was adopted, and she was happy, when my wife died she was just twenty, she always referred to my wife and me as mum and dad."

"I'm sure she did Mr Newman," Chris replied softly. "She seems to have been a devoted daughter to you?"

"She was that," Mr Newman replied wiping his eyes with a handkerchief, and forcing a weak smile. "She was that."

"When was her birthday Mr Newman?" Chris asked as though it had no bearing on the case.

"I know it," Mr Newman replied. "It was the forth of April, I suppose you expected me not to know it?"

"Most men do not remember birthdays, Mr Newman, it seems to be a culture amongst men to forget birthdays," Chris smiled.

"Yes, but not me," replied Mr Newman, a first real smile coming to his face. "Not me."

"She was certainly a pretty girl," Chris continued. "Born in 1890 I believe?"

"That's right inspector, she's only lived a half of her life, dead at twenty five, have you any leads of who did this to my daughter?"

"We are getting there Mr Newman, have no fear we will catch the person responsible."

"I hope you will," Mr Newman sniffed again. "I hope you will."

"Just one more question Mr Newman, then we will leave you in peace, did Gloria ever have a girlfriend to stay overnight?"

Mr Newman shook his head slowly. "I'm sure she would have told me if she had," he replied.

"Well thank you Mr Newman," Chris said rising from the table and looking at George.

"Are you going for a pint?"

"It helps a little," Mr Newman replied. "It helps a little."

Chapter Seven

*C*hris and George left the house, leaving Mr Newman to get ready for his dinner time pint, they walked in silence towards North Walls, at the junction they turned right at the Wagon Inn, into Union Street. Chris took out his pocket watch and looked at it.

"It's almost one George," he said putting the watch back into his pocket. "Let's go in here, the Bird In Hand, I'll treat you to a pint and a sandwich."

George followed Chris through the front door of the pub, and found themselves in a high ceiling bar, the counter was opposite the door, and a well built grey hair man with a walrus moustache welcomed them.

"Two pints please landlord, and do you do sandwiches?" Chris asked.

"Cheese or ham Sir?" asked the landlord, already at work with his pumps.

Chris looked at George, who said, "Cheese."

"Two cheese sandwiches then please," Chris said.

Chris and George sat at a small table with their pint and sandwich in front of them.

"Hardly worth opening, there is no one in here," Chris said looking around the bar.

"Wrong time of the day I expect," remarked George. "You know what you just did back there Chris don't you?" George asked.

Chris who was taking a drink smiled. "Of course," Chris replied putting his glass down. "I made a connection between the two murders, yet I can't believe it."

"It is hard to believe," George agreed. "One girl murdered on Sunday night, aged twenty five, adopted, born on the forth of April 1890, another girl murdered Monday night, twenty five, adopted, born on the forth of April 1890, coincidence or what?"

"Could be," Chris replied as he took a bite of his sandwich. "I don't believe in coincidences in our line of work, still I suppose it could be, but it's unusual," he added as he took a sip of his pint washing down his food.

Chris then told George of his telephone call to the Gosport police station. "When we get his report, who knows," Chris smiled. "Maybe another coincidence?"

"Do you know something that I don't?" George asked as he chewed his sandwich.

"How could I George," Chris replied. "I am wondering however, are we dealing with twins here?"

George shrugged. "They were both pretty girls, but in a different way, they didn't look the same."

"You don't have to look alike to be twins, there are twins who don't look alike, anyway twins that look alike are called identical twins," Chris said. "I keep my mind open, I don't assume, Inspector Noal taught me that, never assume, he told me when you have facts, you have no need to make assumptions."

"Who's Inspector Noal?" George asked.

"My old boss, when I was a sergeant," Chris replied. "He is in France at the moment."

"Was he good, at his job I mean?" George asked.

"He's a legend," Chris replied. "You might meet him in April next year, I hope he will be able to come across for my wedding."

"So you have decided the date?" George replied.

"No I've been told, but it meets with my approval," Chris smiled.

"Where do we go from here?" George asked turning the conversation back to the case.

"When we get back to the office, I'm hoping that Bob, that is Mr Harvey the police surgeon, has delivered his report on the autopsies," Chris replied helping himself to another bite of his sandwich.

As expected, the police surgeon's report was waiting on his desk. Chris smiled at George as he tore the envelope open.

"Now let's see what the autopsy says," Chris remarked as he read, a few moments later he put the report down.

"It seems that Stacey's death was caused by strangulation, we expected, sex had taken place, but there was no suspicion of rape, same as Miss Newman," Chris remarked before continuing.

"Nothing was found on her body, that would have identified her," Chris paused for a while.

"We never found her handbag did we?" Chris asked looking at George who shook his head. "I wonder if she had one, most women don't go out without one," Chris murmured as if in thought. "If Stacey Brown left the house in a temper, she might have left her handbag at home, we slipped up there, not asking Mrs Brown about it."

George made no comment.

Chris continued with the report. "No scars or body adornments were found on the body, she was healthy, and that's about it," Chris finished passing the report to George.

"Strange how both of these cases are familiar, strange also that both these young ladies live miles from each other," Chris added, as he pulled the phone towards.

Taking the receiver off its hook, Chris dialled the number he knew off by heart, then bring the mouthpiece closer to him, he waited.

"Mr Harvey," answered the voice.

"Hello Bob, Chris here," Chris spoke onto the receiver.

"Hello Chris, did you get my report?" Bob questioned.

"Yes, many thanks, but I have a question that you might be able to answer."

"Fire away then Chris," replied Bob.

"Both these girls were twenty five years old, and born on the same day, on top of that both were adopted, could they have been twins?"

Chris heard bob laugh on the other end of the phone. "Don't you read my reports?"

"Of course I do Bob, and study them," Chris said.

"Well on each report I put the person's blood group, if the blood groups of these two women are the same, then they could well be twins, but you would need other proof, such as who the mother is, as well as the father and birth certificate," Bob ventured. "But as you say these two girls were both adopted, so you would need to find out from what agency they were adopted, although adopted children usually have their surname changed, many keep their Christian names, that could help, but twins would have the same blood group," Bob commented.

"Thank you Bob," Chris replied cursing himself for having made another slip. "I just wanted conformation."

"Glad to talk to you any time Chris, as long as it's not a call out," Chris heard Bob's giggle as the phone went dead.

Chris found the folder containing details of Miss Newman, he opened the file, and scanned the contents, and his eyes fell straight on it, below the persons name.

"Miss Newman had the blood group O positive," he said. "What do it say there about Miss Brown?"

George looked at the report. "AB positive," he replied.

Chris felt disappointed. "Well there goes the twin theory, Inspector Noal would never accept all these coincidences, neither do I really, but you can't fight nature."

"We still got the Gosport report to come through yet Chris," George said seeing the disappointment on Chris's face. "It might tell us something?"

"Twins or not George," Chris replied. "We still must find out, why these girls were murdered?"

The telephone rang, and Chris grabbed the receiver off its hook expecting the call to be from Gosport.

"Inspector hardie," he said.

"Constable Shaw here Sir," a voice answered.

"Ah constable," Chris answered slightly disappointed. "I have read your report, and thank you, it was very enlightening as to her character."

"Thank you Sir," came the reply. "However, I wondered where she could have gone in Twyford after she left her house, so I took the liberty this dinner time to go around the pubs in Twyford."

Chris smiled to himself. "How many pubs are there in Twyford constable?" he asked.

"Four," came the reply. "One for each fifty odd people I think," added the constable.

"Really," replied Chris.

"Yes Sir," constable Shaw replied. "It was just a notion, but it paid off, the landlord of the Phoenix told me that

Stacey Brown was in his pub Monday night, he can't remember the exact time she came in but it was late well after eight. She sat with the village doctor, doctor Chapman, you know him you met him at the house."

"Yes I remember constable, please go on," Chris replied.

"Well Sir," constable Shaw continued. "The landlord knew that doctor Chapman bought her a drink, a gin and tonic, and they sat together during the time they were in the pub, he said that the doctor spoke to him before he left at closing time, and he watched the doctor leave by the front entrance. He did not see Miss Brown leave, the pub was busy having a visiting shove halfpenny team playing. He said he might have seen her leave had she left by the main entrance, because the entrance is right opposite the bar, but she could have slipped out by the side entrance that leads to the toilets and parking ground, so he had no idea what time she left, but in any case, the landlord said it was not long before closing time."

"Thank you constable," Chris thanked him. "You have done well, it could be a great help to us, if I need to call upon this landlord, I'll contact you, thank you very much."

Chris replaced the receiver. "That Twyford constable seem to have his wits about him," Chris said turning to George relating the story that the constable had told him.

"At least we now know where she went after storming out of her house, we know she was murdered after ten that night, what we don't know is how long after she left the pub was she murdered, still the constable have given us a start in tracking her movements."

"What about this doctor?" George asked.

Chris spread his hands over his desk. "We will have to check him out now, he was with her before she was murdered,

234

he did not mention that to me when I met him, and constable Shaw's first report gives an interview with the doctor, in which it was not mentioned, I do not think that the doctor could have forgotten being with Stacey in the Phoenix pub that night, so why did he not mention it?"

A knock came on the office door, making both detectives look at it. Sergeant Bloom poked his head around the door.

"Have you a moment Sir?" he asked.

"Come in Sergeant," Chris invited. "What can we do for you?"

"I was talking to the constable on the beat at North Walls last Sunday," Sergeant Bloom said entering the office with his helmet under his arm.

"He told me that it was after midnight on Sunday night, he saw a man hurrying up North Walls. He caught the man in the beam of his torch, but could not see his face, as the man was wearing a topcoat with the collar pulled up and a trilby pulled down over his head, the beat constable did not think it was unusual as it was a very cold dark night and he carried on with his beat."

"Thank you Sergeant," Chris replied deep in thought. "Would there be many people out at that time of night?"

"Not in my experience," Sergeant Bloom replied. "Only those who have been visiting, or those who have been to a party, most sensible people are tucked up in bed at that time of night especially winter nights."

"You know who was on beat duty last Sunday night Sergeant, could you ask them if they can remember seeing anyone after midnight, running, walking, entering a house, or anything, it might help."

"It will take me a couple days Sir," replied the Sergeant. "Most of them on that duty are off at the moment, but I could catch them tonight."

"Good man Sergeant," Chris praised him.

"Thank you Sir," replied the Sergeant Bloom, his eyes lighting up. "You can count on me."

Chris smiled as he watched the Sergeant depart, then looked at George who had a look upon his face. "Well oak trees grow from little acorns," Chris answered his look.

Chris took out his pocket watch. "It's almost six George, I have a dinner date with Elizabeth, so we might as well call it a day, although I was hoping for a call from Gosport."

"Tomorrow is another day," George answered preparing to get up from his desk.

"For you George it's a check up on doctor Chapman, go to Twyford tomorrow morning, call on constable Shaw and see the landlord of the Phoenix pub.

George nodded with a smile. "Have a good meal tonight," he said leaving the office.

Chapter Eight

The lighted candle in the centre of the table enhanced the dim lighting of the restaurant, which at seven thirty in the evening was beginning to fill. The war, and the Hampshire barracks in Winchester had favoured the Winchester restaurants, whose tables were most taken with men in officers uniforms, escorting a lady. A piano in a far corner was playing a melody, which could hardly be heard above the chatter, and loudness of well spoken people, who seem to think that their voices had to be heard. Chris smiled at Elizabeth who face him smelling the small bunch of forget-me-nots, he had bought from a flower girl who had stood outside of the restaurant.

"This is very romantic Chris," Elizabeth said. "Flowers, candle light, and all these well dressed people."

"A bit snobbish for me," Chris replied a smile playing around his eyes. "I could have booked at another restaurant, but your beauty outshine all the other ladies here."

"Oh darling, you say the nicest things," Elizabeth smiled resting the flowers gently to one side. "You may be a detective, but you still don't know that this country has a class culture, poor, middle class, and the wealthy. In the bank, I don't deal a lot with the poorer class, very few have a bank account, but I do deal with the middle class, and the rich."

"What is the difference between the classes being?" Chris asked.

"Money," replied Elizabeth.

"I thought both middle and the rich had money," Chris smiled.

"Well yes they do," Elizabeth said looking at Chris across the table. "The difference being that the wealthy in most cases were born into wealth, they went to a seat of learning for their education. Middle class, some made their money because of this war, some were left it in Wills, most have not had the same education as the wealthy."

"Surely then we must give credit to the middle class for achieving their better way of life," Chris replied.

Elizabeth looked at Chris, she put her hand across the table, resting it on his.

"Are you teasing me Christopher?" she asked.

Chris laughed. "No my darling, just trying to learn, please don't be mad, I really would like to know."

"Well if you're sure," Elizabeth replied a little uncertain. "Rich people born into money and because of their education they are polite and respectful, they have money, which over the hundreds of years before them has been invested in large estates with plenty of land, their money is invested in everything from coal mines to shipping. They know the meaning of money, and know how to use it," Elizabeth paused looking at Chris who kept quiet. "Middle class on the other hand are people who has come into money during their life, through one reason or another, they have no great estates, they have no history of greatness that might have been born by their past relatives, they try to act like wealthy people, many even have big houses that they live in, but they are not educated about money or manners or politeness, those trying to be above their class, I am able to spot straight away."

Chris looked at Elizabeth. "Darling, you're a snob."

"No I'm not Christopher," Elizabeth replied. "I'm just telling you about the class culture of this country, but for all that I prefer the poor, or the very wealthy, I do not like the middle class so much, too rude in my opinion."

"Are we having our first argument?" Chris asked squeezing Elizabeth's hand that still lay on his.

Elizabeth's reply was cut short by the approach of the waiter, who gave menus to Elizabeth and Chris in turn.

"You choose darling," Elizabeth said smiling.

Chris chose a cream of chicken starter, steak with trimmings as the main course. "I think I better have prunes and custard for afters," he said looking over the top of his menu at Elizabeth with a smile.

Apart from the occasional smile, and the odd question and answer, the meal was eaten in silence. Elizabeth pushed her bowl containing three or four prunes away from her, she took a deep breath and smiled as she saw Chris do the same.

"I'm glad you did not order the apple pie," she said. "I don't think I could have touched it, I am so full, it was a great meal wasn't it?"

Chris agreed. "Still it will go down with the walk home."

"I can't move at the moment," Elizabeth said with a smile.

"What about a coffee to finish with?" Chris offered.

"No thank you darling," Elizabeth rejected his offer. "I don't believe that I could even get liquid down at the moment."

Chris felt in his pocket, and brought out his pipe, he looked into the bowl, and saw that it was half full. "I'll finish this pipe then, if you have no objections?"

"Enjoy it darling," Elizabeth replied. "While I go to the little girls room."

Outside the night was dark and cold, Elizabeth clutched hold of Chris's arm, as they made their way to Elizabeth's home, with the collars of their top coat pulled up around their necks.

"Did I put the dampers on the evening by talking about our class culture?" Elizabeth asked.

"I was glad you spoke about something different to that of my job, in fact you gave my mind a breather," Chris replied. "Talking about my job certainly put the dampers on last night, with your mum and dad."

"You mustn't take too much notice of mum darling," Elizabeth replied squeezing his arm a little tighter. "Mum is very sentimental, she feels for everyone, you ought to be with her when she sees soldiers marching, she cries her eyes out and claps at the same time."

"She's seeing a lot of marching men where you live then," Chris stated. "We are getting a lot of troops in town, also we are getting a lot of hospital trains coming in, our hospital is over crowded, it must be going badly over there."

"Dad says it will last a few more years yet," Elizabeth remarked. "I do know that we can't walk over the hill anymore, and I did enjoy our walks over the hill."

"What's happening there?" Chris inquired.

"Don't you know darling, the hill is full of tents, housing the troops, dad says it's a transit camp whatever that means," Elizabeth said.

"It means darling, troops coming in from an area, rest for a while in those tents then move on, my guess is that from here they march to Southampton."

"You are probably right darling," Elizabeth replied stopping at the bottom of the path leading to her house. "Are you coming in?"

"I better not, not tonight, I have a busy day ahead of me tomorrow," Chris replied.

"Thank you for the meal darling, and these lovely forget-me-nots," Elizabeth replied accepting his refusal without comment.

"It was very romantic," she giggled as she offered her lips.

Chris accepted Elizabeth's lips at the front door before making his way home.

Chapter Nine

Chris entered his office as the Guildhall clock was striking nine, George House his sergeant was not there. Chris smiled to himself as he got rid of his trilby, knowing that George was probably at Twyford. Chris sat behind his desk, and took out his pipe, filled the bowl and lit it, blowing out clouds of smoke, he felt contented. He had seen Elizabeth outside her bank, and had got the customary kiss on the cheek.

"It was a lovely evening darling," Elizabeth had said. "I hope we can do it again."

Chris had been pleased with her remark, he had sensed some hostility in her last night, and had laid awake going over their conversation, finding no reason.

"We will," Chris assured her. "When we are married, we must make a routine of eating out at least once a week."

"That will be lovely darling," she had answered. "Will I be seeing you tonight?"

"Yes, if nothing happens, I'll come to the house, that's if you want me to?" Chris replied with a hint.

Elizabeth giggled. "You are a silly man darling, don't you know I always want to be with you."

Chris found himself cheered by her remark, and left her in a happier mood than when he had met her. He put his pipe in the ashtray and picked up the report from Sergeant Bloom. The report did not help, several of the beat policemen reported seeing people, one saw a cyclist walking with his bike, another saw a couple, the odd person was seen here and there, but there was no report about a man hurrying with his collar up and trilby down on his head, covering his face. He put the report to one side. "No little acorn," he thought as he reached for his pipe.

George House decided that before going into the office, he would go to Twyford on his motorbike, and drove straight to the Phoenix Public House. Parking his motorbike, George knocked on the side door of the pub, which was answered by the landlord. George introduced himself, and was invited into the front bar.

"You are the landlord Mr...?" George asked as he seated himself by a small table.

"Ribbons, Peter Ribbons," replied the landlord. "I take it you're here regarding Stacey Brown?"

"That is correct Sir," George replied politely. "I know that you have spoken to constable Shaw, but would appreciate it if you would tell me."

The landlord took a chair, and sat opposite George. "Not much more I can tell you," he said. "Stacey came in Monday during the late evening, and sat with doctor Chapman, who bought her a drink. At closing time doctor Chapman came up to me to say goodnight, I watched him leave from the front door," he continued indication the door. "He left alone, I did not see the going of Stacey."

"You have more than one entrance?" George inquired.

"Yes," replied the landlord. "The other entrance, it has to be used for people wanting the toilets, had she gone out by the main entrance, I'm sure I would have seen her."

"Would you have any recollection as to the time you last saw her?" George asked.

The landlord paused for a moment in thought. "I saw her and doctor Chapman talking, he had bought her a gin and tonic, I remember, that must have been around nine thirty, I'm sorry I can't be more helpful, but we had a shove halfpenny game on that night, and I was occupied more than I would have been on a normal night."

"That's OK," George replied. "How long have you been here?" he asked.

"I took over the pub in 1910, about five years ago," the landlord answered.

"Was doctor Chapman here then?" George asked.

"Yes he was, I am told he has been here for the past twenty years," the landlord confirmed.

"Hmm," George replied. "He seems too young to have twenty years behind him."

The landlord smiled. "He is forty five, or so he told me, came here more or less from finishing his studies, but he did tell me that he did a six month stint at a hospital, I believe he said in Gosport, but I'm not sure, so many people tell me things," the landlord smiled. "It's a job to know who said what."

"I'm sure it is," George replied with a smile. "Is he a good doctor?"

The landlord shrugged his shoulders. "How do one know whether a doctor is good or not, I myself have never had the need to go to him, but the village people seem to like him, don't hear much said against him."

"Is he married?" George asked.

"No, he is single," the landlord replied. "But Sergeant, wouldn't it be best for you to get these answers from him."

"I'm just trying to get a picture of him," George replied. "After all as far as we know, he was the last person to talk to Miss Stacey."

"You mean you suspect him," replied the landlord with an amazed look upon his face.

"No not at all," George replied a smile on his face. "But we have to check on everyone who saw Miss Brown that night, so far we only have doctor Chapman and your good self."

"Also all the people in the pub that night," the landlord offered.

"Yes that's a worry," George said as though he was thinking. "Anyone of them could have followed her out, I'm going to ask you for a list of your shove halfpenny teams, plus any other local you can remember in the pub that night."

"The only strangers in the pub that night, came with the team who played us, they came from the Black Boy pub in Winchester." "Do you know it?"

"No, I'm new to Winchester," replied George. "But my Inspector will, tell me did Miss Brown come in often?"

"I couldn't call her a regular, but yes now and again," the landlord replied.

"On her own?" George asked.

"She was always on her own, don't forget sergeant, there are three other pubs in Twyford, she might have used them?"

George closed his notebook, that he had been writing in, he could not think of any other questions to ask the landlord, who he had thought, had given him honest answers.

"Well thank you Sir," George said. "I can't think of anything else, but I would like that list," George looked at the pub clock. "It's ten thirty now, I have a couple of calls yet to do, do you think, the list could be ready by your opening time, I can call back, perhaps have a liquid lunch," George said with a smile.

"Rely on it," the landlord replied.

George made his way to Mrs Brown in Park Lane, he felt surprise as doctor Chapman opened the door.

"Sergeant," the doctor said with a look of surprise also on his face.

"Doctor," replied George with a smile. "I never expected you."

"No, I just called to see Mrs Brown, she has a lot of grief," the doctor replied. "I think sleep will be the only help for her at the moment."

"I'm sure you are right doctor," George replied. "But I do have a couple of questions to ask her."

"Well come in Sergeant, Mrs Brown is in the kitchen," the doctor offered standing to one side to allow George to enter.

Mrs Brown was sitting at the kitchen table near to the lit range, she looked up as George entered. "Sergeant House isn't it?" she asked.

George nodded. "I'm sorry to call so soon after," he hesitated. "I know it's a silly question, but how are you coping?"

Mrs Brown looked at the Sergeant, her eyes were red and sad, and George could see that her eyes were full of water as she shrugged.

"I have just a couple of questions Mrs Brown, that's if you feel up to it, we want to catch the person responsible, and it's not wise to let too much time elapse, we need to know as much as we can, as soon as we can."

"I understand Sergeant," Mrs Brown replied with a sigh. "Please, seat yourself."

"I had better be on my way," the doctor spoke up. "I have another patient to call on."

George watched as the doctor took his bag from the table. "Doctor before I leave Twyford, I would like a few words with you."

"Certainly sergeant, anything I can do to help, call at the surgery, I should be there after," the doctor looked at his pocket watch. "Eleven thirty."

"It might be a little later than that doctor," George responded thinking of his liquid lunch.

"Not to worry Sergeant, unless I have a call out, I shall be in."

"Thank you doctor," George replied as the doctor left.

George took a chair, and shuffled it up to the table, he took out his notebook, and placed it in front of him. "I'm really sorry to bother you Mrs Brown."

"That's alright Sergeant," Mrs Brown sniffed as she cut in. "I'll answer any questions that I know, all I want is the murderer to be caught."

"He will be Mrs Brown, I can assure you," George replied kindly. "Now as I understand it, your daughter worked at London Bazaar in Winchester, and during the week she would stop overnight in Winchester, to save her the travelling."

Mrs Brown wiped her eyes. "She would stop overnight just two or three nights a week, she had a friend there, the same age, I have no idea where her friend lives, but I believe at the bottom end of the town, Stacey was very fond of her."

"Would you know her name?" George asked.

"Gloria Newman," came the reply.

"Thank you Mrs Brown," George replied, he was surprised at the unexpected answer. "Now you did tell my Inspector that Stacey was adopted."

"That made no different she was my daughter," she said with a worrying look on her face.

"Don't get me wrong Mrs Brown," George hurried to correct the wrong impression. "I only wanted to know, whether she knew she was adopted?"

"We adopted Stacey when she was just a few months old Sergeant, she known no other parents, my husband and I saw no need to tell her."

"I can understand that Mrs Brown," George replied. "I don't suppose you know if she had any brothers or sisters?"

"Sorry Sergeant, if she had we were not told," she replied.

"You obviously went to the adoption agency to apply for adoption, and I suppose that you were allowed to chose the child you took," George continued.

"It was a long time ago Sergeant," Mrs Brown sniffed. "We did apply, Stacey was the only baby at that age up for adoption, we were told both her parents were dead."

"Where did you pick her up?" George asked.

"Children's home at St Cross in Winchester, but we were told that the baby had no Winchester connection," Mrs Brown went on with another sniff. "Stacey was not from a Winchester family."

"So you would not know where she was born?" George asked.

"Afraid not Sergeant," replied Mrs Brown.

"Had she already been named when you adopted her, I mean was her name Stacey, or did you name her?" George asked.

"Not legally, but the nurses called her Stacey, so when we adopted her just a few months old, we had her Christened in our name but we kept the name of Stacey."

"So summing up Mrs Brown," George replied believing that he had asked all the questions. "Stacey did not know she was adopted, did anyone else know?"

"I never told a soul, until I told your Inspector, apart from the four of us in this room on Tuesday night, I haven't mentioned the fact to anyone," Mrs Brown answered.

George closed his notebook. "You have been very helpful Mrs Brown, if there is anything we can do for you, just phone the station at Winchester," George said getting up. "We will of course keep you informed of any progress."

Mrs Brown forced a smile. "When can I start making arrangements for her funeral?"

"We will get word to you when the body is released Mrs Brown, I should not think it will be very long."

"I am told that my husband will be buried in a war cemetery, I am only pleased that he knew nothing about what happened to his daughter, she was the apple of his eye."

Mrs Brown broke down, and covered her eyes with her handkerchief, George felt uncomfortable with Mrs Brown crying, and felt at a loss. "Would you like me to ask the doctor to call Mrs Brown?" he asked politely.

Mrs Brown took the hanky from her eyes, and sniffed. "No Sergeant, I'm alright and my friend Mrs Carter will be over soon."

George walked away from the house feeling a little depressed, he could almost feel the grief Mrs Brown was feeling, it was very hard for anyone to cope with, having had her husband killed at the front, and on top of that having her daughter murdered. He looked at his watch, which told him it was opening time, he decided that he would leave the doctor until after he had a pint, which he felt he needed.

The landlord smiled as he put a pint in front of George. "You look as though you need that one sergeant, have it on the house, I suppose your job is very exciting?"

"Depressive most of the time," George admitted. "Especially when you have a case like this one."

"The Browns were a nice family, her husband used to come in, he was a worker on a farm before he volunteered, but don't worry Sergeant, the village will rally around her, already the pubs have a collection box, and street collections will take place."

"That's one of the nice things about a village, everyone knows everyone, and help each other when it's called for, the towns are too big for this type of closeness," George remarked as he sipped his beer.

George had two pints, then left thanking the landlord for his help, as he passed the list of shove halfpenny players to him.

George found the doctor true to his word, he was in, and he took George into his dining room. "Have a seat Sergeant, would you like tea?"

"No thank you doctor, I have had a pint after leaving Mrs Brown, I felt I need one."

"That poor woman," the doctor said, as he pulled a chair up to the table. "One death is enough to grief for let alone two."

George looked down as he felt a touch on his trousers, and found himself looking at a black Labrador that was sniffing him with his tail wagging.

"That's my dog Butch," smiled the doctor. "I bought him ten years ago, just up the road at Colden Common, there's this chap who breeds gun dogs for the farmers, he told me that his wife had put lipstick on this one, because unlike the other puppies he had, this one liked to be in doors, he was a lap dog, while he normally only sold to the farmers, he sold me Butch because of this, and he's a real friend to me, but very jealous when I pat another dog."

"I can understand that doctor," George said giving the dog a pat.

"Go Butch and lay down," the doctor told the dog, who straight away went to the side of the sofa, where he laid down, putting his head between his outstretched front legs.

"We go for a lot of walks along the river banks, he's very good company, likes jumping in the river, comes out and shakes himself all over you," the doctor smiled.

"Now doctor," George said, cutting the conversation short. "I have to ask you a few questions seeing that you were the last person to see Stacey alive."

"I hope you don't mean that Sergeant," the doctor replied. "It would mean that I murdered her."

"I'm sorry doctor, I should have said the last known person," George corrected himself a little embarrassed.

The doctor smiled. "It's alright Sergeant, in the pub, I was talking to Stacey, I even bought her a drink, but in a village you will find we are all the same, you will find our Priest in for a pint, in fact his name is Richard, and he's called Dick the Vic," George found himself smiling. "What do they call you?" he asked.

"Just the Doc," came the reply.

"Is this why you chose to be a village GP?" George asked. "You are well thought of in the village I know, and I am told you have been here about twenty years."

"I did almost a year training the hospital at Portsmouth after I graduated medical school, but did not like it a lot, too much working inside I suppose, but you do learn a lot in hospital, so I suppose it's very good training for a new doctor just out of school."

"I'm sure it was," George replied. "Do you originate from this part of the country?"

"Not really, my parents brought me over at a very early age from France, we settled in Gosport, which is near Portsmouth."

"Are you married Sir?" George wanted to know.

Doctor Chapman smiled. "Afraid not Sergeant, I have no relations that I know of in England, and if I have some in France, I have no knowledge of them."

"You must get lonely in a small village like this?" George questioned. "What do you do with yourself?"

"Well I do have my patients Sergeant," smiled the doctor. "We have four pubs here you know, but I'm only a social drinker really and I have Butch for walks," he said looking across to where Butch was sprawled out.

George considered that the doctor was now relaxed, he had told George a lot during the niceties.

"Getting back to the murder doctor, you are the only person that we know that spoke to Stacey that night, what was her mood, I mean was she full of life or down in the dumps?"

"She was not happy that's for sure," replied the doctor. "She told me about the war telegram her mother had received, that's why I bought her a drink, I did not see her leave, she must have done while I was at the counter talking to the landlord."

"Do you have a girl friend doctor?" George asked with a smile.

"Not in Twyford Sergeant, it wouldn't be ethical, most people here are my patients, I do pop into Winchester a couple times a week for a meal, I enjoy that," the doctor replied.

"Do you have any knowledge regarding Stacey, I mean can you think of any reason for this to happen to her, did she have a boy friend, or any enemies that you know of?"

The doctor shrugged his shoulders. "Stacey was a patient of mine, although I did not see a lot of her, she was young and healthy, I have not heard of her having a boy friend, although again she was young and attractive, but selection of both boys and girls in a village is limited, if she had a boy friend, I would suppose he came from Winchester where she worked."

George rose to leave. "Thank you doctor, you have been helpful, however this being a murder case, we may have to talk to you again, should you think of anything, no matter how small, I would appreciate it if you will get in touch."

"Count on it Sergeant," replied the doctor as he offered his hand. "One never knows what may come to mind that had been forgotten."

"Just one more question doctor," George said stopping at the door. "Did you know that Stacey was adopted?"

"Was she really Sergeant?" replied the doctor looking surprised. "I had no idea."

Chris signed the last piece of paper, he placed it in a folder and closed it. Dropping his pen, he leaned back with a sigh, glad that he had completed the paper work. He took out his pocket watch, and grunted as he saw it was gone eleven. Chris leaned back in his chair, and automatically took out his pipe from his pocket, he looked at the bowl, and saw it was half empty, and decided it was enough for a smoke. As he lit the pipe and blew out a cloud of smoke, Chris thought of the case he was investigating, it was getting no where, he knew several bits and pieces, but none of them fitted together. He looked around his empty office, George he knew was at Twyford, and expected him back when he saw him, he secretly hoped that George would uncover another bit that might go with the pieces he already knew. He was also waiting for the report from Gosport.

Chris took another drag on his pipe, then looking again at the bowl, decided unless he refilled it, he would be drawing on just ash. He tapped the pipe on the side of the ashtray, and left the pipe in the ashtray. He had made up his mind to see Mr Newman, who would be getting ready at this time to go out for a pint, that's if he was keeping to his normal routine.

Chris knocked on the door just before twelve, which was opened by Mr Newman himself.

"Inspector," he smiled a little surprise. "I was just about to go for a pint, it makes my day go faster, but please come in."

Chris followed Mr Newman to the kitchen, the range was alight, and Chris felt the warmth, it was rather chilly outside.

"How are you keeping Sir?" Chris asked seating himself. "How are you coping?"

"I'm fine," Mr Newman replied. "Can I offer you tea?"

"No thank you Sir," Chris replied. "I called just to ask one or two questions, I won't keep you long."

Mr Newman sat in his rocking chair by the range. "That's alright Inspector, my time is my own now, how are you doing with your investigation?"

"Not well I'm afraid," Chris admitted. "Have you heard that we found the body of a young woman at Twyford?"

"I heard something said about it in the pub, why are they both connected?"

Chris shrugged his shoulders. "I have no idea at the moment, but it might just be a coincidence that your daughter was the same age as this other young woman, and was adopted, I first thought that your daughter and this other woman Stacey could be twins, but medical science has ruled that out," Chris saw that Mr Newman was shaking. "Are you alright Sir?" Chris asked.

Mr Newman hesitated. "It was when you said Stacey," he murmured. "My daughter has a friend at Twyford by that name, she would often spend a night here with Gloria, I did not mind as it was company for Gloria being alone in the house every night, I had forgotten her until you said her name."

"Did you meet her?" Chris asked.

"Only once if I remember, as you know when I get home in the mornings it's early and I go straight to my room, I didn't see my daughter to lunch time, but I knew she stayed here several nights a week, oh dear what's the world coming to," Mr Newman spoke in a broken voice. "I knew that she was the same age as my daughter, but I did not know she was adopted as well," he added.

"Tell me Sir," Chris continued. "When you adopted Gloria, was that her Christian name at the time?"

"Yes, Gloria was her Christian name when we adopted her, you must realise she was eight years old, her name then was Gloria Wellington, after the adoption she took the name of Newman, but we left Gloria, she was used to the name. Her birth certificate however shows her name as Beatrice, which means that her first adopted parents changed it, but then she was a baby, and did not understand names," Mr Newman added.

"Thank you Sir," Chris replied. "I suppose you adopted Gloria from Winchester?"

"Yes at St Cross children's home," Mr Newman replied.

"You have not been able to think of anything that might help us?" Chris asked. "I remember you told us that she did not have a boy friend that was special."

"I'm sorry Inspector, if she had one, she did not tell me, she was twenty five, I often told her she would be left on the shelf, and I always wanted a grandchild, but it wasn't to be," Mr Newman said his voice sadden.

"Well thank you Mr Newman," Chris said getting up. "You know your daughter's body will be delayed just a few days before release, I am sorry about that, but we must be sure that the two murders are not connected."

"I can understand that," Mr Newman replied. "If you don't mind I don't think I will go for a pint now, can you see yourself out."

Chris made his way to the Rising Sun, he decided that he would have a liquid lunch, and did not expect George to be back from Twyford. He felt a little downhearted, he had not wanted to upset Mr Newman, but he knew that he had that was one of the curses to his job, you would often have to upset people who was already coping with grief with more, he did not like it.

Chris found a little relief, on seeing Alfie's smiling welcome.

"Inspector," Alfie said putting a pint glass under the pump. "This is a surprise."

Chris smiled. "Rough morning," he replied. "Just felt like a pint, will you join me?"

"I'll have a bitter," Alfie replied with a smile as he pumped the pump.

"I had young Terry in last night," Alfie remarked as he placed the pint in front of Chris, who put threepence on the counter. "He told me about a body at Twyford being found."

"Did he indeed," Chris said taking hold of his pint and sipping. "What did he have to say?"

"He said he read about it in the evening echo last night, and he knew the girl," Alfie replied. "Still a single man like him would know plenty of girls surely, and she did work in Winchester."

"Perhaps so," Chris said thinking that this was yet another coincidence. "Two murdered women, and Terry knew both, still he thought as Alfie had said, he must know plenty of girls, but then again there was a question about it, would he know plenty, having only lived here a few mouths, did he say anything else?"

Alfie smiled. "No that's all, he normally keeps to himself, never has much to say."

Chris took his pint to his usual seat, he was worried about the case, nothing was coming together, and his suspects were few, with very little to make them suspects, but until he cleared things up, they would remain suspects, and at the moment Terry Sarshall knowing both women took him to the top of the list. Chris finished his pint rather quickly, he checked his pocket watch, and decided that he had time for another pint before going.

It was gone two when Chris left the Rising Sun, and made his way back to the station which was less than five minutes away, he was deep in thought. Entering his office, he put away his trilby, there was no sign of George as he made his way to his desk. The telephone rang, and Chris still standing took the receiver.

"Inspector Hardie" he said onto the receiver.

"Inspector Dodd from Gosport here," came the reply.

"Inspector, nice to hear from you," Chris answered.

257

"Sorry to have kept you longer," Inspector Dodd continued. "But the name of Sarshall held me up, this Terry Sarshall, is actually Terry Sarsh, and the aunty he was living with, was a friend of the family, not an aunty at all, so you will understand that this held us up."

"I'm sure it did Inspector," Chris replied. "Just a moment let me get a pencil and paper," Chris sat behind his desk, and took a sheet of paper from one of the drawers, and picking up a pencil, spoke again. "Right, I'm ready."

"It seems that the Sarsh family was wealthy," Inspector Dodd continued. "Where the money came from, I don't know, but the origin of the family is French, although the name do not suggest this," Inspector Dodd paused a while before continuing.

"Our inquiries takes us back some twenty five years, Mrs Sarsh who was a young woman of about twenty five, had twin girls, unfortunately Mrs Sarsh died in childbirth. Mr Sarsh who was a few years older, blew his brains out, he could not live without his wife, it's a sad case, getting all this down Inspector?" he asked Chris over the phone.

"Yes I'm keeping up," Chris replied.

"Well then, it seems that Mr Sarsh did put all his business in order before he committed suicide, he arranged for the family friends, a Mr and Mrs Sinclare to look after his eight year old son, he made an arrangement for a monthly sum of money to be paid to them up to the time he was twenty six," Inspector Dodd paused again before continuing.

"He also arranged for the twin girls to be adopted, as far as Mrs Sinclare is aware, Mr Sarsh did have a brother, but no idea where he might be, after all it happened twenty five years ago, anyway, whether Mrs Sarsh have any relations alive, she's not sure, but she can remember her talking about her parents and a brother. I thought that if Mr Sarsh made a Will, he might have favoured his wife's and his own relations in France, and Mrs Sinclare was able to tell me the name of the solicitor, because of her monthly income, which of course have stopped now, anyway," Inspector Dodd continued.

"I contacted the solicitor, at Gosport, Blackwell and Blackwell, it seems that they have a Will left by Mr Sarsh, it's a long one and complicated, and of course they saw no reason why they should tell me the contents of the Will that was written in two parts. The first part was about the payments to be made to Mrs Sinclare, and the sum of money the boy was to receive when he reached the age of twenty six. The second part of the Will, is not to opened until Fifth of April 1916, that is four months away, which I am told is the date the twin girls he had adopted reach twenty six."

"You have no idea what the second part of the Will contained?" Chris broke in.

"None at all, I told him why I was making inquiries, but was told it might not concern the second part of the Will, I could not argue with this, and as you know it's not my case, so he clammed up."

"I see," replied Chris a little disappointed voice.

"Cheer up," Inspector Dodd replied.

"Mr Blackwell was more interested than he let on, he asked if he could call upon you, so I gave him your number, fingers crossed he may contact you."

Chris had to accept the situation. "It looks like I owe you a big one," Chris said. "Are you married Inspector?"

"Call me Bill," came the reply, and yes I am married with a son, what about you?"

"I'm Chris, and no I'm not married, but will be in April next year, I hope to see you and your wife at my wedding."

"Thanks Chris will look forward to it, anything else I can do, give me a buzz."

Chris replaced the receiver, then studied what he had written, did it help with his investigation.

Chapter Ten

*C*hris was busy writing the notes he had taken from Inspector Dodd, when George entered the office. Chris looked at him as he sat at his desk.

"Been busy?" Chris asked with a smile around his eyes.

"You could say that, I called on the landlord of the Phoenix, called upon Mrs Brown again and then after a pint, I called upon the doctor, what I have to do straight away is to write up a report," he replied.

"Did you see Constable Shaw?" Chris asked, seeing George taking out a sheet of paper from a drawer in his desk.

"No," sighed George. "I drove straight to the yard of the Phoenix, and saw the landlord, I completely forgot about constable Shaw, I will have to apologise to him."

"I find that village constables are a great help when dealing with an involvement of the village," Chris went on. "The villagers call him by first name, they drink with him, the constable know everyone by their first name, and he knows the village like the back of his hand, it's just a matter of courtesy really."

"I know," replied George. "It just slipped my mind."

"I called upon Mr Newman," Chris continued. "Then I went for a pint at the Rising Sun."

"Two great minds," George remarked with a smile.

"Then I got a call from Gosport, I'm just writing the report, so let us both finish our reports, then we can read each others," Chris said as he looked back to his notes.

An hour later both men had finished and swapped their reports, spending several moments reading.

"Well Mrs Brown and Mr Newman both knew that their daughters were stopping with each other, so that's one thing cleared up," George remarked. "How is Mr Newman?"

"He's coping," Chris replied. "He was shocked when he heard about Stacey, though I think I spoiled his trip to the pub."

"Mrs Brown has more to grief about," George remarked. "The doctor was with her when I called, it's going to take a long time for her, husband and daughter in two days."

Chris fell silent as he read and re-read George's report.

"It's Terry Sarshall," Chris continued after a moment. "That bothers me, apart from him knowing both girls, it seems that he has changed his name from Sarsh to Sarshall, and he came into money when he was twenty six, even the aunty he said brought him up was just a friend of the family, he is capable of lying so it seems."

"Do you expect this solicitor Mr Blackwell to phone you?" George asked.

"I hope so," Chris replied as the phone rang. Chris took the receiver.

"Inspector Hardie," he answered.

"Inspector Hardie, I am Mr Ian Blackwell of Blackwell and Blackwell of Gosport," came the reply.

"Mr Blackwell, how can I be of service?" Chris asked making a face at George.

"Talk of the devil," George muttered to himself.

"I have recently been called upon by Inspector Dodd of the Gosport Police, I gather from what he told me that it was in conjunction of an investigation you had ongoing."

"That is correct," replied Chris.

"Would it be possible for me to pay you a visit, say around ten thirty on Monday morning, I would prefer that not to speaking over the phone."

"Mr Blackwell, if our meeting can be helpful to each other, then by all means I would be glad to meet you," Chris accepted.

"I get you drift Inspector, I am bound by the confidentiality act, but I will be as open as I am able."

"I am bound by the same act Mr Blackwell," Chris answered. "Let's hope our meeting can be positive, I will expect you some time before midday on Monday then."

"Thank you Inspector," Chris heard as the line went dead.

"Let's hope he can put some light on the case," George remarked. "I'm unable to make head or tails of this case yet."

"I see by your report, that Mr Sharpe was playing shove halfpenny at the Phoenix that night, I wonder would it be our Mr Sharpe?"

"Yes it would," replied George "I noticed the name as well, so on my way home I popped into the Black Boy pub and spoke to the landlord, in confidence, I might add, he told me that the Mr Sharpe playing game of life board game at Lower Brook Street."

"Good man," Chris replied very pleased.

"George," Chris said as he took a list of names and addresses from the side of his desk, and studied it. "Do you keep in touch with your friends at the MET?"

"Not really," replied George a bit surprised at the question. "Why do you ask?"

"I was just wondering if you would like a day up in London, I have OK with the Chief Superintendent, I need a little information from London, you can go tomorrow morning, book a hotel over night and come back to take over your Sunday, what you say?"

"Of course I'm easy," George replied wondering. "What is it you want me to do?"

"I have made a list here," Chris said handing George the paper. "I want you to go to Somerset House and find birth certificates and any marriage certificates you can find on the people listed there, it might take you several hours, but you can at least see some of your friends on the Saturday, and of course all expenses paid."

"It will be a break," replied George looking at the list. "But why doctor Chapman?"

"Just that he is connected with Gosport, and I am beginning to think that this case has a Gosport connection as well as a Twyford."

"What do you have in mind for tomorrow then?" George asked.

"Getting no interruptions, I shall be reading, re-reading and reading again these two reports of today, we have too many coincidences with this case, we may have been told what we know already, it only needs connecting one bit of information with another, and that's what I shall be doing tomorrow."

Chris met Elizabeth from her work, it was a cold night, and Chris was wearing his overcoat, after giving Chris her usual kiss on his cheek, she leaned on his arm, as they walked to her home.

"Are you stopping with me tonight?" Elizabeth asked.

"I wish I could," Chris replied with a smile, patting the hand that was clutching his arm.

"Naughty," replied Elizabeth understanding his remark. "I meant are you stopping for dinner, or you have to work?"

"By now you have to know that I may have to work at nights," Chris teased. "And you accepted that."

"I know," Elizabeth replied pretending to sulk. "But I'm a woman, I am allowed to change my mind."

Chris allowed his eyes to look skyward, remembering what Sergeant Willett had told him. "No man will ever understand the mind of a woman."

"No, I'll stop for dinner, but I don't want to be a nuisance to your mother."

"Don't be silly darling," Elizabeth giggled. "You're one of the family, come and go whenever you like."

"I'm glad you said that, I always wanted to be part of a family," Chris replied seriously.

"Well," Elizabeth added. "It's almost Christmas, it won't be long after that, when we will be a family."

"I shall be busy tomorrow, my Sergeant will be in London, and may stop overnight," Chris told her. "And I am on duty Saturday, but off Sunday."

"So I wont be seeing you for a couple days then?" Elizabeth replied.

Chris did not replied. "We could go cycling on Sunday if you wish?" he smiled to himself.

Elizabeth giggled. "Don't be silly darling, we can't go cycling in this weather, it's winter, it's far better you come to my house and spend Sunday, perhaps you and dad go to the pub and have a drink."

"Perhaps you're right," Chris responded, glad that she had not agreed, he had only been teasing her.

They reached the front door, and Elizabeth offered her lips, which Chris took eagerly. "What was that for?" Chris asked as they pulled away from each other.

"A quick one before mother opens the door," Elizabeth smiled as the door opened.

"Chris," Mrs Oborne welcomed. "What are you doing Elizabeth," she scolded her daughter. "Keeping Chris at the door, you have a key."

"I know mother," replied Elizabeth laughing. "I was just getting it out," Elizabeth said a smile on her face.

Discarding their top coats and hats in the hall, Chris and Elizabeth made their way into the front room, where Ron was sitting. He got up and held his hand out to Chris. "Cold out tonight," he said. "Hope you both wrapt up?"

"Yes we did dad," replied Elizabeth. "Now why don't I get you both a beer, before I help mother."

"I have taught my daughter well don't you think Chris," Ron smiled. "There is still room for improvement however."

"Is there?" Chris asked wondering.

"Yes, the beers should be out already, without being asked," Ron smiled at Chris with a wink.

Elizabeth left the room without saying a word but smiled happily.

Mrs Oborne brought in a bottle of beer and two glasses, and placed them on the small table in front of them.

"Elizabeth has gone to her room, to get out of her working clothes," Mrs Oborne smiled at Chris. "It's lovely to see you again Chris, Elizabeth is a different person when you are around, I remember when I was courting Ron."

"Olive," Roy said with a grin on his face. "Chris don't want to know what we went through, it was years ago and things have changed a little."

"Perhaps you're right," Olive agreed. "I'll just go and get your meals ready," she smiled leaving the room.

"I'm afraid you are going to get a mother-in-law that dotes on you, she will pamper you as much as Elizabeth, I hope you are prepared."

"Being an orphan, it is a new experience to me," Chris replied as he watched Ron pour out the beer. "But being an orphan, I did not know what I was missing, just being a part of a family."

"Well you're certainly a part of a family now, how you will manage two bossy women?" Ron laughed and continued.

"Time will tell, but I would not part with either of them, meals ready at regular times, told what to wear on cold days, told what not to wear on hot days, change this and that, don't do this or that, I want this done not tomorrow but today, loads of little things that one retaliates to, but when you sit and think, you realise that without them, you would have no life," Ron said smiling.

Chris did not comment as he sipped his beer. "My last Sergeant was like you a lot," Chris eventually said putting his glass on the table in front of him. "He would always be running his wife down because of her nagging and not being happy where she lived, but he thought the world of her, you could tell."

"A lot of us men are like that Chris," replied Ron.

The silence of the room burst into life, as Elizabeth and her mother entered carrying the meal. "Come along you two," Olive smiled. "I'm afraid it's homemade steak and kidney pie tonight Chris," Olive said without looking at him, while she placed the plates and cutlery.

"She makes a great pie Chris," Ron remarked getting up.

"I'm sure she do," Chris remarked taking his place near Elizabeth, who smiled at him.

For several minutes the meal was enjoyed in silence, then Chris spoke.

"By the way Olive," he said looking at her. "I have another two names to add to my guest list."

"That's nice," Olive replied. "Did you forget them?"

"Not really," Chris replied. "But they are colleagues, Inspector Dodd and his wife from Gosport."

"That's two more at least," Elizabeth smiled. "Have you chosen your best man yet?"

"I'll have to hold back on that one," Chris spoke before putting the last piece of pie from his plate into his mouth.

"I really want Inspector Noal to be my best man," Chris eventually continued swallowing the last of the pie. "But should he be unable to get leave, I think I might ask my Sergeant House."

Elizabeth smiled at him. "You have a few more months yet darling, have you written to Inspector Noal, sometimes a early warning helps."

"You're right," Chris agreed as he wiped his mouth with the napkin. "Perhaps I should drop him a line, Mrs Noal would know his address."

After finishing the prunes and custard afters, Olive and Elizabeth cleared the table, Ron sat in his easy chair, and putting on his glasses picked up the paper. Chris sat in the other easy chair, and took out his pipe and lit it, enjoying the first puffs. Half an hour later, Olive and Elizabeth entered and sat at the table.

"We will have to put the wedding banns read at St John's Church in March," Olive said. "They have to be read three weeks before the wedding."

"Really," remarked Chris. "I'm afraid I do not know too much regarding the routine."

"Oh yes," replied Olive. "You will have to have your wedding banns read in your local church, your marriage will be read out for three weeks running, by the way where is your Church Chris?"

"I've got no idea," Chris replied a little embarrassed. "My landlady will know, do I also have to have these wedding bands read, after all, I am not really known where I live."

Olive smiled. "I don't think so, just in the parish where you are getting married, and that's always the bride's parish."

Chris looked at Ron, who was keeping his head behind his paper. "I have spoken to a member of the council about renting a house," Chris spoke up, as he took his pipe from his mouth, and looked into the bowl. "It seems that I can only apply for a council house when I am married, single people cannot apply."

"I should think not," replied Olive. "But don't worry Chris, we have plenty of room here for you and Elizabeth, after all, you will be family."

Chris looked at Ron who had lowered his paper, and was looking at him over the top of his glasses, a smile playing around his eyes, he looked at Elizabeth who was also smiling at him. Chris cleared his throat, as he looked down at his pipe.

"That's very nice of you Olive, I don't think we will be in your way too long, I was told that I would get a house almost straight away once I am married," Chris replied, knowing that although he felt the world of Olive and Ron, he wanted to start his new life alone with his wife.

"Well that's settled," Olive replied, Ron went back to his paper, and Elizabeth came and sat by him.

"I am not buying a wedding dress," she said holding his hand. "Mum and I are making it, to our own design."

"Really," replied Chris with a smile. "How's it coming."

"It's still in the design stage, but you are not to worry, you will not see it until dad walks me down the aisle."

"Is that so," Chris smiled. "Look Olive, I would be pleased if you could make a list of my own responsibility in our marriage, it would help me."

"I will do that for you Chris," Elizabeth interrupted squeezing his hand. "You don't have to do a awful lot, just make sure of your best man, get your suit, mum and dad will pay for the wedding breakfast, but me and you have car to hire, to collect me and dad and the bridesmaids from here, we pay for the church, and the bridesmaids gifts, we have to book the hall and of course you have to pay for the honeymoon darling, wherever you are taking me."

"Oh dear," Chris muttered.

"Don't worry darling," Elizabeth smiled. "We have plenty of time yet."

"I'll get my suit anyway," Chris replied.

"No you won't darling, I'll come with you when you're ready, I'll help you to choose it," Elizabeth said.

"That's not fair," Chris replied with a laugh. "You're going to choose my suit, but I'm not allowed to see your wedding dress."

"It's all a load of bunkum," Ron cut in, looking at Chris over the top of his glasses. "But it's supposed to be the bride's big day, and I must admit that a woman do look lovelier when she walks down the aisle in her wedding dress, but she promises to love, honour, and obey, and while she might do the love and honour, you will never get a woman to obey."

"Ron," Olive scolded him with a smile. "I've been a good wife to you, have I ever neglected you?"

Ron looked at his wife and smiled. "Out of the three billion women on this earth, you are the most important person in my life, and don't forget we are coming up to forty three years of marriage, you are the only woman in my life and you are the love of my life. I would not part from you for all the tea in china, I love you now more than I did when I married you, but to say you obey me, you only let me think you do."

"We are women dad," Elizabeth butted in. "We have a mind of our own, Chris and I are soul mates we think alike, and I don't think Chris would appreciate a doormat."

Chapter Eleven

*C*hris entered the police station dead on nine, he knew he had reports that he really wanted to study, and hoped for a day without interruptions.

"Morning Sergeant," Chris smiled at the desk sergeant, who managed to mutter a reply.

"Don't disturb me if you can this morning," Chris said watching the desk sergeant as he closed the ledger he was writing in.

"Sergeant House has gone to London and I have several reports that needs studying."

"I'll do my best to keep your fans away from you," smiled the desk sergeant. "I suppose you want tea?"

"Be grateful," Chris replied as he made for his office.

It was a cold morning, and Chris had done what Elizabeth had ordered, that was to wrap himself up warm in the mornings. Chris placed his trilby, top coat and scarf on the hat stand, as the desk sergeant came in with a cup of tea.

"You owe two weeks tea money," the desk sergeant said placing the cup on Chris's desk.

"How much?" Chris asked putting his hand in his trouser pocket.

"Shilling for the two weeks," the desk sergeant replied looking at Chris as he fumbled with the change from his pocket, he chose a coin. "That's for the two weeks I owe, and two weeks in advance," Chris said.

The sergeant took the coin, and left the office saying. "I mark it down."

Chris sat behind his desk, and took the folders holding the reports from a drawer, and spread them out in front of him, he took hold of his cup of tea, and sipped as he started to study. Chris made notes, then re-read the reports time after time, until he leaned back into his chair and sighed, his mind all over the place, he took out his pocket watch, and found that it was afternoon, the time had gone without him realising.

Chris was sure of a couple of things, he would have to visit the Mr and Mrs Sharpe again, and he felt sure that a few more pieces of the puzzle had been found. Chris filled his pipe, and took a few puffs, before putting the pipe in the ashtray, he had made up his mind, he would go now and see Mrs Sharpe, question her on her own, perhaps, he thought it might be better.

Taking his empty cup with him, Chris left the office, stopping at the desk sergeant's counter where he planted the empty cup. "I shall be out for a while sergeant," he said. "I'm not sure how long, but I shall be back."

The desk sergeant nodded as he took the empty cup off of the counter. "I'll enter it," the desk sergeant replied as Chris left the station.

Chris entered Lower Brook Street, apart from the odd person walking, and a horse drawn cart entering from the North Walls, the street was quiet, Chris knocked on the door, which was opened by Mrs Sharpe.

"Inspector," she said with a smile, although Chris could tell she was slightly uneasy. "Would you like to come in?" she offered.

"Thank you Mrs Sharpe," Chris replied taking off his trilby. "I'm sorry to bother you again, but this is a murder investigation."

"Not to worry Inspector," replied Mrs Sharpe making way for him to enter. "I'm afraid my husband is not at home."

"If need be I can always call back," Chris replied sitting at the table in a chair offered by Mrs Sharpe.

"You can remember me calling on Monday evening?" Chris asked.

"Of course Inspector," Mrs Sharpe replied. "I shall always remember it, have you caught the person responsible?"

Chris smiled to himself. "Afraid not, but then it's early days, a lot of questions to be asked, and then sorting out the truth of these questions from the lies."

"Oh dear," replied Mrs Sharpe. "Do people tell you lies?"

"It has been known," Chris replied.

"Would you like a cup of tea Inspector?" Mrs Sharpe asked getting a half way up from her chair.

"No, no thank you, I'm full up with tea, my desk sergeant always bring me in tea," Chris lied. "When I was here Monday night, I left around seven at night, did your husband go out after I left?"

Mrs Sharpe thought for a while before answering. "Why, yes he did Inspector, he had a pub game on, you see he is in the shove halfpenny team."

"Do you know who he plays for?" Chris asked.

"The Black Horse or Boy, I believe at Wharf Hill," came the reply.

"Did you also know that he played at the Phoenix in Twyford that night?"

"I suppose he must have told me, but it didn't sink in, I knew he was playing at another pub, because ten minutes after you left, his friend picked him up, his friend has a motorbike you see."

"Do you know what time he got back that night?" Chris asked.

Again Mrs Sharpe spent time thinking. "I can't really say Inspector, you see I would have been in bed, I don't think I heard him come in."

"So you don't know, whether he came home by motorbike or walked?" Chris asked.

Mrs Sharpe shrugged her shoulders. "Knowing my husband's dislike for walking, he would have gotten a lift back if it had been possible."

"Can you remember if your lodger Terry Sarshall was in before you went to bed?" Chris continued his questions.

"I never hear Terry coming in," Mrs Sharpe laughed nervously. "Is there something wrong Inspector?" she asked.

"No, not really Mrs Sharpe, but it is important to tidy up all the facts, you know of course that another young lady was murdered at Twyford, that night your husband was out there," Chris replied.

"Dreadful," replied Mrs Sharpe. "My husband read it out to us a couple nights ago, it was in the evening standard, Terry was here at the time, and he thought that the two girls could be twins."

"Really," Chris said.

"You don't think that my husband had anything to do with the murders do you Inspector?" Mrs Sharpe asked showing her nervousness.

"Your husband was very near both of the murdered girls Mrs Sharpe," Chris said quietly. "As I said a moment ago,

I have to tidy all the facts up, you see the murdered girl at Twyford was in the phoenix at the time your husband was there, he may have seen her, in fact being in the same room, it would have hard for him not to have seen her, but that do not mean that he remembered her, but he could have glance at her."

"You are worrying me now Inspector," Mrs Sharpe replied. "Do you suspect my husband, because if you are, I honestly think you're barking up the wrong tree, my husband is a gentle man, wouldn't hurt a fly."

"I'm sure you are right Mrs Sharpe," Chris replied kindly not wanting to upset her. "But I must ask these questions in order to eliminate him."

"It's dreadful what happened to these two young girls, one expects only to read about this type of thing, you don't expect it on your own doorstep."

"You are quite right Mrs Sharpe," Chris answered as he put his notebook away that he had been scribbling in. "I would say both were around the same age as yourself."

"If the papers are right," Mrs Sharpe continued. "I am just a few months older than them."

"Really," replied Chris. "How so?"

"I'm a scorpion," replied Mrs Sharpe. "I'm twenty six years old, born in November."

"Ah," replied Chris with a smile getting up to leave. "Then you have a sting in your tail."

Chris stepped outside the house, and put on his trilby, he turned towards Mrs Sharpe who was closing the door. "By the way Mrs Sharpe, do you know a doctor by the name of Chapman?"

"A doctor Chapman, Inspector," Mrs Sharpe smiled. "I'm sorry, never heard of him," she said shaking her head and closing the door.

Chris felt hungry and decided to buy a couple of cheese rolls on his way back to the police station, he was still eating when he entered the station.

"Hungry are we," the desk sergeant remarked with a straight face.

"I don't have regular meal times like you sergeant," Chris replied taking no notice of his straight face. "But I would like a cup of tea to wash this down."

"Constable Shaw from Twyford is in the rest room, he wants to see you, I'll send one in with him," the desk sergeant offered this time forcing a slight smile.

Without comment Chris entered his office, disposed of his trilby and sat behind his desk, finishing his sandwich. Chris brushed the crumbs off his desk into the wrappings of the sandwich, and was screwing the wrappings up into a ball to throw into the waste basket when Constable Shaw knocked and entered carrying his cup of tea.

"Constable Shaw," Chris smiled as he watched the constable place the tea on his desk. "It's nice to see you, what can I do for you?"

"It's about the Twyford murder Sir," replied the constable.

Chris took a sip of his tea. "Have you had a cup of tea constable?" Chris asked.

"Yes Sir," the constable smiled politely.

"Well take that chair, and tell me what you know," Chris replied.

Constable Shaw had been carrying a parcel under his arm, which he put on the desk.

"The dustcart was around emptying the rubbish this morning," the constable stated as Chris touched the parcel, but did not open it. "The driver old Jim Muggins, got onto the back of the dustcart in order to level the rubbish with a rake, and he saw this parcel, he brought the parcel straight to me, he always do if he finds anything valuable."

"That's honest of him," remarked Chris still eyeing the parcel.

"Most of the stuff he brings to me are thrown away on purpose, then I give it back to him, but I do make inquiries first, this parcel however belongs to Stacey Brown, and I thought you better have it straight away, so I cycled here."

"Did this man know where from he collected the rubbish that the parcel was in?" Chris asked hopefully.

"He couldn't say, but he was collecting around the village hall area this morning," replied the constable.

"You know everything about Twyford, don't you constable?" Chris asked.

"Just about," came the reply.

"Tell me if you can about the route that this dustcart takes, after all Twyford is not a big place is it?"

"As far as I know, he collects once a week, he starts from Shawford, then just the pubs and the boarding school at the top of the hill coming into Twyford from Winchester, plus the shops of course and from homes. You see once his dustcart is full, he has to drive to Colden Common where there is a tip," the constable explained.

"This morning or today, he would be collecting around the village hall area?" Chris asked, wanting to make quite sure.

"That's right Sir," replied the constable. "When I saw the handbag, I thought it must have come from the rubbish from the village hall, like someone had thrown it there when the murder was committed?"

"I don't think so constable," Chris replied. "The grounds around the hall was searched, no rubbish bins were found, which implies that the rubbish bins were kept inside the hall, and if what you assume is right the murderer would have the keys to the hall, and our investigation leads us to believe that only two people hold the keys to the hall, one a young woman who looks after children there, and the caretaker, who lives at the top end of Twyford, he is an oldish man, not really capable of having sex and then strangling a young girl."

"I see," replied the constable. "I only thought."

"You thought right constable, even though it may be wrong, in our kind of work, most of the things you think of are wrong, it's the way things are," Chris smiled at the constable. "So now let's see the handbag, see what it holds," Chris said still with a smile on his face, as he stripped the newspaper from the parcel.

The handbag was made of leather, around twelve inches square it had a small handle for carrying, and in the centre under the handle was a brass clip for closing the handbag.

"Looks expensive," Chris muttered as he opened the handbag, and allowed the contents to fall out upon his desk.

Chris moved each article in turn, two combs, a powder compact made of shining brass, a small handkerchief, a small purse, Chris emptied the purse, it contained a ten shilling note and a few other coins. "Well it's obvious that there was not a robbery motive to the crime," Chris remarked aloud as he moved the purse and money to one side, and picked up the remaining object which was a small notebook. Chris studied the notebook without opening it, he felt a tinge of excitement, hoping that the notebook would reveal some help. Chris opened the notebook, then without a word, opened page after page.

"This notebook seems to be a diary of meetings," Chris remarked. "You have looked at this notebook constable?" he asked.

"Yes, that's how I knew it was belong to Stacey Brown," replied the constable.

"What did you make of all these times and initials, take this entry about last Sunday, it says ten thirty, DRT some of them ending with W, now what do that mean?" Chris asked.

"I didn't see that one, but there are several there, that refers to the dates she stopped in Winchester, and they end with the letter W, so I assumed that T meant Twyford and W meant Winchester."

"Good man," Chris replied. "You have to be right, the capitals letters are no doubt the initials of the person she was seeing, and the time mentioned is obvious."

Chris looked at page after page, he knew he would have to study it thoroughly.

"Constable, thank you for bring this in, I'm grateful to you, I will have to study this in detail, but I will keep you informed."

"Thank you Sir," replied the constable getting up to leave.

"Before you go constable," Chris asked. "Have you heard any rumours or talk regarding the habits of Stacey?"

"Not that I take notice of," replied the constable. "You will always get young men boasting who they have had, especially after a couple of pints which loosens their tongues, regarding Stacey, no I can't say that I have."

"Thank you constable," Chris replied. "Before you go, my Sergeant House wants you to accept his apologies for not getting into contact with you last Thursday, he was in Twyford most of the day, and fail to contact you."

The constable smiled. "I heard all about it Sir," he replied. "In a small village police, vicars, doctors, and even lawyers are all friends and know each other, and gossip is a culture."

Chris smiled. "Still Sergeant House should have contacted you, Twyford is your responsibility, it wont happen again."

"Thank you Sir," the constable replied. "Well I better get back to my village."

Left alone, Chris went through the notebook page by page and the afternoon passed without notice, in the end he sat back in his chair, stretched his arms behind his head, sure of one thing at least, that Stacey Brown was meeting people almost every night, many nights two or three, but he understood that these were the nights she spent with Gloria Newman. The meeting she had in Twyford, was always with the same person DR, and mainly during the weekend when she stayed at home, he searched his mind for a person with the initials of DR, but could not think of any. Chris brought up under Inspector Noal, did not accept guesses, nor did he like to assume without the facts, but he could not help thinking that Stacey Brown was selling herself, and if his assumption was found to be the truth, then it would follow that Gloria Newman was also doing the same, it also seemed that as Stacey Brown was staying with Gloria Newman during weekdays, that they were using the Lower Brook Street house for sex, while Mr Newman was at work. He remembered that Terry Sarshall had implied that men were calling at the back of the house during the hours of darkness. He hoped it was just his assumption, he liked both Mr Newman and Mrs Brown, he did not want to add more grief on them that they already had.

Chris lit his pipe as he leaned back in his chair, his mind was trying to understand all the bits and pieces he had about the case, but could not make sense of them. He felt very tired, and made up his mind he would have an early night, he needed sleep, he looked at his pocket watch, and saw it was coming to seven, and knew that he had missed meeting Elizabeth from her work. He knocked out his pipe in the ashtray, took his trilby from the stand, and made his way out of the office, for him it was straight home and bed.

Chapter Twelve

Chris entered his lodgings, and went straight to his room, not even stopping for his evening meal that he knew would be in the oven whether he returned home or not. Within moments of getting into bed, he was fast asleep, but it was a disturbed sleep, his mind would not stop trying to sort out the facts he had on the case. He tossed and turned all night, and jumped out of bed in alarm, as he realised he had overslept. Chris hurriedly dressed, and went to the scullery where he had a quick wash and shave.

"I wondered if you were having a lie in son?" Chris heard his landlady say as she entered the scullery.

"I'm late," Chris replied as he scraped his skin with the open blade. "Didn't sleep well last night," he said.

"You're overdoing it," replied his landlady as she poured out a cup of tea. "I've made you toast by the fire in the kitchen, it's already for you so don't waste it, you must eat, you didn't eat your dinner last night."

"Felt too tired," Chris replied as he dried his face. "But I'll make time to eat the toast."

Chris followed his landlady into the kitchen, it was a cold morning, and the fire in the range had warmed the room. Chris sipped his tea, it tasted good, and he finished the cup.

"Now eat your toast, and before you go out put on your topcoat," the landlady ordered as she poured out another cup of tea for him. "It's very cold outside," she said putting the teapot back on the range. "Should you want me I will be in the bedroom."

Chris smiled his thanks as he watched his landlady leave, he picked up a slice of toast, and bit into it, it was made the way he liked it, buttered with honey.

It was gone ten in the morning, when Chris entered the police station, and saw the desk sergeant looking at him with a slight smile on his face. Chris ignored it, he still felt weary, but the brisk walk to the station in the cold air had awaken him.

"Morning sergeant," Chris greeted. "Any lodgers?"

"Just a couple of drunks," replied the desk sergeant.

"Humm," replied Chris. "A cuppa would go down nice," he said as he went into his office.

Chris hung his trilby and topcoat on the stand, he turned towards his desk, rubbing his hands together, his office was not very warm, he switched on the gas fire that was situated to the side of his desk, struck a match and lit it. "That's better," he muttered.

The room was quite warm when the desk sergeant entered with a cup of tea.

"My we are living in luxury," the desk sergeant remarked feeling the warmth. "I could do with one of those fires at the desk," he continued as he put the cup in front of Chris.

"You have a warm uniform sergeant," Chris said as he picked up his cup of tea.

Chris was incline to agree with him about the gas fire. "I'll speak to Chief Superintendent, see if we can afford to have a gas fire installed behind your desk," Chris offered.

"Call me if you want another cup," replied the desk sergeant, his face smiling, I bring in a couple biscuit as well," he promised as he left the room.

Chris drank his tea, then sat back in his chair, and lit his pipe, he had a restless night, and although he was now fully awake, his mind was weary, he took another puff of his pipe, he had a lot of work still to do, which included a lot of thinking, he shook his head, and taking one last puff of his pipe, laid it in the ashtray.

He took the notebook that had been in Stacey Brown's handbag, and again looked through the pages, it was clear in his mind, that the times and initials entered below each date represented people she was meeting or had met, but were they men or women, the initials told him nothing unless he knew whose initials they were. Most of the times and dates had the letter W following, which could only mean Winchester, and as he knew that she spent her time in Winchester with Gloria Newman, he had to wonder what was going on, it was easy to assume that both these girls were selling themselves. He knew that Gloria Newman did not work, she was more of a housekeeper for her father, yet she must have had a few shillings a week in her pocket, he remembered her wardrobe, she did not have a lot, but what she did have was good and expensive, he had the clothes that Stacey Brown had kept at her place of work, there were also good and expensive, not the type poorly paid shop girls could afford.

Chris took the handbag again and emptied the contents, he opened the compact, it held a layer of powder and a puff, he closed it uninterested, and took the purse containing money, which he absently counted again, he looked into the purse, and his eyes saw a slit in the inside material of the purse, he poked his finger in and felt paper, Chris gently extracted the paper, and pulled out three five pound notes that were neatly folded, and pressed flat.

"Well," he murmured to himself. "If she had saved this sum from her wages, it would have taken her years."

Chris examined the notes, then putting them back in the purse, closed it. Chris was looking at the lipstick when George entered the office.

"Didn't expect you today," Chris greeted him.

"Got back about half an hour ago, I know it my day off, but I have nothing to do, so I thought I would come into the office and write up my report," George said as he went to his desk and sat.

"How did it go in London?" Chris asked looking at him.

"Quicker than I thought," George replied.

"I went to the MET, and found one of my mates, we spent a half hour catching up, then he asked me what I was doing in London, I told him of my errand, and he decided to come with me, and he was a Godsend. He allowed the Somerset House official to know that he was from Scotland Yard, and we got all the assistance we needed. Then I went to his house, and met his family, his wife invited me to stay the night with them which I did. My mate and I went out for a drink last night, and had a real good time, I might have had too much, as I awoke with a headache, anyway, I was given a good breakfast by his wife, and I caught the nine am train back to Winchester, and here I am," George shrugged with a smile.

"I had a full day yesterday," Chris told him.

"I went and saw Mrs Sharpe again," he told George of what was said. "When I returned to the station, constable Shaw from Twyford was waiting for me, Stacey Brown's handbag had been found by the dustman."

"That was a bit of luck," George remarked.

"That was more than lucky," Chris answered. "Had the dustman not try to level his load, the handbag could have been lost forever at the rubbish tip."

Chris then told George what he had found in the handbag, and passed the notebook over to him. "What is your opinion as to the times and dates, it's my thinking that the letter T, following the initials means Twyford, and the letter W, means Winchester."

George took the notebook, and studied the pages for a while.

"The letters W, and T, could mean what you are thinking, at least it would fit in with our case," George eventually said, seeing Chris nod his head in agreement.

"The initials could be men or women," George continued, again seeing Chris in agreement with the nodding of his head. "If Stacey was staying with Gloria Newman during the times followed by W, then that would fit in when Mr Newman was at work."

Again Chris nodded, but waited without saying anything.

"If I was a betting man," George continued. "I would say that these young ladies were women of the night, and that these initials are that of men."

"It's certainly my thought," replied Chris this time without nodding. "You noticed of course that Stacey only had one set of initials followed by T, and always weekend, while she stayed at home."

"Yes," replied George. "DR, who have we in the frame with DR as their initials?"

"No one," Chris said. "But it's just a thought mind you, but in this case could DR possibly mean Doctor, you know capital D with a small r."

"It would certainly fit in with our case," George readily agreed. "But Dr Chapman told me that it would not be ethical to go with a woman at Twyford, because they were all his patients."

"He was telling you the truth George," Chris replied. "He could be struck off if it is found he is having an affair with one of his patients."

"Even if he is paying for it?" George asked.

"I would have thought that was worse, but those letters would not apply to Dr Chapman, he's been a doctor in Twyford for a very long time, he knows all the adults and children, he watches them grow up," Chris replied.

"So what are you doing today?" George asked with a smile.

"I thought I take a walk to the Black Boy pub in Wharf Hill, Mrs Sharpe told me that her husband was taken to Twyford on Monday night by motorbike, just after we left the house in fact, but she did not know what time he arrived home, I thought I might find out who took him."

"Can't you ask him straight out?" George asked.

"I don't really want to, you know how friends stick up for each other, lie for each other," Chris remarked. "I thought I would go and have a drink, and try to get information without suspicion."

"Mr Sharpe might be there?" George said.

"I don't think so," Chris answered. "He takes care of a builders office, he wouldn't leave the office on a Saturday lunch time, at least I shouldn't think so."

"Perhaps you're right," George admitted. "The landlord knows me, but would you like a drinking partner?"

"I would," Chris remarked as George handed him several sheet of papers.

"These tells you everything you want to know," George said. "But doctor Chapman did not have a birth certificate, that's because he emigrated from France."

Half hour later, Chris broke the silence during which time he had been studying the papers. "You done a good job George," he remarked. "I'm beginning to see a little light, I wonder what we will learn from Blackwell and Blackwell Solicitor, on Monday," he smiled.

It was nearing one, when Chris and George entered the Black Boy. "The landlord is serving," George whispered to Chris as they approached the counter.

"Gentlemen," said the landlord with a smile. "Oh hello Sergeant, are you here on business?" he said looking at George.

"I am Detective Inspector Hardie of Winchester CID," Chris spoke quietly.

"It's a bit of both really, perhaps you should call me Chris and my partner George while we are here, it's not uncommon for customers to leave if they know police are in the place, and we are not here to lose you any business."

The landlord smiled understandingly. "What can I get you gentlemen?" he asked.

"I'll have a bitter," Chris said turning to George who nodded. "Make it two landlord."

The landlord took two pint glasses, the beer barrels were placed on a stand at the back of the bar area, the pub did not have pumps. Both detectives watched as the landlord holding both pint glasses in one hand, bent holding one glass below a brass tap that he turned on, the beer came out, and very soon one glass was full, without turning off the tap, the landlord moved his hand and the second glass began to fill.

"Here you are gentlemen," the landlord said, placing a pint in front each of them.

"That must take some learning," Chris remarked. "Holding two glasses at once under a tap, do you ever drop one?"

The landlord smiled. "It's a knack, it comes natural now, I can't remember dropping one."

Chris smiled. "Those pork pies you have in that glass case," Chris indicated. "Can I have two, one for each."

The landlord returned with two plates each holding a pork pie and a small knife.

"Mustard," he said putting a jar of homemade mustard in front of them.

"Thank you landlord, would you have a drink with us?" Chris asked.

"Thank you I'll have a bitter, that will be one shilling please."

Chris gave him the shilling, then while the landlord was serving another customer, cut into his pork pie, his actions was followed by George. Ten minutes later the landlord returned. "How can I help?" he asked.

"It was unfortunate, that your team was playing at Twyford while a murder was committed," Chris said, his mouth half full with pie. "But this is a murder investigation, and I have to follow every line, most of them go nowhere," he continued as he swallowed. "But your team were in the same room with the murdered woman that night."

"I had spoken about it with George," the landlord managed to stop himself saying sergeant. "It was a terrible business, but you don't think my team had anything to do with it do you?"

"At the moment landlord," George said, covering a piece of the pie with mustard he was holding. "We are only interested how your team went and returned from Twyford?"

"Some walked, some went by bicycle," replied the landlord.

"We understand that Mr Sharpe went by motorbike," Chris remarked.

"He may have done," the landlord replied. "I don't really know," the landlord looked around the room. "But I know a man who do."

With the landlord gone again, Chris ate the last of his pie. "That pie was damn good," he said to George who had also finished his pie. "Perhaps I was more hungry than I thought."

Their pints had almost disappeared when the landlord returned to them.

"Two more please landlord," George said. "You draw a good pint."

The landlord took their glasses with a smile, before returning with them full after a few moments.

"Mr Sharpe was given a lift by a rep of the builders he works for, the rep is the son of the Dolphin pub's landlord in Twyford, his name is Carl, that's all I can tell you I'm afraid."

"You have helped us greatly," Chris said with a smile of thanks. "It will most likely clear up another loose end, but at the moment, I would appreciate it if you will treat our visit in confidence."

"I will Inspector," the landlord replied forgetting. "I'm sorry he said smiling apologetically."

Chris lifted his glass and drank.

"We had five people in the frame when we started this investigation George," Chris remarked as they made their way back towards the station. "We still have five, no one else has come in."

"You feel that one of the five is the murderer?" George asked.

"Too many coincidences in this case, so far each one of them could be the murderer?" Chris replied not answering the question. "We still don't know whether this is a double murder or two single murders."

"Perhaps the solicitor on Monday will be able to answer that," George replied. "But then I wonder how or if he can tell us anything?"

"We will have to wait and see," Chris replied with a sigh. "Now you get off, you are on duty tomorrow, and I shall be with Elizabeth."

"Lucky dog," remarked George. "By the way what are we going to do about the Dolphin landlord's son, do you want me to go?"

"I'll get constable Shaw to pop in and see him, you go along and do what a young single man needs to do," Chris said with a grin on his face.

Chris entered his office, he hung up his coat and trilby, then crossing to his desk, he dialled constables Shaw's number.

"Twyford police," came a voice over the phone.

"Inspector Hardie of Winchester here," Chris spoke into the mouth piece.

"Sir," came the answer.

"I hope I haven't caught you at a bad time constable, but I need you do me a small favour."

"Gladly Sir," came the reply.

"The son of the landlord of the Dolphin, do you know him?" Chris asked.

"Carl Kirby, yes I know him, is he in trouble?"

"I'm not sure constable, could you be discrete and ask him if he gave a lift to a Mr Sharpe on Monday night, I am told he did, but I really would like to know if he gave Mr Sharpe a lift home that night?"

"It will give me a chance to have a pint Sir," the constable replied. "I'll do my best tonight if he is around."

"Thank you constable, I appreciate it," Chris replaced the receiver.

It was Saturday, he could not meet Elizabeth, because the bank was closed in the afternoon, he went out to the sergeant's desk.

"No trouble of any sort, sergeant?" he asked.

"None that uniform can't handle," the desk sergeant said with a smile. "But the Chief Superintendent has just come in, should you have time to see him?"

Chris remembered his promise about the gas fire. "Good, I'll pop and see him, seeing that you have everything under control."

Chris returned to the desk half hour later.

"Chief Superintendent is not too pleased with you sergeant," Chris said hiding back a smile. "He could not understand why you could not have gone straight to him, he told me his door was always open to his staff."

"I bet he did," replied the desk sergeant with a straight face. "So?"

"Well," Chris answered with his hand slapping the top of the desk. "Get it done."

Chris smiled to himself as he went to his office.

"I'll bring you a nice cup of tea Sir," he heard the desk sergeant.

"Don't forget some biscuits you promised," Chris said with a laugh.

Chapter Thirteen

C hris met Elizabeth by the Butter Cross.

"I got away a few minutes early," Elizabeth smiled giving Chris his usual kiss on the cheek.

"I was on my way to meet you," Chris replied as they walked towards the King Alfred Statue. "I am not fond of these dark nights."

"Oh I don't know," Elizabeth remarked. "Darkness hides a lot of things, for instance, no one would see you taking me in your arms while you have your wicked way with me," she giggled.

"I'm sure the few people passing would realise," Chris replied with a smile.

Chris very used to the way Elizabeth teased him whenever she could. Actually Chris enjoyed her teasing, and wondered just what Elizabeth would be like when they were married, at the moment he had to control himself, knowing that sex between them would only happen after they were married, due to the respect Elizabeth and for her parents.

"How did your day go darling?" she asked.

"It's been a long day, I have all the pieces, the difficulty is fitting them altogether, I never seem to get an open and shut case," Chris replied.

"I have faith in my soon to be husband," Elizabeth replied squeezing his arm and giggling. "I am sure you will solve it."

Olive was at the door waiting to welcome them home, with a quick cheek kiss for both of them, Olive helped them with their top coats, then almost pushed them into the warm dining room, where they found Ron already at the table, and the food laid.

Chris sat at one side of the table, with Elizabeth at his side, they faced Ron and Olive, Chris felt happy, he was part of a family, and they were lovely people.

"This looks good Olive," Chris praised as he looked at his steak and kidney pie with all the vegetable.

Chris remained quiet as he ate the his steak and kidney pie, his mind pondering over the case, grinning a few times at the banter between Olive and Ron. Finally he pushed his empty plate away from him, feeling so full that he declined the prunes and custard afters.

Chris leaned back and put his hand over his stomach. "I am absolutely full Olive, couldn't get any more down, I really enjoyed the meal," he said. "Ron is very lucky to have such a cook," he flattered her.

"Thank you Chris," Olive replied. "It is nice to be appreciated," she smiled looking at her husband.

"I was just about to praise it my sweet, but Chris beat me to it," Ron smiled teasingly.

"That would be a first," Olive remarked looking at Elizabeth with a slight smile.

"You know dad is only teasing you mum," Elizabeth smiled. "You know he appreciates you."

"It wouldn't hurt for him to say so now and again," Olive laughed as she cut into the steak pie.

With the meal over, Elizabeth and her mother cleared the table, and went to the scullery to wash up. Ron retired to his favourite chair, put on his glasses then picked up the paper and started to read, the paper covering his face as he held it up, it was a usual routine with him. Chris sat in the remaining armchair, and took out his pipe, lit it and puffed contentedly.

Ron and Olive relaxed in front of the fire, while Elizabeth and Chris relaxed on the sofa, the afternoon passed quickly into evening, and after saying goodnight to Ron and Olive, Chris accepted Elizabeth's lips at the front door before making his way to his lodgings.

Chapter Fourteen

hris entered the Police Station the next morning, he was smiling and shaking his head, after having his instructions from Elizabeth.

"If you go out, wrap up," with "I love you," and his usual kiss on the cheek, she had walked away with a smile towards to her bank.

Chris entered the office, and found Gorge already at his desk.

"You have been here all night?" he spoke jokily as he hung up his trilby. "It's only ten to nine now."

"I'm single," George answered with a teasing smile on his face.

"What sort of day did you have yesterday?" Chris asked.

"Quiet," George replied. "I managed to get my paper work under control, I went to my lodgings for dinner, my landlady had a roast ready for me."

"Glad to hear it," Chris replied settling into his chair, and taking out his pipe lit it. "We have the solicitor coming this morning," Chris remarked blowing out smoke.

"What's your thinking with this case Chris?" George asked. "Have you any opinion yet?"

"I have," Chris replied. "But because it's just an opinion, I'm keeping it to myself, what about you, have you an opinion?"

"Not knowing whether it's a double murder or two separate murders, I have no idea," George answered.

The telephone rang, and Chris lifted the receiver.

"Constable Shaw, nice to hear from you," Chris spoke into the mouth piece.

"I'm sorry that I did not get back earlier, but I was only able to find the landlord's son to speak to last evening, it was late, so I decided to phone you this morning," said the voice of constable Shaw.

"Thank you constable, what's the verdict?" Chris asked.

"Well the landlord's son Carl said although he gave Mr Sharpe a lift to the Phoenix, he made no arrangements to take him back, he presumed that he had made other arrangements," constable Shaw answered.

"Thank you constable, that's all I wanted to know, it clears up a loose ends," Chris replied. "Thank you again," Chris said replacing the receiver.

"That was constable Shaw from Twyford," Chris said to George who was watching him. "He spoke to the landlord's son who gave Mr Sharpe a lift on Monday night, but did not bring him back to Winchester, so he must have walked," Chris concluded.

"It also makes him a suspect," replied George. "He only lives a couple houses from Gloria Newman, and he was at Twyford when Stacey Brown was murdered."

"Agreed," replied Chris. "But what would his motive be, did he know that Stacey Brown would be at Phoenix that one particular night that he happened to be there, as far as we are told Stacey stormed out of the house because she had just learnt about her father, so it was not arranged if indeed it was him, then going back, we are forgetting Terry Sarshall, who had as much opportunity as anyone, he knew men were going to Gloria Newman's house at nights, he could have been one, as he told you he could have done it and why did he change his name?"

George thought for a while. "I guess you're right, each and everyone could have done it, but no one has a motive."

"Apart from a fight that starts suddenly, and one is killed," Chris continued. "Murder is normally committed with a motive, you just do not go around murdering without a reason."

"I agree," George replied. "So where do that leave us?"

"Up a creek without a paddle," Chris replied with a smile.

Sergeant Bloom put his head around the office door.

"Sergeant Bloom," Chris greeted. "You on desk duty this week?"

"Afraid so," replied the sergeant. "There is a solicitor here to see you, he said his name was Ian Blackwell."

"I am expecting him sergeant, can you show him in, he has come from Gosport, perhaps a cup of tea can be arranged?"

"Certainly Sir," replied sergeant Bloom. "I'll show the gentleman in first."

Chris smiled as the sergeant left. "What a difference in attitude between him and sergeant Dawkins," he said to George.

"Both very helpful though," George laughed.

Chris rose from his chair as Mr Blackwell entered. He was a short thick set man wearing a dark overcoat over his navy pin stripe suit, he wore a bowler hat and carried a rolled up umbrella, and a briefcase.

"Thank you for coming Sir," Chris said holding out his hand, which Mr Blackwell took.

"This is my colleague Sergeant House, please take a chair," Chris offered pointing to the interview chair.

Mr Blackwell returned the greeting from George, then unbuttoning his overcoat, he crossed to the chair, that Chris had indicated.

"Did you have a pleasant journey down?" George asked.

"A bit slow and noisy," smiled Mr Blackwell with a sigh. "But these things have to be done," he said making himself comfortable as he could on the hard chair.

Sergeant Bloom entered carrying a tray.

"Thank you Sergeant," Chris said to the departing sergeant. "Now Mr Blackwell, I'm sure you would like a cup of tea?"

"I would appreciate it," Mr Blackwell said. "I came here straight from the railway station."

Chris poured out three cups, offering sugar and milk to Mr Blackwell.

"It's a cold day Mr Blackwell," Chris said as they all sipped their tea.

"It was colder at Gosport when I left, Mr Blackwell replied. "Blows in from the sea, you see."

Not wanting to hurry him, Chris waited for him to empty his cup, before speaking.

"I am investigating the murder of two women Mr Blackwell," Chris began. "I have no idea what your interest is in the case, but we do have a connection with you, as one of our inquiries have led to a man who calls himself Terry Sarshall, we now understand that this is not his real name, unless of course he had changed legally."

"I'm afraid it's the two girls that I am more interested in Inspector," Mr Blackwell replied. "I could not tell Inspector

Dodd all I knew, because it would not be my place, and of course he was not investigating the case, but I feel I must tell you."

"Thank you Mr Blackwell, perhaps we can help each other," Chris said with a smile.

"Let's hope so Inspector," replied Mr Blackwell unlocking his briefcase and taking out several papers.

"I will start from the beginning," Mr Blackwell continued. "Mr Sarsh who I will tell you about, was not originally my client, he was Mr Blackwell senior, my father's client, on his death, my brother and myself divided his clients between us, and Mr Sarsh became mine," Mr Blackwell paused for a while as he shifted his papers.

"I understand Mr Blackwell," Chris said keen for him to continue.

"I have studied the case, spent many hours doing so since your Inspector Dodd called upon me, and I think I can now tell you the whole story," Mr Blackwell continued.

"Mr Sarsh emigrated to England from France with his wife in 1889, and settled at Gosport. He had a son at that time who was about six or seven," Mr Blackwell spoke while still studying his papers.

"Mr Sarsh was a very rich man, where he got his money, is not recorded in our documents, but he was very rich. He had one brother in France, Mr Ronald Sarsh, and as far as I know had no other relations, although one would suppose he had aunts and uncles somewhere, however they are not mentioned so we can forget them."

Chris was secretly cursing, urging Mr Blackwell to get to the main reason for his visit, but he knew that solicitors had their own way.

"Did Mrs Sarsh have any relations?" Chris asked.

"I was about to inform you Inspector," Mr Blackwell replied, his tone telling Chris that he hated being interrupted.

"Mrs Sarsh also had a brother, Mr Raymond Chapman but he was already in England studying to be a doctor, I believe that both Mr and Mrs Sarsh families way back had immigrated to France from England, that is why they both have English sounding names, Mrs Sarsh's maiden name was Chapman."

"I see," murmured Chris feeling excitement mount within him. "Please go on."

"I was about to Inspector," Mr Blackwell replied. "In 1890, Mrs Sarsh who was pregnant was taken to hospital where she gave birth to twin girls, the sad thing was that Mrs Sarsh died shortly after the births, Mr Sarsh, unable to bear his grief, shot himself in the head."

"Oh," George who had been listening intensely remarked.

Mr Blackwell looked at George. "I agree Sergeant," he said. "Not a pleasant task for anyone to do to oneself."

"But he did put everything in order before doing so," Chris said taking a chance of Mr Blackwell rebuff.

"Partly," replied Mr Blackwell, deciding that all police were ignorant, and could not stop themselves from interrupting.

"He never saw the twin girls, he just gave instructions to the hospital to have them adopted, he wanted no part of them. He met with my father, and made out a Will," Mr Blackball paused again and pulled a document from his papers. "I have the original Will here," Mr Blackwell said holding up the document. "I have made you a copy, which I shall allow you to keep, should you want it."

"Thank you," replied Chris, making no other comments.

"Blackwell, and Blackwell, was charged with both their funeral arrangements," Mr Blackwell continued.

"It was a very sad day, and one had to feel for Mr Sarsh, here he was a wealthy influential man, with a nice home and a son he idolised, but his grief of losing his wife, was I suppose," he said trying to find the right words. "Far greater than even the love for his son," Mr Blackwell sat silent for a while.

"Would you like more tea Mr Blackwell?" Chris asked.

"No thank you Inspector, I must complete my story, anyway," he continued. "We, that is Blackwell and Blackwell, was unable to read the Will after the funeral, because we could not contact the brother of Mr Sarsh who benefited through the Will, our private detective however did trace him in France, he was shocked he had no idea what had happened to his brother, however to cut a long story short, my father did read the Will to his brother Mr Ronald Sarsh, to Mr Raymond Chapman, and Terry Sarsh to the son of Mr Sarsh. You will understand that Terry was far too young to understand, but we allowed his presence accompanied by Mr and Mrs Sinclare who was to be his guardian, as they also benefited with the Will," Mr Blackwell paused for a while and licked his tongue.

"George," Chris said seeing this. "Perhaps Mr Blackwell would like a glass of water."

George turned to his desk, and poured out a glass, he always kept water and a glass on his desk when a long interview was expected to happen. Mr Blackwell took the glass, and smiled his thanks.

"Now I am coming to the part, to which I have no authority to tell, but it is not a secret," Mr Blackwell continued putting the glass on the desk in front of him.

"Mr Sarsh left ten thousand pounds each to his and Mrs Sarsh's brother, he left twenty thousand to his son Terry, to be kept in trust until he became the age of twenty six. To the Sinclare who became Terry's guardians, he left five hundred a year until the time that Terry reached twenty six, now all the above has been dealt with, Terry received his money some six or seven years ago, which with accumulated interest was in the region of over thirty thousand pounds."

"Well Mr Blackwell," Chris responded. "It do seem that your client Mr Sarsh, and our case are connected in some way, we have a Dr Chapman, and a Terry Sarsh, but for reasons we don't yet understand, he goes by the name of Sarshall."

"I fail to understand why Inspector?" Mr Blackwell replied.

"But," Chris continued. "If as you said, all monies had been paid to the beneficiaries, why are you still interested?"

"That's where my problem comes in Inspector," Mr Blackwell answered. "You see as I understand it, Mr Sarsh told my father, that although he did not even want to see the twins, that caused his wife's death, he knew his wife would turn in her grave, if he did not provide for them, after all they were his daughters as well as hers, they had not asked to come into the world."

"Did your father know the intentions of Mr Sarsh?" Chris asked.

Mr Blackwell spread his hands. "If he did, he did not mention it."

"I'm sorry to interrupt you Mr Blackwell, please continue," Chris apologised.

"Mr Sarsh left his daughters thirty thousand pounds in trust between them, they would receive the money at the age of twenty six, with the added interest for twenty six years, that amount has now risen to around fifty thousand, a very nice sum, due to be collected on the forth of April 1916, just a few months away."

"Your problem then is finding the twins?" Chris remarked.

"Yes, and it's a big problem, you see the twins I am told were separated, most people only like to adopt singles, twins are a bit harder to get adopted, when your Inspector told me that you had a case of two girls being murdered, both born on the forth of April 1890, both adopted you can understand my interest."

"I certainly can," Chris expressed himself. "Was there any other clauses concerning the money?"

"If the girls are dead, then the money goes to Terry, if only one of the girls are alive, then the remaining one gets the lot, the trouble is, I have no idea who or where they are?"

"Who knew about the Will and what the twins were getting, besides who you have already mentioned Mr Blackwell?" Chris asked.

"In fact I'm sure no one else know apart from those at the Will reading, of course," Mr Blackwell argued. "Anyone of them at the reading could have told other people, for myself, I would not even tell your Police Inspector Mr Dodd that called upon me."

"Do you think it's possible for someone to know where the twins are today Mr Blackwell?"

"Again, I can't say for sure, but I would doubt it, of course there is no reason for either one of them getting in touch with me, because they have no knowledge of what was left them, that's assuming that the girls know they were adopted," Mr Blackwell remarked.

"I can see your predicament Mr Blackwell," Chris answered. "We are investigating the murder of two young woman, born on the same day, both adopted, and both single, however medical evidence tell us that they are not twins, the coincidence however is that we have a Dr Chapman and Terry Sarsh involved in our case."

"It's a puzzle," remarked Mr Blackwell disappointment showing in his voice.

"Mr Blackwell," Chris continued. "I am sure that your problem is connected with our case, is it at all possible for someone to find out, where the twins went from the hospital, and to who they were adopted?"

"I would doubt that very much Inspector," Mr Blackwell replied. "Records are kept of course, but for a stranger or even a relative would not get access to the reports, they are kept very secret, after saying that, there must be someone at the hospital that know where the twins were sent, but he would not know who adopted them, the adoption society would of course know who adopted them, but, I can't believe that they would inform anyone, they have to protect the adoption family, but then why would anyone want to know," Mr Blackwell shrugged his shoulders. "No one knew of their windfall if you can call it that, and then again Inspector, the twins are now twenty five years old, who would carry a desire to want to know where adopted twins were all that time?"

"Family," George remarked.

"I can't believe you're right Sergeant," Mr Blackwell smiled weakly. "I am only sorry that my visit here was not more positive."

"I thank you for your frankness Mr Blackwell, I'm sure you have helped us great deal," Chris said. "I will however phone you by the end of the week, keep you up to date, one never knows, I might have news for you."

Mr Blackwell stood up after he had closed his briefcase, and laid a document on the desk. "That's a copy of the Will Inspector, but as you have already got two girls born on the forth of April 1890, and not a twin to each other, I can't see this document any good to you."

Chris stood up, he wished Mr Blackwell a safe trip back to Gosport, and thanked him again. "I will phone you by the weekend regardless," Chris promised.

"I hope you kept notes of what he said," Chris said to George. "it's a lot to digest, I need to study it."

"I'll rewrite it," George smiled, you would not understand my shorthand writing.

"I believe you were right when you said family would be the only interested wanting to know where the twins were," Chris remarked. "Remember we have a couple of the family connected with our case, but the clause states that if anything happens to the twins, their demise, then all the money go to Terry Sarsh, now that's something to think about."

Chapter Fifteen

Chris took out his pocket watch. "Good God George," he remarked. "Do you know it's almost one."

"It must be," George answered.

"Do you want to go to dinner?" Chris asked him.

"No, I think I will get on with this report, while it's still fresh on my memory," George replied

"Your shorthand, is not clear to you then," Chris replied with a smile.

George made no comment as he concentrated on his writing.

"I think I will go into the Abbey Grounds and clear my head for a while," Chris said as he got up and went to the hat stand and took his trilby.

"You better put on your topcoat then," George remarked without looking up. "It's bound to be a bit nippy out there."

"Good thinking," Chris replied, taking his overcoat, and putting it on. "If Elizabeth caught me without a overcoat on cold days, I would be in for a ticking off, well, I wont be long," Chris said as he left the office.

Chris stopped at the edge of the Fire Station, and pulled up his collar, he was glad of the reminder that George had given him, it was nippy. He crossed Abbey Passage, and walked through the high iron gates of the grounds, the path forked, one going to the right, Chris decided to follow the half circle path straight on, that took him past the rear of Abbey House, ending at the gents toilet, where it turned right, running along the side of the narrow river. A few yards along Chris came to a bench seat and sat. With his collar up around his neck to protect himself from the winter air, and his hands dug deep into his coat pocket, Chris looked at the small river, that was separated from the Broadway pavement by a tall wrought iron railings, he lifted his eyes, and looked at King Alfred Statue directly in front of him, but it did not register in his mind, which was deep in thought on what Mr Blackwell had told him.

Chris sat on the bench as though in a trance, he did not see the people walking by on the opposite side of the railings, he did not notice the horse drawn traffic that was busy moving around the statue, his mind was twisting and turning all the evidence he had on the case. It was a good hour later, that Chris stood up, and walked back towards the police station, he thought he now knew who the murderer was.

Chris entered the office, George looked up and smiled. "You look cold."

Chris hung his trilby, he took off his overcoat which he hung, he shivered and rubbed his hands together as he went to his desk.

"Didn't realise how cold it was," he said, taking out his pipe and filling the bowl from his pouch, before lighting it.

"Is this your report George?" he asked seeing the sheet of paper on his desk.

"It's all there Chris," replied George. "Word for word."

"Thanks," Chris replied, picking up the paper and reading it while he puffed on his pipe, George did not interrupt the silence that followed.

Chris read and re-read the report, and finally placed it back on the desk, he laid his pipe in the ashtray.

"I think I can solve this case George," he said which made George look at him in wonder. "But I have just a couple of things to do before I do, so don't expect me in tomorrow, certainly not during the morning."

"You're not going to tell me," George accused him, knowing the way Chris worked, keeping things close to his chest, until he was perfectly sure.

"Not yet George," Chris looked at him and smiled. "Write these names down, I want them in this office on Wednesday morning at ten, you can go around and tell them tomorrow, but don't frighten them, tell them they can have a solicitor present if they want one."

"What about if they can't make it?" George asked.

"Then you will have to tell them, that this is a murder investigation, if they don't turn up, then the police will come and get them, wherever they are," Chris advised. "They have a clear day to make arrangements."

"Scotland," George replied.

"I see your point," Chris answered with a smile, thinking of his Scottish trip. "By the way, when do I go and give evidence in the Goldsmith case, it's soon I know?"

"Second Monday in December," George spoke from memory.

"That will be almost Christmas," Chris murmured. "Blast I have to be in Portsmouth to give evidence."

"It won't take long Chris, you do have confessions, it has to be a guilty case."

"I know," Chris replied. "But so near Christmas, and some of these cases can go on, and on, especially if the accused change his plea, have you got any plans for Christmas George?" Chris asked.

"When I went to London last week, my mate and his wife invited me, but I told them I would have to wait and see how things work out regarding time off, there being only two of us."

"Well we will do our best," Chris said as he lean forward and took his pipe from the ashtray, then leaning back in his chair, and taking a puff. "Anyway, get these names down George."

George laughed as he took up his pencil.

"What?" Chris asked.

"I was thinking," George replied still grinning. "You have to go to Portsmouth during December to give evidence in the Goldsmith case, the spy connected case comes up at the end of January, if my memory serves me right, and if we solve this case this week, you could be giving evidence again in February or March, your time will be taken up just giving evidence."

Chris thought as he puffed his pipe. "We must pray that we get a calm period after this one," Chris remarked. "The last three cases have followed quickly I admit, the trouble is, we have such a wide area to cover, never mind," Chris said. "We can't do anything about it, now pencil these names in. Mr and Mrs Hanks and their daughter Linda, Mr and Mrs Sharpe, and Terry Sarshall, and Dr Chapman."

"No Mr Newman or Mrs Brown?" George asked.

"No," Chris replied. "I don't want to add to their grief, but if I am right, they will get the go ahead by Friday, to bury their daughters."

Tuesday came and went, Chris carried out his errands, and George managed to see all those who Chris wanted to attend his office the next day. George went to Twyford on his motorbike, and managed to catch Dr Chapman just before his surgery.

"For what reason would I need to attend Sergeant?" Dr Chapman asked. "After all, I have nothing to do with the murders."

"Inspector Hardie wants to clear the case," George told him. "He wants everyone involved to be there."

"That implies that he knows the murderer," Dr Chapman replied. "In that case he would know it was not me, in fact, I am offended in thinking that I was even a suspect."

George flapped his arms. "I'm only carrying out orders doctor, you must attend."

Doctor Chapman sitting behind his desk sighed. "Very well Sergeant, against my will, what time?" he agreed.

"Ten o'clock doctor," George answered. "If you feel you need a solicitor, then by all means bring one."

"I'll think on it Sergeant," replied the doctor ungraciously. "But now I have a room full of patients to see, so if you will excuse me."

George managed to see Mrs Hanks who seemed a bit flustered. "I can get in touch with Linda's employers," Mrs Hanks said. "But I don't know about my husband, he won't get the sack taking a day off will he?" she asked.

"The police can verify his absence," George assured her. "Now don't worry, it's only a formality, all will be over in an hour."

"I'm glad you have caught the murderer," Mrs Hanks continued. "I get scared to go to sleep at night, it being so near."

"Just make sure you and your husband and your daughter attend, should your husband want a solicitor present, it's quite alright," George said trying to comfort her.

"We cant' afford a solicitor Sergeant," Mrs Hanks answered.

George smiled at her. "Don't worry Mrs Hanks, you don't have to have one, but I have to tell you have a right to bring one."

George left Mrs Hanks bewildered, playing on her mind was her husband, would he get the sack.

George had to wait to see the Sharpe, as Mrs Sharpe was out, he knew that Mr Sharpe worked until late, but was not sure about Terry Sarshall, however, with his second call Mrs Sharpe was in.

"Come in Sergeant," she offered. "How about a nice cup of tea?"

"I can't stop long, I have a lot of calls to make," George lied.

"Well sit a while then," responded Mrs Sharpe, Chris took the offer and sat.

"You, your husband, and Terry are needed to attend the police station tomorrow morning at ten Mrs Sharpe," George said.

"Oh," replied Mrs Sharpe. "Can you tell me why?"

"Inspector Hardie hopes to close our enquiries regarding the murder of your friend Miss Newman tomorrow," George half told the truth. "I'm afraid your presence along with your husband and Terry are needed."

"Have you caught the murderer then?" Mrs Sharpe asked, George sensed a little excitement in her voice.

"We will have to wait and see," George replied. "Can you all be there?"

"I can't speak for Jack or Terry," Mrs Sharpe replied. "But I shall be there, will anyone else be there?"

"Mrs Sharpe," George said, hoping to calm her excitement. "There is no option about your husband and Terry attending, it's a must, if they do not turn up, then the police will come and get them, wherever they are."

"Oh I say," replied Mrs Sharpe. "It's serious then."

"If your husband or Terry are worried regarding their work, then we will verify their absence to the employer, also Mrs Sharpe," George continued. "Should any of you feel that you want a solicitor with you, then you will be within your rights."

"Don't be silly Sergeant," replied Mrs Sharpe. "We can't afford one, but even if we could, why would we want one, but it should be interesting, I have never been to anything like this before, I can't wait."

"Just as long as all three of you attend," George remarked getting up to leave.

"Don't worry Sergeant we will all be there," Mrs Sharpe said grinning and almost pushing George out of the door.

George smiled to himself, he had no doubt that Mrs Sharpe was anxious to tell her friends.

Chapter Sixteen

$\mathcal{C}$hris was in the office on time on the Wednesday morning, he found George already there, Chris took off his trilby, and after taking off his overcoat and hanging it, he walked to his desk smoothing his hair with his hand as he did so.

"Morning George, another nippy day," he greeted him.

"I don't have far to come," replied George.

"Did you manage to catch everyone yesterday?" Chris asked as he started to fuss over the papers he had taken from his drawer.

George told Chris about his errands. "Doctor Chapman was very indignant being forced to attend, he said he would be here under duress, Mrs Hanks seemed bewildered, and was afraid her husband would get the sack, and Mrs Sharpe was very excited."

Chris who was still sorting papers smiled. "She might have good cause to be excited."

"Anyway," continued George. "They all know that they have no option but to be here."

"Good," Chris replied. "Now what about the chairs, have we enough," he asked looking around the room.

"I think so," replied George. "Sergeant Bloom brought these in when I arrived, we have eight chairs, just in case

315

someone brings a solicitor, Sergeant Bloom told me he could always get another couple if needed."

"Well we seem to be ready," Chris remarked. "The shorthand typist will have to sit with you at your desk, at least we won't have the noise of the typewriter," Chris said.

Chris felt nervous, he only hoped that he had a tight case to put, he sat back in his chair, and took out his pipe and sucked on it without lighting it.

"Are you nervous Chris?" George asked.

"Yes," replied Chris. "This is your first case with me, I hope to have the murderer in a cell before long, but if I make a balls up, I could lose him for all time."

"You are still not telling me?" George asked.

"No, not yet, I need to bring everything out, that we have learnt, have you any idea?"

George thought for a while. "I think I know, who it is not," George smiled. "I'm sure Mrs Sharpe had nothing to do with it, nor Linda Hanks."

Chris grinned. "Keep those two in mind for after, you may be surprised in a way."

George wondered what Chris meant, but had no chance of asking, as sergeant Bloom entered the room.

"Your people are here," he informed them.

"Good," Chris replied getting up, and pocketing his pipe, knowing that it was not alight. "Show them in then please sergeant Bloom."

The typist was first to enter, carrying her notebook, she was followed by the Mr and Mrs Hanks, and their daughter Linda, who was followed by the Mr and Mrs Sharpe, Dr Chapman entering last, with Terry.

"Please seat anywhere," Chris offered.

Chris waited for all to be seated, no solicitor was present.

"You may all be wondering why I have called you all together," Chris began. "It is because, each and everyone of you are in someway involved with either Miss Newman or Miss Brown, either by knowing or being with them," Chris paused allowing the murmur that had started to stop.

"I am going to tell you a story," Chris said, a picture of Inspector Noal flashing through his mind.

"It's a very sad story, greed brings grief, this case is full of coincidences, this greed was also the reason why two young innocent young woman were murdered."

Again Chris paused to allow the murmur subside before continuing, he studied the faces before him, most was looking at him with blank expression, while others were looking into their laps. He looked across to George who sat by the typist, George winked, and Chris smiled to himself.

"My story starts back in 1889, about a wealthy man Mr Sarsh and his wife Mrs Sarsh, who emigrated from France to live in England, they settled at Gosport," he said while most were listening to him with interest, Chris noticed that the doctor and Terry were looking at each other.

"Mrs Sarsh became pregnant, and gave birth to twin girls on the forth of April 1890, but sadly Mrs Sarsh died in childbirth," a murmur went up mainly from the women attending. "Filled with grief, and unable to live without his wife, Mr Sarsh shot himself."

"Oh, poor man," came a cry from Mrs Sharpe.

"Yes Mrs Sharpe," Chris said in agreement to her cry. "However before he died, he made a Will, making arrangements for his son, who he was very close to, and make arrangements for his twin girls to be adopted, as I have told you he was a wealthy man."

"What happened to the twins?" Mrs Sharpe asked.

Chris smiled to himself at the interruption, but ignored it. He looked at the faces in front of him, and he realised that none of them had any idea what he was talking about, apart from doctor Chapman, and Terry, he decided he would tell them the good news first, then the bad, but at least in this way, they would have each other for comfort.

"Coincidence and fate, caused the death of Miss Newman and Miss Brown," he started. "And apart from a few lies, most of what each of you told us was the truth, we ran around in circles, because you may be aware that anyone committing murder would have a motive, and that motive we were unable to find," Chris paused looking again at the faces in front of him, most with still a blank look.

"Mrs Sharpe," he said looking at her. "You lied to me over your age, you were born on the forth of April 1890, and not as you told me fourteenth of November, that lie did not help us at all," he remarked starring at her.

"I'm sorry," Mrs Sharpe replied. "I knew that Gloria was also born on the same date, and when I heard that Miss Brown was also born on the same day, and both were murdered, I became frightened."

"Plus the fact that you were also adopted Mrs Sharpe," Chris said.

Before Mrs Sharpe could comment, Chris turned to Mr Hanks.

"You also did not tell the complete truth to me Mr Hanks, you told me your daughter was twenty four, knowing full well that she was twenty five, born on the fifth of April 1890, you also left out that your daughter was adopted."

"Fortunately Inspector, my daughter do know that she was adopted, but I told her never to tell anyone,"

Mr Hanks said holding his daughter's hand who was looking at him.

"My wife and I idolise Linda, but when she started school, we realised that she was not as bright as other school children, and her classmates would abuse her with calling her names. We felt, my wife and I, if the children knew she was adopted, they would tease her even more, so I told her never to tell anyone, she is intelligent in other ways, she's very healthy and bright, it's just that she's a little slow in learning, when she have learnt, she never forgets."

"I am sure you are right Mr Hanks," Chris replied understanding Mr Hanks.

"Both you and Mrs Sharpe wasted a lot of our time in not telling the truth, now doctor Chapman, you are the brother of Mrs Sarsh who died in childbirth, aren't you?" Chris asked in a loud voice, which everybody could hear.

Doctor Chapman nodded his head in agreement.

"Like Mr Hanks, you did not lie, but left out the important detail to tell us," Chris said.

"I saw no reason," doctor Chapman replied. "These murders were nothing to do with me."

"Perhaps more than you think," Chris answered turning to Terry.

"Now Terry Sarshall, or should I say Terry Sarsh," Chris said. "You are the son of Mr and Mrs Sarsh of Gosport, you were born in France, and with your parents emigrated from France to England, why did you alter your name?" Chris asked.

"I've hated my surname than anything," Terry replied. "I loved my father, we did everything together, when he killed himself, I hated the name Sarsh, and added a few more letters on the end."

"You told Sergeant House when he spoke to you about the death of Miss Newman, that you could have done it, what exactly did you mean by that?" Chris asked in a stern face.

"I don't remember saying it," Terry replied. "But if I did I must have been thinking of the twins my mother had, which caused her death, at the beginning I could have killed both of them, I knew Miss Newman had the same birthday as the twins."

"Do you still hate them?" Chris asked, the room fell silent, and all eyes were on Terry.

"When I got my inheritance," Terry continued. "I travelled the country, even went back to France for a while, I came back to England just over a year ago, and eventually found lodgings with Mr and Mrs Sharpe, fate must have brought me to these parts, because although until I got my inheritance, my uncle doctor Chapman and I, had kept in touch, we lost touch when I started travelling, this is the first time I've seen my uncle for a number of years."

"Well at least you have the start of a family," Chris remarked. "Much better than not having any family at all."

Chris looked toward George, who had not said a word, George had been at many interviews during his time at the MET, but this one was unusual, as no mention of the murderer who ever it was, had not been named.

"I'm glad of that," Terry replied.

Chris then turned to Dr Chapman.

"You also have twin nieces, don't you doctor?" Chris dropped the bombshell. "You know that Mrs Sharpe is one of the twins, don't you?"

Mrs Sharpe just looked at the doctor, then at Terry, she was in shock, the Inspector was telling her Terry is her brother, while Terry sat up and looked at his uncle, as doctor Chapman coughed to clear his throat.

"Did you know this uncle?" Terry interrupted, a look of surprise upon his face. "Did you know this?" he repeated looking at doctor Chapman.

"It can't be," Mrs Sharpe shouted. "He's a lodger with me, I would have known if he was my brother."

"Please calm down, Mrs Sharpe, I will explain," Chris said.

"When Mrs Sarsh died in childbirth, her brother who we now know was doctor Chapman, was studying medicine to become a doctor, after he passed out, he took a job as a locum in the hospital where his sister had died, he stopped there just about a year, during which times he managed somehow to read where the twins of his sister had been placed, and found that both of them had been sent to Winchester, children's home at St Cross. Now the doctor was not short of funds owing to Mr Sarsh Will, he could afford to wait a while, and eventually bought Twyford practice, where the original doctor was about to retire. Doctor Chapman has been Twyford doctor for about twenty years."

No sound was coming from the people in front of him, but he noticed that Mrs Sharpe was looking at Terry, wondering.

"During this time, doctor Chapman offered his service free of charge to the adoption board to look after the children at the children's home, which they readily accepted, how long it took, I don't know, but it must have taken years for doctor Chapman to find out about the first twin, which as I have told you was Mrs Sharpe. But doctor Chapman only had information on who adopted her, and the name was Mr and Mrs Smith, he could not find out the address.

Every week doctor Chapman would come into Winchester, and call upon anyone with the name of Smith, he had no motive other than he wanted to find his sister's twins, and become their uncle. After perhaps years of searching, he did find the adoption parents, but their adopted daughter, who was then twenty two, had married a Mr Sharpe, to his disappointment, they refused to tell him where they were living, which meant another few years of searching for doctor Chapman, they could have been anywhere in the country. To cut a long story short, after years of trying to trace his nieces, doctor Chapman found Mrs Sharpe living at Lower Brook Street in Winchester, when he found her I might add, Terry was not a lodger of hers."

Chris paused for a while, and saw by the faces in front of him, they were looking at him with a total confused look on their faces, he smiled to himself as he continued.

"Somehow doctor Chapman made contact with his niece, and I suppose after telling her that she was his niece, he told her about the large sum of money she would inherit when she became twenty six, and if the other twin was dead, or could not be found, she would have all the lot. He also told her that he had a young lady at Twyford as a patient who was born on the same day, but did not know whether or not she was adopted, so while he was finding out he asked Mrs Sharpe to say nothing to anyone, Mrs Sharpe in return must have told him about her friend Gloria Newman who lived a few doors away, who was also born on the same day and had been adopted."

Chris took a drink of water, he knew he had an audience attention, he looked at George, who had a slight smile on his face, wondering what was coming next, he thought of Inspector Noal, and hoped he would approve.

"Unfortunately," Chris continued having drank half glass of water. "Mrs Sharpe did not obey doctor Chapman's advise when he asked her to keep it quiet for a while."

"Yes I did," Mrs Sharpe remarked. "I didn't tell a soul, only my," her voice trailed off.

"Yes Mrs Sharpe you told your husband," Chris continued for her.

"But that's only natural," Mrs Sharpe responded. "He is my husband."

"Normally I suppose," Chris replied. "But in this case a disaster, your husband is in charge of a builders office, he knows all about taking and pricing orders etc, he also knows about accounts, he knew that the money left in trust to the twins twenty six years ago, would now be, allowing for the yearly interest a vast sum of money, enough to live on without working or worry, he also knew that should you be the only surviving twin you would get in the region of fifty thousand, a very large sum of money."

"Are you accusing me of the murders?" Mr Sharpe stood up and spoke for the first time.

"Sit down Mr Sharpe," Chris ordered. "Your greed have ruined what could have been a joyful reunion, yes my Sergeant will charge you with the murder of Miss Gloria Newman."

"You have no proof," Mr Sharpe shouted.

"What are we talking about?" Mrs Sharpe screamed. "You don't seriously think my husband murdered Miss Newman do you?"

"I'm afraid I do Mrs Sharpe, let me continue, your husband knew the birth date of Miss Newman, he also new about Miss Brown of Twyford because of what you had told him, and greed got the better of him."

"How can you prove I killed any of these girls?" shouted Mr Sharpe, with the audience looking at him in disbelief.

"That's right Inspector," Mrs Sharpe sobbed. "Miss Newman was killed around midnight you said, my husband was in bed with me at that time."

"Mrs Sharpe," Chris spoke kindly. "Since you were told about having a possible sister, you have suffered a kind of depression, when you go to bed you are unable to sleep, and you are having restless nights sleep, you felt alone and depressed unable to get the thought of having a sister out of your mind, for this reason you were given sleeping pills by your GP, you told me yourself that you never heard Terry enter the house at nights, that was because you were under the drug."

"I still don't believe it," she sobbed.

"He can't prove it," Mr Sharpe remarked. "You are trying to get a scapegoat for the crime."

"I can assure you Mr Sharpe, you are the only one with opportunity and motive, you were at Twyford on the Monday night, when Miss Brown was strangled to death, you even saw her in the pub, you were playing shove halfpenny, by the way, when you play shove halfpenny, do you play with your own disc, or the one's supplied?"

"I can't see what that has got to do with anything," Mr Sharpe remarked angrily. "I play with my own disc, if you really want to know."

"I am well aware of that Mr Sharpe, I have one of your own disc here," Chris replied holding up the disc.

"That could be anyone's," Mr Sharpe replied, my set is at home in a pouch.

"No, this one belongs to you Mr Sharpe," Chris replied, his voice was showing certainty. "I spoke yesterday to the engineer that engraved your initials on them so that the weight would be the same."

"Where did you find it then?" Mrs Sharpe asked dabbing her eyes with her handkerchief.

"I found it myself, under Miss Newman's bed," replied Chris. "At the time neither Sergeant House or myself knew what it was, thinking it was a foreign coin."

Mrs Sharpe looked at her husband. "Tell me Jack, are you telling the truth, how did that disc get under Gloria's bed, you told me you have never been in her bedroom."

"I haven't," her husband replied. "I can't explain it."

Chris took a small paper bag, laid beside him, he emptied it in front of them.

"Mrs Simpson cleaned the room for Mr Newman after his daughter was murdered, she found other coins under the bed, also this ring, it's broken, it seems that you must have spilt these items from your pocket Mr Sharpe."

"That's my ring," Mrs Sharpe exploded seeing it. "It had worn thin, and Jack was taking it to be mended," she swung her handbag at her husband's head. "You filthy liar," she shouted as she swung her handbag again. "You killed her didn't you?" she screamed her eyes full of tears.

"I did it for us Ellen," Mr Sharpe moaned as he lifted his arms, and ducked to protect himself. "I did for us."

"You mean you killed my sister, who I never knew, just for money," Mrs Sharpe cried out repeating her action with her handbag.

George left his seat, and gently held Mrs Sharpe. "Come along Mrs Sharpe, this is getting us nowhere."

Mrs Sharpe allowed George to place her in her seat, she was bewildered and very upset, her husband is a murderer.

"Is he responsible for Miss Brown's death as well?" Mrs Sharpe asked sniffing.

"Well," Chris said as he watched doctor Chapman and Terry pull their chairs nearer to Mrs Sharpe, each holding one of her hands.

"He was at Twyford that night, doctor Chapman and Miss Brown were in the same bar, hearing the doctor called Doc, he could have enquired who they were, he could have seen her leave, and he could have followed her, we know he walked back to Winchester, but because Mrs Sharpe took sleeping tablets, we do not know what time he arrived home. I can't proof that he murdered Stacey, but he is still the only person with a opportunity and a motive for the murder."

"You will never know," Mr Sharpe shouted. "Ellen will be the only twin left."

"I'm afraid I have to disappoint you there Mr Sharpe," Chris answered. "You see doctor Chapman miss one vital bit of information in his search, Mrs Sharpe was born at ten minutes to midnight on the forth of April 1980, her twin was born at ten past midnight on the fifth of April 1980, so Mrs Sharpe is a day older than her twin, although in reality only twenty minutes, your mistake was thinking that twins had to be born on the same day, unfortunately because you made that mistake, innocent lives were destroyed."

Mr Sharpe looked at him desperately. "God," he muttered. "Then who is Ellen's twin?"

"She has been living a few doors away from you for years," Chris replied. "Mrs Sharpe's twin sister is Linda Hanks."

Linda had listen to all that had been said, she took her time, but managed to keep up, with her eyes full of tears, she left her father and went to Ellen, and with a smile and a sob, embraced her, all these years she thought she had no one only her adopted parents, now she had a twin sister, a brother, and a uncle. They did not notice Sergeant House, take Mr Sharpe outside, where his rights were read and charged with the murder of Miss Gloria Newman.

It was some time later, when the office was cleared, George looked at Chris.

"You let him off easy Chris, he made love to them both before he killed them."

"I'm sure you're right George," Chris replied. "But I thought Mrs Sharpe was upset enough without knowing that her husband had made love to them, also I didn't know what difference it would make, he will be found guilty, and it's a hanging offence."

"You didn't bring up about the two murdered women's life as women of the night either," George remarked.

"There was no need George, and it save a lot of grief for Mr Newman and Mrs Brown not knowing that, it would have upset them, it would be silly of Mr Sharpe to bring it up at the trial, because he assaulted both of them, and that would go against him, I can't see his solicitor bringing it up."

"I don't know how you placed it altogether Chris, it was certainly a case of coincidences, who would expect three girls born on the same day, and all adopted, living so close to each other, with one not knowing the other."

"Four if you include Miss Hanks," Chris agreed with a sigh. "I don't want another case with so many coincidence, I don't believe in them, still I have one last thing to do, phone Mr Blackwell the solicitor in Gosport," Chris said with a grin.

"We still need the signed confession from Mr Sharpe," George reminded him.

"We will have him in as soon as I speak to Mr Blackwell," Chris replied. "I would like his confession regarding Miss Brown's murder but first of all we will get a bite to eat, what you say?"

George agreed with a smile.

Chris and George having had a bite to eat entered the station, Chris stopped at the desk and spoke to sergeant Bloom. "Bring Mr Sharpe into the office sergeant, he has to be interrogated."

"Will do Sir," sergeant Bloom replied. "I like to add my congratulations Sir, a job well done."

"Thank you Sergeant," Chris replied with a smile. "But we are all a team here, yourself included."

Sergeant Bloom smiled. "Thank you Sir, any help I can give I am only to willing, I'll bring Mr Sharpe in straight away."

Chris looked at Mr Sharpe sitting in the interview chair, Mr Sharpe had the look of a person who had given up all hope, very dejected.

"Have you been fed Mr Sharpe?" Chris asked taking a quick glance at George, who was sitting facing Mr Sharpe.

"Yes," Mr Sharpe replied nodding his head.

Mr Sharpe, you are being interviewed regarding the murder of Miss Newman, a murder you have already confessed to in front of many witnesses, also the murder of Miss Brown of Twyford, you can if you wish to have a solicitor present."

"I don't have a solicitor," Mr Sharpe replied.

"Would you like us to provide one for you?" Chris asked.

"What's the use?" Mr Sharpe replied. "I have already confessed."

"It is for your own benefit to have one present," George spoke up.

Mr Sharpe looked at his hands, clasped in his lap. "The way I see it, I am already doomed, a solicitor would be of little use, he won't be able to stop the Judge passing the death sentence on me would he?"

Chris glanced at George, who was shaking his head. Chris picked up his pen, and dipped it into the ink bottle, he picked up a typewritten document that had already been prepared by the typist.

"This is your confession to the murder of Miss Gloria Newman, Mr Sharpe, if you will please sign it," Chris said, placing the document in front of Mr Sharpe and offering him the pen, at the same time hoping that Mr Sharpe was not going to withdraw his confession. Chris felt relieved as Mr Sharpe signed the document without even reading it.

"Thank you Mr Sharpe," Chris said taking the document and pen from him. "Now you understand Mr Sharpe," Chris continued. "You will face a court trial, with your confession you will almost be sure to be found guilty, the Jury will give their verdict almost immediately, the trial for Miss Newman's murder will be short."

"I will be hung," Mr Sharpe answered his face showing no signs of any emotion, only sadness in his eyes. "I did it for my wife," he continued in a whisper.

Chris leaned back in his chair, he did not believe Mr Sharpe murdered Miss Newman simply for his wife, he was sure that there was some degree of greed involved.

"I cannot speak for the Judge Mr Sharpe, you have confessed, saved the court time and money, he may be lenient and give you a jail sentence."

"Well what ever will be, will be," Mr Sharpe sighed accepting what Chris had said. "They were only prostitutes after all."

"I never mentioned the fact Mr Sharpe, I was thinking of your wife's feeling, I could not bring myself to tell her that you raped them before killing them," Chris replied.

"Actually I never raped them, I mean Miss Newman," Mr Sharpe hastily corrected himself. "She was quite willing, but my wife would never believe that now, so I owe you for not mentioning the fact," Mr Sharpe replied.

Chris leaned foreword. "Now Mr Sharpe we still have the murder of Miss Brown, you refused to say whether you have involvement with her murder, we believe you did, in fact you have just convinced us."

Mr Sharpe looked at Chris, but said nothing, just shrugged his shoulders.

"Mr Sharpe," George remarked. "If you did commit the murder of Miss Stacey Brown, it may be in your best interest to own up now, you are already charged with one murder, and the Judge will always consider the circumstances which made you commit the crime."

"You mean the Judge will put on his black cap?" Mr Sharpe replied, looking at George with a weak smile on his face.

"It's a possibility," George replied.

Mr Sharpe looked at his hand again. "I will take your advice and have a solicitor," he said.

Chris leaned back, a little disappointed, he had almost a confession he thought for a little while, it was always harder having a solicitor present when interviewing a suspect, but the suspect was entitled.

"Very well Mr Sharpe, we will arrange one for you," Chris replied taking the receiver from his phone. "You will have to go back to your cell until we have arrange one."

Chris spoke into the receiver. "Sergeant Bloom," he said into it. "Mr Sharpe can now be taken back to his cell."

"I wonder why he changed his mind," George remarked as Sergeant Bloom and his prisoner left the room.

"Perhaps he considered what you told him George," Chris replied. "He probably thought that he would have more chances of getting a prison sentence confessing to one murder, however in my opinion confessing to one or two murder don't make any difference both these murders were premeditated, both hanging sentences."

Sergeant Bloom returned to the office. "I have arranged for a solicitor Sir," he remarked. "Would four o'clock this afternoon suit you?"

"Perfect I would say," Chris replied with a smile and looking at George. "Thank you sergeant."

"At least we can get on with our paper work while we are waiting," George remarked.

Both Chris and George spent the afternoon studying the paper work.

Chris looked at his pocket watch. "Well George it's almost four, the solicitor is keeping it close."

George was about to answer as a knock came on the door, and Sergeant Bloom entered. "Mr Sharpe's solicitor is here Sir," he said.

"Thank you sergeant, show him in, and get Mr Sharpe from the cells."

Wearing a blue top coat, and a bowler hat, and carrying a briefcase and umbrella the solicitor was ushered into the office, he unbuttoned his overcoat, and took off his bowler, and approached the desk behind which Chris was standing.

"I am Mr Bradley, solicitor, here to be with you during your interview with my client Mr Sharpe."

"I know," Chris replied offering his hand. "I am Detective Inspector Hardie, and my colleague Sergeant House," he said indicating George. "Please take a seat, Mr Sharpe is being brought in."

Chris waited until Mr Bradley was seated comfortably. "Mr Bradley, we were interviewing Mr Sharpe this morning about the murder of Miss Stacey Brown of Twyford, and that is all."

"I see Inspector, I am familiar with the details of the case, also Miss Newman."

"Mr Sharpe has already been charged with his own confession regarding Miss Gloria Newman's murder, no need to waste time going over that, you may in your own time go over it with Mr Sharpe as you will be defending him, as far as we are concerned he is guilty of Miss Newman's murder, however we have to make sure he is guilty of the murder of Miss Stacey Brown."

"I understand Inspector," Mr Bradley replied as the office door opened and Mr Sharpe was brought in. Sergeant Bloom, leading him by the arm sat him in the chair beside the solicitor.

"Thank you Sergeant," Chris said as the sergeant retired. "Please make sure we are not disturbed."

Chris rested his hands on the desk, and looked at Mr Sharpe.

"Mr Sharpe, I ask you again in the presence of your solicitor, whom I believe you had already had a few words with, did you kill Miss Stacey Brown at Twyford Village Hall?"

"No I didn't," Mr Sharpe replied without hesitation.

"But you were at Twyford, at the time she was murdered," Chris said in a very calm but stern voice.

Mr Sharpe looked at his solicitor, who just nodded.

"I was playing a league match at the Phoenix pub that evening, but I don't know if I was in Twyford when this young lady was killed," he replied.

Chris looked at George who was listening, he had a knowing smile on his face, Mr Bradley had obviously grilled Mr Sharpe with answers.

"What time would you say you left Twyford?" Chris asked.

"After the pub shut," Mr Sharpe replied, leaning back in his chair.

"Village pubs, close the same time as town pubs, do they not?" Chris asked.

"I suppose, half past ten," Mr Sharpe replied.

"Autopsy reports states that Miss Brown was murdered between ten pm and midnight, so that one point we can agree that you were in the village at the time of Miss Brown's murder?" Chris said.

Mr Sharpe looked at his solicitor, who again nodded.

"Agreed," Mr Sharpe answered.

"How did you get home?" Chris asked.

"I walked," replied Mr Sharpe without any hesitation.

"Can anyone vouch for that?" Chris asked.

Mr Sharpe shrugged. "I don't know."

"But surely you spoke to your team members about getting home, how did they get home anyway?" Chris asked.

Mr Sharpe shrugged again. "I don't know, some had bikes and probably some walked the same as me," he answered.

"You don't know?" Chris asked.

"No I don't," Mr Sharpe replied. "What does it matter?"

"It's several miles from Twyford to Winchester, why didn't you walk with your team mates who was walking home?"

"I didn't say they did, I only said probably," Mr Sharpe said fidgeting in his chair.

"OK then you left at closing time, started to walk home, if any of your team mates walked home, you did not see them, or walk with them, I am correct?"

"That's right," Mr Sharp said.

Mr Bradley sat looking at his client without interruption, seemingly contented with his answers. Chris took up a sheet of paper from his desk and read it.

"Mr Sharp, did you leave before your team mates, or did you leave after them?" Chris asked.

"I must have left before them, because I did not see them," Mr Sharpe replied.

"But you did see Mr Charley Coven, who cycled home, even if he had left behind you, on a cycle he would have overtaken you," Chris said.

"Old Charley," Mr Sharpe smiled. "He always drinks too much, shouldn't be riding a bicycle after drinking, yes I waved to him as he rang his bell going by me."

"He did have a accident on his way home," Chris said.

"Yes I heard he had, the silly man," replied Mr Sharpe.

Chris saw Mr Bradley straighten himself, with a concerned look on his face.

"Where is this going Inspector?" Mr Bradley asked.

"Simple Mr Bradley, Mr Coven would have been in front of Mr Sharpe, who tells us he left ahead of the other walkers, now Twyford Road, is quite a straight road, without any turn offs, it stretches perhaps a half mile or more. Now Mr Coven came off his bike, buckled his front wheel, the walkers behind Mr Sharpe found him sitting by the road side, shaken a bit, I have no doubt, and helped him home," Chris turned to Mr Sharpe. "Had you left in front or behind your team mates, you would have come across Mr Coven and your other team mates, now please let's have the truth."

Mr Sharpe felt a little flustered, he had made a mistake.

"Well," he shrugged. "I had had a few pints, I must have forgotten what happened, I said what I thought had happened."

"Come Mr Sharpe," Chris remarked. "You don't expect us to take that as the truth you know perfectly well what you did that night."

"Why don't you tell me then, you're the detective," Mr Sharpe shouted defiantly.

"Very well, I will tell you what I believe happen," Chris replied. "You were with your team mates playing shove halfpenny, as a matter of fact," Chris continued picking up a sheet of paper from his desk and reading it.

"You lost your games, perhaps because of lack of concentration, but fortunately your team won the game. You saw Stacey Brown in the bar, talking to doctor Chapman, she took all your concentration, thinking that she might be the twin standing in the way of your wife getting all the inheritance."

"The doctor could have done it," interrupted Mr Sharpe. "After all he was the one with her."

"But why would the doctor want to kill her, who he believed may have been one of his missing nieces, who he had searched for twenty or more years?" Chris commented. "What would be his gain?"

Getting no answer, Chris continued. "I believe you watched Stacey all night, you knew her, because you had seen her visit Miss Newman at nights, when you saw her leave by the back entrance you followed her, no one would have noticed you, the teams were engrossed in the game going on, any other person in the bar would have been strangers to you and they would not have noticed you going. You caught up with her outside, perhaps offered her money to go somewhere with you."

"She had just lost her father damn it," Mr Sharpe said in an outburst. "Would you expect a girl to go with you having just learnt that?"

"Never the less, you did do that, and because she was vulnerable that night she agreed, perhaps because she wanted a little love, anyway, I believe you took her behind the village hall, had sex with her, then strangled her."

"All fantasy," Mr Sharpe shouted. "Can you prove it, I have never met the girl."

"But you just told us, she had just lost her father, how would you have know had you not met her?"

"They were talking in the pub about it," Mr Sharpe replied.

"I'm sorry Mr Sharpe, but the only people in the pub that night that knew about Mr Brown having been killed, was doctor Chapman and Stacey, you did not speak to the doctor, so you must have heard it from Stacey."

"Well I didn't, I never spoke to the girl," Mr Sharpe replied. "And you can't prove that I did."

Chris looked at the solicitor who remained silent, he looked at George who also remained silent with a look of frustration on his face.

"You have no real evidence Inspector that my client murdered Miss Stacey Brown have you?" Mr Bradley said breaking the silence just as the phone rang.

Chris lifted the receiver, he felt angry, and had to agree with the solicitor, also with the interruption of the phone call.

"Detective Inspector Hardie," he said into the mouthpiece.

"Bob Harvey here Chris," came the reply. "I have got the result's of Mr Sharpe blood test, he is AB negative."

"Really Bob, that is good news, thank you very much," he said replacing the phone. He moved papers on his desk and picked up the autopsy report on Miss Brown and read it over, then looked at Mr Sharpe.

"Although you had it in your mind that you were going to kill Miss Brown, you did not expect to do it the night you played at Phoenix, Twyford, in fact it was a big surprise to you finding her in the pub, she was not a regular there, and only would pop in now and again, so I believe you were unprepared for what you did."

"What did I do then, tell me," Mr Sharpe interrupted.

"Please allow me to finish," Chris replied to the interruption. "When you killed Miss Newman which you have already confessed to, you took precautions, in other words, you left no sperm in her vagina or womb. When you surprising found Miss Brown in the Phoenix that night, you were unprepared, you made love to her without using a condom."

"I don't understand what you are saying," Mr Sharpe said looking at his lap.

"You should know Mr Sharpe," Chris continued. "That the sperm left can tell us the blood group of the sex partner, Miss Brown had sex with a person whose blood group is AB negative."

"So," Mr Sharpe replied spreading his hands, worried because he did not know his own group.

"Your group is AB negative Mr Sharpe, don't you find that a coincidence?"

"Inspector," Mr Bradley said. "Do you think I can have a few moments alone with my client?"

"By all means Mr Bradley, you can use my office, Sergeant House and myself will step outside, knock the door when you have finished."

Sitting on the chairs outside his office, Chris lit his pipe, after taking a puff he looked at George. "What do think?" he asked.

"I'm sure he is guilty," George replied. "But have we enough proof?"

"Yes I know," Chris answered. "If only we could get some evidence that he was seen around the village hall."

Deep in thought, Chris had finished his pipe when the office door opened, and Mr Bradley looked out. "I have finished Inspector," he said.

Chris looked around wondering where he could knock his pipe out, seeing no place, he carried it back into the office and put it in the ashtray, before seating himself.

"I have spoken to my client Inspector," Mr Bradley spoke. "He would like to tell you of the truth."

"I shall be glad to hear it," Chris replied.

Mr Sharpe sat uneasily in his chair, and Chris could see he was shaking a little.

"I saw Stacey Brown in the Phoenix that night speaking to a man," Mr Sharpe started hesitantly. "I did not know who she was, although I had seen her visit Miss Newman. During the game, I heard someone said.

"The Doc is alright tonight, with the village bike, then I realised who she was."

Mr Sharpe paused for a while, and swallowed, his throat feeling dry.

"I saw her leave by the back door, and the doctor went and stood at the bar, I followed Stacey out, as you said, no one noticed me. To keep the story short, outside I offered Stacey money, and we did it in between two carts that were in the ground outside. While we spoke, she told me of her father being killed in action in France."

Chris looked at George, who just shrugged at him, knowing that their case against him for the murder of Stacey Brown was being taken away.

"How was it that you did not see Charley Coven on your way back to Winchester, you said yourself that you waved at him?" Chris asked.

Mr Sharpe cleared his throat. "After I had finished with Stacey, she left saying she was going home, it must have been around ten then, I decided that I had enough to drink and I had played my games, to start out for home, I did not return to the pub. When I got to corner of Hockley golf club, I had just passed the houses there, when a cyclist went by, it was pitch black, I could not make who it was, and as I told you I waved to him in the darkness. Charley I knew was riding a bike, and when you mentioned him, it came into my mind that he was the one that overtook me, however thinking on it, because I had left early, I was well out of Twyford Road, before he had left the pub."

Chris felt despair, Mr Sharpe had neatly got himself out of the three bits of evidence that they had against him. "You are telling me that you were no where near the village hall that night with Stacey Brown?" Chris asked.

"Well I did have to pass it on my way home," Mr Sharpe answered. "But I did not enter the village hall grounds, nor was Miss Brown."

"You took Miss Brown behind the village hall and strangled her," Chris almost shouted loosing his composure.

"No I did not," replied Mr Sharpe.

"I think my client have told you his movements for that night Inspector," Mr Bradley interrupted.

Chris picked up the pencil in front of him, and twisted it between his fingers, he looked at Mr Sharpe, who was now looking quite relaxed. Chris was mad with himself for almost losing his temper.

"Very well," Chris said straightening up.

"There will be a court hearing early next week, where you will be charged with the murder of Miss Gloria Newman, the murder of Miss Stacey Brown is will still have to be investigated."

THE END

BOOK THREE

INSPECTOR
CHRIS HARDIE

THE SMELL OF
TALCUM POWDER

Chapter One

*C*hris stood outside the Police Station, it was cold, and darkness was descending. Chris pulled the collar of his top coat up, he was pleased that George on the way back from Twyford had taken him by his motorbike to his lodgings to fetch his topcoat. It was a trip he had not looked forward to, he had to inform Mrs Brown that although he knew the murderer of her daughter Stacey, it was unlikely that he would be unable to charge him of it. However he would be charged with the murder of Miss Gloria Newman. Chris glad to get away from the house, he had left a very distraught woman.

Chris has frozen on the back of the motorbike, and wondered how George had stood it being the driver. With neither of them having had dinner, Chris told George to call it a day, as he was meeting Elizabeth.

Elizabeth smiled as she saw Chris approach. "Hello darling," she said planting a kiss on his cheek.

"You've been out," she continued fussing with his overcoat, which Chris had not bothered to button up. "I keep telling you, to keep your overcoat buttoned up," she scolded.

"It's not that cold," Chris replied still with Mrs Brown in his mind. "I have just had a very unpleasant duty to perform," he added.

Elizabeth looked at Chris. "You do look sad darling," she replied grabbing his arm. "You don't have to go into the station now do you?"

"No, we'll go home," Chris replied.

Elizabeth grabbed his arm as they walked towards home.

"I wonder what mum is cooking for tonight, I'm starving," she changed the subject.

"We will soon find out," Chris replied disengaging himself from Elizabeth so that she could go in front up the path to the front door, where Olive was already standing with the front door open welcoming them.

Olive served up pork chops and vegetable, with spotted dick pudding and custard for afters.

"Olive, I must say you are a good cook," Chris flattered her on her cooking pushing his empty pudding dish away from him."

"Service is the best thing that ever happen for a woman," Ron interrupted.

"My Olive here," Ron continued reaching for his wife's hand.

"She did her time in service, she is a good housekeeper, and cook, and knows how to look after her husband," Ron said proudly, his face expressed emotion of caring and love.

"You can stop your flattery," Olive turned on him. "Service do not teach one how to look after a husband, husbands should be taught how to treat their wives, you are lucky, having made me your skivvy."

"She loves me you know Chris," Ron laughed.

"I know that Ron," Chris replied looking at Olive who was blushing.

"Women have a way of pretending their feelings I might add," Olive said with a wink at Elizabeth as she rose from the table. "Come Elizabeth let's clear the things away before your father makes more of a fool of himself."

Elizabeth rose with a smile on her face. "Don't take them seriously Chris, they have been like this all my life, anyway they like a little banter."

Chris smiled. "I know that," he agreed.

Chris enjoyed the meal, after which he followed Ron and sat in the armchairs that face each other. Chris took out his pipe and lit it, and puffed on it contentedly. While the women cleared the tea things away and washed them up, Chris and Ron exchanged a few words about the ongoing was, until the women made their appearances.

"You seem very quiet tonight Chris, are you wrapping up warm, it's very cold these days, you must make sure you have regular meals, and keep warm," Olive said in a concerning voice.

"I'm alright Olive," he replied blowing out a cloud of smoke towards the ceiling. "I have just completed my investigation of two murders, it was a bad case, I've seen a lot of grief, and I suppose it got to me."

"Two young women were murdered by the same man, one young woman from Lower Brook Street, and one from Twyford, both were adopted, and both were of the same age," Chris paused as he heard a gasp escape both Mrs Oborne and Elizabeth.

"The trouble is," Chris continued. "While I have his confession regarding the Winchester murder, I cannot charge him with the Twyford murder, I know he did it, but I cannot find the proof."

"What will happen to him do you think when he stands trial for the Winchester murder?" Ron asked.

"It was premeditated, I would expect him to be hung," Chris replied.

Ron got up from his seat, he wanted to change the sad atmosphere of the room. "I have some beer bottles under the bath Chris, what about one?"

Ron brought in a bottle of beer and two glasses, and placed them on the small table in front of them.

"You look as if you could do with one," he said as he started to pour two glasses. "This will help you Chris," he said.

"I can certainly do with one," Chris replied smiling, with his free hand Chris lifted his glass, and smiled his thanks at Ron then took a long drink.

For Chris the evening passed in a relaxing atmosphere, in which he sat on the sofa with Elizabeth close to his side, with the radio playing dance tunes, Elizabeth had fallen asleep at times, and Chris himself had felt very sleepy. It was gone ten when Chris kissed Elizabeth goodnight at the front door.

Chapter Two

ohn Paris was a creature of habit, he would leave his office in Lower Brook Street at the same time every night, making his way to the saloon bar of the Indian Arms public house where he would enjoy two pints and a whiskey, while chatting to other regulars. This night was not an exception, he entered the tiny saloon bar, but his mind was troubled.

"John," came a voice from a man sitting to the right of the opening used as a bar, that separated the saloon bar from the public bar.

"I've ordered you a pint," he said.

"Thanks Roger," John replied as he discarded his trilby and overcoat on the hat stand provided. "It's getting colder, but it can be expected this time of the year," he added as he walked to the bar rubbing his hands. John took the pint, which the landlord seeing him enter had already pulled, and sat down by Roger.

"Something on your mind John?" Roger asked sipping his drink.

"No, not really, business worries you know," John replied taking a drink.

"How's that lovely wife of yours and that attractive step daughter of yours?" Roger asked with a smile.

"They are both well thank you Roger," John replied with a serious face. "Although my step daughter is causing concern to her mother."

"Sorry to hear that," Roger answered. "Serious?" he asked.

John took another drink before answering. "She is attractive as you say, I believe the problem lies with the school she attends, she is a day student at St Swithuns girls school, God knows what the girls get up to, but one thing is sure they know more than I do about sex."

"She's at a girls school John," Roger replied. "Girls will always talk about boys, the same as boys do about girls, it's the way of things, I sometime wonder whether we should be more open regarding sex, sweeping it under the carpet leads to curiosity."

"I'm incline to agreed with you Roger," John said getting up and taking the two empty pints glasses to the bar for refill.

"Since her own father died, her mother has relaxed in her strictness with her," John continued as he brought back two fresh pints. "I keep out of it as much as I can, I feel she has a resentment towards me."

"Come John, you must be imagining it," Roger smiled taking a drink.

"I think she is making up things about me and talking to her mother about me, I find Linda very cold sometimes, yet she will not tell me the reason."

Roger smiled taking a drink. "You know John, girls like a father figure, give it time, she will come around, you have only been married a few months."

"I guess you're right Roger, anyway that's enough about me, how's life treating you?" John asked.

"Well apart from what we both know, things are as usual, not a word has been said," Roger replied.

"I have carried out my promise," John replied. "From next week you will have to make your own decision on what you do, it will be rough."

"I understand John, and thanks," Roger answered.

The next hour passed with small talk, John finished his whisky and soda.

"Well I'm off Roger," John said getting up and crossing the saloon for his overcoat and trilby which he put on. "Glad it's not raining, see you tomorrow," he smiled at Roger as he turned towards the door.

"I'll be here John, and don't worry," Roger replied to the back of John.

Once outside John stopped, he fumbled with the collar of his top coat, and did up the buttons, it was cold, the Broadway was almost deserted apart from a few soldiers, who seem to be enjoying themselves following a young woman. John smiled at his thoughts, and walked as he always did towards Middle Brook Street, where he turned right into it, and walked the entire length, eventually crossing the North Walls and entering Park Avenue. It was not quite dark, but the light was fading, John knew that he had ten minutes before the Park Gates were closed. Going through the Park was a short cut to his house in Monks road.

John entered the park, the darkness seemed more tense, there not being a single lamp in the Park. He took the centre gravel path, crossing over a small flint sided bridge, he saw the canoes tied up in the centre of the river he was walking along side. He passed the edge, beyond which he knew to be the bowling green he felt a shiver run through his body, and he wondered why, he was not really cold, his walking had warmed him. John reached the iron bridge which he had to cross, but as was his habit, he stood on it for a while looking at the river below in the semi darkness.

He made a sharp look at the weeping willow, to one side of the bridge, he was sure he heard a noise, then relaxed feeling a fool when the noise was not repeated, considering that the noise had been made by the dipping branches of the weeping willow, rustling in the breeze. John smiled to himself, and was about to leave when he heard the noise again. He turned towards the sound, and recognised that shadowy figure approaching him. "What are you doing here?" he asked.

Chapter Three

hris and George were both in the office, it was Thursday.

"Perhaps we will have a period of peace now," Chris remarked as he leaned back in his chair puffing his pipe. "The funeral of Miss Newman and Miss Brown is tomorrow."

"Are we going?" George asked. "I hear they are going to be buried beside each other."

Chris leaned forward over his desk, and took his pipe from his mouth. "No, the case has been solved, we are no longer investigating it, to be honest there will be too much grief there."

Before George could comment, the desk sergeant knocked and entered the room.

"What is it sergeant?" Chris asked politely.

"We had a missing person call, he was missing since last Monday night," the sergeant explained.

"You carried out the usual routine?" Chris asked.

"Yes we did," replied the desk sergeant with a faint smile. "And we might have found him."

"How do you mean we might have found him," Chris asked a little confused.

"A man have been found under a weeping willow tree, by the iron bridge at the back of the park, it might be our missing person," the sergeant explained.

"Is he alive or dead?" Chris asked taking an interest.

"Dead," replied the sergeant. "That's all I know."

Chris looked at George. "You are not the pipe piper are you George, in the couple weeks you have been with me we have had three murders, should this one be?"

George shrugged his shoulders. "We never had this many in such a short time in London," he replied.

"How do you know this last one is murder?" the desk sergeant asked.

"He would not crawl in under a weeping willow tree just to die," Chris replied getting up and crossing to the hat stand. "People who normally kill themselves where they are easily found, what's the name of your missing person?" Chris asked taking his trilby.

"A John Paris, lives at 6, Monks road, a few minutes walk from where the body was found," replied the desk sergeant.

Chris looked at George who was already on his feet. "I know the bridge George, we had better use our bikes, who is at the scene?" Chris asked turning to the desk sergeant.

"A constable is there, and I have already phoned the police surgeon Mr Bob Harvey," came the reply.

Chris and George dismounted when they reached the bridge, and saw the constable.

"The body is under the weeping willow tree," the constable pointed out. "It's like a little room once you go through the dipping branches."

Chris followed by George, push the branches to one side, and saw by the trunk of the tree a body of a man laying on his back fully clothed, a closer look proved the desk sergeant's words, no signs of the reason the man was dead, no struggle seem to have taken place.

"It was raining during the night wasn't it?" Chris asked.

"Yes," replied the constable. "I was out in it."

"He could have fallen into the river, and grabbed hold of one of these overlapping branches, and pulled himself out," Chris said bending over the body. "But I doubt it, his cloths are damp, not saturated with river water."

"But what killed him?" George asked agreeing with Chris.

"Perhaps he suffered a heart attack," Chris murmured unconvincingly as he stood up and went to the river bank, and studying it by moving aside branches of the tree.

"However I think we can rule both those ideas out, first if he fell into the water, his clothes would have at least been wet through, and if he climbed out the water, he would have left some sign, the river bank is quite muddy here."

"You know this is the first time I have been in the centre of a weeping willow," George remarked.

"Same as me George," Chris remarked. "It's quite dry here, he was pulled in here, look at the heels of his shoes, covered with mud and grass," Chris stood up, and stepped carefully around the trunk of the tree so that he was facing the bridge.

"Can't see the bridge plainly from here George," he remarked. "So we must assume for the moment that whoever shot him was standing outside the tree, whoever it was would not be standing that side," Chris indicated the river. "The branches dip almost into the river, he stood this side on the field."

"What makes you say he was shot?" George asked alarmed at the statement.

Chris gave a smile. "Look behind his left ear George."

"I see," George agreed as he tilted the man's head."

"I've only noticed it when I stood that side," Chris said as he pushed back the over lapping branches and stepped out into the field, he look around, for any marks.

"I wonder how long he has been here?" Chris muttered as he bent and examined several impressions in the ground. "Perhaps the last few nights being cold and frosty have helped us, what do these marks look like George?" he asked.

George bent and looked at the marks. "Wellingtons boots, someone wearing wellingtons have stood here," George replied.

Chris looked towards the constable who was standing on the bridge. "Who found the body constable?" Chris asked.

"A runner Sir," the constable replied. "He runs around the park every morning, but today he wanted a pee, so he went in under the branches, knowing that he would not be seen."

"Where is he now?" George asked.

"He was cold, and told me his name and address, saying that should he be needed, he will be back from work around five this evening, then ran off."

Chris shook his head as he continued to examine the impressions on the ground.

"The trouble is George," he remarked. "This is the edge of the sports field, they never mow the edges, so we have turf, which spoils any impression, we have only the heel part to go on," Chris stood up and looked towards the bridge. "We have a clear view of the bridge from here, how far away do you think?"

"No more than fifteen feet," George replied.

"It was likely that he was shot while he was on the bridge, then dragged into this tree to hide it, the question remains, was it dark or light when he was shot?" Chris murmured.

George shrugged. "No way of telling."

"Well we better empty his pockets while we are waiting," Chris said as the back firing of Bob Harvey's motorbike and sidecar drew up.

Bob got off his motorbike, he took his bag from his sidecar and walked towards Chris and George who were watching him.

"Unable to get here sooner," Bob apologized with a smile as he approached them.

"We have only been here a few moments," Chris replied.

"Hello George," Bob smiled. "You are having a very busy couple of weeks aren't you?"

"It keeps one busy," replied George.

Bob smiled back. "Well let's see the body," he said as he followed them both between the overlapping branches of the willow tree.

Chris and George kept quiet as they watched Bob examine the body.

"Well, there is no question in my mind how he died, but I still need to make an autopsy," Bob said as he stood up.

"How long has he been here?" Chris asked.

Bob fingered his chin. "Hard to say straight out, but I would put it at about two or three days."

"The time would be about right," Chris remarked.

"With what Chris?" Bob asked.

"A missing person," Chris answered.

"You know who he is?" Bob questioned.

"We were about to search him when you pulled up," Chris replied.

"Well get on with it then Chris," Bob scolded. "I'm a busy man."

George bent down, he searched the man's overcoat pockets, and found only a hanky which he put in a brown bag, he undid the overcoat, the man was wearing a three piece suit. George examined all the pockets, he found several articles in different pockets, then found the one main thing he was looking for, the man's wallet which he handed up to Chris.

Chris opened the wallet, he did not look at the contents within, for a card laid in a small transparent compartment of the wallet, told him all he wanted to know at the moment.

"It seems to be the missing person," Chris spoke to George and Bob who were both watching him. "The address is also right," Chris handed the wallet back to George, who put it in the brown bag.

"I will send you my report," Bob informed. "But it will be a while before I am able to do the autopsy I'm afraid, this is the third body you've given me in ten days," he smiled. "I do have many other patients in the Hospital."

"Well the body is yours now Bob, I am going to make a plaster cast of the heel print outside, then we will call at his address. Should you want to go, the constable will stay here until your wagon turns up."

"It would help," Bob replied. "The porters have their instructions, and should be here at any time," Bob replied closing his bag, and making for his motorbike.

Bob put his bag in the sidecar, took a pair of goggles from it which he put on after he was seated on the motorbike. "Not another one tomorrow Chris, I haven't got the time," he shouted as he started the engine which backfired, and moved off.

Chris opened his detective bag, and took out a small bag of plaster of Paris, plus a small bowl. "You're younger than me George, get me some water without falling in," Chris said with a smirk on his face.

George took his own bowl from his detective bag, and holding on to one of the branches, leaned over the edge of the bank, and scooped up some water, and took it to Chris who mixed the plaster of Paris with it, before spreading the mixture over two of the heel impressions.

"Let that dry for a while, then we can lift it, you got your camera in your bag, take a couple of shots of the body, and a couple of these prints I have not covered, while I speak to the constable," Chris said to George. "I've a good mind to give him a telling off allowing the finder to run off, but then, perhaps this is the first time he has experience a crime scene."

George smiled watching Chris approaching the constable.

Half hour later, Chris and George closed their detective bags, George had taken several snap shots of the body, and around the crime scene with his box camera, and Chris had lifted his plaster cast to his satisfaction. "We will get to his address now, no good hanging around here, the constable will stay he knows what is expected of him," Chris said.

A few moment later, Chris and George rode into Monks Road, a street of bay window houses, that looked directly onto the pavement. Number Six they found was about in the centre of the row on the right hand side. They parked their bikes by the kerb, and took off their cycle clips before approaching the front door and knocking. The door was opened by a well groomed woman of about forty, her dark hair was neatly combed into a bun at the back of the neck, she wore a long brown dress, with a matching short coat that was waist high. Her blouse was yellow, that frilled out at the neck.

Chris showed his police badge, as he introduced himself and George.

"Are you Mrs Paris?" Chris asked.

The woman nodded. "Have you found my husband?" she asked her face had the look of concern on it.

"I wonder Mrs Paris, may we come in for a moment?" Chris asked.

"Certainly Inspector," she replied opening the door for them to enter.

Taking off his trilby, and followed by George, Chris entered a wide hall way, the stairs faced him, and a passage ran along side the stairs towards the back of the house.

"Please," Mrs Paris said, having closed the front door. "Come into the front room," she offered opening a door on the left of the passage. "It's cosy in here, can I get you tea?" she asked.

Chris looked at George before declining the offer.

The front room was furnished for comfort, a wireless stood on top of a walnut sideboard, there were table and chairs to match, it was a large room, and two sofas used the rest of the room which was carpeted.

"Let's sit at the table," she offered.

When all was seated Chris looked at Mrs Paris, who seemed to have a puzzled expression.

"Have you found my husband?" she asked again.

"We have found a body," Chris said. "But we are not sure that it is your husband, the body will have to be identified before we are sure."

"Oh God," moaned Mrs Paris tears appearing in her eyes, as she put both hands to her mouth. "It can be my husband," she choked on her words.

"What was your husband wearing when he disappeared?" Chris asked.

Mrs Paris got up, and finding her handbag took a small hanky from it, she put it to her nose and sniffed, before returning to her seat. "My husband was a creature of habit," Mrs Paris started to tell them as she dabbed her eyes with her hanky, as she felt tears flowing. "He also liked all his clothes to match, on Monday, he left for work wearing a brown suit, with matching overcoat and trilby, oh God, are you sure it's my husband you found," she sniffed.

"The description you have given of his wear, matches the body we found I am afraid Mrs Paris," Chris replied feeling awkward, this was one piece of police work, that he did not like. "In his wallet we found a card with his name and address, that is how we came here."

"Well what was the cause of his death, he is a very fit man," Mrs Paris cried.

Chris looked at George, who had his notebook open, he could tell that George was feeling sorry for Mrs Paris.

"The body we found Mrs Paris, died we believe of a gunshot to the head," Chris replied."

"Good God," Mrs Paris cried pressing her hanky to her face.

"Where was he found Inspector?" Mrs Paris sobbed.

"By the iron bridge in the park," Chris replied. "The body was found by a runner, it was under a weeping willow tree."

"You are saying that my husband's body has been laying out there under a tree for almost four days," Mrs Paris sobbed uncontrollably.

"Have you got any children Mrs Paris?" George asked.

"I have a daughter," Mrs Paris replied.

"How old is your daughter?" George asked.

"My daughter is hardly fifteen years old," she replied.

"These questions has to be asked Mrs Paris," Chris remarked gently.

"Assuming that who you found is my husband Inspector," Mrs Paris replied.

"As I have already said in his wallet he had a card with his name and this address on," Chris continued gently. "Even without your identification, I am sure that the body we found could be that of your husband."

"Oh God," moaned Mrs Paris again covering half her face with her hanky. "Why would such a thing happened to him, he was not an aggressive man, very mild in fact."

"Mrs Paris would you be prepare to identify the body?" Chris asked.

"You are so sure Inspector, then I must," Mrs Paris replied with a sob in her voice.

"The body is now at the hospital," Chris carried on. "I will send a constable to inform you when it will be possible."

"What do I do until then?" Mrs Paris asked dabbing her eyes.

"I can call a doctor to give you something to make you sleep," Chris advised.

"Where is your daughter?" George butted in.

"My daughter is at home, she has had permission to do so from school since my husband disappeared, she is out at the moment," replied Mrs Paris sobbing.

"Then we will take our leave Mrs Paris," Chris said gently. "Should it be your husband, we will have to call again, it's routine."

Mrs Paris sniffed as the detectives got up to leave. "You are certain that it is my husband Inspector aren't you?"

"I'm afraid I'm unable to say for certain Mrs Paris, I never met your husband, though the description tallies, there are other possibilities," Chris replied.

"Name one," Mrs Paris asked as she opened the front door dabbing her eyes with her hanky.

"The simples one that comes to mind, is that the dead man could have stolen your husband's wallet."

Chris and George cycled back to the police station, Chris felt angry with himself.

Once in the office, after ditching his trilby Chris was on the phone.

"You can't question anyone without being a hundred percent sure about who you are talking about," Chris said to George as he was dialling. "I must have Mrs Paris identify the body before we proceed, we jumped the gun a bit."

"Chris Hardie here, Bob," Chris spoke onto the phone receiver. "I was wondering Bob, could Mrs Paris identify the body, there is not much I can do until."

After a few moments Chris put the phone down.

"Tomorrow morning," Chris said to George. "Bob will get the body presentable, I will send a constable to Mrs Paris, and George a job for you, I want you to be with her."

"That's OK," replied George.

361

Chapter Four

*C*hris entered his office as the Guildhall clock was striking nine, his sergeant George House was not there. Chris smiled to himself as he got rid of his trilby, knowing that George was probably on his way to Mrs Paris. Chris sat behind his desk, and took out his pipe, filled the bowl and lit it, blowing out clouds of smoke, he felt contented. He had seen Elizabeth outside her bank, and had got the customary kiss on the cheek. The desk sergeant entered with a hot cup of tea, spoiled his recollection of his meeting with Elizabeth.

"I do have other work to do, you know," the desk sergeant said with a smile on his face as he placed the tea in front of Chris.

"Leave your other work for a moment sergeant," Chris said. "Just run me through your routine on Mr Paris."

"Mr Paris is the owner of the Wool Factory in Lower Brook Street," replied the sergeant.

"Really," replied Chris.

"Yes he leaves his office at half past six punctually every night after the workers left, every night after leaving work he pops into the saloon bar of the Indian Arms, he drinks two pints and a whisky, then he leaves for home, he never alters his course, he walks Middle Brook Street into Park Avenue, through the park into Monks Road."

"I did the route this morning sergeant," Chris said. "He never alters his routine?"

"Not that I can find out," replied the sergeant.

"Does he meet anyone in the Indian Arms, or is he a loner?" Chris asked.

"The night he disappeared he sat with a Mr Roger Argue, I spoke to Mr Argue, he told me that his friend John had entered the pub at the usual time, and left the pub at the usual time, having had his usual drink."

"Seems straightforward," Chris remarked. "Perhaps this habit of his caused his death."

"I wouldn't know," replied the sergeant. "Mr Argue did say that Mr Paris seemed depressed on Monday night, something about his step daughter being resentful about him, but Mr Argue did not take too much notice, John Paris was pleasant to everyone, he was well liked."

"Do you know how many he employs?" Chris asked.

"As far as I can make out, it's about half dozen," answered the desk sergeant.

"Mr Paris always locks up?" Chris said verifying what the sergeant had told him.

"That was only an assumption," replied the sergeant.

"Thank you sergeant," Chris said with a grin. "I have your report here, so don't let me stop you doing all that work you said you have to do."

The morning was half way through when George entered the office, Chris who was studying all the reports in front of him looked up with a smile.

"How did it go?" he asked.

"Mrs Paris fainted as she recognised her husband," George replied. "Mr Harvey had laid him out, he looked like a man sleeping, he said he had not extracted the bullet yet, but would send it with his report."

"Really," Chris replied. "Is Mrs Paris here with you George?"

"Outside, with her daughter," replied George.

"Then we better have them in," Chris said.

"What about me Chris, do you want me at the interview?" George asked. "I do have a couple of calls to do."

Chris thought for a while. "The interview will only give us a picture of Mr Paris's life, I think, your job is very important, so if you don't mind, just show Mrs Paris and her daughter in, then off you go."

"You'll be here when I get back?" George asked.

"Unless I'm called out, heaven forbid," Chris replied with a smile.

George ushered Mrs Paris and her daughter into the office, then making excuses left.

Chris rose, and indicated a chair for Mrs Paris, and a chair for her daughter. Chris thought Mrs Paris looked every inch a lady with the she was wearing, nothing seemed out of place, he looked at the daughter, she was attractive teenager, but looked older that her fifteen years.

"Thank you for coming Mrs Paris," Chris started. "I am sorry, very sorry that you have identified the body."

Mrs Paris who was holding her hanky in a gloved hand, touched her nose with it.

"It was a shock Inspector, your sureness yesterday that it was my husband, prepare my mind a little, but seeing John laid out like that was still a terrible shock to my system."

"I'm sure it must have been," Chris replied. "Now that we are sure that the body is of your husband, are you prepared to answer a few questions, or shall we put it off for a day?"

"Let's get it over with, what I can tell you, I have no idea, but please ask," replied Mrs Paris dabbing her nose again.

Chris with pencil in his hand and paper in front of him leaned forward in his chair.

"Your husband's name was John, just John?" Chris asked.

"John Albert," replied Mrs Paris, as Chris started writing.

"Your full name Mrs Paris?" Chris asked.

"Linda," came the reply.

"Your daughter?" Chris asked.

"Rosemary," came the reply.

"Thank you Mrs Paris," Chris said looking up from his writing. "We are treating your husband's death as suspicious Mrs Paris, as he was shot."

Chris looked at Rosemary who was sitting, just looking at her mother, she showed no grief. "Suicide is not considered because of the nature of his fateful wound, and no gun was found, nor I might add was his trilby."

"That is obvious to me Inspector," Mrs Paris agreed.

"Because of this I do have to ask personal questions," Chris said gently. "I was wondering if you would like your daughter to leave the room?"

"My daughter can stay," Mrs Paris replied, without looking at her daughter. "My background will verify my breeding, I have nothing to hide."

Chris mind went back to the evening before, the small argument he had with Elizabeth regarding the middle classes, and wondered about Mrs Paris.

"I understand that your daughter was Mr Paris's step daughter," Chris said.

"That is correct Inspector, Rosemary is the daughter of my first husband," Mrs Paris replied.

Chris summed Mrs Paris up in his mind, he knew he would have to pump her for every bit of information, he had been very sorry for her over the ordeal of verifying her husband's body, but was now growing a little wary over her answers to his questions.

"Mrs Paris, I did explain that my questions might be personal," Chris said. "Could you give me a brief rundown regarding your husbands and your own relationship."

"I am unable to see what the relationship I had with my husbands have to do with this, with one of my husbands died of natural causes, and as you say, my second died in suspicious circumstances, however, my two husbands Mr Thomas Grice, and Mr John Paris, and I, grew up together. Both my husbands went to Peter Symonds for their education, I went to St Swithuns School for mine. On leaving school, both Thomas and John decided to go into the wool business, they rented this building in Lower Brook Street and they started the business. I became their business secretary, which I am still, and the business soon became a success. Both Thomas and John wanted to marry me, and in the end I chose Thomas, that was twenty years ago. We waited almost five years before deciding to expand our family, and we had Rosemary," Mrs Paris explained this time looking at her daughter with a weak smile.

"Middle class," thought Chris allowing his mind to travel back to the evening before with Elizabeth.

"My husband Mr Grice died some four years ago, with lung trouble, and after a respectable waiting period Mr Paris asked me to marry him, which I did some six month ago."

"Thank you Mrs Paris," Chris said. "That's a very clear picture, your first husband Mr Grice, he left you his half share of the firm?" Chris asked.

"If that question is relevant, then yes he did, I own forty nine percent."

"With the death of Mr Paris, you could become full owner?" Chris asked.

"I have no idea what is in John's Will Inspector, but I would say yes to that question."

Chris twisted his pencil between his fingers. "Tell me Mrs Paris, I am not very well acquainted with the wool trade, exactly what do your factory do?" Chris saw Mrs Paris's face light up, he knew this was one subject that she was pleased to discuss.

"Thomas or John would travel the county," she replied. "They would use their own judgement, and buy wool from the sheep's back, so to speak. With the delivery of the wool, it would go into lime pits and the skin and lime later separated from the wool, then it would be separated into different grades, the wool is separated into four main categories. The wool would then be sent off to different manufacturers with the grade of wool they needed. All our workers are very skilled, and all live locally."

"Really," Chris replied. "I did not know."

"Your relationship with both husbands were good then?" Chris asked.

"Perfect," Mrs Paris replied, the light having gone out of her face, and resulting to being pumped to answering questions.

"You realise Mrs Paris, I have to ask these questions, your husband was murdered by someone, I need to know who might have been an enemy," Chris said.

"Mr Paris was a well liked, and very polite man, I assure you he had no enemies," Mrs Paris replied.

"What about business rivals and such?" Chris asked.

"I would doubt that Inspector, we have no rivals in Winchester," Mrs Paris replied. "The wool bought by us is bought from auctions at fairs, markets, I would not think that would make enemies."

"What about personal friends?" Chris asked.

"John did not have much time to make friends, he must have had a few, naturally, when my first husband Thomas died, John had a double load to bear you might say," Mrs Paris dubbed her nose. "Apart from when he was travelling around the county, the only people he is likely to see would be his workforce, or perhaps representatives from manufacturers, no Inspector, John had no enemies."

"Unless we find that he was mistakenly shot for someone else, then he did have one person who wanted him dead," Chris replied warily.

"Your thinking might turn out to be the truth Inspector," Mrs Paris replied twisting in her chair. "In fact being mistaken for some other person would coincide with my own opinion."

"When you reported your husband missing Mrs Paris," Chris continued. "We did everything we could to find him, it seems your husband Mr Paris was a creature of habit, he left his office last Monday night as usual, he went for his drink as usual, and he left to go home as usual, finding him where we did tells us that his routine did not differ in any way, that of his usual routine."

"I must agree with you Inspector on that point, John was very habitual in everything he did."

Chris looked at Rosemary who seem to be taking very little interest in what was being said.

"Mrs Paris, would you tell me where were you on Monday night?" Chris asked.

"Really Inspector," replied Mrs Paris anger in her voice. "Where else would I have been but at home preparing my husband's dinner."

"I am sorry to have to ask you, but I must," Chris continued ignoring her outburst. "Can anyone verify that?"

"My daughter," Mrs Paris replied.

Chris looked at the daughter. "That's right, my mother was in all night, she rarely go out during the evenings," her daughter replied.

Chris smiled at the girl. "Thank you," he said.

"What time do your husband usually get home Mrs Paris?" Chris continued his questioning.

"Always by eight fifteen," Mrs Paris answered.

"You phoned the station reported your husband missing just before midnight last Monday Mrs Paris, why did you wait so long if your husband is always home by eight fifteen?" Chris asked.

Mrs Paris spread her hands over her lap. "Inspector, because for once my husband is late home, I do not automatically think he is missing, I suppose there could be many reasons for a person in my husband position to be late home," Mrs Paris replied without given examples.

"Do you or your husband own a handgun?"

"What would we need a handgun for Inspector," Mrs Paris said with alarm in her voice.

"I have to ask Mrs Paris," Chris replied. "I will take then that you do not, what about wellingtons boots Mrs Paris, do you own a pair?"

"I believe not Inspector," Mrs Paris replied with the toss of her head.

Chris looked at Mrs Paris, sitting in front of him, her back straight in the chair, keeping up an appearances. Chris wondered why she did not act normally, breakdown, cry, after all she had just identified her husband's body, who she had said, she had a perfect relationship with. Chris thought of the conversation he had with Elizabeth the evening before, and was incline to agree with her.

"I want to ask your daughter a couple of question," Chris said to her.

"I don't see the need, she is only a young girl," Mrs Paris responded.

Chris thought that there was many young men who would disagree with her, Rosemary was a very attractive young lady, he thought, had she not been in her school uniform, she could easily be taken for eighteen.

He looked at Rosemary. "Rosemary," Chris said, his voice gentle. "I am Detective Inspector Hardie, it is my job to find out, who is responsible for what happened to your stepfather, you would not mind me asking a few question would you?"

"Not at all," replied Rosemary. "But please don't treat me as a child, I have been listening, and I am aware that my stepfather was murdered."

"I'm sorry," Chris replied with a slight smile. "I can see that you are an intelligent attractive young lady."

"She is not a young lady Inspector, she is a young girl," Mrs Paris repeated herself.

Chris looked at Mrs Paris with a weak smile, without comment.

"You were of course close to your natural father?" Chris asked Rosemary and he saw her face lit up.

"Oh yes, he would play with me, buy me dollies, and would make me laugh, he would sing to me when he put me to bed, I thought him very romantic, I loved him."

"Really," Chris murmured. "He would sing to you?"

"Yes, he had a very nice voice," replied Rosemary.

"Did you get on with your stepfather, I mean you did not resent him, taking the place of your father?"

"He was never my father," Rosemary almost shouted. "But I never resented him, he made mother happy, but never me."

"Rosemary, your stepfather gave you everything, you are a very very privilege young girl," Mrs Paris butted in again.

Chris thought he had better change the subject before Mrs Paris objected to his questions, he had learnt that Rosemary was not too fond of her stepfather.

"Mrs Paris," Chris said politely. "Thank you for allowing your daughter to answer questions, what she has told me is very important, and I must thank her again," Chris said turning to Rosemary with a smile.

"Thank you young lady," he said to Rosemary with a smile, knowing the he had defied her mother by calling her a young lady.

"I am glad she have been of help Inspector, now is there anything else?"

"No Mrs Paris, thank you both for coming in."

"One last question Mrs Paris, do you ever travel abroad, on your holidays?"

"Inspector," replied Mrs Paris alarm at the question. "We have no time for holidays, it must be years since I had one, no we never travel abroad, Inspector do you suspect me of murdering my husband?" she asked.

Chris clenched his hands, resting on his desk. "Mrs Paris," he said. "Where there is a murder, everyone is a suspect at the beginning, murders are normally the action of a family relation or a friend. Unless a murder is carried out by a person that has been paid, or for some other reason, it is rare for one stranger to kill another unless by accident. My questions to you Mrs Paris were to enable me to eliminate you from being a suspect, I complimented you, having the intelligence of knowing that," Chris smiled inside as he saw colour come to her cheeks knowing that he had taken her down from her high horse.

"Before you go Mrs Paris," Chris added. "I have the contents of your husband's pockets etc, I have been through them, I can find nothing that might have a bearing on his death, I will send a constable with them to your home."

Mrs Paris nodded, Chris watched as Mrs Paris and her daughter left the room, Rosemary allowed her mother to leave first, and as she followed, she turned and smiled at Chris.

Chris sat writing his notes when George appeared.

"How did it go with Mrs Paris?"

"I had to pump her to get answers," Chris replied.

Chris then enlighten George on his interview with Mrs Paris.

"We could do without this case, it's come too quick on the tail of our last one, there are only two of us, perhaps it's time to have another chap in this office."

George shrugged. "It's the paper reports that take the time."

*I*t was Saturday with George on his day off. Chris sat at his desk writing reports, he cursed the nib pen, every so often it would make a blot on the report, as without thought he would dig the pen into the ink too deep, his thoughts being with the present case, he thought of Mrs Paris, it was proving a difficult case, he would have to go to the factory to speak to the workers, but that would have to be on Monday, he did not expect a lot employer do not usually converse with their workers about their worries. He opened the files, and started to study when the desk sergeant came in without knocking.

"I have a young man outside Sir," he spoke respectfully for once. "He found a trilby, with a gun inside."

Chris stood. "Get him in here then sergeant," Chris ordered excitedly.

The desk sergeant ushered in a young man, perhaps about twenty, dressed in a grey pin stripe suit, wearing a tie, that Chris thought did not match.

"Mr Simpson," said the desk sergeant as he left closing the door behind him.

Chris offered his hand, and then offered him the interview chair.

"I am Detective Inspector Hardie," Chris introduced himself. "I take it you have found a gun?"

"That's right Sir," Mr Simpson replied respectfully, placing a wrapped parcel on the desk.

Chris looked at the parcel, and felt an instinct to open it, but held himself back.

"Where did you find this parcel Mr Simpson?" Chris asked, his eyes still on the parcel.

Mr Simpson smiled. "I was taking my girlfriend for a boat ride around the park, I have been in the boats several times, I like them."

"Yes they must be enjoyable for those who like rowing," Chris said unhurriedly. "But please continue."

"Well as I said I took my girlfriend for a boat ride, perhaps I was looking at her too much, she was sitting facing me as I rowed, anyway, I found myself almost hitting the riverbank, I had strayed from the middle of the river, the riverbank is shallow with reeds, and as I put in my oar in order to push myself away from the riverbank, I dislodged from the shallows, what looked like a very large cash bag, after I got it aboard, I found that it was a trilby that had been tied around the brim."

"You untied it then?" Chris asked.

"Oh yes," replied Mr Simpson with a smile. "It was kind of heavy I wondered what it could be."

Chris smiled at him, knowing that it was a very natural thing to do. "Did you touch the gun?" Chris asked.

"Yes I did, I have never held a gun before," he admitted.

Chris took the parcel and unwrapped it, and found an out of shape trilby tied up around the brim. "You retied it then?" Chris asked.

"Yes," replied Mr Simpson, I showed the boat owner what I had, he told me to bring it straight to you which I have done."

"You did right Mr Simpson," Chris replied untying the string.

Inside Chris saw a blood soaked cloth, he opened his desk drawer, and took several sheets of paper from it, which he laid in a square upon one side of his desk, then holding the cloth between two fingers, placed the cloth upon the paper. Underneath the clothe, Chris saw the gun, and a heavy flint, taking his pencil, he poked it into the barrel of the gun and lifted it out, putting it on the paper beside the clothe. He did not touch the flint.

"Your girlfriend Mr Simpson, did she touch the gun?"

"Oh no Sir, she was much too frightened," he replied.

"I will need your fingerprints before you leave Mr Simpson, so that I can eliminate should there be others on it," Chris said, feeling excitement.

"That's OK Sir," Mr Simpson replied. "Am I in trouble for touching it?"

"No Mr Simpson, but it would have been better had you not touched it," Chris replied with a smile. "But I would probably have touched it myself if I had found it."

Chris looked for his detective bag, and found it in the corner behind his desk, he took from it a ink pad and a card.

"Now Mr Simpson, if you will allow me, I will take your fingerprints," Chris said as he rose and walked around to where Mr Simpson was sitting.

"Now Mr Simpson," Chris said. "If I understand it you were rowing and looking at your girlfriend, that tells me you were facing away from the direction in which you were going, what side of the river were you on?"

"I had just hired the boat, we were on the left hand side," Mr Simpson replied.

"That means you passed under the iron bridge," Chris replied.

"That's right inspector, my girlfriend giggled as we had to bend our heads," Mr Simpson smiled.

"After you had passed under the iron bridge, how far had you gone before you saw this object in the water?" Chris asked.

"Up to the bend," Mr Simpson replied. "It was my fault, I was watching Hayley that's my girlfriend, licking her ice cream, and drinking her Tizer, I forgot I had to make a right turn, when I realised, I suppose I panicked a little, and in the event, I turned to quickly, not taking a full turn so to speak, and so I hit the riverbank."

"Then allowing for the way you were facing, you hit the left hand side of the riverbank," Chris remarked.

"That's right," replied Mr Simpson. "And it was then while I was struggling with my oars that I saw it."

Chris thanked Mr Simpson, as he spoke into the receiver of the phone.

"Sergeant," he said into the receiver. "Will you come in a moment."

"You will need to wash your hands," Chris said to Mr Simpson as he replaced the receiver.

"Sergeant," Chris said as the desk sergeant entered. "Take Mr Simpson to the wash room, he needs to wash his hands, Mr Simpson will you give the sergeant your address, just in case I need to talk to you again."

Mr Simpson nodded as he rose.

"Mr Simpson," Chris said as he was following the sergeant. "Thank you very much, this may be very important," he said indicating the trilby on his desk. "It was perhaps a hundred to one shot, anyone finding it."

Mr Simpson smiled leaving the office.

Chris got busy powdering the gun, but as he expected he found only one set of prints on it, which at first study seem to be those of Mr Simpson, he looked up as the desk sergeant re entered.

"The address of Mr Simpson," he said putting a slip of paper before Chris.

"Thank you sergeant," Chris replied. "Don't touch, but where would one buy a gun like this, you know the area better than me," Chris asked touching the gun with his pencil.

"Looks like a handbag gun to me," replied the sergeant bending over and looking at the gun. "Just a guess, but Southampton might be a good place."

"I've no idea of the calibre," Chris replied. "You could be right, what one might call a woman's gun."

"The clothe looks covered in blood," remarked the sergeant.

"Yes," Chris replied. "Mr Paris had little blood on him, you had to look before you saw the wound behind his ear, as though someone had cleaned him up, I don't understand why?"

"In the dark as well," the desk sergeant remarked. "Any fingerprints on the gun?" the sergeant asked.

"Only Mr Simpson's as far as I can tell," Chris replied. "But then no one today leaves fingerprints."

"Do we have any book or chart on handguns Sergeant?" Chris asked.

"We have somewhere," the sergeant replied. "Hang on I'll have a look," he said going out of the office.

Chris studied the gun, it was indeed very small, he had never seen one before, he picked the gun up, having tested it for fingerprints, and studied the chamber, it fired six shots, but the chamber was empty, and only one shot had been fired killing Mr Paris, where were the other bullets he wondered, or was the murderer so sure that he only needed one shot.

The desk sergeant entered carrying a small book. "This book covers all handguns available in this country," he said placing the book before Chris.

Chris studied each page with the gun, and finally closed the book. "Well it's not in the book," Chris said looking at the sergeant. "Is this book up dated?"

"Two years old," replied the sergeant.

"Well it's not in here, must be an illegal," Chris said as he taking out his pocket watch. "If I go now I might just catch the gunsmith in Southgate street, I'm off now, Sergeant House will be in tomorrow, I'll leave a note for him."

"Anything I can do?" asked the desk sergeant.

"It's Saturday sergeant," Chris replied. "Not a lot anyone can do with half of the places closed for the weekend."

Chapter Six

Chris entered the Rising Sun, he was late, he felt the warmth of the large log fire but was unable to see it, as the area was crowded with men drinking, smoking, and in general making a noise. He looked to the right and saw Ron looking at him smiling. Chris went to him taking off his top coat as he did. "Cold out there," he said folding the coat and putting it on a spare chair, then followed it with his trilby.

"I've put one in for you Chris," Ron informed him.

Chris smiled his thanks, then went to the counter where the smiling Alfie was already pumping his pump.

"Crowded a bit this morning," Chris said to Alfie as he watched his pint filling.

"Yes," replied Alfie. "It's usually the same Sunday mornings, darts, they like playing dart," Alfie smiled as he put the pint in front of Chris. "They only have two hours Sunday dinner times, they will be gone by two."

"Perhaps a good time for their wives and mothers who are cooking their Sunday roast," Chris answered.

"Perhaps," replied Alfie. "These men work long hours six days a week, perhaps they deserve a break."

"I think we both scored a point there Alfie," Chris remarked taking his pint, and sitting with Ron.

"Cheers," Chris said taking a sip, before putting his glass down. "I'm a bit late, walked down with the march parade, another lot going to France I expect."

"I thought I heard a band," Ron said. "But over this din."

"How are our ladies?" Chris asked.

Ron grinned. "They are OK, slaving away getting our roast."

"Do you think wives mind if their men go out on a Sunday dinner time for a drink?" Chris asked a bit shyly, seeing a grin appear on Ron's face.

"Getting worried already Chris," Ron laughed.

"No just a thought," replied Chris seriously.

"Well I suppose some do," Ron replied afterthought. "Especially if the man has no work, and the wife is struggling to keep food on the table, and that would go double if they have children. Some I expect realise that they will never change their husbands ways, and just accept it, then you get wives like my Olive," continued Ron a broad smile on his face. "She more or less orders me to go out because I get under her feet."

"You are very happy with Olive aren't you?" Chris remarked taking another drink.

"Chris," Ron replied his face serious. "I love my wife dearly, give my life for her, but if I was to lose my Olive, I would not want to live, you know that I am fifteen years older than Olive, so the chances are that I shall go first, and that is my wish," Ron picked up his pint and drank.

Chris fell silent, and felt a little guilty.

"Married life is what you make it," Ron continued putting his glass down. "Olive was the daughter of the bank manager where I began work, when I first met her she was about nineteen, and I was thirty five, single and living in lodgings just as you are, my parents had both died. During the next three years I rose to deputy manager, and I saw more of Olive, for me it was love at first sight, Olive told me it had been the same with her, but of course in those days she could not reveal her feelings for me to her parents," Ron said with a smile. "Her father the manager might have sacked me."

"Go on Ron, how did you manage to marry?" Chris urged interested.

"Well," Ron replied spreading his hands. "Olive's father retired, and I became manager, I was a bit young for the job, but with Olive's father recommending me, I got the job at thirty nine."

"Is that young for the manager's job?" Chris asked.

"Oh yes," Ron replied. "About ten years too young."

"Well go on," Chris said.

"During the time I was deputy, I was invited many times to his house for a meal, and at times I was left alone with Olive, and during those times I told Olive of my feelings for her, and no one was more surprised than I was when she said she returned my feelings, by this time Olive was almost twenty five. When I became manager, I bucked up courage, and asked her parents if I could marry their daughter, and to my surprise, they agreed without any argument," Ron grinned. "That was back in 1880, and her father knew that I had a job for life and how good it was, after all I had taken over from him."

"That's a lovely story Ron," Chris remarked. "I fell in love with Elizabeth the first time I saw her, by the way, where did your in-laws live?"

"Where I'm living now," Ron replied.

"That must have been a great help to you both," Chris replied. "But when you think about it, there is no gain without pain, Olive losing her parents."

"That is life Chris," Ron said finishing his pint. "We all have to go sooner or later, Olive still have her parents memories in the house, which I hope you and Elizabeth will have when our times come."

"I don't want to hear that," Chris said getting up. "I get another in, we have time before we go."

Ron allowed Chris to go first up the path to the front door, Elizabeth was standing there with the door open, in her ankle length dress of purple, Chris thought she looked the most beautiful girl in the world, and his love for her flooded him.

"Just in time," she said already unbuttoning his overcoat, then planted a kiss on his cheek. Chris saw Olive appear.

"I hope my Ron is sober?" Olive said teasingly.

Chris thought how lovely it was, when either of them spoke each others name, it was always preceded by My.

"Yes he is," Chris replied. "I have never seen him any different."

"Well come along," Olive said as she was about to disappear into the kitchen. "Dinner is on the table."

Olive had overloaded the plates with her Sunday roast, and Chris wondered if he would be able to eat the lot, but intended to try.

"I saw another parade of soldiers this morning," Chris opened the dinnertime conversation.

"Yes he was late coming in," Ron said with a smile. "I was thinking I would have to drink his pint."

"No chance of that Ron," Chris replied. "I like a march with the band in front."

"Those poor boys,'" Olive said with a sad look. "What must their parents or wives feel?"

"They are all volunteers Olive, they go with their own free will," Ron replied.

"I know, but I can't help to feel for them, they are brave lads," Olive said.

"I'm glad you're not going to fight," Elizabeth looked at Chris. "I wouldn't be able to sleep with you out there in danger," she said.

"My feet stopped me," Chris replied. "Otherwise I would already be out there, perhaps with Inspector Noal, my biggest worry was, could I take the discipline, would it be too strict?"

"Your job must have a certain discipline," Ron remarked.

"Mainly of the mind," Chris answered.

"That's where discipline starts surely," Ron replied.

"I agree Ron," Chris answered. "But the army discipline is different, in order to train us, I didn't have a sergeant calling me names that would have insulted my parents, and that kind of discipline can arouse anger, even hate."

"It's the nurses I fell sorry for, you see them scrubbing floors, washing bed pans, always fearing the sister, who in turn is always fearing the matron," Olive remarked.

"But being a nurse or a doctor mum is a calling, they want to do the job," Elizabeth replied. "Their wages and hours, and the strict routine, they don't care about, they just want to tend people who are ill, it wouldn't be any good for me doing nursing, I'm not made that way."

"Perhaps discipline is important in a hospital, the staff is dealing with people's lives, one mistake, and a patient could die," Chris replied. "That's why sisters and matrons are strict, but I doubt if there is much name calling?"

"Elizabeth is right, to do anything medically must be a calling, I would hate to think of a time when people enter the medical profession for money, then we will see a difference in the service," Ron remarked pushing his plate away from him. "Anyway Olive, that was a big dinner, I'm full, so no sweet for me."

"I'm afraid Olive, I agree with Ron, I have had too much, it was lovely," Chris pushed his plate a little away from him.

"Thank Elizabeth, she did the roast, while I did the bedrooms," Olive said with a smile.

Chris looked at Elizabeth, surprise showing on his face, Elizabeth giggled and put her hand on his arm. "I'm not just a pretty face," she smiled a twinkle in her eyes.

While Olive and Elizabeth cleared the table, Ron made for his easy chair, and within a few moments was fast asleep.

"You and Chris go into the front room, listen to the radio, I wash these things up, then I'll sit by Ron and read his paper, it's the only chance I get to read it when he's asleep," Olive offered.

Chris sat on the sofa, as Elizabeth switched on the radio, very low, then she snuggled up against Chris, and tucked her legs up under her.

Tea time came, but they both refused any, Chris found himself relaxed, he did not think of the case he was on, with his arm around Elizabeth, he was happy, as the radio playing light music. He felt the warmth of Elizabeth close to him, then looked down in mild surprise as he heard a gentle snoring, Elizabeth snuggled in his arms had fallen asleep, Chris smiled to himself, as he felt his own eyes closing.

Chapter Seven

Chris entered the office on the Monday morning, and found George already at his desk.

"You look bright and breezy," George remarked as he entered.

"I feel as though I have been on holiday," Chris replied with a smile. "I was with Elizabeth yesterday, I felt so relax, that believe it or not, I fell asleep on the sofa," Chris said hanging up his trilby, and crossing to his desk.

"That was a waste of time then," George replied.

"Not really, Elizabeth did the same," Chris replied. "I learnt one thing however, I shall be marrying a great cook, she cooked the dinner."

"I thought girls were trained to do so, don't they go into service when they leave school?" George asked.

"Elizabeth didn't," Chris replied taking files from his drawer, and placing them before him. "Elizabeth went straight into the bank."

"Lucky then," George remarked.

"I suppose," Chris answered. "What sort of day did you have yesterday?"

"Quiet," George replied. "I managed to get my paper work under control, I went to my lodgings for dinner, my landlady had a roast ready for me. I got your note, it was a lucky find the rower, though it don't tell us much, no fingerprints."

"You did look at the inside band of the trilby, the letters JP was embossed in the band, tells us that the trilby belonged to Mr John Paris," Chris replied.

"Where it was found puzzles me," George replied. "Surely who ever it was would not have just dropped it near the river edge."

Chris smiled. "Unforeseen mistakes George, the one reason how murderers are caught."

"How so?" George replied wondering.

"Well the murderer wanted to get rid of the gun, the park river is a mucky river, what better place to get rid of it, but it must have been very dark, he walked along the riverbank on the left hand side, when he came to the bend, which is the widest part, he threw the trilby in weighted down by a flint and the gun, it should have disappeared into the mud below, in the centre, but as I said, it was dark, he must have over threw it, as it landed close to the riverbank on the other side."

"I see," replied George imagining. "By the way, I did see the landlord of the Indian Arms, this Mr Roger Argue is in the saloon bar every evening from six until closing time on weekdays, a regular you might say."

"Glad to hear it," Chris replied settling into his chair, and taking out his pipe lit it, I'll call and see him tonight."

"I thought he had already been interviewed by uniform," George replied. "Do you think he has any connection with the case?"

"Not really," Chris replied as he puffed on his pipe, he felt a feeling of sadness as he spoke.

"Inspector Noal and myself dealt with two cases just before he went to war," Chris continued, sitting up and placing his pipe in the ashtray. "One of them was a rape case, that we knew was connected with the shoe trade, anyway to cut a long story short, I called on one of the two shoe makers in Winchester, I questioned him, and he willingly gave all correct answers. Inspector Noal later was to call upon him, he asked the same questions that I did, but his answers to the odd question that I did not ask, led us to the rapist."

Chris took his pipe from the ashtray, Elizabeth was on his mind, he puffed in silence.

"About the gun, what make is it?" George asked.

Chris took his pipe out of his mouth and smiled.

"It's called at Baby Browning 25ACP 6,35 calibre," Chris replied.

George looked at Chris with surprise on his face. "You are into guns then?" he asked.

"No not really," Chris replied smiling. "I went to the gunsmith shop on my way home Saturday night, he was closed but he lives above the shop, he was very willing."

"Well the police hold all serial numbers of gun owners," George replied.

"I know, but there is no licence for the import of this gun into this country, it is used on the continent, it's made in Belgium," Chris told him. "Perhaps who ever brought this gun into this country, did not register it with the police."

"So we are looking for someone who have been abroad then?" George asked.

"Perhaps," Chris replied thoughtfully as he puffed on his pipe. "But to cover ourselves, I will get Sergeant Bloom to phone police stations around, to see if it had been registered."

Sergeant Bloom knocked and entered carrying two cups of tea. "Thought you might welcome a cuppa," he smiled placing a cup before both of them.

"You thought right sergeant," Chris replied. "Sergeant," Chris said stopping him as he was about to leave. "I want you to phone around police stations, Southampton, Andover, Basingstoke etc, see if they have a Baby Browning handgun registered with this serial number," Chris said handing sergeant Bloom a piece of paper with the number on.

"Will get on to it straight away Sir," sergeant Bloom replied as he left the office.

Chris smiled as he left. "What a difference in attitude between him and Sergeant Dawkins," he said to George.

"Both very helpful though," George replied.

Chapter Eight

*C*hris tidied his files on the cases in hand, and arranged them neatly to one side of his desk, he looked at his watch, it was almost six pm, he knew he had missed Elizabeth, but was unable to help it, he needed to see Roger Argue at the Indian Arms. Chris took out his pipe, and lit it leaning back in his chair, he had a lot of bits and pieces on his mind, the murder of John Paris was a puzzle, he had no idea, or even clues as to who killed him.

Sergeant Bloom entered the office.

"Glad I caught you before you left Sir," the sergeant said. "I have phoned all around the county, no luck I'm afraid, some had guns and rifles registered with them, no one had a Baby Browning, none of them knew of the gun."

"Thank you Sergeant," Chris replied disappointed yet it was what he expected.

"It's what I expected, there is no licence for it to be imported into this country, the only Baby Browning in this country has to be brought in by travellers, and I doubt if any of them are registered."

Sergeant Bloom smiled. "Anything else I can do?"

"Not at the moment Sergeant," Chris replied knocking his pipe out in the ashtray.

"I have to see a man now, but I know you are around should I need you," Chris replied.

Sergeant Bloom smiled and left the office.

Chris got up and went to the hat stand, and without rush put on his overcoat and trilby. He left the Police Station, it was almost quarter past six, and crossed the Broadway to the Indian Arms. He went under the arch that lead to the rear of the pub, and entered the saloon door on the left. At a glance he saw only one man in the bar, sitting at a small table to the right of the bar. He walked to the small opening used as the bar, at which the landlord was waiting with a smile on his face.

"Good evening Sir," he said as Chris approached. "What can I get you?"

"I'll have a bitter please," Chris replied.

The landlord brought his pint, and Chris paid his twopence. "Would a Mr Roger Argue be in this evening?" Chris asked, his voice low.

"He's the only one in the bar apart from you," the landlord replied taking the money.

Chris smiled, and taking his pint, turned towards the man sitting at the table.

"Are you Mr Roger Argue?" Chris asked the man as he stood in front of him holding his pint.

The man looked up, Chris saw that the man was clean shaven, he looked about the same age as Mr Paris, his hair was well groomed, and the greying around the temples gave him a distinguish look.

"That's me," he said.

"I am Detective Inspector Hardie, of Winchester CID, I wonder would you mind me asking a few questions about Mr John Paris."

Roger indicated the empty chair at the table. "I always thought you chaps always interviewed people in their homes or at the station," he said as he watched Chris sit and placed his pint before him.

"We do normally," Chris replied taking a sip of his bitter. "But I did not really want to upset your wife, I knew you came in here, and crossing the road for a pint is no hardship to either of us."

Roger smiled as he picked up his pint. "Thoughtful of you Inspector," he replied. "But although I welcome your company, I am afraid I told your sergeant everything I know."

"Yes thank you I know that Mr Argue, but then it was a missing person's case, it is now a murder enquiry."

Roger shifted in his chair. "Yes that was a surprise to me, I had been drinking with him that night, as you know, when I heard about it, you could have knocked me down with a feather."

"I am afraid that you are also the last person that we know of that spoke to him," Chris commented.

"Well someone else must have spoken to him after he left here, what I hear he was killed while I was still here drinking a pint."

"We put his death down as around eight or eight fifteen that night," Chris said.

"Well there you are then, very rarely I do leave before closing time," replied Roger.

Chris smiled. "You say that as if you need a alibi Mr Argue."

Roger shrugged. "Just stating a fact," he murmured.

Chris took another drink of his pint, before speaking again. "Mr Argue," Chris began. "An investigation into a murder, is very different to that of a missing person, what you told the police officer that spoke to you, was accepted, and I am sure it was as you remember, but sometimes a person knows that which can be very helpful without realising."

"Ask me anything you need to Inspector," Roger said with a weak smile on his face. "I would dearly love to help catch John's murderer, believe me."

"Thank you Mr Argue," Chris replied. "Just tell me the conversation you had with Mr Paris that night, also was he looking happy or depressed?"

"He was not looking happy," Roger replied. "He looked down in the dumps, I asked him what was wrong, and he told me business worries, I then asked him how his beautiful wife and step daughter was," Roger continued with a smile on his face. "He told me that the step daughter was causing some concern, he said she knew more about sex than he did, and blamed the school she was attending."

Chris smiled. "There you go Mr Argue, you did not tell the police officer that."

Roger hesitated. "Well when he spoke to me, I could not really believe that John was missing, I was sure he would turn up, and what John told me about his step daughter was kind of personal."

"Do you know Mrs Paris and her daughter?" Chris asked.

"Not really," Roger replied. "They are not in my circle of friends, I am just a hair barber, I only met John because he has his hair trimmed in my shop, we do see each other in here most nights, if we are both without company, we sit together."

"I see, what did you make of his remark regarding his step daughter?" Chris asked wondering why if they were not close friends, Mr Paris would share his personal business with him

"Well it jumps into your mind don't it, she was having sex, and she was only fifteen, John did say it was a concern to his wife who had gone cold on him," Roger replied.

"Is there anything else you can think of?" Chris asked.

"Not really, after that was said, we spoke about this and that, John had his two usual pints and a whisky, and left," Roger said.

Chris finished his pint. "Thank you Mr Argue, I think you may have been helpful, now allow me to buy you a drink, I like at least two myself."

Chris went to the counter, and ordered the drinks, then placing them on the table.

"You are in every night Mr Argue?" Chris asked.

"Apart from when I am on holiday," Roger replied taking a sip of his pint. "I do not come in weekends, Saturday I take the wife out for a meal, and Sunday of course is Church day."

Chris smiled. "Where do you take your holidays, I haven't been on one for two years," he said.

"I don't suppose you can go on holiday should you be on a case," Roger remarked.

"That's true," Chris replied. "Sometimes cases take months and months to solve, other just don't get solved."

Roger feeling more relaxed, smiled. "Are you married Inspector?" he asked.

"Will be next April," Chris replied with a smile thinking of Elizabeth.

"Take my advice, take your bride to France, it's a lovely place to spend a honeymoon, I always go to France every year for two weeks."

"Really," Chris replied.

"Yes Paris is the place," Roger replied smiling all over his face. "I've never seen so many beautiful women as there are in France, but I have to be careful noticing them," Roger winked. "Wives don't like that."

"I'm sure," Chris replied, finishing his drink. "How did you become a barber, did you take an apprenticeship?" Chris asked.

Roger smiled. "Oh no, I picked it up during the Boer War, I started to cut my mate's hair, and as I became more skilled all generals, officers, and soldiers started to come to me to have their haircut. When I left the army, I decided to carry on as a barber, you see I was a batman, and had plenty of time to myself, when I could practice."

"Well I'm afraid I will have to leave you Mr Argue, work to do you know, thank you for being so cooperative, appreciate it," Chris smiled.

"Won't you allow me to buy you a drink?" Roger asked.

"No thank you Mr Argue, I have to keep a clear head, two pints is just right for me," Chris replied. "Just one thing to clear, you are sure you never met Mrs Paris and her daughter?"

"Afraid not," Roger smiled.

"Goodnight Mr Argue and thank you," Chris said standing up and offering his hand. "I have to go."

"Just before you go Inspector, just how was John killed?" Roger asked.

"He was shot in the head by a handgun," Chris replied. "Goodnight and thank you Mr Argue."

Chris felt the cold as he left the pub, he pulled up his collar as he made his way up the high street, his mind twisting and turning all that Mr Argue had said to him, and to him it did not seem to add up.

Chapter Nine

Elizabeth was standing outside her bank, when Chris approached her, it was a chilly morning and Chris saw that Elizabeth was well wrapped up, she smiled and kissed his cheek, then started to button his overcoat, that he had left undone.

"You must keep warm darling," she scolded. "You need a good woman looking after you."

"I got one," Chris replied with a smile.

"I missed you last night," Elizabeth said satisfied that his overcoat was buttoned up.

"Did you have to work late?" she asked.

"I went to the pub," Chris replied.

"Oh," replied Elizabeth disappointment showing on her face.

"Police work," replied Chris smiling. "I also did work in the office, until gone six," he added.

"Oh Chris," Elizabeth remarked holding on to his arm. "I did miss you, will I be seeing you tonight?"

"I can't promise very much this week darling," Chris said looking down at her and wishing he did not have to leave her. "I have this murder on my hands, that I cannot seem to get into."

"I understand Chris," Elizabeth said faking a sulk. "I will be glad when we are married, so that I can cook you a breakfast and that."

"I like the sound of, and that," Chris said laughing. "I can hardly wait."

"You are naughty Chris, I did not mean what you are thinking," she teased.

"Never mind," Chris replied. "I have you, I can't expect to have everything."

"Don't be like that darling," Elizabeth giggled. "I shall give you everything you want, once we are married."

"I know darling," Chris replied looking down at her and becoming serious. "I will try to see you, but the next two days will be hard for me, but cheer up, I shall have Saturday off, we can go to Southampton if you like."

"I would love that darling," Elizabeth smiled. "But I must go in now, I'll see you when I see you," she said, planting another kiss on his cheek. "Keep warm," she ordered as she entered the bank.

George was at his desk when Chris entered the office.

"How did it go last night?" George asked watching Chris taking off his overcoat and trilby, which he placed on the hat stand.

"Good, I saw Mr Argue last night," Chris replied going to his desk. "A lot of doubts are in my mind, I have been over and over our conversation, and I am still full of doubts," Chris replied.

"What is he like?" George asked.

"A likeable chap," Chris replied. "It's just what he told me that makes me have doubts of the truth."

"Run it pass me, see what I think," George said.

Chris took out his pipe and lit it, he blew out a cloud of smoke before he spoke.

"If you had not met a man's wife or daughter," Chris asked, taking his pipe from his mouth. "Would you ask the man, how his beautiful wife and step daughter was?"

George did not take time to think. "I would probably ask, how his wife and step daughter was, or how was the family," George replied. "Is that the cause of your doubts?"

"No," Chris replied after taking another suck on his pipe.

"He also told me that the step daughter was causing concern to her mother, then Mr Paris had said to him that his step daughter knew more about sex than he did, and blamed the school she was attending."

"So," replied George.

"I was just wondering what that statement meant, I mean what made Mr Paris to think that way about his step daughter."

"She is a privilege girl," George said. "Perhaps she has a dirty mouth, perhaps that was her mother's concern."

"Mr Paris it seems also told Mr Argue that his wife was cold towards him and thought the daughter resented him," Chris continued. "Why would she turn cold even if the daughter resented him, Mrs Paris told us herself that her marriage was perfect."

"Did Mr Argue say anything else?" George asked.

"What I have said was the main conversation, but I did get out of him that he spent his holidays in France, the way he said it, I realized that he was a ladies man, however he could have brought in that handgun."

"I can understand your mind Chris, a lot of assumptions can be assumed out of the conversation you had, but can we get proof of any of it?" George said shrugging his shoulders.

"Mr Argue is a barber, his shop is in Upper Brook Street, can you see what you can dig up on him George, he could not have killed Mr Paris, he was in the Indian Arms at the time, anyway Mr Paris left before him, but there might be a connection?"

Before George could answer, the phone rang, Chris laid his pipe in the ashtray, then lifted the receiver, without saying anything, he listened to what the desk sergeant was saying.

"Put him through then sergeant," Chris finally said.

"Good morning doctor, I am Detective Inspector Hardie, you have a problem?"

"Only with a call I went out to this morning," came the reply. "I was called to Mr Argue's barber shop an hour ago, I found Mr Argue in one of his haircutting chairs, I am afraid he was dead."

Chris felt a shock, he looked at George, before answering.

"How did he die doctor?" Chris asked.

"That's why I am phoning you Inspector, he died of a gun wound."

Chris moaned to himself. "Did you move him doctor?" he asked.

"Well I did examine him," came the reply.

"Which end of Upper Brook Street is the shop?" Chris asked.

"The town end," came the reply. "A few yards in from Dolcis Shoe shop, I have told Mrs Argue that I shall have to phone you, so she will be expecting you, should she be in a bad way, give me a call, I had to leave I have other emergencies to call upon."

"Thank you very much doctor, I might want to talk to you again," Chris said.

"I have given my number to your sergeant," doctor Foster replied as he put the phone down.

Chris replaced his receiver and looked at George.

"No need to check on Mr Argue George," Chris said. "He's been found dead in his shop, that was a doctor Foster on the phone who attended him, we better make haste,

Mrs Argue it seems have been left on her own, I hope she don't touch anything."

Chris grabbed his overcoat and trilby, and followed by George hurried out of the office. "You know where we are," Chris said to sergeant Bloom as they passed.

"Mr Harvey has already been notified," sergeant Bloom spoke loudly as the two detectives hurried from the police station.

Mr Argue's barber shop was only a five minute walk from the police station. The detectives mounted the two steps that led to the shop door, it opened with the sound of a bell ringing. Mrs Argue was sitting in an ordinary chair, looking at her husband who was in the barber's chair, laid back as though he was being shaved, she did not move as they entered.

Chris looked around the shop, he assumed rightly, that the shop door was the only entrance to the house beyond, the shop itself was a largest room on the street side, dominated by one large window and the front door. A curtain was hung across the window that covered the lower two feet of the window, that kept the gaze of passers-by from looking in. Behind the barbers chair was a simple sink, above which was shelves with several shaving mugs displayed, by the side of the sink was a small cupboard, on which several combs, scissors, cut-throat razors etc. laid, several chairs stood in a row on the side of the front door.

Mrs Argue turned her head and looked at Chris as he stood before her, she was a woman of about forty, one side of her hair was falling over her cheeks, Chris noticed that she had a rosy complexion, and at first glance thought that she was a pleasant type of woman. Chris noticed that she had not been crying, yet a sadness was showing in her eyes.

"I am Detective Inspector Hardie, and my colleague Detective Sergeant House," Chris spoke gently.

Apart from the sadness in her face, Mrs Argue showed no other emotion.

"I will go to the back," she said. "No doubt you will want to ask questions, and you can be sure that I will," Mrs Argue said as she stood up, and moved to a door at the rear of the shop. "Can I make you tea?" she asked as she opened the rear door.

"No thank you Mrs Argue," Chris replied. "I am expecting the Police Surgeon in a few moments, he will want to see you."

Mrs Argue gave a faint smile and disappeared through the door.

Chris looked at George. "This is definite unexpected," he said. "Who would have thought," he said spreading his arms. "I was only speaking to him last night."

"Shot behind the ear," George said as he studied the body. "Same as Mr Paris, no blood apart from that on his shoulder."

"Probably, the doctor is responsible," Chris replied. "He did examine the body."

Chris looked at the lino floor, which was clean apart from a splatter of blood by the side of the barber's chair.

"It seems identical to that of Mr Paris," George remarked looking at the wound.

"Can't be the same gun," Chris replied. "We have that one in custody."

The shop door made the detectives turn as the small bell above door rung, Bob Harvey entered.

"Morning," he said smiling at Chris and then George. "I just haven't got room for all your bodies Chris," he continued with a smile. "I haven't finished with Mr Paris yet, well let's have a look at this one," he said approaching the body. "At least I can examine him in the dry, not a muddy wet field," he added.

"Looks very much like that of Mr Paris," George remarked, stepping aside for Bob. "Behind the left ear."

Bob examined the wound, not bothering with anything else. "Mmm," he murmured, as he stood back from the body. "Do we know who he is?" he asked.

"I can identify him," Chris responded. "I was speaking to him only last night, he is Mr Roger Argue, a barber, he owns this shop."

"Well, George is right, it do look identical to the wound of Mr Paris," Bob confirmed.

"We have the gun that killed Mr Paris," Chris remarked.

"Then there must be two of them," Bob replied.

"I agree," Chris replied. "But it is a bit of a coincidence, two people killed with an illegal handgun don't you think, of the same make," Chris added.

"Perhaps a pair was brought into the country," George voiced his opinion.

"That would make this murder and that of Mr Paris connected," Chris remarked. "As far as I know, Mr Paris and Mr Argue knew one another because Mr Argue trimmed Mr Paris's hair, apart from that they only saw each other when they were in the Indian Arms."

"You don't connect the two then Chris?" Bob asked.

"No reason to at the moment," Chris replied. "However both of them knowing each other, gives a weak connection, we will just have to wait for further information, by the way, can you give a time?"

Bob smiled. "Always the same question Chris, at a guess I would say about twelve hours."

Chris looked at his pocket watch. "Well it's just gone ten now, so we can work on around ten o'clock last night that he was killed."

"That's about it Chris," Bob replied. "Can the body be taken, I have a lot of work to do, I don't know why I bother about my patients, you give me enough work with your bodies."

"I wish I didn't," Chris replied. "Yes the place is too clean, I'm not going to find anything to help me here, would you see Mrs Argue before you go Bob, she seems calm for my liking, she is in the room through the rear door there," Chris said.

Bob picked up his bag, and disappeared through the door. George looked at Chris whose eyes was still examining the room.

"We only had Mrs Paris and her daughter in the frame," George remarked. "Mr Argue could have been in the frame had we proved that he was the one to bring these guns into the country, but now he is dead."

"I'm wishing that Inspector Noal was here," Chris replied.

"He had a knack of hitting on the unexpected truth. Let's examine what we have, Mr Argue said that he was not in the Mr Paris's circle of friend, which means they were not close, Mr Argue on the other hand is the only person we know to do with the case who travelled abroad, if he did bring in the guns for a present shall we say for Mr Paris, then they must have been closer than we know, it's not a present you would bring in just for an acquaintance is it?"

"Mr Paris could have known that Mr Argue went abroad, and asked him to bring it in," George argued.

"Accepted," Chris replied. "But why would Mr Paris want the guns, he is not known as a gun collector."

"Protection," George offered. "He do have a factory."

"Why would a burglar burgle his factory, it's doubtful he has many on the property, it's not as if people go to the factory to buy goods, his wool is sent off to certain manufacturers, the payment is probably paid straight into the firms bank account, besides what would a burglar do with a stack of wool?"

"He travels a lot," George continued his thoughts. "He must carry money on him."

Chris smiled. "I'll give you that," he said. "The money we found in his wallet would match both our pay for several months, but somehow, I don't feel that he needed protection in that way."

George spread his arms. "It's all assumption," George replied. "Perhaps Mr Argue is not connected with the Mr Paris's case at all."

"It is a coincidence however," Chris replied. "Both men being killed by an illegal gun, it is called a ladies gun, can you imagine Mrs Paris doing it?" Chris asked.

"Not really," replied George.

"But someone did George," Chris remarked. "Someone it seems managed to get hold of a pair of handguns, that they are illegal in this country."

"I've given her a couple of tablets to take, should she need it," Bob said as he entered the room. "She seems a strong woman, but she is in shock now, but anytime she will realise the reality of what has happened to her husband, then she will grieve."

"Can I ask her a few questions?" Chris asked.

"Better now than later," Bob advised. "Now I must get going, see you both again," he smiled as he opened the shop door to the ring of the bell. "But not too soon."

Chris followed by George made their way behind the rear door, the room was warm, comfortably furnished, about the same size as the shop, Mrs Argue was sitting at the table, her head in her hands, she looked up as they entered.

"Please take a seat," she offered.

"Mrs Argue," Chris said gently as he took a seat facing her. "I do need to ask you a few questions, but it can wait if you feel you are not up to it."

"Inspector I don't know what I am up to, I don't understand anything what's going on, I don't have any feeling, I feel sort of numb."

"Would you like me to make you a cup of tea?" Chris asked concerned.

"No thank you, the doctor offered, I don't want any," Mrs Argue replied. "But thank you."

"Do you have anyone who can stay with you Mrs Argue, anyone I can get in touch with?" Chris asked.

"I do have a sister in Parchment Street," Mrs Argue replied. "I will have to get in touch with."

Chris had noticed a phone standing on the sideboard. "May I use your phone?" Chris asked.

"Of course, but my sister is not on the phone," Mrs Argue replied.

"What number does she live?" George asked, getting up knowing exactly what Chris wanted to do.

"Number 24,in Parchment Street," Mrs Argue replied.

George phoned the police station, and sergeant Bloom answered. George explained briefly, before replacing the receiver and seating himself at the table.

"A constable will fetch her for you Mrs Argue," George told her. "It won't be long before she is here."

"Now Mrs Argue, can you tell me the events of last night?" Chris asked in a gentle tone.

"Nothing unusual," Mrs Argue began. "Apart from that loud bang everything was as usual."

"What bang was that Mrs Argue?" Chris asked.

"I don't know," came the reply. "I was awoke by a terrible bang, I could not understand it, I thought it might have been from one of those motorise machines, they make a bang sometimes, then I thought perhaps I dreamed it, so I went back to sleep."

"Was your husband in bed with you?" Chris asked.

Mrs Argue gave a weak smile. "No Inspector, I go to bed early, and get up late, Roger, my husband comes to bed late, and gets up early, we are sort of opposite," she replied.

"So you would not know when your husband came to bed?" Chris asked.

"No, my husband goes out during the weekdays for a pint, he is rarely home early," Mrs Argue replied. "By the time he is in, I'm fast asleep."

"What about this morning Mrs Argue?" George butted in. "Could you not see that his side of the bed had not been slept in."

"I'm a restless sleeper," Mrs Argue replied. "I twist and turn all night, Roger is always telling me I pull the clothes off him during the nights, you see I do myself up in the sheets, like I'm in a cocoon, I have often told him he will have to sleep in another bed," Mrs Argue smiled for the first time. "So I really could not tell, I did not take notice."

"Do you know what time that loud bang woke you up Mrs Argue?" Chris asked.

"No idea," Mrs Argue replied. "It was very dark, I could not make out our alarm clock, but having said that, before

I was able to get back to sleep, I heard the Guildhall clock strike ten, I counted the chimes, trying to get back to sleep."

"So it would have been a few minutes before ten last night," Chris said.

Mrs Argue nodded.

"Tell me Mrs Argue," Chris said his voice very gentle. "Tell me what you did this morning, if you will."

Mrs Argue looked at her hands, Chris thought bringing the memory of the morning back to her, might start her up, but was pleased seeing she was still calm.

"I rose just about nine this morning, washed, dressed and came downstairs, I did not see Roger, but guessed that he would be in the shop, he's always in the shop," she added. "I made him breakfast, he likes just toast, then went into the shop to tell him his breakfast was on the table, then I saw him, then I called doctor Foster."

Chris looked at George who was busy with his shorthand writing.

"Tell me Mrs Argue, do you know a Mr and Mrs Paris?"

The bell of the shop sounded, Chris looked at George, who got up and left the room.

"Mrs Argue, that will probably be the hospital men to take your husband away, there will have to be a post-mortem, would you like a few moments with him?" Chris asked in the kindness voice.

"He will come back won't he?" Mrs Argue asked.

"Oh yes," Chris replied.

"I will wait then," Mrs Argue replied. "I can't bear to see him again as he is."

Chris smiled. "He will be taken well care of Mrs Argue, the doctor who saw you a while ago will look after him."

George came back in the room, Mrs Argue looked at him, her eyes moistened.

"If you are unable to carry on Mrs Argue, we can come back in a couple days?" Chris asked kindly as George re seated himself.

"No please, get it over with," came the reply. "I can't tell you any more, than what I have already said."

"You have been very helpful Mrs Argue," Chris continued. "I only have a few more questions, now about Mr and Mrs Paris do you know of them?"

"I can't say I do," Mrs Argue replied. "I may have met them, but it don't come to mind, my husband of course know hundreds of people."

"You go to France often on holiday, don't you Mrs Argue?" Chris asked.

"How do you know that Inspector?" Mrs Argue asked amazement showing on her face.

Chris smiled. "I knew your husband Mrs Argue, in fact I had a couple pints with him only last night."

"Yes he likes his pint, every week night, I am shut in this shop all day long apart from shopping, sometimes I walk with him to the Indian Arms, then walk back just to get a breath of fresh air, we do go to France on holiday, I like Paris," Mrs Argue forced a smile. "Roger of course like the women, I know my husband has a roving eye Inspector but I'm not the jealous type of woman, I know my husband was mine, he would not have left me for another woman, so why should I stop what was his innocent enjoyment."

"That is a nice attitude to take Mrs Argue, though I doubt if many women would have the same attitude," Chris remarked. "Tell me did your husband ever bring home gifts for friends?"

"Roger brought home a lot of things that he bought, I never interested myself in them, I have no children unfortunately, otherwise I might."

"But your husband did," Chris prompted.

"Yes I believe he did as favours to customers," Mrs Argue replied.

Chris looked at Mrs Argue, with her smooth complexion, he thought her an attractive woman at her age. He noticed that she had choked back the tears that he thought was coming, when she was told her husband was being taken to the hospital, and in his own way admired her.

"When you went into the shop Mrs Argue," Chris said. "Did you touch anything, or see anything on the floor?"

"I might have touched my husband, that would have been all," she replied. "What should I have seen Inspector?" she asked.

"Your husband was shot Mrs Argue, we found no gun," Chris replied.

"No I didn't see anything on the floor," she replied looking at her hands resting on the table. "I would have noticed a gun, although I can't say I have ever seen one, only in books."

Chris smiled understandingly. "When you went into the shop, was the door open?"

"It was closed, I would have noticed that," Mrs Argue replied. "I saw my husband lying back in the barber chair, I saw the blood around his neck, I immediately ran back in here and phoned the doctor, but the shop door was closed."

"Why did you call the doctor not the police?" Chris asked.

"I don't know what I was thinking Inspector, I saw my husband who I thought had an accident, the police didn't enter my mind, I wanted a doctor."

"When the doctor arrived Mrs Argue, did he enter straight away, or did you open the door for him?" Chris asked.

Mrs Argue thought for a while. "My mind is not with it Inspector, but it was the bell, yes I heard the bell, I was not in the shop at the time, I was getting a blanket to cover Roger, to keep him warm, I went back into the shop and found doctor Foster."

"I noticed your shop door Mrs Argue, apart from the lock, it has two bolts, bottom and top," Chris said. "So the door must have been open when you first saw your husband."

"That's right Inspector, my husband opens the shop at nine every morning, then that bell hardly stops ringing, funny, it's hardly rung this morning."

"That is because a close sign is still showing on the door Mrs Argue," Chris replied, just as the bell sounded.

Chris looked at George, who was about to rise from his chair when the door of the room flew open, and a woman rushed in.

"Oh you poor dear," she cried rushing over to Mrs Argue, and putting her arms around her shoulder. "The constable told me all about it, what a terrible thing to happen."

Chris rose, and took hold of his trilby that he had put on the table, he looked at George, who also stood up.

"This is your sister Mrs Argue?" Chris asked.

Chris saw her eyes were tearful as she nodded to him.

"Then we will take our leave Mrs Argue, please contact us if you need anything, we will do our best to help, now don't get up, we will find our own way out."

Chris and George stood for a while outside the shop, while Chris buttoned his overcoat.

"Well George what do you think?" he asked, turning towards the high street.

"She never faltered in her answers to your questions," George replied. "She showed little or no emotion, we never found the gun, in my opinion, it could have been an inside killing, and also from the outside."

Chris did not comment, as they turned left at the H&C Food Shop, making their way towards the police station.

"I feel out of my depth on this one," Chris admitted. "But I'm sure of one thing, both Mr Paris and Mr Argue knew their killer, they were not shot from yards away, the gun was touching the skin on both when the shot was fired, which means very closeness, Mrs Argue was right about the very loud banging, the gunsmith who I visited told me that although it was a very small gun, that could easily be hidden in a handbag, or slid down in your sock, even carried unnoticed in a coat pocket, it had a very loud noise."

"Surely someone else heard it," George responded.

"I expect someone did George," Chris replied as they crossed Middle Brook Street. "But I would doubt if many people were about at that time, the shop is isolated to a certain degree, stuck in between the rear of Dolcis Shoe shop, and Woolworths side at the other end, there are no pubs in the area."

Chris stopped at Cross Keys Passage. "Look George," he said. "Hundred yards from this passage is Lower Brook Street, where you will find Mr Paris wool factory, I want you to interview all his workers, find out as much about Mr Paris as you can, remember in a group you won't get a response, use your authority and interview each employee separately."

George looked at the Guildhall clock. "Well it's eleven now, so I'll see you when I see you," he said walking away from the passage.

Chris crossed the Broadway into the police station, and was welcomed by sergeant Bloom.

"Did the constable find the Mrs Argue's sister?" sergeant Bloom asked with a smile.

"Yes, thank you sergeant," Chris replied. "She came in just as we were leaving."

"Anything else I can help you with?" asked the sergeant.

"Well there is as a matter of fact," Chris answered. "First, the Bobby on the Beat around Monks Road, if you can trust him, ask him to ask information discreetly about the Paris family at number six, all bobbies have houses they call at for a cup of tea."

"Will take care of it Sir," sergeant Bloom replied respectfully making a note.

"Also, when I came out of Mr Argue's barber shop, I noticed a drain in the kerb, can you find out from the council, perhaps it comes under the sewer department, I would like the drain lifted, to see if a handgun has been dropped into it."

"I'll get on with that, a drain is a good place to hide a gun," sergeant Bloom said making a note.

"Thank you sergeant," Chris replied with a smile. "If you have any problem with the council, you can use my name," he added as he went into his office.

Chapter Ten

eorge found it easy to find the wool factory, on the left hand side of Lower Brook Street, going towards the North Walls. He looked at the two large closed doors, then spotted a smaller door, built into one of the larger doors. He tried the unlatch, and it opened, he stepped inside, he found himself in a large spacious area, there was little noise apart from a radio playing dance music, he saw a few men, all wearing boiler suits, and several wearing caps, and ankle length wellingtons boots, they all seemed busy, he saw high bins on wheels, that was overflowing with wool. He looked up to his right, and saw what he took as the office, and Chris thought that anyone sitting in the office could see the entire work floor. Several wooden steps had to be mounted to reach it. George started to climb, until he was looking through a glass pane of a door, and could see a smartly dressed man sitting at a desk, smoking a pipe. Chris knocked on the door, made the man turn his head towards him, he got up and came to the door.

"Can I help you?" he asked, holding his pipe.

"I'm hoping you can," George replied, pushing back his bushy black hair with his hand. "I am Detective Sergeant House of Winchester CID, I'm here regarding the death of Mr Paris."

"Come in then," the man replied. "Please take a seat," he offered indicating a chair to the front of the desk.

George could see all the factory floor from where he stood. "Nice view from here," George smiled as he seated himself.

"Yes we need the view, can't have smoking in a place like this," the man said putting his pipe in the ashtray. "You always get one who likes taking a risk when he feels it's safe," the man smiled.

George seated comfortably looked at the man. "You are?" George asked.

"I am Mr Trever, Tony Trever," the man replied. "Floor manager, although I am in charge this week owing to Mr Paris's tragedy, I am taking charge of the office as well this week while Mrs Paris takes a break, it was a terrible killing, and Mrs Paris is very upset."

"I'm sure she is," George replied.

"Well Sergeant how can I help you?" Tony asked.

"I need to interview all your employees," George replied.

"You want me to stop them all working Sergeant?" Tony asked. "We have a heavy schedule to carry out."

"No, one by one, and in private, if that is possible," George replied.

"I doubt if the men can tell you anything Sergeant," Tony answered. "Perhaps I can be of more help?"

"So you might be Mr Trever, but I also must interview the men regardless to what they know," George replied.

"Very well Sergeant, you can use this office, I will be on the floor, you want me to send one man at a time?"

"That would be fine Mr Trever, and thank you for the office use," George answered.

For the next hour, George spoke to all the six employees, none of them threw any information as to the killing of

413

Mr Paris, they all spoke highly of him as their boss, and they were very modest in telling George that they were skilled people. George closed his notebook, in which he had written nothing, he looked up as the door open, and saw Mr Trever entered, George rose from Mr Trever's seat at the desk at which he had been sitting during his interviews, allowing Mr Trever to sit.

"Did you have any luck Sergeant?" he asked with a smile.

"No nothing that could help," George replied a little disappointed. "It was what was expected but we have to ask all the people that knew Mr Paris, now Mr Trever, as foreman, you must have known Mr Paris better than the rest?"

"I suppose I must have done," replied Mr Trever. "But I don't talk about my employer, I try to be loyal."

"You can be as loyal as you like Mr Trever," George spoke sharply. "But I must warn you, should this case get solved, and if it's found that you have information that could have helped, and not devolved it, then you would not have an employment, you would be charged with wasting police time, and perhaps send to prison, remember this is a murder investigation."

"Sergeant," Mr Trevor said alarmed. "I haven't had a question from you yet, I just meant that I hate being disloyal to my employer."

George looked at the man, he kicked himself for having lost his coolness, he decided he might get more from Mr Trever by being a nice cop.

"Mr Trever," George replied in a pleasant voice. "I need to ask you questions, and I do need honest answers, should you wish, I can get in touch with Mrs Paris, but remember she wants the killer caught, it was her husband that was killed, and I don't think she would be grateful to any of her staff, that did not cooperate regardless."

"I see what you mean Sergeant," Mr Trever said taking out his pipe and sucking it unlit. "Please ask what you will."

"Did you know Mr Paris socially?" George asked.

"I would at times have a drink with him in the Indian Arms," Mr Trever replied still sucking on his unlit pipe. "But that would be the extent of it."

"I see," replied George. "Now when he took a holiday, did he go abroad or stay in England?"

"I'm not sure whether it was on holiday or business, but he would sometimes go to France, no, I'm sure it was not holiday, as he always went alone," Mr Trever replied. "And I am sure Mrs Paris would not have trusted him going holiday without taking her."

George looked up. "Are you saying he was a ladies man?" he asked.

"Sergeant," replied Mr Trever leaning forward. "Do what I say have to get into the ears of Mrs Paris?"

George thought for a while, he needed to be careful. "Let's say this Mr Trever, what you say to me is confidential apart from my boss, I would not tell Mrs Paris of our conversation, but it could come out in court."

Mr Trever leaned back in his chair. "Mr Paris was a good-looking man, a hard worker, and a very fair man to us his workers, also with his good looks he had money to match, it's only natural that some woman would make a play for him, married or not."

"But you don't know that for sure?" George asked.

"Not really," admitted Mr Trever. "It's only my assumption, it's not my place to criticise my employer."

"But you must have other ideas in your head," George encouraged him. "Come on Mr Trever, going to France don't mean he is meeting a woman over there, I mean did he go more than once?"

"No, just once a year for the last two," Mr Trever replied. "But some nights when I leave here, I see a woman standing a little way off, I could not make out what she looked like, and to be honest for the first few times I saw her, I took no notice, but I have seen her standing there about twice a week, and I became curious, but at that time I did not connect her with Mr Paris."

"But now you do?" George questioned.

"Well one night, as you know it gets dark at nights, I walked towards North Walls, the way I always go, and stopped to look back, I saw her disappear into our factory door, I am positive it was our factory door."

"Did you do anything else?" George asked.

"Oh no, I think I smiled, and silently called him a dirty old man. Mrs Paris is a gracious woman, but I would not like to be married to her, she believes she is a better class person, what you may call a real snob, but whatever you do, don't tell her I said that, she would kill me," he said.

George smiled back. "What is the working hours here?" George asked.

"Seven in the morning to six at night," Tony replied. "One hour for dinner."

"Mr Paris always left about six or just after didn't he?" George asked.

"That's right," came the reply. "I leave with the men, having made sure everything is secure."

"Tell me Mr Trever, when was the date Mr Paris went to France this year?"

Tony took a diary from his desk, and turned the pages. "Twenty fifth July," he replied closing the book and throwing it back on the desk. "He was gone for ten days."

"Well thank you very much Mr Trever, thank you for your cooperation, is there anything else?" George asked.

"I think I have said too much already Sergeant," Mr Trever said getting up. "I hope you catch Mr Paris's killer, he was really a good and kind man you know."

George offered his hand, and left with a feeling of having accomplish a little.

Chris was studying papers as George entered the office, he looked up without comment as he watched George cross to his desk, and sat.

"I interviewed each employee separately," George began, taking out his notebook, and putting it on the desk. "I didn't get much from them, all they really said that they were happy with him as a boss, but socially knew nothing about him."

"That was to be expected George" Chris replied. "But we had to see them, it was possible that one might have had some information, but never mind," he said looking back at the papers he was studying.

"That's not all Chris, the foreman was far more obliging," George remarked, making Chris once again look up from his papers.

"He seemed a bit nasty at first, I think I lost my cool a little, and told him what he could expect should it be found that he was holding information back relating to the case, he seem to come around a bit after that, and started talking."

Chris looked at George with a smile on his face, but made no comment, as George reading parts from his notebook related his talk with the foreman.

"So," Chris remarked after George had told all. "What have we got now?"

"Well we know that Mr Paris might be a ladies man," George replied. "We know Mr Paris went to France."

"The France bit interests me," Chris replied. "I wonder why Mrs Paris did not mention it when I asked her if she went abroad for her holidays, she said no, also I wonder about the date Mr Argue went to France, that might prove interesting."

"Mrs Paris did not go with her husband," George reminded Chris. "He went on his own on business, perhaps that is why she said no about going on holiday to France."

"Thank you for correcting me George, I am being carried away in my thoughts," Chris replied annoyed at himself.

"What about this woman that Mr Trever saw her enter the factory after he had left, remember he had seen her several times standing near the factory entrance about twice a week," George argued.

"I know George," Chris replied. "That is what makes it interesting."

George closed his notebook, not grasping the meaning of what Chris had just said.

"What do you think we should do now George?" Chris asked.

"I think we should see Mrs Paris again," George replied. "Get to the bottom of his French trips, and try to find out if he was a ladies man, and whether she knew?"

"OK George," Chris agreed. "Should we find out what you believe might be true, then it would give us a motive for Mr Paris's killing, but what about the killing of Mr Argue, Mrs Argue did not know the Paris family, so it's likely that Mrs Paris do not know the Mr and Mrs Argue."

"Perhaps the killings are not related," George replied.

"Perhaps," Chris agreed. "I have a strong hunch that they are."

Chris looked down at his papers, then dropping his pencil, he looked at George. "Give me a half hour to finish these papers, then we will get on our bikes and see Mrs Paris."

Chris looked at his pocket watch. "In the meantime, it's now one thirty, the pubs are still open George, could you pop over to the Indian Arms, ask the landlord what time Mr Argue left on the night Mr Paris was killed, and perhaps he may have heard a little of their conversation."

"Any particular reason?" George asked getting up.

Chris shook his head. "Just an idea forming at the back of my head," Chris smiled.

George crossed the Broadway, he entered the Indian Arms saloon bar. The bar was empty, most workmen used the public bar, only the well off used the saloon bar, as the drinks were a halfpenny dearer, the saloon bar had to be kept clean and tidy, and well furnished, no straw or spittoons were seen in the saloon bar.

The landlord smiled at him as George approached the small opening.

"Afternoon landlord," George greeted him.

"Sergeant," smiled the landlord. "What can I do for you?"

"Just a little more information if you don't mind landlord," George smiled back.

"I have no idea about my customers social life Sergeant," the landlord replied. "After they leave the pub, they could be become strangers to me in that respect, but ask away."

"When Mr Paris left that night he was killed, can you remember what time Mr Argue left?" George asked.

"Mr Argue always stopped until nearly closing time," the landlord replied.

"I see," replied George, wondering to himself, why Chris wanted to know. "About their conversation, did you hear any of it?"

"No, afraid I didn't," remarked the landlord. "I am kept too busy this side of the bar, anyway, I hear bits and pieces of conversations all evening long, they are just a lot of jumble to me, but they were both talking, and bought each other a drink."

"Well thank you landlord, forgive me for not having a drink, not allowed to drink on duty," George smiled.

"I understand Sergeant," the landlord returned the smile. "Any movement on Mr Paris's murder case?" he asked.

George thought for a while, he thought the landlord was friendly enough. "Keep this to yourself for a couple of days landlord, but I am afraid you have lost two of your customers, Mr Argue was also found dead this morning," he said.

"God," replied the landlord staring at the George. "What's going on, he left early last night, he left about a half hour after your Inspector left, I was wondering if he was cutting down his drinking, I remember thinking at the time, that was very unusual, well, well, well," he said wiping his hands in his waist high apron.

While George was in the Indian Arms, Chris phoned Elizabeth at the bank. On hearing her voice. "Hello, this is Chris," he spoke onto the receiver.

"Chris darling, what a lovely surprise, or is it?" she asked her tone of voice dropping.

"We will have to leave tonight out," Chris said.

"Are you going to the pub to think?" Elizabeth asked.

"Never had the thought," Chris replied. "But I do think better when I have a pint in my hand."

"Oh Chris, do you have to?" Elizabeth replied.

"No, you got it wrong," Chris smiled into the receiver. "I had another murder this morning," he explained. "Now don't say a word about it to anyone."

"Of course I won't darling," Elizabeth replied, her voice full of concern. "You are working yourself to hard."

"I have George," Chris replied. "He is a good man, but with this new case, on top of the one I already have, it's hard to see when I will be free."

"Don't you worry about me darling, mother and myself have plenty of things to do, but I shall miss you."

"I always miss you darling," Chris assured her as he replaced the receiver.

George returned to the office, just as Chris had put down the receiver. "Just phoned Elizabeth," Chris said to George as he entered. "No date tonight."

"You're going to lose that girl if you are not careful, it will be hard enough on her when you are married, being a detective Inspector's wife," George replied smiling.

"So you're a marriage councillor," Chris teased returning the smile.

"Seriously Chris," George replied. "I have seen marriages break up because their husbands are at the office all the time, and not only policemen wives."

"I'm sure you are right George, and thanks for the warning, I have told Elizabeth what she can expect, but you are right, I must try to see her more often, anyway," Chris sighed. "I hope to take her to Southampton on Saturday that I'm off."

"With your wedding not far off Chris," George said. "I can always change your Sundays with you, Saturdays are the better days for shopping for you both."

"That real decent of you George, thank you very much, if I tell that to Elizabeth, you won't have a Saturday off for many weeks."

"Tell her then, my offer will not put me out," George replied smiling. "Now let me tell you what the landlord told me."

"I'm all ears George," Chris replied.

"That at least tells us one thing," Chris said to George after he had related what had been said between the landlord and himself.

"Mr Argue is clear of murdering Mr Paris, he was in the pub until closing time that night, but it was unusual as the landlord said, Mr Argue leaving early last night he was with me and what made him leave the pub early after I spoke to him?" Chris said thoughtfully. "When we know we might know the murderer, so for now, let's get on our bikes."

The Monk Road house was a double bay window house, with the front door situated between. Chris knocked the door, and it was opened as expected, by a well groomed Mrs Paris. Showing no surprise, not even commenting on why they were there, she opened the front door to its full, and offered them in, Chris took off his trilby, and followed by George, stepped into the well decorated hall way.

Chris took it all in at a glance, he had not really noticed the last time he had been in the house. The hall was wide, and facing him was a staircase with a banister of highly polished wood, he saw two doors on the left of the hall, and one on the right, at the foot of the stairs, all the doors seem to be highly polished.

"We will go into the lounge," Mrs Paris said having closed the front door, she opened the door at the foot of the stairs. "The cleaning lady has already finished, and I have a fire burning."

Chris looked at George, and both exchanged a smile, as they entered the lounge.

"This is what one would call posh," Chris thought to himself as he looked around at the comfortable sofa, and highly polished furniture.

"Would you like me to take your overcoats," Mrs Paris offered. "You will feel the benefit when you leave, it's quite warm in here," Mrs Paris continued without a smile.

Both Chris and George took off their overcoats, and gave them to Mrs Paris, who went outside to hang them up.

"Now before you tell me why you are here," Mrs Paris said as she re entered. "Would either of you like a cup of tea?"

"Thank you no Mrs Paris," Chris replied, wondering what would happen if he accidentally spilt from a cup.

"Please make yourselves comfortable," she offered taking a hard chair herself.

Chris and George did the same, so that they were all seated together at the same table.

"You have news?" Mrs Paris asked.

"Your husband's trilby has been found Mrs Paris," Chris informed her.

"Has that helped you uncovering the murderer?" Mrs Paris asked.

"No, not really Mrs Paris," Chris replied. "But what was inside might, we found a small handgun inside, tell me Mrs Paris, did Mr Paris own a gun?"

"You have already had my answer of the question Inspector, the answer is again no," Mrs Paris replied. "Do not weapons of that kind have to be registered with the police?" she asked.

"Certainly they do," Chris agreed. "However there are those who bring them in from abroad, and keep them secret."

"Are you saying this gun that my husband was shot with, is a foreign gun?" Mrs Paris asked clenching her hands in front of her.

"Not only foreign Mrs Paris," Chris replied. "But also illegal, they are not imported in this country, you can understand why this gun would not be registered with the police, it can be bought anywhere on the continent however, do you ever travel abroad?"

"You have already asked me, had I taken a holiday abroad Inspector, and my answer is still no," Mrs Paris replied sarcastically. "Did you have this gun when you asked?"

Chris gave a weak smile. "No, Mrs Paris, it was just an out of the blue question."

"I see," Mrs Paris replied. "So you assumed that whoever killed my husband, had at some point travelled abroad?"

Chris ignored the question. "During our investigation, since I saw you last, we have called at your business premise, and questioned your staff."

"I know," Mrs Paris butted in. "I see no benefit in that, however you do what you must, but notice of your visit would have been appreciated."

"We did find out that your husband had gone to France for ten days this year Mrs Paris," Chris said.

" I had told my staff to cooperate with you should you call, I had anticipated that you would," Mrs Paris spoke unclasping her hands, and spreading her arms on the table.

"My husband was trying to expand our business into the export business, he was not there on holiday and I did not go with him."

"I am already aware of that Mrs Paris," Chris replied. "Tell me Mrs Paris, do you know a Mr Argue?"

Mrs Paris sat for a while without answering, then got up, and walked to the window, where she fiddled with the curtains, Chris looked at George who was making notes and smiled, Chris knew instantly that she knew Mr Argue.

"I cannot recall the name Inspector, should I?" she asked returning to her chair.

"Not really Mrs Paris, only Mr Argue as far as we know was the last person to speak to your husband, Mr Argue is the barber who trimmed your husband's hair."

"I see," replied Mrs Paris, clasping her hands in front of her again. "My husband might have mentioned his name in passing, I might even have met him, but it has not registered, do you think that this man is involved?" she asked.

Chris thought she looked a little nervous. "We don't think that Mrs Paris, Mr Argue was still in the Indian Arms when your husband was shot."

"Then what?" Mrs Paris asked unclenching her hands.

"Mr Argue was found dead in his barber shop this morning," Chris explained. "It seems that he was shot the same way as your husband, and with we believe the same type of handgun."

"You told me you had the gun that killed my husband," Mrs Paris replied quickly.

"Correct Mrs Paris," Chris replied. "We are working on the theory that there was a pair of these handguns."

"Inspector," Mrs Paris said lifting her hands from the table in a suggestion of hopelessness. "I am lost, what you tell me is that you are no closer to catching the person who shot my husband than you were a week ago, and that this new murder has put you farther behind."

"We are here to keep you updated with our progress Mrs Paris," Chris said politely.

"Which is none, the way I see it Inspector," Mrs Paris answered.

Chapter Eleven

ack in their office, Chris and George discussed the interview.

"She is certainly a difficult person to interview, she gives nothing away," Chris said.

"I agree," George replied. "But she did call Mr Argue's death murder, you only told her, he was found dead."

"That could have been a slip of the tongue," Chris remarked. "After all murder is in her mind at the moment with her husband's death."

"Do you think she had anything to do with her husband's death Chris?" George asked.

Chris shrugged. "She is a snob, she tries very hard to make people think she is superior, I don't honestly know, she remain a suspect however."

Both detectives looked towards the door as a knock came, and sergeant Bloom entered carrying a large brown envelope.

"It seems your hunch paid off Sir," he said respectfully placing the envelope before Chris on his desk. "I did what you asked, I went to council, saw the sewer department and the men opened the drain, and they found the gun."

"Really," replied Chris taking the envelope and looking inside. "Well done sergeant," he said as he saw a handgun inside.

"The constable I was able to get in touch with and sent there, arrived after the sewer department men, I am afraid I don't know how the gun was handled," sergeant Bloom said awkwardly.

"Don't worry Sergeant," replied Chris. "Any finger-prints would probably been washed off," Chris replied as he allowed the gun to fall onto his desk from the envelope.

Sergeant Bloom left the office, Chris looked at George, who was looking at him wondering.

"When we left Mrs Argue this morning George," Chris started to explain. "I stood on the kerb, and did up my over-coat, looking down I saw a drain, when you went to the factory, I asked sergeant Bloom to get the responsible department to lift the drain outside the shop, to see if any-thing had been dropped into it, it was only a hunch, with no expectations really, but it paid off."

"Good thinking," replied George. "We now know that there was a pair of handguns, it looks the same," George remarked as he stood over the desk, while Chris match it with the one he had.

"I'm sure it is," Chris remarked. "Being a pair, it is likely they were in a case of some kind."

George returned to his seat. "We are still no further ahead," he remarked as he watched Chris examine the chamber.

"Empty," Chris remarked. "The same as the gun that shot Mr Paris, only one shell was used, this murderer must have been so sure of carrying the crime out using just one bullet."

"Perhaps whoever it was only had one bullet," George commented.

"Then that would imply that the murderer intended to kill, whoever it was must have been very close to the victims," Chris murmured.

"Like a wife or a lover," George offered.

Exactly George, like a wife or a lover," Chris replied. "Pity we can't search Mrs Paris and Mrs Argue's houses," Chris remarked. "Do you realise that these two wives are the only people in the frame."

"What about Rosemary Paris, or Grice, whatever name she uses?" George asked.

"I have wondered about her myself," Chris admitted. "I always come back to her being too young, and for her to commit murder, she would have to be deranged in her mind."

"She's tall enough," George replied.

"There has to be a connection between Mr Paris and Mr Argue, at the moment all we know is that Mr Argue cut Mr Paris's hair, and they drink together, but there has to be something else. Both the wives seem not to know each other, it's puzzling."

"Perhaps the girl know something, we really have not interviewed her have we?" George remarked.

"No we have not," Chris agreed. "Perhaps we should, but how do we do it without her mother around?"

Chris thought for a while. "Let's put it behind us for a while George, we have a couple of reports to get on with, at least we can give all our attention to the Mr Paris's case tomorrow, but there is one other thing," Chris said lifting the phone.

"Sergeant can you come in?" he spoke onto the receiver.

Sergeant Bloom entered the office almost immediately. "How can I help you Sir?" he asked.

"I want to find out some information about a Mr Thomas Grice, he died some four years ago, he was the husband of Mrs Paris, you know of the case sergeant?"

"I do Sir," replied sergeant Bloom.

"Of course you are thinking why I don't just ask Mrs Paris," Chris said.

"It did cross my mind Sir," sergeant Bloom replied with a slight smile.

Chris picked up his pencil and twisted it around his fingers. "Mrs Paris is an obstructive person when you are asking questions to her, in other words she is not forthcoming with answers, unless you force her, so it might be best to find out these things, without asking her."

"I understand Sir," sergeant Bloom replied. "What do we know about him?"

"Not much I'm afraid, Mr Grice having died four years ago, did not seem to be a part of the case, so I asked no questions about him," Chris replied. "All I know is that about twenty odd years ago, he attended Peter Symonds School with the late Mr John Paris, on leaving school, both Thomas and John decided to go into the wool business, they rented a building in Lower Brook Street and they started their own business, Mrs Paris became their business secretary, and I was wondering if the school kept records of their pupils?"

"I'll get in touch with them Sir, I would think all schools keep some sort of records," sergeant Bloom replied.

"Thank you Sergeant," Chris replied. "Also find out if you can, when and where one can meet all the dustcart men together, will you?"

After Sergeant Bloom had disappeared, Chris continued with his report, with the case of Mr Paris, having finished the report, Chris held the letter in front of him and re-read what he had written, he had to pick and chose his words, but a smile came to his face as he felt satisfactory with the report.

"I will get this report to the typist," he muttered as he put the statement into a folder.

Sergeant Bloom knocked and entered the office, carrying his notebook, which was already open.

"I contacted Peter Symonds School Sir," he said standing in front of Chris looking at his notebook. "The headmaster was very helpful, they keep records of all their students," he said looking at Chris.

"It seems that Mr Thomas Grice was the son of General Grice, who retired to Winchester after leaving the Army from India. Thomas his son, started at Peter Symonds in 1892, he was fourteen years old. He has no idea where they live at the moment, but their address was a house in Chilbolton Avenue, called "Retreat," sergeant Bloom looked at Chris. "That's all I can get I'm afraid," he said.

"You have done well Sergeant," Chris replied. "Was the headmaster sure it's the right Thomas Grice."

"He was in the same form as Mr Paris," sergeant Bloom replied. "And the only one with the name of Grice at that school at that time, so it's as certain as we can get."

"Good work Sergeant," Chris praised him with a smile. "Anything else?"

"I phoned the council Sir, dustcart men are all together on Saturday mornings, when they work a half day cleaning their vehicles, at the city council yard," sergeant Bloom answered.

"Very good work Sergeant, you have been a big help and thank you," Chris smiled.

Sergeant Bloom smiled back as he put his notebook in his top tunic pocket. "Oh and I have constable Grimshaw waiting to see you Sir, you remember asking me regarding the Beat Bobby at Monks Road?"

"I do Sergeant, thank you, will you asked him in," Chris smiled.

"That's a good man George," Chris said as sergeant Bloom left the office.

Constable Grimshaw was a large man, whose uniform seemed too tight for him, he had a red face, he looked every bit a man who liked a pint, a jolly sort of man. Chris thought he seemed out of breath as he stood in front of him.

"Have a seat constable," Chris offered smiling to himself.

Constable Grimshaw sat in the interview chair, and rested his helmet on his lap.

"Now constable," Chris said. "What are you able to tell us?" he asked.

Constable Grimshaw cleared his throat. "Sergeant Bloom told me to be discreet Sir," he answered. "So I did not ask questions, just tried to make pleasant conversations around instead of asking direct questions, if you understand Sir."

Chris nodded his head.

"Monks road is mainly middle class Sir," constable Grimshaw continued. "The residence speak very loud when they talk, in their lardidar way, I mean snobbish forms of behaviour or speech, they don't seem to gossip, they praise their own ego really, any problems that they have, they keep secret behind their own doors, life for them is all pretence, so you will understand that there is not a lot one can find out."

Constable Grimshaw paused for a while, he took out his handkerchief and wiped his brow before continuing. "Mr and Mrs Paris, are respected, Mr Paris is liked better than Mrs Paris it seems, as Mrs Paris cannot stop believing that she is better class than any of the others, but Mr Paris acts differently, he speaks softly, he jokes at times, and is well liked by his neighbours. Miss Rosemary Paris the daughter however is spoken about, many call her a hussy, I have heard, it is said that she goes with men, but that is only talk Sir."

"So there is not much slander then constable?" Chris asked.

"Afraid not Sir," came the reply. "Outside their homes, they are too high and mighty to gossip if they have any problems, they are kept behind closed doors."

Chris smiled. "Thank you constable, should you hear of anything else, please let me know."

"What did you think of the daughter when you interviewed them?" George asked Chris after the constable had left.

Chris smiled, as he remembered her flirty smile at him when she was in the office with her mother. "I don't want to speak ill of the girl," he replied. "But she strikes me as being a bit of a flirt."

Sergeant Bloom knocked and entered. "I was able to speak to the constable on the Beat along Chilbolton Avenue, he knows the house called the Retreat, he told me that the gentleman of the house had died a few years back, but his wife, is still living at the address."

"That's handy to know Sergeant," Chris replied. "Good work."

Chris looked at his pocket watch. "The time is getting on George, not much we can do today, tomorrow morning you can drive me on your motorbike to Chilbolton Avenue, it's a fair way from here, and up hill," he smiled.

"I'll bring my motorbike with me," George replied with a grin. "Will this Mrs Grice be able to help us, I mean so far we seem to be up the creek."

"Yes," Chris replied deep in thought. "It's this Mr Paris's case that is baffling, take away Mrs Paris, and her daughter

433

and Mrs Argue, we have no one in the frame," Chris shrugged as though putting his thoughts behind him.

"Anyway, I'm off to see Elizabeth so I'll see you in the morning George," Chris said crossing the room where he put on his overcoat and took his trilby from the stand.

George smiled. "Have a nice time," he remarked turning back to the paper work on his desk.

Chapter Twelve

Chris saw Elizabeth as he approached the Butter Cross. "Am I late?" he asked as he stood in front of her.

Elizabeth gave him a kiss on the cheek, "No, I might be a few minutes early," she replied with a smile, already buttoning the buttons of his overcoat. "There that's better," she said. "You must wrap up warm."

Chris smiled to himself, he thought he rather liked being fussed over by this beautiful woman. Elizabeth grabbed his arm, and they began to walk down town.

"Are you stopping tonight darling?" she asked. "I missed you last night."

"All night if you want me to," Chris smiled as he patted Elizabeth's hand that was holding his arm.

Elizabeth hugged onto his arm with a smile and a soft giggle.

"I have been thinking," Chris said as they reached the bottom of Magdalene Hill. "When we are married, and I am on a case, I will put you in quarantine."

"Whatever for?" Elizabeth asked. "Do you find me contagious?"

"To my mind you are, when I am with you, I can't think of anything but you," Chris answered.

Elizabeth giggled. "You say the nicest things darling," she said. "But then," she continued after a thought. "It do give your mind a rest, not thinking about crime and crooks, and when you get to bed, your mind is relaxed, and you picture things in a different light."

"That's the trouble," Chris continued with his teasing. "When I do get to bed, whether I have seen you or not, you play on my mind worse than ever."

"I love it when you say things like that darling," Elizabeth replied as they come to a stop at the bottom of the pathway leading to her house. "I am restless with the same thoughts every night."

Chris laughed as he allowed Elizabeth to go in front towards the front door. "I know one thing," he said. "By the time we are married, I shall be completely worn out, just with my thoughts."

Elizabeth stopped and turned back to him, she gave him a quick kiss on the lips. "You poor darling," she said smiling at him. "Are you sure you don't mean after we are married," she giggled.

Chris turned towards her, and playfully tapped her bottom, making her smile. "I have to talk to your mother about you, wherever do you get these ideas from?"

"I thought I heard laughing," Olive said as she opened the front door. "You both must be chilled, get your coats off and come into the front room, it's nice and warm there."

Still smiling, Chris allowed Olive to fuss, and entering the front room, Chris found Ron, who stood up and welcomed him. "Been reading the list of casualties," he said indicating the paper on his chair with his head. "Awful lot of casualties we are getting, a wise man once said that it is right to kill one man, if the killing meant the saving of several, but is the killing of one man justified in the slaughter of thousands."

"I agree," Chris replied. "There are enough deaths without war."

Ron smiled weakly. "You see many of them I suppose in your work, but we are unable to change things, what do you say to a glass of beer before dinner?"

"I'm with you all the way Ron," Chris answered as the door opened and Elizabeth entered carrying two glasses and a bottle of stout.

"You read our minds Elizabeth," Ron said to his daughter.

After a dinner that filled him up, Chris and Elizabeth settled on the sofa, Chris took out his pipe, and puffed it contentedly.

"Now how do we work it for Saturday?" Chris asked.

"We can go early darling," Elizabeth answered. "I am off this Saturday morning."

"Of course you are going to Southampton aren't you," Olive butted in as she sat in an armchair by her husband. "I hope it will be warm for you."

"I'm not worried," replied Elizabeth. "It will be a lovely break."

"Shall I pick you up?" Chris asked Elizabeth.

"No need for you walking all the way from your lodgings and back again, Elizabeth will see you on the platform," Olive spoke for her daughter.

Ron looked over the top of his paper, and smiled knowingly at Chris.

"Thank you mother," Elizabeth scolded her mother. "But she is right darling, I will see you at the railway station, I have already checked on the trains, there is one at nine o'clock."

"I think I can manage that," Chris smiled.

Chris whistled as he entered the Police Station on the Friday morning, he had seen Elizabeth before she had entered the bank, he felt please with himself, and was looking forward to his day off on Saturday with Elizabeth. He hoped she was not catching a cold.

"You look like a cat who have found the cream," George remarked as Chris took off his overcoat and trilby, hanging both on the stand.

"Thinking about tomorrow, my day off," Chris replied sitting behind his desk, he looked at his in tray, and saw an official letter, and picked it up.

"This is Bob's report on his post mortem on Mr Argue," he said to George passing the letter over. "No more than I expected, the same as Mr Paris, both these men were shot in the same manner, behind the ear, would someone who have never handled a gun before, shoot two victims the same way I wonder?"

"Unlikely I would say," replied George. "But whoever it was, must have been known by both victims, you could not get close to a person and shoot him behind the ear, unless perhaps the killer approached from behind."

"That's a thought George," Chris replied. "But if you are right, then it implied that the killer knew how to use a gun."

Chris looked at a few papers on his desk then took out his pocket watch. "It's almost ten George, did you bring your motorbike?"

"Around the back," George replied. "Are we ready to go?"

"Better get it over George," Chris answered, getting up.

By the time George had come to a stop outside the house called the Retreat in Chilbolton Avenue, Chris who had been sitting on the pavilion seat, felt numb with the cold, he eagerly got off, and stamped his feet, and blew into his cupped hands.

The Retreat stood quite away back from the road, a gravel path leading to the front door, separated the large front garden into two. Chris knocked the door, which was opened by an elderly woman in an apron.

"Are you Mrs Grice?" Chris asked taking off his trilby.

"No, I am her maid," the woman replied.

"Is it possible for me to see Mrs Grice then?" Chris asked.

"I will see," replied the maid without a smile. "Who might I say is calling?"

"Just inform your mistress that we are from the Police," Chris answered.

"Very well," replied the maid a little taken back. "Please wait there."

Within a couple of minutes the maid returned. "Mrs Grice will see you," she said opening the door wide for them to enter.

Chris and George entered, and waited while the maid closed the door behind them. "This way please," the maid said walking in front of them.

The hall was wide with a wide spiral staircase with a open centre. The maid opened one of the doors on the left hand side. "If you will go in, Mrs Grice suffers with a hip complaint, she gets pain while rising from her chair," she said.

"Thank you," Chris replied as he followed by George entered the warm well furnished room, and saw a woman sitting in a comfortable chair close to the coal fire that was burning in the grate. The woman was elderly, well wrapped up even with the fire. She looked very thin and frail, her face showed signs of wrinkles, and Chris thought this was due to the heat while being in India, her hair was silvery white.

"Please don't get up," Chris smiled as he approached the woman. "Am I speaking to Mrs Grice?"

"You are," replied the woman in a firm but pleasant voice. "But I am at lost."

"You must forgive us for our interruption Mrs Grice," Chris apologised. "I am Detective Inspector Hardie of Winchester CID, and this is Detective Sergeant House."

"Pleasure to meet you both," Mrs Grice replied. "You must forgive me for not rising, my hip you see, can I get you a drink?"

"No thank you Mrs Grice," Chris refused the offer politely.

"Well then please be seated, pull up a chair near to the fire," Mrs Grice offered. "And tell me what I have done to warrant an Police Inspector to call."

Chris and George smiled as they obeyed, Chris undid his overcoat, and was feeling quite warm. "We are investigating the murder of your ex daughter-in-law's husband," Chris spoke as gently as he could.

Mrs Grice bowed her head, and Chris thought he saw a sadness appear on her face.

"I'm sorry if our visit brings back distressing memories," Chris said gently.

Mrs Grice looked up, she smiled. "That's kind of you Inspector, but thinking of my son always bring me good memories, although he died now five years ago, my sadness is that he is not here, but yes Linda was married to my son Thomas, and what a dreadful thing to happen to her again having her second husband killed, they had no marriage at all, just a few months."

"Do you see much of Mrs Paris?" George asked.

"Occasionally," Mrs Grice replied. "But my grand-daughter Rosemary often pops in," she smiled at the thought. "She is my only living blood line now."

"She is certainly a beautiful young lady," Chris offered.

"Yes she is, she turns after my son, he was a handsome boy," Mrs Grice answered with a proud look on her face.

"What we are wondering Mrs Grice," Chris said coming straight to the point.

"Did your husband, who I believe spent a lot of his army career in India, did he bring back to England a pair of ladies handguns, perhaps in a case?"

"My memory is not like it was Inspector, but yes, he did, he bought them for me while we were in India, for my protection."

"Could you use a handgun Mrs Grice?" George asked.

"I was a good shooter, my husband made me practice," she answered proudly. "My husband being a General, I had to be a good host, but other wives thought that handling a handgun was beneath them, but not me, I'm not that much of a snob, it was dangerous times out there, one needed protection."

"I'm sure you did," Chris replied, knowing very little of the past situation in India. "Do you still have them?"

"I'm sorry Inspector, but my husband gave them to his old batman, a couple years before he died."

"Do you know his batman Mrs Grice?" Chris asked perhaps a bit to hastily.

"No Inspector, the man was a mere boy when I knew him, I would not recognise him now, he must be so much older now, like us all," she smiled. "Is it important?"

"It could be Mrs Grice," Chris replied disappointed. "This batman of your husband, was that in India?"

"Oh no Inspector, it was in the Boer war, my husband took to him, as he was just a few years older than my son and they seem to like each other, as far as I know he lives in Winchester, my husband kept in touch with him, I forget when, but I do remember my husband sending him the pair of guns as a present with my son."

"Would you know the batman's name?" George asked hopefully.

Mrs Grice shook her head slowly. "No I don't think I do, such a long time ago, but as I said before, I do know that he lives in Winchester, and that he met with my son, while he was alive."

Chris looked into the fire, he was disappointed.

"You haven't had the answers you expected Inspector," Mrs Grice remarked. "I am sorry that I can't remember the name, it was such a long time ago, are the handguns important?"

Chris looked at Mrs Grice who was looking at him with concern.

"Mr Paris was shot with a handgun Mrs Grice, these handguns are illegal in this country, what I mean by that is that this country do not import these handguns, so they would have had to be brought in, possible by someone not realising that the guns were illegal."

"Oh dear," Mrs Grice moaned. "I'm sure my husband would not have done anything dishonourable."

Chris took a package from his overcoat pocket. "I have one of the handguns here Mrs Grice," Chris said taking the handgun from the package. "Do you recognise it?"

Mrs Grice took the gun and examined it. "Yes," she finally said. "That's one of them."

"Are you sure Mrs Grice?" Chris asked.

"I'm sure, but I am now worried, my husband I am sure never thought he was bringing illegal guns."

Chris took the handgun from Mrs Grice, and replaced it into its package.

"Please Mrs Grice," Chris continued. "Please do not worry yourself, the guns your husband gave as a present to his batman, may have been illegal but we are not interested in that, all we are doing just trying to find out who is the murderer of your ex daughter-in-law's husband."

"I see," Mrs Grice replied. "I am really sorry I cannot think of the name you want, but should I suddenly remember, and I do sometimes," she added. "I will let you know straight away."

"It would be appreciated," Chris said standing up. "We won't take up any more of your time Mrs Grice, thank you for seeing us, without knowing it, you may have been a big help to us."

"I certainly hope so Inspector" came the reply.

Back in their office, Chris looked at George and smiled. "Well we do know now that the guns were brought in by General Grice."

"Do it take us any farther with the case?" George asked.

Chris shrugged. "Mrs Grice said that her son who died around five years ago had met with the batman, now who is could be that man?"

"Mr Argue was a batman," George replied. "But he is dead now all we have is two women and a young girl, could Mr Argue have killed Mr Paris, then say, killed himself," George added.

"I see how your thinking George," Chris replied. "But think of the evidence, Mr Argue was in the pub about the time Mr Paris was killed, and if he killed himself, who move the gun and dropped it down the drain?"

"I see," George agreed. "If only we knew the name of the batman," he said.

Chris clasped his hands in front of him. "The guns were given to a old batman by the General, the guns were used a few days ago on two victims, whoever the batman was or is, he is still in Winchester, and is known by the Paris family and the Argue family, who the devil can he be?" Chris blurted out.

"The batman who got the guns could have sold them," George offered.

"I'll agree with that George," Chris admitted the possibility.

"Mr Argue was in the Boer War," George commented.

"Yes," Chris replied. "Do you think there might be a connection with the Boer War?"

"Anything possible," George replied. "But then again Mr Paris was not in it."

"No," Chris replied.

Chris looked at his pocket watch. "Let's go and have a liquid lunch at the Rising Sun."

"Suits me," George replied with a smile.

Chris stopped at the desk sergeant. "This is your last day as desk sergeant?" Chris asked sergeant Bloom.

"Yes Sir," he replied with a smile. "Be glad to get back on the streets again."

"Pity," Chris replied giving him a slip of paper. "You have become very good at checking, I shall miss you, can you check on this list of men's background, they all work at the Mr Paris's wool factory in Lower Brook Street, just find out whatever you can find about them, George and I are off for a bite to eat, we will be back by two."

Making their way to the Rising Sun, George looked at Chris with a manful look.

"Just a precaution," Chris said understanding his look was about the instructions he had given sergeant Bloom. "We are not getting far on the shootings, might as well know about those who are not a suspect."

Chris and George entered the Rising Sun, and felt warm with the large log fire that was burning happily in the fire place, only a few regulars were in the pub.

"Well, I thought you two have been ill," Alfie greeted them with his usual smile. "I was beginning to worry."

The detectives leaned on the bar, smiling. "Thank you for your concern landlord," Chris smiled. "Now a couple of pints of bitter, and a couple of cheese sandwiches would be welcome."

"Your wishes are my command," Alfie replied as he put a glass under the pump, and started to pull.

With the pints drawn, and paid for and Alfie having ordered his wife to make the sandwiches, the detectives sat at their usual seat, under the window that looked out on Bridge Street and took a drink of their pint.

"Alfie," Chris asked. "You do seem too young, but were you in the Boer War?"

"Yes, I was Chris," he smiled. "I have had my fortieth birthday."

"Really," Chris smiled. "You keep your age well."

"It's being cheerful," replied Alfie.

"Who was your General?" George asked.

"Oh God," replied Alfie. "It was fifteen years ago you know, let's see, he was a Winchester man, yes, his name was Grice if I remember, a decent chap, one of the boys, you might say."

445

"Was many Winchester men in the Boer War?" George butted in.

"Quite a few, work was not easy to come by, many joined to get a wage," Alfie replied seriously.

Chris took another drink before speaking. "Do you keep in touch with any of your mates in that war Alfie?" he asked.

"A few, mostly those that pop in for a drink, I don't get out much, I have too much here to do, I go up town about once a week, that's about all, the funny thing is when you are bunched together in the army you bond with your mates, it's a strong bond, many soldiers died protecting their mates in one way or another, but when you come out, that bond disappears."

"What were you Alfie?" George asked, as the sandwiches arrived, and Alfie handed them to him.

"Just a Rifleman," Alfie replied. "I didn't get any stripes."

"Really," replied Chris smiling. "I would have thought you would have made sergeant."

"If I had, I would have got busted down," Alfie replied. "I was a handful in those days, I had a sort of love for fighting."

"That's what you were there for Alfie," George replied.

"I don't mean fighting the Boers, one wrong word and I would fight with my mates that's what I mean."

"Did officers all have batman in those days?" Chris asked as he bit into his sandwich.

"Yes they did, God knows where some of them would have been without the batman, most of the officers were well off you might say, bought their rank, and was brought up with servants doing everything for them, but to give them credit, when in a battle, they showed courage, they did not want shame on their families back home."

"Was that the reason for their courage Alfie?" Chris asked interested.

"For many I would say," answered Alfie.

"Officers are no different from their men, everyone suffers with fear, if as you say these officers only put up a good show so that they brought no shame to their families, then they were certainly not cowards, it takes a brave man to fight when frightened," Chris replied.

"Never thought of it that way," Alfie admitted. "The Boers were certainly scary, even frightened me."

"Who was General Grice's batman?" George asked.

"You're asking a lot," Alfie said, putting down the glass drying clothe, and leaning on the bar.

"It's a long time ago, I remember a Argue, because he would cut our hair, he was a officer's batman. He's still in Winchester, has a shop here somewhere in the Brooks, let's see who the hell was the General's batman, I can picture him in my mind, where he is now, I don't know, if he is in Winchester, he has never been in here, Winchester is only a small place, no it won't come," Alfie gave up. "But Argue was a Captain's batman, I'm sure of that."

"Never mind Alfie," Chris replied. "So this Argue who used to cut your hair was not a General's batman?"

"No," Alfie replied with a smile. "Of course, Argue is the name suited him, he was always arguing if I remember, I'll have to pop up and see him."

Chris and George finished their drink, and got up to leave, Chris collected the empty glasses and took them to the counter. "I wouldn't bother about seeing your old mate Alfie," he said. "He died a couple days ago."

Alfie opened his mouth about to say something, but Chris cut him short.

"Ask me no questions Alfie, I am unable to answer them, but should the name of General Grice's batman come back to you, please let me know."

Chapter Thirteen

"Information comes from the most unlikely places," George remarked as the detectives made their way back to the Police Station.

"I have found Alfie a help in the past," Chris replied. "I only hope he remembers the General's batman name, it would be a great help."

Sergeant Bloom looked up and smiled as they entered, and handed Chris a paper.

"I managed to do what you wanted," he said with a smile. "You will find details about all the men who works at the wool factory."

"Thank you sergeant," Chris said taking the paper. "You are back on the street tomorrow aren't you?"

"Monday," sergeant Bloom answered. "I am off Sunday."

"You have been a big help to me sergeant," Chris replied.

"Well I shall be around Sir, if you need me," sergeant Bloom replied going back to his desk.

Chris looked at the paper, he read down the list of names, by each name there were details of how long they had worked for Mr Paris, where they lived, whether they were known to the police etc. Chris passed the paper to George.

"Two of them were in the Boer War," George said after reading the paper.

"I saw that," Chris remarked. "The foreman being one of them."

The phone rang while Chris was still studying the list of information given to him by sergeant Bloom.

Chris took the receiver as the phone rang. "Detective Inspector Hardie," he spoke onto the receiver.

"Chris, this is Olive," came the reply.

"Olive," Chris replied wondering, Olive had never before phoned him.

"I'm sorry Chris, but Elizabeth urged me to phone you, I'm afraid she is in bed with a bad case of the flue," Olive continued. "She won't be able to go to Southampton tomorrow."

"I'll be right up," Chris said concern in his voice.

"No, no, Chris," Olive replied hastily. "I have had the doctor in, he confirms it's a bad case, and she needs to stay in bed for a few days, she don't want you to come."

"Why not?" Chris answered worried.

Olive gave a small laugh. "Chris love, Elizabeth is a young woman, I know she loves you deeply, there is no way she will allow you to see her like she is, she is not at her best, also she do not want you to catch it."

"That won't bother me Olive," Chris replied.

"Chris love," Olive begged. "As a woman, I can understand my daughter, perhaps you could leave it a day, Ron said, if you are stuck on Saturday, he will be in the Rising Sun midday and bring you up to date."

"Are you sure I have no need to worry Olive?" Chris asked worried himself.

"It's just a case of flue Chris," Olive assured him. "A few days in bed with plenty of liquid, the doctor said would do her the world of good, I'll look after her for you."

"I know you will Olive," Chris replied. "I feel a little helpless, but on your assurance, I'll leave it at least until tomorrow, I'll see Ron then."

"I know Elizabeth is dying to see you Chris," Olive continued. "You will have to put it down to vanity, young women only want their love ones to see them at their best, so please Chris do not worry."

"I'll try not to Olive, give Elizabeth my love, tell her I shall miss seeing her, and hope that she recovers quickly," Chris said into the phone feeling uneasy as he did.

Chris replaced the receiver. "That was Elizabeth's mother," he said looking at George. "Elizabeth has a bad case of the flue, so it won't be a trip to Southampton tomorrow."

"Bad luck," George replied.

"She don't want me to see her," Chris said disappointed.

"That's natural," George smiled. "Woman are like that."

"I wouldn't care what she looked liked," Chris answered. "I don't love her for her looks, well not wholly," he added thinking that his words had come out wrong. "I love her for who she is."

George smiled. "Women don't understand that," he remarked. "They think a man falls in love with them because they are attractive and desirable, they don't seem to realise that it is the complete make up of a woman that a man falls in love with, it's probably the same with us."

"Well, whatever," Chris answered. "My day has changed for tomorrow, so I might as well help out with this case, tomorrow before I meet Ron, I want to go and see this Tony Trever, and call upon Mrs Paris again, you never know, might find out something that will help this case."

On the Saturday morning, Chris knocked the door of Mrs Paris's house in Monks Road, which was answered by Rosemary.

"Inspector," she smiled.

"Good morning young lady," Chris returned her greeting. "I'm here to see your mother."

Rosemary's eyes smiled. "You will have to put up with me for a while Inspector," she replied. "Mother have just gone to the shops, why not come in, I'll make you tea."

Chris took off his trilby and entered, finding that he had to squeeze by Rosemary, who had not moved, nor had she opened the door wider for him to enter.

Chris smiled to himself as he waited for Rosemary to close the door, and show him into the front room.

"I'll make you tea," she offered, a smile playing on her face.

"No need young lady," Chris replied finding himself a chair. "I had one just a few moments ago."

Rosemary threw herself on the sofa, Chris thought it was a bit unladylike.

"Anything can I do for you Inspector?" she asked a suggestive smile playing on her face.

Chris wondered if what he had heard about her going with men was true, then dismissed the thought, she was just a young girl, who knew she was attractive and flirting harmlessly.

"I just wanted a few moments with your mother," Chris replied.

"Mother treats me like a child," Rosemary said. "But as you can see, I am a woman," she smiled allowing one her arms to sweep over her body form.

"But you're still very young," Chris replied feeling a little uncomfortable. "Your mother is only protecting you,

I suppose you miss your stepfather," he continued hoping to get away from her flirting.

"I had no problems with my stepfather, only that he married my mother, I loved my dad very much, we had fun together, it's my dad that I miss," she replied the smile having left her face.

"I can understand that," Chris replied gently.

"I never heard my mother and my real dad row, perhaps I was too young, but my stepfather row with my mother a lot of," Rosemary continued.

"Really," Chris said.

"The day my stepfather was killed, I heard them rowing, something about the Talcum Powder I couldn't hear what was being said as the bedroom door was closed, but I did hear my stepfather saying she was imagining, and I wondered why, Talcum Powder seems a silly thing to argue about, don't you think?"

"It is rather," Chris replied wondering.

"Did you knew Mr Argue?" Chris asked absently still wondering about the Talcum Powder.

"Oh yes," replied Rosemary moving her body that was relaxed across the sofa.

"Dad used to take me with him, I was young then, I would sit in a chair watching his hair being cut and Mr Argue would always ask me if I thought he had cut my dad's hair satisfactory I liked that."

"It must have been fun," Chris replied.

"I enjoyed going with my dad, but my step dad never took me," Rosemary said.

"But I have often seen Mr Argue in the town," she smiled. "He always lifted his trilby when we meet."

"Your stepfather had only been married a few months to your mother Rosemary, perhaps he had not had the chance, with you away at the girls school," Chris remarked, as he heard the front door open.

Chris was on his feet as Mrs Paris entered the room, having already disposed of her coat and hat.

"Inspector," she uttered as she caught sight of him.

"I'm sorry Mrs Paris, I wanted a moment with you, you were out and your daughter kindly offer me in I hope you don't mind," Chris apologised.

"That is quite alright Inspector," she replied looking at Rosemary.

"Rosemary sit up straight, one do not flop on a sofa when guest are present," she turned to Chris. "You will forgive my daughter Inspector, children have no manners these days."

"I am not a child mother," Rosemary almost shouted before Chris had a chance to replied, and stormed out of the room.

Mrs Paris watched her daughter run from the room, then turned to Chris. "I'm sorry Inspector for her actions, please take a seat and tell me how I can be of help?"

Chris re-seated and Mrs Paris took a chair opposite to him across the table. "In your husband's business, I take it you yourself did the office work, such as keeping the books, and doing all that would be needed for orders coming and going."

"That is correct Inspector, wages of the men, and employment of them when needed," Mrs Paris replied.

"Did you employ your manager as well?" Chris asked.

"We have no manager Inspector," Mrs Paris replied. "But we do have a floor foreman, Mr Tony Trever."

"I'm sorry Mrs Paris, I understood from my sergeant that he was the manager."

"He is acting temporary manager at the moment, but his works title is floor foreman," Mrs Paris answered.

"Perhaps that is how I made my mistake," Chris apologised. "Did you employ him?"

"No as a matter of fact," Mrs Paris replied. "We were just settle the business up, and my first husband Thomas gave him a job, if I remember correctly, Mr Trever was in the Boer War with Thomas's father General Grice, he was his batman I believe."

"Would you know whether Mr Trever knew Mr Argue the barber?" Chris asked.

"I'm afraid I do not interest myself with the affairs of my staff," Mrs Paris replied. "They do their work, I pay them their wages, apart from that I know nothing, why Inspector is it relevant?"

"I have no idea as yet Mrs Paris," Chris replied with a weak smile. "It could be just a coincidence, but Mr Argue was also in the Boer war with General Grice, he cut the chaps hair."

"You can find out easily Inspector, go and ask Mr Trever," Mrs Paris offered. "I do not know."

"General Grice's wife told me that her husband gave her son Thomas, your first husband a case of two handguns, to give to his batman, can you remember anything about this, I know it must have been a few years ago."

"Are these guns involved?" Mrs Paris asked.

"I'm afraid so Mrs Paris, Mrs Grice recognised the gun that shot your husband, as one of a pair that her husband had bought for her in India, for protection," Chris replied.

"Oh dear," Mrs Paris gasped. "I must go and see her, she must be feeling terrible."

"Can you remember anything about Mr Trever's promoted?" Chris asked.

"I'm afraid not Inspector," Mrs Paris replied looking serious. "It was John, not Thomas that promoted Mr Trever to floor foreman, they got on well I'm sure."

"I'm just stating the facts as I know them at the moment Mrs Paris," Chris said. "Mr Trevor, if as suspected was given the guns, could he have sold them on?"

"I see," replied Mrs Paris slowly. "Then you do not really suspect him?"

"I'm afraid everyone involved are suspected Mrs Paris," Chris answered.

"Even myself Inspector?" Mrs Paris responded with a stare.

"Mrs Paris, I have a case of two murders, somehow they are connected, because both guns bought in India by General Grice and they are the murder weapons, and including your goodself, I have only a handful of people involved."

"I am alarmed that I should be a suspect Inspector," Mrs Paris replied. "Deeply alarmed, but I do understand."

"I suppose Mr Trever would have the keys of the factory?" Chris asked trying to get away from the suspect questions.

"Yes he would," Mrs Paris replied. "He lets the workers in at seven in the mornings, and locks up after they gone home, it is his job to make sure that the premises are secure in all respects at night."

"I understood that your husband locked up at nights," Chris replied.

"When he was here yes, but do not forget my husband was often away buying wool, and I leave the office about four in the afternoon I have Rosemary to think about, of course when both Thomas and John were there, it was worked differently."

"I see," murmured Chris slowly his mind going over and over what he had learnt.

"Would it be possible for me to have a look at your husband's desk at the factory?" he asked.

Mrs Paris stared at Chris. "What possible help that could be, I fail to understand," she replied.

"Someone killed your husband," Chris replied. "As far as I am able to find, your husband was a pleasant man, and spoke well of as an employer, so there must be a reason for his killing, I must check all sorts of things to get to the truth, sometimes a person will write a few words, or a letter that can prove to be helpful, and what better place that one might find this than his office desk, should he have one."

"Oh very well," Mrs Paris replied impatiently. "You are quite right about John's character, I get you John's keys, he keeps his office desk drawers locked, when do you expect to do this?" she asked.

"As soon as I leave here, I take it that your employees work Saturday mornings?" Chris asked

"Until one pm" Mrs Paris replied handing Chris a set of keys, which Chris took.

"I will get these back to you without delay," he promised.

"May I ask you a personal question Mrs Paris, although I can realise that it would be one that you would not care to answer, it could have a bearing on the case," Chris spoke gently.

Mrs Paris looked at Chris, she felt unsure how to answer, but did not want to seem uncooperative. "You may Inspector," she finally answered.

"Was there any trouble between your husband and yourself?" Chris asked.

Chris saw colour appeared on Mrs Paris's face, and she just stared at him. "You have a nerve Inspector, I will give you that, but I will also tell you I was very happily married to both my husbands."

"Thank you Mrs Paris," Chris replied. "Believe me I am not being nosy."

Chris looked at his watch as he left the house, it was five past eleven, he decided to walk back through the park, his mind going over all that had been said, he wondered about the row Rosemary had heard between her parents, the words Talcum Powder interested him, also far as he knew, Mrs Paris and Mr Argue did not know each other, but Rosemary did. Chris came out of Park Avenue, and stopped at the main road North Walls, he turned left, crossing the road as he did so, within a hundred yards he turned right into Lower Brook Street, and in five minuets he found himself opening the small door of the wool factory.

Chris found himself in a large, lengthily enclosure, he look to his right and saw the upstairs office, further in he could see men at work, and wondered what they could be doing, a man came towards him with a smile on his face.

"Can I help you Sir?" he asked.

"Yes," Chris replied. "I am looking for Mr Trever."

"I am Tony Trever," answered the man. "How can I help you?"

"Mr Trever, I am Detective Inspector Hardie of Winchester CID, I want to ask you a few questions about the death of Mr Paris if you can spare a few moments."

Mr Trever considered for a moment, before answering.

"Well you better come up to the office," he offered walking towards the stairs where he stopped and took off the Wellingtons boots he was wearing and putting on shoe that were at the ready.

"Why do you wear Wellingtons?" Chris asked as he waited.

"Wool dipping," Mr Trever explained slipping his feet into the shoes. "The liquid we use rots the shoes."

"Take good care of your wellingtons then," Chris smiled. "Are they supplied or do you have to supply your own?"

Mr Trever looked up with a smile. "All supplied thank goodness, every member of the staff, have their names are on the inside," he said. "No one can pinch them, please come up, I have already had one of your chaps here, a Sergeant House, I think his name was," he continued as he mounted the stairs and entered the office with Chris following.

Mr Trever sat at the desk, that overlooked the work floor, a position from which he could see the whole of the depot. Chris noticed that there were two more desks in the room.

"Take a seat," Chris was offered as Mr Trever indicated a chair at the side of his desk. "Now how can I help you?"

"I know my Sergeant has seen you Mr Trever, but since then other information has come, to which I need answers," Chris said seeing Mr Trever nodded his head. "You were I believe a batman to General Grice during the Boer War."

"That's right," Mr Trever replied with a smile. "I was very young then, and the General was very good to me, he died a few years back."

"So I understand," Chris replied. "I also understand that before he died he gave to his son Mr Thomas Grice a pair of handguns as a present to give to you."

"That's right Inspector, a pair of handguns, worth a few bob I can tell you," Mr Trever replied. "Mrs Linda Grice was here when her husband Mr Thomas gave them to me, so was Mr Paris."

"Really," replied Chris. "Mrs Paris knew about the guns?"

"Oh yes, she was very interested in them, I remember she took them out of their case and pretended to be some kind of cowboy girl, pointing them out through the office window," Mr Trever smiled as he remembered.

"Can you remember the number of shells that were with the guns?" Chris asked.

"There were two," Mr Trever replied. "I took it that Mrs Grice had used all the shells for practice while in India, there were places for twelve."

"Did you have a desk in this office at that time?" Chris asked.

"Oh no, I was working on the wool dips at that time, I got promoted by Mr John after Mr Thomas had died."

"I see," Chris murmured. "Do you still have these guns?" Chris asked.

Mr Trever looked at Chris, he seemed a little sad. "No, I sold them, I know they were a present, but I was trying to buy a little place around that time, I wasn't earning a lot, so I sold the guns to an old friend of mine that was in the army with me, Roger Argue, sadly he is dead as well."

"Yes I know," Chris answered feeling shocked, he had never given it a thought that Mr Argue had been the owner of the guns, one of which killed him. "Would Mr Argue have sold them do you think?" Chris asked.

"No, not Rodger, he never sold anything, but was always open to a bargain, he was what you might call a hoarder, never threw away anything, not even newspapers, which he tore up and used in his barber shop for wiping the cut-throat when shaving a customer," Mr Trever laughed.

Chris could not see anything funny in what Mr Trever had said, his mind was tormenting him. "Your job now is to secure the building at night and lock up, am I right in thinking that?" Chris asked.

"Well at the moment it is with no boss around, but when Mr John was here, he would sometimes lock up," Mr Trever answered.

"You told my Sergeant that you often saw a woman waiting a little way off as you closed up for the night, and that one night you saw this woman enter the factory."

"That's correct," replied Mr Trever his face unsmiling. "That what I told him, and it's the truth."

"That must have been one night that Mr Paris locked up?" Chris asked.

Mr Trever nodded his head. "That's right Inspector."

"What was your opinion of this?" Chris asked. "Did you think Mr Paris was having an affair?"

"I'm a man who have seen a lot of the world Inspector, why would any woman sneak into a building at night, I had my thoughts," Mr Trever answered.

"Did Mrs Paris have any suspicion of what was going on?" Chris asked.

"No idea," Trever replied. "But when they were both in the office, there seem to be an atmosphere."

"I see," Chris muttered thinking of nothing more to ask.

"Thank you for your cooperation Mr Trever, which is Mr Paris's desk?" he asked. "I want to look through it."

"I can't let you do that Sir," Mr Trever said with authority. "It's not my place to allow you."

Chris smiled dangling a set of keys in front of Mr Tever. "It's alright, I have permission from Mrs Paris, phone her if you must."

"Well seeing you have the keys, I suppose it's alright," Mr Trever said hesitantly. "His desk is the one on the left."

Chris moved to the desk as indicated and sat down behind it, it was a seven drawer desk, three down each side, and a narrow drawer across the centre. Chris pulled to open the centre drawer, it contained what he imagined. Rulers, pencils, pens without nibs, and pens with nibs and assorted rubbers, he moves the articles around with his fingers, small boxes of paper clips, and pen nibs, nothing of interest to him. He pushed his chair backwards a little, and studied the three drawers on each side, and saw that the bottom drawer on the right hand side was fitted with a lock, he checked his bunch of keys, selecting one, he bent right over and inserted the key, it fitted. The drawer contained several red covered ledgers.

"A set of books for the firms accountant," Chris thought to himself, as he lifted the top one out, income and expenditure, Chris read on the front of the ledger. Chris had no interest in the business side of the firm, he ruffled through the pages without reading a word before putting it to one side. The next ledger he took out, was a record of orders, and deliveries, ruffling through the pages as he had the previous one, he put it to one side, and took the next one from the drawer. It was the wages ledger, he followed his previous procedure, and a loose sheet of paper poked out from the pages. He opened the ledger to where the loose sheet was hiding, it was a carbon copy of a letter on the firms business heading to the firms accountant. Chris read it, and a smile crossed his face. He looked towards Mr Trever, who had his back to Chris, seeing that Mr Trever was unconcerned, he folded the letter and put it in his overcoat pocket. No longer interested in the other contents, Chris replaced the ledgers, and re locked the drawer.

"Don't seem to be anything to help me here," Chris said, making Mr Trever turn in his seat and look at him.

"What did you expect to find Inspector?" Mr Trever asked.

"I was just hoping that if you were right regarding him having a woman here at nights, a letter perhaps, or even an article belonging to the woman, you never know?"

Chris got up from the desk. "Anyway Mr Trever, I must be off, thank you for your cooperation, now just one other thing, I need your statement as to what you told me and my Sergeant, can you pop into the station about ten, Monday morning."

"Well," replied Mr Trever. "I don't know, I will have to get permission from Mrs Paris, I am running this place at the moment."

"Yes you do that Mr Trever, I doubt if there will be any trouble, Mrs Paris will be there as well," Chris informed him.

"Oh I say Inspector, what I told you about her husband seeing a woman, she could sack me," Mr Trever said looking worried.

"I can promise you she won't sack you Mr Trever," Chris replied.

A weak smile appeared on Mr Trever's face. "I hope you're right Inspector."

"Trust me," Chris replied leaving the office.

Chris stood outside the building, he felt very happy, he put on his trilby, then looked at his watch. "Time," he muttered to himself he wanted to call into the police station before going to meet Ron in the Rising Sun. He turned towards Cross Keys Passage, buttoning his overcoat as he did, he patted his overcoat pocket and smiled.

He entered the station, and saw Sergeant Williams staring at him.

"Can't keep away," the sergeant greeted Chris without a smile.

"Is sergeant House in?" Chris asked ignoring the desk sergeant's remark.

"No, he had a place to go, said if it took time he would have a bite to eat before returning," replied the desk sergeant without any expression.

"Is Sergeant Bloom on today?" Chris asked.

"Not on the desk, he is off tomorrow," came the replied.

"Let him know that if he has nothing on I want to see him tomorrow," Chris commanded.

"I'll make a note of it Sir," Chris heard the reply as he made for his office.

Chris hurried to his desk and sat taking out paper and envelope from his desk drawer, and hastily wrote Mrs Paris's address on the envelope. On the paper he wrote a short letter, asking Mrs Paris to be at his office at ten on Monday morning, and explain to her that he had already asked her manager to be there as well. He put the letter and the keys she had given him in the envelope and seal it. On his way out of the station, Chris stopped at the desk.

"Sergeant Williams, I want this envelope delivered today, will you see that it is done," Chris asked putting the envelope before him. "It is urgent."

"Leave it to uniform," remarked Sergeant Williams taking the envelope and looking at it. "It will be done, running errands keep uniform fit," the sergeant replied.

"Work as a team Sergeant," Chris remarked leaving the station.

Chris felt the warmth as he entered the Rising Sun, the large open fire was well alight. He saw Alfie grinning at him, and he caught sight of Ron sitting in his usual place.

"Ron," Chris said approaching him with his arm outstretched. "Sorry I'm a little late."

"No problem," Ron replied standing up and taking the hand of Chris. "I have ordered you a bitter."

"Thank you," replied Chris unbuttoning his overcoat, and turning to the bar at which Alfie was busy pulling his pint. "Alfie how are you?" he asked.

"I'm always healthy and happy," Alfie replied, with his usual grin putting the drawn pint before Chris on the bar.

"Lucky you," Chris replied. "It must be that good lady of yours that keep you so."

"Typical remark coming from someone not married," Alfie replied still grinning. "By the way, I thought of General Grice's batman, it came to me in a flash last night while I was serving, funny how these sort of things happen?"

"Yes Alfie it is," Chris replied impatiently. "Who do you say it was?"

"I don't know his full name, but we used to call him TT, is that any help?" Alfie asked, his grin having left his face. "I don't think he was a proper batman, he was very young, and I think the General made him some part of his staff."

"It helps a lot Alfie, and thanks, thank you very much," Chris said picking up his pint and taking it with him to join Ron.

"Well how is Elizabeth?" Chris asked before he had taken a drink. "Is she allergist?"

Ron laughed. "Red eyes and a red nose, but otherwise getting better, the doctor is pleased with her."

"I'm so glad," Chris smiled taking up his pint. "She has been on my mind, so I can see her."

"I should let it go until Monday," Ron advised. "Women are silly things, they only want to be seen at their best, look at the time they take over themselves when they are going out on a date, one wonders just what do they do to themselves."

"All I want is for her to get well Ron, I miss her, but I will be up some time Monday, you can tell her that," Chris said as he took a drink.

"Also tell her I love her and miss her, and whatever she looks like is OK with me."

"I'll tell her that, it will cheer her up," Ron replied lifting his glass.

Chapter Fourteen

*I*t was almost closing time when Chris and Ron parted outside the Rising Sun.

"Olive will be going on to you when you get home," Chris said with a smile as he and Ron shook hands.

Ron grinned. "She who must be obeyed, has commanded me to stay with you as long as you want, she realises that you want to see Elizabeth, and you will worry over her."

"I am worried over her Ron," Chris replied. "I also know that Olive is the best person in the world looking after her."

"You got that right," Ron remarked.

"I can not understand why Elizabeth do not want me to see her?" Chris muttered.

Ron grinned again. "You have a lot to learn about women Chris."

"I don't see why?" Chris replied his face serious. "After all when we are married I don't expect to be pushed out of the house should she become ill, as her husband I would want to be with her."

"It's all vanity at the moment Chris, when you are married, she will expect you to be by her side, at the moment however, nothing must come between you seeing her at her best, she is after all a woman," Ron grinned again.

"It do not make sense to me, I am not marrying her for her looks, even if she is the most beautiful girl I have ever seen," Chris remarked.

"Men are inclined to be attracted to looks, more than a woman, and women are aware of this, otherwise why would they go to all the bother of making their face up," Ron argued. "Then at night take an hour getting it off their face."

Chris shrugged. "Anyway Ron, I will leave you here, thanks for having a drink with me, I am at a loose end at the moment."

"No plans for the rest of the day?" Ron asked as he buttoned his overcoat.

"Might pop into the station and see how George is getting on, will you give Elizabeth my best, and of course Olive as well," Chris said as he followed Ron in doing up his overcoat.

"Elizabeth will want to know word for word what we talked about, don't you worry," Ron laughed as once again he offered his hand. "Take care Chris, and you will be calling on Monday?"

"That's a guarantee," Chris grinned taking Ron's hand.

As Ron walked towards Alresford Road, Chris walked away from him towards the police station, apart from Elizabeth on his mind, he also had the Mr Paris case, he passed the entrance to the Abbey Grounds then he changed his mind, a few minutes later he turned back and entered the Abbey Grounds, deciding he would sit and think about his case.

Chris seated himself on the bench that facing King Alfred Statue, he pulled his collar up and pulled his trilby down over his head, although it was extremely cold, there were plenty people in the town, Chris took out his pipe, finding the bowl half full he lit the pipe and sucked it contentedly blowing out smoke, his mind went to his case, although he was looking at the traffic and people walking by, he was not seeing them, as his mind was now fully exploring the murder of Mr Paris.

He had two dead men, both shot, he had two wives in the frame, and Mr Trever who worked for Mr Paris, and was a buddy of Mr Argue as a soldier in the Boer War. The only other person in the frame was Mrs Paris's daughter Rosemary.

Both the dead men had been shot with handguns that had been given to Mr Trever by General Grice who had been his commanding officer in the Boer War, but Mr Trever had told him that he had sold the handguns on to Mr Argue, but Mr Argue was dead and unable to verify the fact.

His thoughts went to the wages ledger of the wool factory that he had seen that morning, which told him Mr Trever had been given the sack by Mr Paris, and wondered if this would have cause Mr Trever to kill Mr Paris, it could have been a motive, but then, who was this mysterious woman who Mr Trever says he saw entering the factory while Mr Paris was still there. He wondered about the Talcum Powder that Rosemary had heard her stepfather and mother argue about, and wondered if there was any significance in it.

Mrs Paris, although difficult seemed to have answered his questions in a plausible acceptable way, and so had Mr Trever, unless he found out to the contrary, he had to accept what they told him.

With his pipe out, and getting no where in his thoughts, Chris decided that he would give the police station a miss, and go back to his lodgings. Chris crossed the Broadway, and walked past the police station on the opposite side. He stopped outside the Indian Arms, where he bought a newspaper from the newsboy standing by the arch entrance to the saloon bar. Further on he put a penny in the organ players hat, walked a few steps further and bought himself an apple from the barrow boy on the corner of Middle Brook Street. Chris bit into the apple as he made his way to his lodgings oblivious to all those he passed.

Chapter Fifteen

*C*hris entered his office on the Sunday Morning, he had not seen George the day before. Chris had gone home to his lodgings, eaten the dinner his landlady Mr Dobson had put out for him, then he had retired to his bedroom, where he eventually fell asleep.

Chris hung up his overcoat and trilby, then seated himself behind his desk, a note was there for him from George. It told him that George had no luck with the dustcart men, that he had gone to the council yard to see them, no gun case had been found, although one man had found a cutlery case, Chris laid the note down on his desk.

Chris had already decided that he would call upon Mrs Argue that day, Mr Trever had told him he had sold the handguns to Mr Argue, and he wanted to know just what had happened to them through the years. He remembered that Mr Argue had told him that his wife was a church goer on Sundays, so he decided to put his visit off until the afternoon, he had plenty to do, the paper work of the two interviews he had done on Saturday, plus trying to piece together what he had been told during those interviews, he also had Elizabeth on his mind.

Sergeant Williams came in with a cup of tea during the morning, and apart from that Chris was not interrupted, busy with his paper work, the morning went quick. Chris leaned back in his chair after completing his report, he fingered his moustache then looked at his pocket watch, which told him it was almost one o'clock. Chris spared a minute tidying his desk, then collecting his coat and trilby which he put on and left the office.

"I am going to Mrs Argue's house at Upper Brook Street," he told Sergeant Williams as he past to the station door. "Should I be wanted."

"Sundays, always quiet until two," replied the sergeant. "I'll make a note."

Chris mounted the two steps to the shop door, and knocked and within moments Chris saw Mrs Argue leave the back room and come to the door, she was smartly dressed, and she touched the back of her hair as she opened the door.

"Inspector," she said a smile appearing on her face. "I haven't long been in, I go to church you know, come, come in, I have a nice pot of tea on the table."

Chris took off his trilby and entered, following Mrs Argue to the front room back of the shop.

"I must apologise for interrupting your Sunday," Chris said as he seated himself at the table.

"That's alright Inspector," Mrs Argue replied. "I am glad of a bit of company, I get that in the church, but the church is not open for service twenty four hours a day, is it," she smiled as she poured out two cups of tea. "Sugar and milk she asked?"

"Milk with one sugar, thank you," Chris replied.

"Nothing like a nice cup of tea to warm you up," Mrs Argue continued pushing a cup towards him, and sitting herself at the table. "Now Inspector how can I help you?" she asked.

Chris took a sip of the tea, it was hot. "Yesterday, I was talking to a man by the name of Mr Tony Trever, do you know him?" Chris asked putting the hot tea down for a while to allow it to cool.

Mrs Argue sipped her tea before answering. "Yes I do Inspector he was a friend of Roger, they were both in the Boer war together."

Chris smiled deciding not to take up his cup for a while. "Yes he did tell me that, he also told me that he sold your husband a pair of handguns, and I had to call today to ask you if you knew of this?"

Mrs Argue took another sip of her tea, then replaced the cup into the saucer. "My husband buys a lot of things Inspector, I have never really been interested," she turned her body towards the sideboard.

"The bottom of that sideboard belongs to my husband, what he has in there is nobody's business, I believe he has razors, comb sets, tweezers, and what have you, concerning his business, much of it unopened," Mrs Argue smiled. "As for the handguns I do not know, if I had seen them I would soon had them out of here," she said lifting her cup again.

Chris smiled to himself and picked up his cup, the tea was cooler, and he drank it willingly.

"Can we take a look Mrs Argue?" Chris asked his cup going back in his saucer. "It would help me if they were still in the sideboard."

Mrs Argue looked at Chris and hesitantly spoke. "Well, what Roger has in the sideboard is no good to him now, I will soon have to sort out his business papers he puts in there, go ahead Inspector have a look."

Chris knelt before the sideboard and open the doors of the cupboards, it was full of boxes mainly small ones and packages, on the right he saw ledgers and papers were piled neatly, which he took to be business books. Chris more or less knew the size he was looking for, and the fact that the case would be similar to that of cutlery case, he felt disappointed finding no kind of case at all.

"It do not seem to be here Mrs Argue," Chris said getting up and closing the cupboard doors. "Would he keep things anywhere else?" Chris asked.

"No," Mrs Argue replied. "We had this agreement, that he would use the sideboard as his own, and not fill other drawers up around the house, I know what's in all my drawers Inspector," she said.

Chris finished his tea.

"Another cup Inspector?" Mrs Argue offered.

"No, no thank you Mrs Argue, I am not a big tea drinker."

"You like a pint that I'm sure Inspector," Mrs Argue smiled.

"I have been known to have a pint," Chris informed her absently, his mind wondering about the guns. "Are you sure you know nothing of your husband buying the guns, I mean he could have sold them on?"

"I'm sorry Inspector, I know very little of what my husband did, or bought or sold, I am sorry."

"You said you knew Mr Trever didn't you?" Chris asked.

"Inspector," replied Mrs Argue pouring herself another cup of tea. "My husband was a soldier with Mr Trever, of course I knew him, he would have his hair cut here, and when the shop was empty, he would often come back here with Roger and have a cuppa," she said pouring milk into her tea.

"Would he ever have been in this room alone?" Chris asked.

Mrs Argue did not answer straight away, she took a sip of tea. "I really can't remember, is it important?" she finally replied.

Chris smiled. "I need to know all I can Mrs Argue, a matter of routine, I have two dead men, both killed with the guns that as far as I am aware was kept in that sideboard," he said indicating the sideboard with his head.

"As I said Inspector, I know very little of what was in that sideboard, surely it's a guess on your part that they were ever there at all," Mrs Argue said as she took another sip of her tea.

"You are right there Mrs Argue, tell me do you have many visitors, I mean those you would leave alone in this room?" Chris asked.

"Not really Inspector, perhaps the only one I can think of is my sister, who you have met," Mrs Argue replied. "What my husband did while I was out shopping, of course I wouldn't know."

"Your sister did not know Mr or Mrs Paris, and perhaps not Mr Trever?" Chris asked.

"She might have met Mr Trever, if he was here when my sister was, but like myself, I do not think she knew Mr and Mrs Paris," replied Mrs Argue becoming a bit irritated with the questions. "You are not thinking that my sister had anything to do with the deaths are you?"

"No, no, Mrs Argue, please forgive the questions, it's not only routine me asking them, it's necessary if I am to solve the case."

Mrs Argue smiled making no comment, she sat with her arms on the table looking at Chris and wondering what he was going to ask next.

Chris shifted in his chair. "Well I must get along now Mrs Argue," he said.

"Just to re-cap, if the guns were indeed in the sideboard, apart from your sister and Mr Trever, no one has been left alone in this room, during the day or evening while your husband is out?"

"As far as I'm aware Inspector," Mrs Argue confirmed.

"Well thank you for being so patient with me, I know my questions can sometime irritate people, but," Chris said standing and spreading his arms. "It's a part of the job."

"Think nothing of it Inspector, it was nice of you to call," Mrs Argue replied getting up.

Chris picked up his trilby and was about to leave, when he turned back facing Mrs Argue. "Would you be able to call at the police station tomorrow morning around ten?" he asked.

"I'm sure I can," Mrs Argue said. "But can you tell me why?"

"Statements Mrs Argue," Chris replied. "Mr Trever and Mrs Paris will both call and make their statements as well."

"I see," Mrs Argue answered, her mind racing. "Well if the other two are going, then I will be there."

"Thank you Mrs Argue," Chris smiled. "I'll see myself out."

Chapter Sixteen

C hris's sleep was restless, his mind tormented with the jigsaw of the case, one of the three had to be the murderer, but which one. Monday was the crunch day, he had to know what he was doing when the three suspects were in his office, if he made an error then he might never really know who the murderer was, and like the last case with Mr Sharpe, he would be unable to charge anyone with the crime, not having convincing proof.

Dressed, shaved and having had breakfast, Chris left his lodgings, with the thoughts of the case still occupying his mind, interrupted at times with the thought of Elizabeth. He looked at her bank as he strolled pass, and was wishing she was outside waiting for him, but she was not there. He dug his hands into his overcoat pockets and walked quickly to the police station.

Chris entered the station to the smile of sergeant Williams, who looked at him as he entered. "You look as though you have been up all night Inspector," he voiced as Chris entered.

"One could say that I have," Chris replied not wanting to get into sarcastic remarks. "My sleep was restless, and a nice cup of tea would do wonders."

"All your orders have been carried out, and I have a couple uniforms standing by, I will send you a nice cup of tea in," sergeant Williams remarked not being sarcastic.

"Appreciate it," Chris answered as he entered his office where he discarded his overcoat and trilby, then crossed to the gas fire and lit it with a match. It was a cold morning, and he crossed to his desk rubbing his hands, and found the instant warmth of the fire. He had just sat when the office door opened, and George entered carrying a cup of tea.

"Compliments of the Sergeant Williams," George smiled placing the cup before Chris.

Chris took up the cup with a smile. "Thanks George," he said. "Just what I need, help to keep me awake," Chris drank the hot tea in one go, and replaced the cup in its saucer.

"Now George, I have asked Mrs Paris, Mr Trever and Mrs Argue in at ten this morning to make statements, I have not had time to tell you yet, I did not see you yesterday."

"I heard you have been in on Saturday," George replied. "You got my note, the council dustcart men were of no use."

"I expected the result, but it had to be done, one never know. With Elizabeth ill, I felt lost without her on Saturday, so I made the time up by seeing Mrs Paris and saw Mr Trever, and on Sunday I saw Mrs Argue, I believe I can solve this case," Chris told George his thoughts.

"How is your Elizabeth?" George asked as sergeant Williams brought in three chairs, and placed them in front of the desk.

"I had a drink with Ron Saturday, he told me she was on the mend, and that I could see her later today," Chris replied. "Funny how women don't like you to see them at their worse."

"That will change when you are married Chris, there would be no way out for Elizabeth to stop you seeing her."

Chris made no comment as he looked at sergeant Williams who had arranged the chairs. "Thank you sergeant, it's almost ten, I want to see them altogether, not one at a time."

"Understand Inspector," replied sergeant Williams with a grin as he was about to retreat.

"When Sergeant Bloom comes in, ring my phone," Chris added as he left.

Chris sat back in his chair, and studied the three people seated in front of his desk, he looked at George, and saw that the shorthand typist was ready with his notebook, he leaned forward.

"Thank you all for coming," Chris opened the meeting. "I hope Mrs Paris and Mrs Argue will not find it too painful, both of you having lost a husband. Now this case has baffled us, mainly because apart from the three of you here today, we can find no one else who might or could be involved."

"You asked us here to make a statement," Mr Trever interrupted. "Now you are insinuating that one of us is a murderer."

Chris smiled. "I do not recall asking you Mr Trever to come and make a statement."

"Well I took it at such," replied Mr Trever knowing that he had made a slip up.

Chris looked at him then at Mrs Argue who coloured a shade, Chris smiled inwardly.

"Well you are quite right Mr Trever, I do want a statement from each of you, but I thought before doing so I would give you all a update on the case," Chris saw them relax at his words.

"With two deaths and only just the three of you that seem to be involved, you will understand that the case baffled us, however we were able to get a start, it seems that you Mr Trever," Chris said looking directly at him. "Was given perhaps a very unusual present from General Grice, who I believe took you under his wing during your time in the Boer War."

"I was his batman," Mr Trever remarked interrupting again.

"You were certainly a part of his staff Mr Trever, but not as his batman, you were of course too young for one thing, and a General would normally have a soldier with stripes as his batman," Chris replied. "However you were given a pair of handguns from General Grice, and these were the guns that killed Mr Paris and Mr Argue."

"I told you I sold the guns," interrupted Mr Trever.

"Indeed you did," Chris answered. "However when I saw Mrs Argue, she knew nothing of her husband buying these guns, and Mr Argue is not here to verify that he did buy them, however I do believe that you did sell Mr Argue the weapons."

"Well thank you very much," Mr Trever remarked sarcastically. "He keeps them in the sideboard in his front room, look in there," advised Mr Trever.

"I can assure you I have, I did so myself, and found no signs of any guns," Chris replied.

"He must have sold them on then," Mr Trever argued.

"He might have," Chris agreed. "But Mrs Argue told me he was a hoarder, you yourself told me he was crafty when it came to a bargain, I doubt very much he sold them on, we are talking about firearms, and unregistered ones," Chris then looked at Mrs Argue, who was sitting silent her hand clasped in her lap.

"Mrs Argue, I have no doubt that Mr Trever did sell your husband these guns, which he kept them in the sideboard. Although you told me that you did not know anything about them, I cannot believe you, after all, they had laid in the sideboard for several years," Chris paused waiting for an objection, but none came. "You told me of course that you knew Mr Trever, but did not tell me you were having an affair with him."

Mrs Argue could not comprehended what Chris had just said about her. "I was most certainly not," Mrs Argue spluttered, her rosy cheeks redder than ever. "What could have gave you that impression?" she shouted, there being anger in her voice as she looked towards Mr Trever.

"It seems that your husband knew of your association with his friend Mr Trever, he spoke of it to Mr Paris, and Mr Paris sacked Mr Trever because of it," Chris explained.

"Where do all this rubbish come from?" Mr Trever jumped to his feet. "Mrs Paris can vouch for me."

"I have no doubt she can, but please Mr Trever take your seat," Chris spoke commandingly.

"Now Mrs Paris," Chris looked at Mrs Paris. "You doubted your husband infidelity."

"How would you know that," Mrs Paris shouted. "And how dare you bring my marriage into this, I consider it very disgusting."

Chris gave a weak smile. "Nevertheless Mrs Paris, you did think that your husband was having an affair, you smelt Talcum Powder when you entered your office in the mornings."

"How would you know what I smelt in the office?" she asked her voice a little calmer.

"I'm afraid your daughter told me on Saturday morning," Chris replied.

"How dare you question my daughter while I am out, she is just a child," Mrs Paris replied angrily.

"I can assure you Mrs Paris, I did not question your daughter on any matter, what she told me was innocently volunteered," Chris answered back.

"Now if we can get on," he said turning back to Mr Trever. "You told both Sergeant House and myself that you saw a woman enter your work place, a short time after you left, implying that this woman was seeing Mr Paris."

"That's right," Mr Trever answered. "So much for trusting the police, you promised not to mention it."

"Had it been the truth I would not have," Chris answered. "But you were lying, you did not see a woman enter the factory when you left, in fact the woman entered only when Mr Paris had left, the woman in question being Mrs Argue."

"So it was your fancy woman's Talcum Powder that I smelt, and all the time I blamed my husband," Mrs Paris stormed angrily. "Well you can certainly say you are sacked now."

"How can you say the woman was me, many woman uses talcum powder," Mrs Argue pleaded.

"I would agree Mrs Argue," Chris spoke quietly. "When I saw you yesterday, you had just come from church, no one would have missed the smell of talcum powder on you, and as I have said before, you three are the only ones involved in this case."

Mrs Argue looked at her hands, that she was twisting in her lap, since the death of her husband she had felt guilt, she had betrayed his trust. She knew that her husband had an eye for the beautiful looking woman, but knew also he had not gone as far as she had, by having an affair.

"You are quite right Inspector," she said tears coming to her eyes.

"I was having an affair with Tony, I can't help my feelings, I was very bored as a wife, Roger, he was in the shop each day, and every night during the week he was in the pub until closing time, I'm afraid my feelings for Roger vanished when I met Tony, but even then it took time, but I did not kill my husband Inspector."

Chris looked at Mrs Argue, he felt a little sorry for her, knowing that emotion was the cause of many crime, he turned back to Mr Trever.

"Mr Trever, with permission I searched Mr Paris's office desk, as you know, you were there, I opened the wages ledger, by the side of your name Mr Paris had put discharged with one week's notice."

Chris saw Mr Trever stare at him and was about to say something, but Chris cut him short. "We have already established why Mr Paris sacked you, but I would like to know the meaning of this letter," he continued holding up a sheet of heading paper.

"I found this inside the ledger, it is a copy of a letter sent by Mrs Paris to her accountant."

Chris heard a gasp come from Mrs Paris. "It seems that Mrs Paris had re-employed you with a managerial job, and requesting a raise in pay, can you tell me how this came about?" Chris asked.

Mr Trever looked at Chris then at Mrs Paris, he started to mutter, when Mrs Paris interrupted.

"Inspector," she said with anger in her voice.

"Why, who I employ and what position I employ them at in the firm have anything to do with this case is beyond my understanding, but I am the one you should ask, not an employee."

"Very well Mrs Paris, can you give a reason?" Chris asked smiling to himself, knowing that Mrs Paris in her anger might drop her guard.

"As you know," Mrs Paris replied. "Both my husbands were the wool buyers, I have lost both of them now and have no one experience in wool buying, I myself not able to be at the work all day, Mr Trever is the most experience man, and I knew that he was sacked by John, because of an affair he was having, but did not know with whom, or that he was using our premises for that affair, I had re-employed him with a managerial job, and a raise in pay. The wages rise was appropriate to his new position, so I do need a general manager, I would however say to Mr Trever," Mrs Paris continued looking at Mr Trever. "That I did allow my temper to get the better of me, and withdraw my remark about him being sacked."

"Thank you Mrs Paris, that was very informative," Chris commented.

He looked at Mr Trever as the phone rang, he lifted the receiver, and after a moment spoke into it. "Thank you, tell him to wait until I need him," Chris replaced the receiver.

"I'm sorry about that," he apologised without further comment.

"Now Mr Trever, would you say that Mrs Paris gave a fair account of the reason for your re-employment?"

"Apart from my indiscretion, I have and always been and will continue to be a trusting loyal employee," Mr Trever responded.

Chris leaned forward, he clasped his hands in front of him as he looked at Mrs Paris.

"I am lost for words Mrs Paris," he remarked. "A moment ago you blamed your husband for having an affair with someone, now you are saying you knew it was Mr Trever who was having the affair and you have reinstated him."

Chris waited for the expected outburst from Mrs Paris, which did not come.

"OK," Chris remarked. "Now let's get back to the gun that killed Mr Paris, as we know Mr Trever was given a set of handguns as a present, Mr Trever later sold them on to Mr Argue, so that in fact the guns were in the Mr Argue's household. So who could get hold of one of these guns I wonder, Mrs Argue of course, but she has told me she knew nothing of the guns, that would leave only you Mr Trever, you were often in Mr Argue's front room perhaps carrying on with your, as you call it indiscretion."

"Well I didn't take it," Mr Trever almost shouted. "How would I have a chance of searching for them, while Mrs Argue was in the room, they could have been kept in the bedroom, or anywhere in the house."

"You have already told us that he kept them in the sideboard Mr Trever, I can have your word said back to you if you wish."

"Had I known what sort of meeting this was to be I would have brought my solicitor," Mrs Paris interrupted.

Chris looked at Mrs Paris. "You were asked if you could attend Mrs Paris, you were not under arrest or force, you came voluntarily."

"Yes but had I known, I would have had my solicitor with me," Mrs Paris replied angrily.

"I am just trying to sort out the facts from the untruths," Chris answered. "I have not accused any of you of anything, had I arrested you, then you would certainly have been entitled to have your solicitor with you."

"I must get back to my business, with Mr Trever and myself away, how much longer will this take?" she asked, fidgeting in her chair.

"Not too long Mrs Paris, but we will be quicker without interruption," Chris replied, then ignoring her, turned again to Mr Trever.

"If Mrs Argue is telling the truth Mr Trever, you are the only one here today that could have taken the gun, and remember Mr Trever this is a murder investigation, a hanging offence," Chris went on a little anger showing in his voice.

"You keep going on about Mr Paris being killed by one of the guns, who killed Mr Argue with the other, or are you suggesting that I shot him as well," shouted Mr Trever.

"Allow me Mr Trever to tell you a story about Mr Argue," Chris offered. "Now we have established that you were having an affair with your army friend's wife, you did not know however that your friend was aware of it, Mr Argue did tell this to his other friend Mr Paris."

"I know that, that is why I was sacked," Mr Trever said.

"What you did not know Mr Trever," Chris replied. "I chatted with Mr Argue, just hours before he died, I did not know at the time that Mr Argue had bought the guns from you, and when he asked how his friend had died, I told him shot with a small ladies handgun," Chris paused, he looked at George, who was leaning on his desk, listening intensely.

"Information told me that Mr Argue left the pub about half an hour later, this was unusual for him, as he would always stay until closing time. However he made his way home, deeply worried. I have no idea where Mrs Argue was when he arrived home, but he went straight to the sideboard cupboard where he kept the guns, and saw one gun missing.

One can only guess what was going through his mind, his friend who he had served with in the Boer War, was carrying on with his wife, and now he had taken a gun and shot his other friend Mr Paris. Whatever was in his mind, Mr Argue went back into his shop, sat in his barber chair, and shot himself."

Chris looked at Mrs Argue who was sitting, sobbing before continuing. "At first we thought it was murder, it had the same hall marks of Mr Paris killing."

"But why would he kill himself?" Mrs Paris asked curiously.

"What did he have to live for," Chris answered. "Although he was a man, who got pleasure out of looking a lovely women, he was a kind man, and as far as I'm aware very loyal to his wife, who he had now lost to another man, his army friend, then his drinking friend also was killed by that same friend. I feel that had this friend been a stranger, he may have handled things differently, he might even had confronted his wife about her affair, but Mr Argue was dealing with a man, who in war time he would have given his life for to save him."

"Why do you keep on referring to his friend, I did not kill Mr Paris or Roger," Mr Trever swore. "And anyway, how do you know it was suicide, it could have been a burglar?"

"I thought of that Mr Trever, but dismissed it, you see Mr Argue had no back way to his house, apart from climbing over other buildings, one could only get into Mr Argue's shop or house from the front, but the front door was locked and bolted from inside. Mrs Argue of course, wherever she was in the house would have heard the bang sound of the gun, which I am told is very loud, I have no idea what Mrs Argue did on finding her husband, but in her panic, she thought her lover had done it, so she washed the floor, took the gun outside and dropped it down the drain, then somehow got rid of the case, perhaps putting it on the fire."

"You are very clever Inspector," Mrs Argue remarked. "I was actually in the bedroom, I never waited up for my husband, I did not hear the door bell ring, but I heard the bang. I did think Tony had done it, so I cleaned the place up, and as you said dropped the gun in the drain outside. I was in a panic, or my mind was, for now I remember unlocking the front door to go outside with the gun, had I not panicked, I would have realised that Roger took his own life, partly as you said, because of me," tears fell from Mrs Argue's eyes as she remarked. "That knowledge will be a punishment to me for the rest of my life."

"There you go Inspector," Mr Trever added to Mrs Argue's speech. "I did not kill my mate Roger."

"I have always been aware that Mr Argue shot himself Mr Trever, but regarding the murder of Mr Paris, you are the only one with motive, been given the sack, you had plenty of time to get to the park, and having the weapon which you did steel from the house of Mr Argue, I will have to charge."

"Just a minute," Mr Trever shouted standing up. "I'm not taking blame, yes I did take the gun but gave it to Mrs Paris."

"Shut up you fool," Mrs Paris interrupted. "This is all so ridicules," she stormed.

"No Mrs Paris, I was going to tell Mr Trever that I was charging him only with stealing the gun, until he interrupted me, I am quite sure you killed your husband, let me tell you a story."

"You are a very strong woman Mrs Paris, you give all the impression that you are high born, but I have checked your family history and find out this was not true, you grow up poor, you often look at wealthy families feeling jealous, but you had high ambitions for the future. Mr Thomas Grice was for you the first step of the ladder, there is no doubt that during the first struggling years, you did pull your weight until the birth of your daughter Rosemary. Mr Grice however was to die young, and left you with forty nine percent of the firm, but you wanted it all. The firm was doing well, you had a nice house, in a nice part of town, you married Mr Paris, who had always wanted to marry you, but you married him with the hope of getting the other fifty-one percent of the business."

"Utter rot," Mrs Paris shouted. "Just utter rot."

Ignoring the remark, Chris continued.

"Where you live Mrs Paris, any sort of scandal is kept behind closed doors, you have to keep up appearances, but then you started to smell Talcum Powder in the office, you reasoned that your husband was having an affair with a woman, and using the office to carry it out, you tackled him over it, and naturally he rejected it, but your mind became twisted, another woman would be the greatest threat to you, especially should he leave you for this other woman, he could have vote against you just to make it hard for you to work there because of the fifty one percent of the business he held. Your attitude towards him changed, changed so much that your husband was quite worried, so worried that he told his friend Mr Argue of the situation the night you killed him. Mr Paris however who thought the world of you, partly blamed his step daughter, he told Mr Argue that perhaps Rosemary was saying things to her mother," Chris paused and took a sip of water before continuing.

"Your husband had told you that he had terminated Mr Trever's employment, he was not a man to tell you that it was because Mr Trever was seeing a woman in the office at night, because he respected Mr Argue's confidence."

"You knew about the guns that General Grice had given to Mr Trever, although you told me you had not, I do know that you did, you were in the office when your first husband Mr Thomas gave them to Mr Trever, so was Mr Paris," Chris paused again and took a sip of water before continuing.

"Oh yes, I do know that you were very interested in them, you took them out of their case and pretended to be some kind of cowboy girl, pointing them out through the office window," Chris smiled weakly.

"When Mr Trever told you that he had sold them, you asked him if he could get you a gun, but Mr Trever wanted to know why, what you told him, I do not know, but you had to reward him well, you promised to reinstate him with a higher position, and a good rate of pay. Mr Trever as we now know got you your gun, and on the night of Mr Paris's death, you were waiting for him behind the weeping willow tree by the iron bridge at the back of the park."

"All conjecture and assumption," Mrs Paris shouted feeling frightened.

Chris lifted the receiver of the phone. "Send in Sergeant Bloom now please," he replaced the receiver.

Sergeant Bloom entered carrying a pair of wellingtons, and a plaster cast, he put them on the desk in front of Chris. "Thank you Sergeant," Chris said. "I will call you later," without a word Sergeant Bloom left the room.

"What are my wellingtons doing here, how did you get them?" Mrs Paris said angrily.

"From your premises, with the authority you gave me on Saturday," Chris replied.

"This cast Mrs Paris, is one I made at the scene where your husband's body was found, and it matches the soles and heels of your wellingtons exactly, you were waiting for your husband that night by the side of the weeping willow tree wearing your wellingtons."

"Anyone could have worn them," Mrs Paris almost shouted. "They are never locked up."

"Who could have worn them exactly Mrs Paris?" Chris asked.

"I don't know, perhaps one of the workmen," Mrs Paris answered.

"These are women's wellingtons Mrs Paris, all the men that work for you have tried them, none of them could get their feet into them, they did inform us, no woman hardly set foot in the factory, so there you have it Mrs Paris," Chris said ending the conversation.

He turned to Mrs Argue. "By moving evidence you have committed a crime Mrs Argue," Chris said in a serious voice.

Mrs Argue who had started sobbing again, nodded her head without looking up from her lap.

"Also you wasted police time, however you will have to live with your indiscretion, I am letting you go after you have made a statement, on the understanding that I might have to see you again, you will also probably be needed to give testimony at the trial."

Chris took the receiver from the phone. "Send in Sergeant Bloom," he asked then replacing the receiver.

Sergeant Bloom entered, and with a nod from Chris, he took Mrs Argue by the arm and led her sobbing from the room.

"Now Mr Trever, you will be charged with the stealing of a fire arm, but other charge could follow," Chris continued.

"Such as?" Mr Trever asked worriedly.

"Well," Chris answered. "I am not convinced that you gave Mrs Paris the gun without knowing her intentions, I believe you knew, and went along with it knowing that you would have a higher position in the firm for life. You will be kept at least overnight Mr Trever, you will be interviewed tomorrow afternoon, get yourself a solicitor, we will see what arises from it."

"Now Mrs Paris," Chris continued turning towards her. "You will have your rights read, and charged on suspicion of murdering your husband. You will be kept in a cell, and face a court hearing within two or three days."

"You can't do that, I have responsibilities," shouted Mrs Paris. "My daughter and business."

"I will see that, your daughter is taken to her grand-mother, arrangements are already being made," Chris told her. "As for your business, you would do better to talk about it to your solicitor."

Chris looked at Mrs Paris, in his mind he admired her, here she was charged with murder, yet she was still keeping up appearances. Mrs Paris looked up and stared at Chris.

"You seem very good at jigsaws Inspector, but I am not only ambitious, I am also a fighter, let's see how many pieces of your jigsaw are forced into place."

Chris looked at her and shook his head, then looked at George and nodded.

George took Mr Trevor and Mrs Paris from the room, then Chris fell back in his chair, took a deep breath and sighed, took out his pipe, filled it and puffed contentedly.

Chapter Seventeen

Some time later George returned to the office, and found Chris relaxed in his chair smoking his pipe.

"They have had their rights said to them, and are now lodgers, you know Chris," George said with a smile on his face.

"Clearing this case was the last thing I expected this morning, how did you do it, you must have got a lot of information on Saturday."

"Some which helped," replied Chris putting his pipe in the ashtray, and leaning forward onto his desk. "It cost me a few hours sleep however, Inspector Noal always said that if you are stuck, re-read all the statements you have over and over, sometimes a picture will emerge."

"It must have done," George remarked relaxing in his chair.

"You see," Chris continued. "It eventually stuck out a mile, Mr Trever had the guns, sold them to Mr Argue. Now Mrs Argue did not know Mr Paris, but was having an affair with Mr Trever, so unless Mrs Argue shot Mr Paris, which can be dismissed because of not knowing him, it had to be Mr Trever, and Mr Trever who was the only one connected with the case that could have taken the gun."

"But it wasn't Mr Trever that killed him," George replied baffled.

"I have previously tried my own shoes against the cast I took at the scene, mine was far too large, which told me that it had to be a woman," Chris answered. "I saw Mr Trever take off his wellingtons Saturday as I went to his office, and knew straight away that he could not have made the impressions, so I had to look at it from another angle, how did a gun given to Mr Trever, then sold to Mr Argue, end up in the hands of a woman who shot Mr Paris. It was perhaps pure luck that I saw the wages ledger, and this note fell out, it fitted with my thoughts."

"I was not sure who the murderer was," George admitted. "It could have been any of them."

"That's the way I wanted it to seem," Chris carried on. "You see I was sure that Mr Trever stole the gun, also sure that he did not murder Mr Paris, but unsure what he had done with it, the letter Mrs Paris wrote to her accountant, reinstating Mr Trever with a higher position and a wage increase made me think on another track, but I had to get him to say who he gave the gun to."

"What other charges do you expect to bring against Mr Trever?" George asked.

"I do believe he knew what Mrs Paris had in mind, you see George both Mr Paris and Mr Argue was shot in the same way, a bullet behind the ear. Now this way is what the soldiers are taught to do in the army, both Mr Paris and Mr Argue knew that a bullet behind the ear means instant death. Mr Argue used same method when he committed suicide, the only way Mrs Paris could have known how to do it, she was being told by Mr Trever, remember, she only had one bullet she had to make sure."

"So did Mr Argue," George replied.

"Exactly George," Chris replied. "It has turned out to be a simple case, but I can't help feeling it could have been a perfect murder."

"How so?" George asked.

"If Mrs Paris had thrown the trilby with the gun and flint in it, into the centre of the river, it could have laid there for years, when finding Mr Paris's body we never had a clue as to who or why he was killed, it could have been anyone, a passing stranger perhaps, that gun gave us the break we wanted, without it the case would still be unsolved."

"What about Mrs Paris's business?" George asked.

"With the right people acting for her, she should be able to keep it going, there is little doubt in my mind that Mr Paris's Will, will show that he had left his share of the business to Mrs Paris, but if convicted, she will never be sole owner, a murderer does not inherit anything from someone you murdered."

"That will only leave Rosemary her daughter," George remarked.

"Perhaps the courts will pass the share down to Rosemary, who knows, but if they did, and she eventually inherited her mother's shares, she would be the complete owner."

"What about Mrs Argue?" George asked.

"I don't know George," Chris replied. "She could be charged with destroying evidence, and when you think about it, it was really all her fault, had she not carried on with Mr Trever, her husband would not have ask his friend Mr Paris to help him stop it. Had Mrs Argue not gone to the wool factory, then Mrs Paris would not have assumed that her husband was having an affair, Mr Trever would not have been sacked, Mr Paris would not have been shot, and Mr Argue would not have killed himself, so you see although at fault, she will get off the lightest apart from having to live with her memory for life."

"It all seems so simple now," George remarked. "Perhaps it was fate that your Elizabeth would go down with the flue on Saturday, one thing for sure we have a lot of interrogating to do."

Chris looked at George and smiled. "Everything is simple when it's known," he said.

"As for the interrogation, it will wait until tomorrow, I'm off for the rest of the day, I'm spending it with Elizabeth."

THE END

Lightning Source UK Ltd.
Milton Keynes UK
UKOW04f0610230216

268928UK00002B/99/P